Enemy Embrace

Luci tried to get out of the barn but the big Pawnee scout blocked her way. "Stop treating me as if I were your woman!" she spat. "I'm not yours! I'll never be!"

"And that's what's driving me *loco*," Johnny Ace admitted grudgingly. He reached out, grabbed her as she tried to run past, and dragged her to him. Luci struggled to break free as his big arms enveloped her, pulling her hard against his wide chest. His mouth covered hers and she gasped at the sensation.

He was an enemy. The Cheyenne and the Pawnee had forever warred on one another. But Luci couldn't stop her body from molding itself against the Pawnee all the way down their legs.

"Star Eyes, oh, Star Eyes . . ." Johnny's mouth was hot as a comet's trail across her mouth.

At that moment, Luci was lost. She slipped her arms around his sinewy neck, clung to him, shaking with sobs, and begged him to please her . . .

FIERY ROMANCE

CALIFORNIA CARESS (2771, $3.75)
by Rebecca Sinclair

Hope Bennett was determined to save her brother's life. And if that meant paying notorious gunslinger Drake Frazier to take his place in a fight, she'd barter her last gold nugget. But Hope soon discovered she'd have to give the handsome rattlesnake more than riches if she wanted his help. His improper demands infuriated her; even as she luxuriated in the tantalizing heat of his embrace, she refused to yield to her desires.

ARIZONA CAPTIVE (2718, $3.75)
by Laree Bryant

Logan Powers had always taken his role as a lady-killer very seriously and no woman was going to change that. Not even the breathtakingly beautiful Callie Nolan with her luxuriant black hair and startling blue eyes. Logan might have considered a lusty romp with her but it was apparent she was a lady, through and through. Hard as he tried, Logan couldn't resist wanting to take her warm slender body in his arms and hold her close to his heart forever.

DECEPTION'S EMBRACE (2720, $3.75)
by Jeanne Hansen

Terrified heiress Katrina Montgomery fled Memphis with what little she could carry and headed west, hiding in a freight car. By the time she reached Kansas City, she was feeling almost safe . . . until the handsomest man she'd ever seen entered the car and swept her into his embrace. She didn't know who he was or why he refused to let her go, but when she gazed into his eyes, she somehow knew she could trust him with her life . . . and her heart.

Cheyenne Caress

GEORGINA GENTRY

ZEBRA BOOKS
KENSINGTON PUBLISHING CORP.

Zebra Books

are published by

Kensington Publishing Corp.
475 Park Avenue South
New York, NY 10016

First printing: January, 1990

Printed in the United States of America

*To my darling "Murph,"
to commemorate a very special anniversary,*

and

*To the "Dirty Half-Dozen + Two," with fond
memories of a brief, golden time in Phoenix—
never to be forgotten, but never to be
recaptured. . . .*

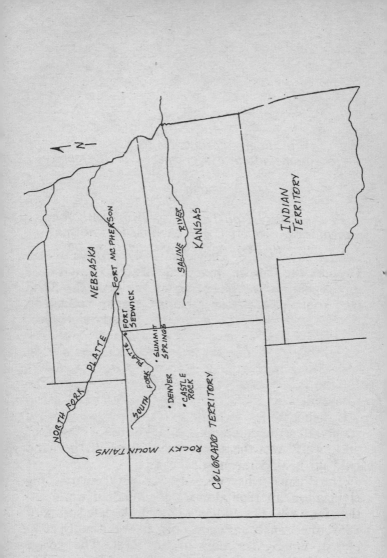

Prologue

Human sacrifice. Only one tribe above the Rio Grande, the Pawnee, practiced this cruel ritual with any regularity. In the spring of the year, the Skidi clan sometimes offered a captive enemy maiden to the Morning Star in a gruesome, bloody ceremony.

Because the Pawnees were a small tribe with few allies, they chose to align themselves with the whites, often using their skills as trackers to work as scouts for the U.S. Cavalry against their old enemies, the Cheyenne and the Dakota (Sioux). So well known was their skill as "wolves," as the other tribes called scouts, that the universal sign language for "Pawnee" and "wolf" was the same, two fingers of the hand held up behind the head like ears.

The Plains tribes were at war with encroaching civilization. In 1868 alone, eight hundred white settlers were killed by Indians. During the late spring of 1869, the transcontinental railroad was finally completed, linking the East to the West. The savage Plains Indians, especially the Outlaw Dog Soldier warrior band of the Cheyenne, realized this train would be the final destruction of their way of life.

7

They stepped up their attacks on rail work crews, passing wagon trains, stagecoaches, and settlers, rampaging across Nebraska, Kansas, and eastern Colorado.

General Carr's Fifth Cavalry with its three troops of crack Pawnee scouts, was sent to Fort McPherson, Nebraska, to deal with these warring renegades. The Fifth's chief scout was "Buffalo Bill" Cody, who, nine years before, had been a Pony Express rider.

But according to legend, their most skilled tracker "wolf" was a big, virile Pawnee nicknamed Johnny Ace by the whites, who couldn't remember his Pawnee name, Asataka. Johnny had good reason to hate the Cheyenne. As a youth, he had been orphaned when a Dog Soldier killed Johnny's warrior father in hand-to-hand combat.

The day he rode into Fort McPherson, he spotted a half-breed Cheyenne girl with bright blue eyes. Lucero. An unusual name that meant Morning Star—the star revered by the Pawnee. At their first encounter, she spat on him with scorn and hatred. The tough tracker reminded himself that she was the enemy and he was paid to hunt down her people. But from the moment Johnny Ace saw her, nothing else mattered but possessing her, body and soul. . . .

Chapter One

Fort McPherson, Nebraska
Late Spring, 1869

Sunrise Woman lay dying and there was nothing Luci could do but sit by the cot in the back room of the trading post and hold her mother's hand. *What would happen to her when her mother died?*

Luci sighed and leaned over to pull the ragged blanket up around Mama's thin shoulders.

What a place to die, Luci thought forlornly, looking around at the heaped-up burlap bags, piles of potatoes, and cartridge boxes. If she craned her neck a little, she could see the group of men playing cards by the pot-bellied stove in the main room.

Oblivious to her trouble, the men slapped cards down, drank, and laughed.

"Damn, Johnny Ace! For an Injun, you sure know how to play!"

"Whose deal is it, anyway?" A third man snapped.

"Mine," said a fourth.

The first man slammed his glass on the table. "Is there any more whiskey?"

"That we always got!" Old Mr. Bane cackled, pushing his chair back.

The noise seemed to disturb the feverish woman on the cot. Sunrise twisted restlessly and cried out.

"Please, Mama, be quiet!" Luci implored. "Else Mr. Bane is liable to throw us out and we have no place to go."

Miserable as the storage room was, being out in the raw spring weather here in Nebraska would be worse.

The big Indian at the card table twisted around curiously, looking her way. "What's going on in there anyway, Bane?"

Bane shrugged, scratched his chin stubble. "Aw, just that squaw who showed up a couple of weeks ago, Johnny. Does laundry for the soldiers. I been givin' her and her half-breed daughter a cot in exchange for cleanin' up the place."

"Oh, that pair." Johnny Ace looked her way again and she thought she saw disdain mixed with sympathy on his bronzed face. "Cheyenne?"

Of course she was Cheyenne. And he was Pawnee: blood enemy of her people. Luci's lips curled in scorn. She'd heard he was the best of the cavalry's Pawnee scouts.

Sunrise moaned again and thrashed. "I—I sorry about the money. . . . When I get well, we earn more. I promise this time, we buy clothes and books for you. When your father returns . . ." Her voice trailed off as she lapsed back into unconsciousness.

Automatically Luci brushed back her mother's gray-streaked hair. Sunrise looked so old, but she was not yet forty. *When your father returns.* Her mother was such a pathetic fool. Once Sunrise had been a pretty, young girl and a cavalry captain had promised her everything. But all he had given her

10

before he left was his child.

"There, there, Mama, it doesn't matter about the money." Tears overflowed Luci's bright blue eyes. How many times had Sunrise made that promise and how many times had she broken it as she drowned shattered dreams in whiskey?

For her seventeen years, all Luci could remember was the miserable existence of drifting from fort to fort while Sunrise looked for the love who had deserted her. If it hadn't been for a kindly chaplain's wife at Fort Leavenworth, Kansas, Luci would have gotten no schooling at all.

If she only had money for the doctor. Luci sponged off her mother's face with a wet rag. Anyone could see Sunrise had caught pneumonia hanging laundry out in the raw spring wind. At least she might die more comfortably. But without money, the post doctor had refused to come.

Sunrise moaned loudly and some of the men in the next room grumbled. "Damn, how can we enjoy ourselves with that squaw moanin' and carryin' on? Bane, can't you shut her up?"

"I could throw them out, I reckon."

"No." She heard the Pawnee scout's deep voice. "Let me see about it."

Luci heard his chair scrape back and felt the vibration of his large frame crossing the floor boards. Then Johnny Ace towered over her in his moccasins. "Can I do anything to help, Star Eyes?"

"A Pawnee help a Cheyenne? And don't call me that!" She sneered and glared up at him.

"Why not? It fits you." His chest was broad in the butter-soft buckskin shirt over a pair of blue cavalry pants. "Stop bristling like a porcupine. I'm trying to keep them from throwing you out in the weather." Johnny Ace ran one big hand through his ebony hair,

11

which was cut short like a white man's.

She jumped to her feet. "Go away! I don't need help from a tracker and killer of my people!" If she snarled at him, maybe he wouldn't see how alone and helpless she felt. The soldiers knew Sunrise Woman carried a knife and could use it expertly. But with her mother dying, Luci felt like a baby rabbit in a pen of coyotes.

"Small One, you dare insult me? I ought to . . ." His voice trailed off and his big hand reached out, grabbed her shoulder.

His fingers burned through the worn, faded calico of her dress. *Was his mouth as hot as his hand? If he pulled her close and ripped the calico away, would his body be warm and hard on her soft breasts?*

Immediately she was furious with herself for the feelings that rose in her. But she had affected him, too. Innocent as she was, she understood the way he looked at her, and saw the hard bulge in the tight blue pants. If the scout decided to drag her over in a corner on a pile of burlap bags and ravish her, no one in the next room would come to her aid. In fact, they'd all want their turn.

Would he share her with the others? He gazed down at her intently as his strong fingers dug into her flesh. Luci had a sudden feeling he was going to pull her to him and kiss her; molding her pliant body all the way down his virile hardness whether she wanted it or not. What made her so confused and angry was that she wasn't sure she didn't.

He was a enemy, a killer of her people. If she didn't pull away, he was going to jerk her into his embrace and she didn't know if she could stop him . . . or wanted to.

With effort, she twisted out of his grasp. "You big, stupid Pawnee. How dare you touch me?"

12

Before her withering words, he seemed to falter—unsure of himself for the first time. He rubbed his hand across his left ear absently. "That's what I get, I guess, for pitying a Cheyenne."

If nothing else, Luci was proud. That was all she had; her pride. "Get out of here, you soldier scout; you wolf for the army!" She spat at him and backed away, bristling like a small, scared kitten.

For a moment she thought he might strike her and she realized the big man could be pushed only so far before he was dangerous. Everyone on the frontier had heard of the scout called Johnny Ace who was known for his remoteness, his ability in a fight.

From the next room, a voice called, "Hey, Johnny, shall we deal you in or not? Need any help with that little gal?"

He just stood there, shaking with anger, rubbing his head as if it hurt. "I ought to take that pride outa you," he almost hissed, "but damn, the pride is what I like best!"

Then he turned on his heel and strode back into the other room.

"Deal you in, Johnny?"

"No, I've got to see Major North. Weather looks like we'll be getting a late snow."

Luci craned her neck, and saw the tall scout pause with his hand on the doorknob. "If any of you have ideas about that girl; don't." The unspoken threat of his tone was evident.

"Sure, Johnny, sure," a chorus of voices mumbled.

The big scout went out, leaving Luci glaring after him. A Pawnee. A damned Pawnee. A scout for the soldiers who hunted down her people. Luci reached over, took the small knife from Sunrise Woman's belt, and tucked it in her own clothing. Before she let a hated enemy take her virginity, Luci would kill him!

Her mother's eyes flickered open. "I — I heard," she whispered weakly. "Luci, you must find your father. He have same name. . . . Look after you."

"Like he did you?" Luci retorted with sudden anger and was immediately contrite. "Oh, Mama, I'm sorry, I didn't mean—"

"I know." Her trembling hand stroked Luci's hair gently. "You not be safe with me gone. If nothing else, go back to our people. I have a brother with the outlaw Dog Soldiers, Ta Ton Ha Haska. He disowned me because of my love for the white soldier."

"Yes, Mama, yes." Luci only half listened. She had been raised around the white forts, had seldom been among her tribe. She barely spoke her own language. Could she fit in, find happiness among the Cheyenne, who were now on the war trail, fighting a losing battle against the Iron Horse that whistled and smoked across the vast buffalo plains? Well, maybe. . . .

The other alternative was to risk the same fate as her mother — become a pretty plaything to warm some soldier's bed until his frontier duty was over. Then he would go back East, deserting her without a backward glance. But there were worse things. That big Pawnee might force himself on her, make her submit as warriors had always conquered enemy women.

She'd kill him if he tried. Holding the small knife in her red, work-worn hand, Luci buried her face in the tattered blanket, and wept softly so as to not disturb her dying mother.

Johnny Ace hesitated outside, looking toward the major's office. The wind picked up out of the north.

14

He felt it blow cold on his dark, high-cheekboned face. *There was a good chance of a late storm moving across the barren plains.*

He leaned against a post out of the wind and slowly rolled a cigarette. Without thinking, he rubbed his ear again. *Big, stupid Pawnee.* Once again he was in the white man's boarding school, an orphaned boy with no one to protect him. When he made mistakes in his lessons because he knew so little English, the stern Miss Platt had struck him again and again along side his head with her ruler.

The teacher's pale eyes had almost seemed to relish her action. *Big, stupid Pawnee boy,* she would say in front of the others. *Big, stupid Pawnee.* He didn't know which hurt worse—the ruler slammed with all the white woman's strength across his ear, or the humiliation of her words before the other students.

So why was he putting himself in a position to be humiliated again? Johnny finished rolling the cigarette and lit it, relishing the taste. The other Pawnees would be gathering to eat now, but Johnny always felt like an outsider. The years in the boarding school had made him a white man in a brown man's skin.

His mind went back to the fiery half-breed girl, wondered about her. She had pride, like he himself. Even when Miss Platt had made his head bleed, he had never cried. His pride would have kept him silent if she had tortured him to death.

Damn little Cheyenne. He was Pawnee in his heart after all because he thought of her as his enemy— just as the two tribes had been enemies for many generations. The Pawnee were a small tribe, struggling constantly to withstand their old enemies, the Cheyenne and the Sioux. Almost the only ally the Pawnee had found was the white cavalry so the braves tracked and scouted for the soldiers. Without

15

the army, the Pawnee would have long ago been wiped out. The Cheyenne and the Sioux were as many as the snow flakes that were beginning to swirl from the sky onto his eyelashes.

He took a deep puff, watch the occasional snowflake fall in the growing twilight. Lights flickered on gradually in the buildings of the fort. Across the square at the trading post, the card game had broken up. He watched handsome Chief Scout "Buffalo Bill" Cody come out of the door with some of the others and stride toward the barracks where dinner and maybe a snort of whiskey awaited them.

Johnny studied the glowing tip of the cigarette. Cody was a good sort, but not a close friend. The Pawnee, Asataka, whom everyone knew as Johnny Ace, didn't have any close friends. He was a loner.

Star Eyes. He couldn't get her off his mind. What he ought to do was go back over there, throw her down on some burlap bags, and rape her until his body was sated. Then he could forget her. He'd break that pride of hers, make her submit and beg mercy. He wouldn't ask, he'd take.

That was what he ought to do. But he didn't move. He thought about the girl's mother with a twinge of pity. Same old story. Everyone had heard about the drunken Cheyenne woman who wandered from fort to fort like a crazy woman, looking for some soldier who had used, then deserted her. She had a little white blood in her background herself, he thought, remembering Sunrise Woman's light skin. Somewhere a long time ago, some trapper had enjoyed Sunrise Woman's grandmother or great-grandmother. And now the result of all this was a small, slight girl with eyes the color of stars. *A damned Cheyenne.*

With annoyance, he flipped the cigarette away,

strode toward Major North's office. For a long moment he hesitated before rapping sharply on the door.

"Come in."

Johnny entered and stood with feet wide apart, one hand resting on the knife in his belt. The slightly built young officer looked up from behind his cluttered desk. Frank North wore a small mustache to make him appear older than his late twenties, which was also Johnny's age.

"Hello, Johnny, my heart is glad to see you." Major North spoke fluent Pawnee, better than Johnny himself. He stood and held out his hand to shake, then gestured to a chair. "Sit down. We'll smoke, and talk."

"We did not get much chance to talk on the last campaign, Pani Le-shar."

Pani Le-shar. *Pawnee Chief.* Only one other white man besides Frank North had ever been honored with that title—Fremont, the Pathfinder—and that was long ago, before Johnny's time.

"No wonder." The major smiled, switching to English as he seemed to remember Johnny's language problem. "The Cheyenne have been raising hell all up and down, haven't they? Just one scrimmage after another."

Johnny hesitated, looking from the major's piercing eyes down to the floor. He had an overpowering urge to get up and leave. But as he hesitated, he saw bright blue eyes in his mind, eyes the color of stars, full of desperation . . . and hate for himself. "Pani Le-shar, we have ridden together much time, fought the enemy of the whites and Pawnee together."

"More than two years," North mused, scratching his head in memory. "Remember Plum Creek?"

"Who could forget how the Cheyenne Dog Sol-

17

diers lay in ambush for the inexperienced blue coats they thought were riding into their trap?"

North laughed aloud. "And the looks on their faces when those green troops they thought were riding in formation suddenly threw off the blue coats and were Pawnee warriors instead! You gave them more than they bargained for!"

"And will again, next time we go out, Pani Le-shar."

"Cheyenne," North mused, and made the sign language for that tribe absently, his right fore finger making stripe marks against his left. "My Pawnee brothers are the world's best scouts." He made the sign for Pawnee and scout: two fingers held up behind his head like ears.

How was he to ask this? While Johnny pondered, the major reached for a box on his desk and offered Johnny a cigar. Then he lit it for Johnny and leaned back in his chair, waiting patiently. It was good manners among the tribes to sit quietly, waiting for the other to finally bring up the reason for his visit.

Johnny took a deep drag of the savory smoke and wondered how to bring it up. "Pani Le-shar, did you see the girl carrying the laundry basket across the square when we first rode in several days ago?"

"The small one with the bright blue eyes?" He tipped his chair back, and put both hands behind his head. "That's Lucero. The pair hangs around first one fort, then another. Her mother is a little crazy, I'm told, and keeps searching for the soldier who deserted her."

"The mother is dying," Johnny said, blowing smoke toward the ceiling. "She lies in the dirty storage room of the trading post. There doesn't seem to be anyone who cares."

Frank North's eyes were bright with curiosity, but

18

he only shrugged. "The pair are tame Cheyenne, but we fight their people every day. Is the girl so desperate for help, she asks you, an enemy of her people?"

"Hardly." Johnny smiled in spite of himself, remembering the girl's spunk and fire. "She spat at me and acted like a kitten cornered by a dog. She called me a big, stupid Pawnee."

Without thinking, he put his hand protectively to his head, almost as if he could feel the white teacher's ruler striking and humiliating him before the whole class.

Frank North chewed his lip. "If you're asking me to throw that pair out into the cold or run them away from the fort because of the way she treated you—"

"I do not ask that, Pani Le-shar," he blurted without thinking, although it was rude among Indians to interrupt someone who was speaking.

"I see," North said, but the expression on his puzzled face betrayed that he did not understand what it was that Johnny wanted. "Very well, I will punish the girl in any way you ask, short of throwing the pair out into the cold. Although I fight her people, I cannot do that to helpless women. For you, my best and bravest scout, I will take action against her."

Johnny studied the tip of his glowing cigar. He should get up and leave now. He owed the little spitfire nothing. Her people and his had been enemies for generations. She had been so pathetically brave, snarling at him when he could break her small back across his knee with one stroke of his big hands. "As far as action, Pani Le-shar, there is one small quarters for soldier families available on this post. Could—could the army pretend not to notice while you move the pair into that?"

Major North brought his chair down on all fours

with a loud bang. "Let me get this straight, after she spat at you and insulted you, you ask that I do her a favor?"

"Not even a Cheyenne should have to die like a dog," he mumbled. He had known the major would be surprised and curious. No one hated that tribe like Johnny Ace. And he had good reason.

The major only stared back at him in wide-eyed shock.

Johnny looked away. "I admire her spunk, her pride."

"Ahhh!" The major nodded and his smug tone said that now he understood. "She is very pretty, too. Well, the victors have always enjoyed the losers' women. It's just one of the spoils of war."

Johnny tried to appear careless. "I have not looked at her much. She is just a girl, that's all. Someone should make her more obedient, break that pride." He thought about it a moment. Her stubborn pride was what he liked best about her. He, too, had pride. That was the only thing that had sustained him all those miserable years in the white man's school.

North shrugged. "You're my best scout, Johnny. If you want her, take her a couple of times until you're tired of her. No one will listen if she tries to complain to me or General Carr."

Johnny had a sudden image of her small, slender body spread beneath his big, dark one. *Was she a virgin?* Possibly, as young as she was and with her mother a little *loco* and always carrying a knife. The men would be afraid to bother Luci. That's what he should do—drag her into his room and humble her, smear her with his seed, force it deep into her womb until she was dominated and begging for mercy.

He pictured her on her knees as he stood before her. He would grab that long ebony hair and force

20

her to kiss his manhood, to take it between her hot, moist lips to show complete submission. He would do anything he wanted to her while her mother lay helpless and everyone on the post would look the other way . . . or offer to help him humble her.

The thought of her on her knees naked before him made his groin tighten and he moved restlessly in his chair. "Maybe that is what I will do, Pani Le-shar. But the dirty storeroom is no place for what I have in mind. Can't you get her the quarters?"

North groaned aloud and rolled his eyes. "Not for anyone else would I do this, Johnny. I'll get her and her mother into those quarters if I have to list her name as Mrs. O'Brien, here to meet her soldier husband. I just hope we don't both get in trouble over it."

"No one cares about an enemy girl," Johnny said.

"You're *loco* to get mixed up with a Cheyenne, Johnny. It's bound to lead to grief. She might stick a knife in you."

"I'll take that chance." He would put his knife in her, driving deep and hard, pinning her against a bed while his lips sucked her nipples into hard, pink nubs. He tossed the cigar into the cuspidor, stood up. "One more thing. If her mother dies, the girl is all alone. Each of the white soldiers will try to force himself on her."

North stood up, nodding. "I'll speak to General Carr about the quarters, Lord knows what I'll tell him. The paperwork will delay it 'til morning, but I wouldn't want to move a sick woman while it snows anyway."

"And the white soldiers?" Johnny persisted as he got up from the chair, "Otherwise . . ."

"I'll pass the word around that no man is to touch her until Johnny Ace has had his fill of her and is

21

ready to trade her off."

As someone must have done to Star Eyes' mother, Johnny thought with a frown. But that wasn't his problem. He nodded. "After I've enjoyed her a few days, I may not care who has her next . . ." He let his voice trail off. When he thought of another man even putting his hand on her arm, much less lying between her thighs or kissing her breasts, he got an angry, burning feeling deep inside.

"Is that all?"

Abruptly Johnny came out of his thoughts, saluted smartly. "Thank you, Pani Le-shar."

Frank North leaned against the door post. "Get her out of your system fast. We'll be going after Ta Ton Ka Haska and his Dog Soldiers again soon, and the quicker I move her out of the quarters, the less explaining I'll have to do. I'll get them moved first thing in the morning when the snow stops."

Johnny nodded, turned to open the door, and walked out into the cold spring night. The snow fell steadily now on the green grass that had just started to come up after the long winter.

He had felt pity for the dying mother, perhaps because he had barely known his own. What difference did it make if Major North thought he was setting the girl up to be used for his lust? But wasn't that exactly what he was doing and using pity as an excuse? He didn't know himself.

It occurred to Johnny that she might be just grateful enough to him for making her mother more comfortable that when he told her his body hungered for her, she might let him make love to her without a fight. Maybe she would even respond, make love to him. Johnny had had many women, white and brown, but he had never loved any of them. Of course, he could never love this enemy girl either; he

22

could only slake his lust on her slim body.

He went next to the post doctor and promised to pay for medicine if the man would see about the Indian woman — at least making her rest easy if there was nothing he could do.

There was one more thing that someone would have to take care of in case. . . . With a sigh, Johnny looked around at the lights of the fort reflecting off the swirling snow. Hunching his broad shoulders against the chill, he went off to find the post carpenter. If the mother died, there was no chance of doing a Cheyenne burial on a raised platform with a fine horse killed beneath it to take the dead one on her journey up the Hanging Road to the Sky. No doubt the soldiers would wrap the body in a ragged blanket and scratch out a shallow hole on the edge of the fort graveyard. Even a dog should be buried with more dignity than that.

He found the man and paid him to build a good pine coffin. Lumber was dear on these plains, much too dear to waste on an Indian squaw, the man informed him. Johnny refrained from hitting him in the mouth and demanded he build the coffin if needed.

It was dark now, the wind whipping his buckskin coat as he hunched against the cold and walked across the parade ground. He stopped and looked toward the trading post. Should he go back over? Johnny hesitated and stopped. He didn't feel like being spat on and screamed at anymore tonight. Besides, the doctor would do whatever he could. Reluctantly Johnny trudged back to his quarters.

He should stop thinking about getting the small beauty into his blankets. After all, she was the enemy and her people had killed his father, leaving him and his brothers orphaned. His brothers now

23

scouted for Custer and Crook.

He stripped down to a scanty breechcloth and went to bed. But he couldn't sleep. Johnny lay staring at the ceiling, restless and listening to the fire crackle. He worried about Luci and her mother in that storage room. His own mother had died in the cholera outbreak of 1849 that a passing wagon train had brought among the Pawnee. At least in the morning, the pair would be moved to quarters that were clean and warm.

He almost got up in the middle of the night and went over to see about them; then he shook his head and settled back onto his cot. Star Eyes would never believe that he had good intentions. She would think he was coming to force himself on her. *But were his intentions all that noble or did he just want to feast his eyes on her again?*

Star Eyes. Romantic name for an enemy girl. Nothing could come of this attraction he felt for her unless he raped her and was done with it. But Johnny had never raped a woman, not even an enemy female. He knew some of the others would laugh if they knew he thought it a despicable and shameful thing to do. Still he wanted the blue-eyed one badly enough to be tempted by the idea.

Johnny rolled over on his belly, trying not to think about her. Were her breasts small and delicate with soft pink buds that would harden when he put his mouth on them? With a curse, he felt his manhood harden at the thought and wished he had her beneath him right now.

As he dozed off, he pretended he did have. Her mouth was hot and moist, sucking his tongue deep into her throat. Her slim legs locked around his hips, pulling him deep within her. But best of all, her small arms were around his neck and she whispered over and over, . . . *I need you, Johnny, I want you . . . make love to me. . . .*

But then the wind picked up and rattled the building as he slept and the wind seemed to cry and wail through his troubled dreams.

Johnny jerked up with a start, listening. As a scout, often sleeping in hostile territory, his life might sometime depend on his ability to hear the slightest sound, come awake in an instant. *What was it that had awakened him?*

He slipped on his moccasins and crept silently as a lynx to the window, staring out at the night. The light snow still swirled in the darkness and the wind blew. Standing there in nothing but a breechcloth, he shivered in the cold. The faint sound drifted on the wind again. It sounded like a small, hurt animal, or a lost child . . . or a bereaved woman.

Then he saw her collapsed on the parade ground, a small shadow against the snow. With a curse, he swung open the door and raced into the night, heedless of the snowflakes melting on his bare skin.

"Luci! What are you doing out here? What . . . ?" Then he saw the torn clothing, the hair hanging loosely around her small shoulders, the blood smeared on her skin and the torn clothes. For an instant, he thought she had been attacked. But then she raised her eyes to his and he saw the grief, the tears freezing on her cheeks.

"She's dead! My mother's dead!" The wind carried away her weeping.

He tried to raise her to her feet but she struggled with him and fell back to writhe in the snow. "She's dead! Aiyee! She's dead!" Luci tore at her clothes, then brought out the small knife and began slashing at her arms in the traditional way of expressing grief.

"You'll freeze to death out here!" He twisted the

knife out of her hands and tried to pick her up. Her blood ran hot and red on his bare skin. When he swung her up in his arms through sheer brute strength, she fought him. Her torn dress came open and he felt her bare breasts warm and soft against his chilled skin.

"I don't care! She's dead! I don't care what happens to me!" The girl tried to fight her way out of his grasp, smearing them both with her hot blood. He could feel it sticky on his body, smell the coppery scent of it.

"Dammit it, small one, I care and I'm freezing!" He swung her up in his arms and started walking swiftly toward his quarters, glad only that the wind and the cold had everyone inside and asleep so they couldn't witness this struggle. The soldier on guard duty must have dozed off at his post.

She fought to get away from him, but he held her easily, cradling her against his bare chest, protecting her shivering body from the wind with his big one.

"Dirty Pawnee!" she cried, struggling. "You're glad she's dead, aren't you? I hate you, you killer of my people! You wolf for the bluecoats!"

He marched doggedly across the parade ground while she fought and scratched and bit him. It seemed a million miles through the snow to his quarters with the struggling girl. Finally he made it and kicked the door closed with his heel before he dumped her unceremoniously on his cot. "I'll stir up the fire and make you a pot of coffee."

She looked up at him with wide, frightened eyes, then glanced toward the door.

"Star Eyes, don't try it," he said patiently, stooping to stir up the coals of the fireplace and add another pile of buffalo chips. "I can outrun you and I'd only bring you back. I'm sorry about your mother."

"No, you aren't!" She raged at him, oblivious to her torn clothes that left her half-naked on his cot. "You're the enemy! And now you'll finish by raping me!"

He paused and looked over at her as he put a kettle of water on to boil. "Don't tempt me, Blue-eyed One. I'm cold as hell and those blankets look good to me!"

"You wouldn't dare!" She scurried to the far edge of the cot and stared back at him.

He stood up slowly, frustrated and angry at himself because of his urgent need of her. She was fast becoming an unquenchable fire in his soul. "I am Asataka, Major North's best scout. If I want you, the army will turn its head and pretend not to notice until I've had my fill of your body and toss you aside."

He was sorry then for his outburst because of the haunted, terrified look on her small face. She drew herself up into a ball and burst into exhausted tears, hiding her face against her knees.

She had brought him nothing but trouble from the first moment he laid eyes on her. With a sigh, he went over to the wash stand, got a big bowl and pitcher of water, came over to the cot. "Luci, let me help clean you up. In a minute, there'll be coffee ready and we'll talk."

He set the bowl and pitcher on the table next to the bed and reached out his hand to her.

"Damned stupid Pawnee!" She knocked his hand away and slapped his face.

He had to fight to keep from grabbing and shaking her. Johnny stood glaring down at the small girl, his cheek still stinging. "Men have died for less than that."

"Then kill me!" she challenged. "Make war on a woman!" She tried to slap him again. He caught her hand and they struggled.

As he pulled her against his bare chest, trying to keep her from striking him, her ripped, faded dress tore away. He realized suddenly that she was warm and smeared with blood—completely naked and defenseless in his arms.

Chapter Two

Luci stopped struggling and looked back up at him. She suddenly realized from the heat of his gaze how her nakedness had affected him.

"Star Eyes, you have the most beautiful breasts . . ." He seemed to be fighting for self-control, battling an impulse to lift her up so that his lips could taste her nipples.

Now was her chance. In one abrupt move, she jerked away from him, ran to the door, flung it open, and looked out uncertainly as the cold gust blew in.

He sighed loudly behind her. "Small One, close the door. You have my word I won't lay a hand on you."

"The worthless word of a Pawnee!" she sneered, but she couldn't stop her teeth from chattering.

He got up, grabbed a blanket, and came over to where she stood. While she tried to decide whether to run out the door naked, he reached out, slammed the door, and wrapped the blanket around her.

"It's too cold to stand here fussing in the doorway," he said gently. "Now come back to the fire and have some coffee. You hungry?"

Tears ran unchecked down her face. Her mother's death had caused a pain of grief deep inside that wouldn't stop hurting. She was also starving. She'd had nothing but a little corn pone all afternoon. "No! I eat no Pawnee's scraps!"

He shrugged and went over to the fire. "Too bad. I've got a big hunk of beef I roasted this morning. I'm going to have some with my coffee and leftover biscuits."

She stood there uncertainly, watching him fix himself a tin plate, smelling the coffee and food. "I—I suppose you intend to humble and humiliate me—make me beg for it."

He looked at her a long moment in the firelight. Then he fixed a second tin plate and put it on the cot. "It's there; eat it. Don't expect *me* to beg *you*."

For a long moment she hesitated, watching him eat. Her grief was deep and hurting. But she was also hungry and cold. The food and the fire drew her closer.

She wondered for a long moment if she looked as sad and forlorn as she felt. "Is there—is there sugar for the coffee?" Sugar was a delicacy that she and her mother could never afford.

In answer he reached over, dumped two spoonfuls into a cup, poured the coffee in it, and set it next to the tin plate.

She thought of Sunrise Woman. Her mother wouldn't want her to accept food from a hated enemy. Even when her mother had been drinking, she would have nothing to do with a Pawnee. Her mother had pride, Luci thought sadly, perhaps more than her daughter had.

The big scout turned away, sat down on a stool before the roaring fire, and went back to his plate of food.

Perhaps he wouldn't notice if she sneaked just a few bites behind his back.

Quietly she tiptoed over, sat down on the cot, and pulled herself into a little ball inside the blanket. He didn't look around. *Was she being a traitor, taking his food?* The only person in the world who had loved her lay dead over at the trading post and here she sat, wolfing down the enemy's beef. Her grief was nothing compared to her guilty conscience, but she couldn't stop herself from eating. The coffee was very hot and sweet. Luci warmed her cold, red fingers around the mug and sipped it.

The scout finished eating and sat drinking his coffee, staring into the fire. Luci savored the taste, wondering what to do about her mother. She couldn't go back over there, not with her mother lying dead in the storeroom. The Cheyenne always burned the lodge and personal belongings of the dead, but she knew she couldn't set fire to the trading post without getting into trouble. Besides they had been so poor, there were no personal possessions to burn.

He got up slowly and Luci cowered back against the wall behind the cot, clutching the coffee mug in both work-worn hands. But he only came over, poured more coffee for her, put sugar in it.

"*Hahoo,*" she whispered, then said it in English. "Thank you."

"Well, it's a start," he muttered. "At least you aren't spitting at me." He seemed to see the fear in her eyes as he reached out with his free hand, hesitated, dropped his arm to his side. She had a distinct feeling that he had been about to touch her face.

She stared at him while pretending not to. He was so big and muscular and naked except for that brief loincloth. Now that he had eaten, would he rape

31

her? She was almost too exhausted and saddened to care. But she couldn't keep the tears from overflowing as she looked up at him.

"For God's sake, stop that!" he snapped. "I'm not going to hurt you."

"What kind of Pawnee are you?" She didn't try to hide the contempt she felt. "You act and talk more like a white man."

"And you are arrogant and rude as any white girl," he retorted, "not soft-spoken and shy as is proper in an Indian maiden of any tribe."

The insult stung a little because her mother had often admonished her that she needed to learn better manners if a Cheyenne warrior were to ever want her for a wife. Thinking of her mother again, Luci began to weep softly, unsure if she wept for her mother or for herself.

He hesitated as if uncertain what to do next. "Here, one of my shirts is big enough to cover you." He tossed her a butter-soft deerskin shirt, and as she watched, he reached for his pants.

She clutched the shirt against the blanket and watched him dress. "Where are you going?"

"It's not long 'til dawn," he answered as he continued to dress. "There'll be things to be taken care of—"

"I don't want to go back over there." She was in a panic, not wanting to see her mother dead, wanting to remember her as Sunrise Woman had been the few good times they had had.

"I'll take care of things," he said gently. "It looks as if it's almost stopped snowing. Maybe we can have the burial at dawn. That would be fitting because of her name." He put on his coat then paused with his hand on the doorknob.

She couldn't keep from weeping at the thought. "I

don't know what will become of me now."

"Get some sleep," he whispered. "When I go over there, I'll bring you a dress."

"I—I don't own another," she said, shame-faced.

She felt the pity in his gaze. "Maybe one can be bought at the trading post."

"Mercy! I have no money for that. I—I don't even have money for a burial."

His face betrayed nothing. "Don't worry about it. I'll be back after awhile."

When he left, she slipped into the oversized deerskin shirt, marveling at how big it was. It came halfway down her thighs while the sleeves completely covered her fingertips. She wore an enemy's clothes. Perhaps it was just as well her mother hadn't lived to see Luci's shame. But it was either that or run about naked, tempting him.

With her belly full and the room growing warmer, she snuggled down under the blanket and put her head on his pillow. The slight masculine scent of him was on the pillow when she put her face against it. She would not sleep. She would only lie here until she got warm. Then before he returned, she would leave his quarters.

Where would she go? There really wasn't anyplace to run. She and Sunrise Woman had been at this fort only a few days and knew no one. Luci had not had much rest since her mother had become ill. Now exhaustion and grief descended on her although she struggled to keep her eyes open. The big Pawnee wanted to sleep with her; she knew that by the way he looked at her. She would not do that, of course. As she yawned and snuggled deeper into the pillow, she wondered suddenly how it would feel to sleep in his arms with her face on that wide chest. She would rather die first.

33

She came awake in an instant at the creak of the door, but she did not move. If only she had her mother's knife, but she had dropped that in the struggle on the parade ground.

Who was in the room? She tensed but lay still, ready to fight to defend her virginity. She opened one eye and peeked. It was the big Pawnee. He looked down at her a long moment, then he picked up another blanket and spread it over her gently. His fingertips brushed along her hair almost as if he were reluctantly caressing her.

Luci sat up in bed suddenly. "Don't touch me, scout! Did you think to take me unawares before I could do anything about fighting you off?"

He smiled wryly. "I told you I wouldn't hurt you. If I decided to force myself on you, you wouldn't have much chance of fighting me off."

That was true. The fact of her vulnerability and helplessness made her angry, and she got up and went over to sit on the stool before the fire.

He held out a bundle. "I got you a dress. I've also made burial arrangements. The snow's let up but I figure it'll start back up again heavy later today by the way the sky looks."

She would not take a gift from this killer of her people, and yet she could hardly go around in his shirt. The frustration of her situation brought tears to her eyes.

He lay the bundle next to her. "Old Mr. Bane gave it to you."

He was lying, she thought, knowing she would not, could not, take a gift from a Pawnee. She picked it up, opened it, ran her work-worn hands in wonder over the blue-flowered cotton. "Mercy! It's

34

the most beautiful dress I ever saw!"

"I thought of the color of your eyes," he blurted, and then he cleared his throat and spoke matter-of-factly. "It was the only ready-made dress he had."

She knew that was a lie. When she was cleaning for Mr. Banes, she had seen that rack of women's dresses. "I—I never had a new dress before."

"You're too pretty to have to wear some white woman's castoffs."

That reminded her then how she would be expected to repay the scout for the dress. Well, she'd fool him. She'd take in extra washing and pay him back so she wouldn't obligated in any way.

"I'll go outside so you can change," the scout said. "Later the army has found a small quarters for you."

"In exchange for what?" she asked sharply. "If some young officer thinks I'm going to warm his bed and take care of his needs as my mother did until he goes back East—"

"You know I wouldn't let that happen." His voice sounded sharp and threatening, as if the idea annoyed him.

"I'm not a whore to be bought and paid for." She swallowed hard. "Especially not by a Pawnee. I'd rather sleep out in the cold and freeze to death."

"We'll talk about that later." He paused in the doorway, "I'll wait outside for you to dress."

She had no underwear, but she put on the dress and took his comb from the bureau, rebraided her hair, and washed the tearstains from her face. Her moccasins were worn ragged, but she had nothing else.

When he came back in, he stood looking at her a moment. "Small One, you are even more beautiful than I imagined in that dress. I'll take care of final details. When I come back, we'll have the burial."

She was too sad to do anything but slump on the stool and stare into the fire until he returned.

"Luci, do you have a coat?"

She was too embarrassed even to look at him as she shook her head. "We were so poor and Sunrise Woman drank . . ."

"You don't owe me any explanation." He draped his own coat over her shoulders and took her arm. "They are ready for the burial."

"You're going with me?" Somehow she had not expected this.

"If you don't want me to—"

Luci shrugged. "What does it matter? Sunrise Woman won't know."

He took one of her small, work-worn hands, looked at it a long moment, and frowned before draping it through his arm. "No girl should have to work so hard."

"We had to eat." And there had been her mother's drinking. Luci had tried to save for a dress, thinking that if she ever did find her father, she wanted to look pretty. But that dream had died a long time ago. What a twist of fate. When she finally did get a nice dress, it had been paid for by an enemy and bought to wear to a funeral.

They went out and Johnny Ace led her to his big, black stallion, held out his hands to her. She hesitated a long moment.

"Don't be afraid," he said. "Katis is gentle with women."

She wondered suddenly if his master was. "Katis? That's a strange name for a horse."

"It's Pawnee; means 'black.' "

Luci decided she didn't want his hands on her waist, so she struggled up into the saddle alone.

He didn't say anything, just led the horse across the parade ground, out through the fort gates where two soldiers waited with a horse-drawn wagon. On the wagon was a newly made wood coffin. She had been so afraid they were only going to wrap her mother in burlap bags and throw her in a hastily dug hole. She wouldn't ask who had paid for the coffin. She was certain she already knew.

The sunrise was starkly scarlet on the white snow of the eastern skyline. The soldiers drove the cart out to a windswept rise with a few scattered headstones sticking darkly through the white snow. A grave had been dug already. There was even a wooden marker with her mother's name and a carving of a sun coming up.

Johnny reached up his hands to her, but she brushed him aside and dismounted awkwardly in the long skirt. The snow came into her moccasins and she gasped at the cold on her feet as she trudged to where the soldiers were already lowering the wooden box into the freshly dug grave. A tear ran down her face though she struggled to hold it back.

The scout came over next to her, standing awkwardly with feet wide apart, his hand on the hilt of the knife in his belt. "I—I tried to get the chaplain, but he . . . was off the post."

She knew better than that. Probably the man didn't want to get out in this early cold over a drunken squaw. "It doesn't matter. Sunrise Woman would have rather done it the way of her people."

But of course there was no fine horse to kill on the grave even if the army would have allowed it and she was sure they wouldn't. Luci would have hated to kill a horse. Still the Cheyenne liked to send possessions and food with the dead.

The Pawnee walked to the wagon and came back

with a small bundle. She recognized her mother's few pitiful possessions. "Luci, you can do what you want with these."

Some of the items Luci really could have used, but she would not have Sunrise Woman start up the Ekutsihimmiyo, the Hanging Road to the Sky, with nothing at all. Luci stepped forward, dropped the pitiful bundle in on top of the box and watched stoically as the bored men began to fill the grave.

The sun came up slowly as the soldiers heaped the black dirt on the mound. The Pawnee stood with his arms folded. "Do you want to say anything, Luci?"

"She—she was born at sunrise. That's how she got her name. Funny, isn't it?" Luci choked on the knot of grief in her throat and shook her head. If she began to weep, she might not be able to stop and she would not lose her pride before an enemy.

They stood there in the silent red dawn, the only sound the jingle of the harness and the stamping of the horses. The wind blew about them, and the soldiers, who had gone back to sit on the wagon, muttered under their breath.

Finally the Pawnee cleared his throat. "Great Father, we return Sunrise Woman to you. She came into this world at sunrise and now she returns to you at that exact same time. It is fitting, maybe, that this should be in completing the cycle of life."

He paused awkwardly, looking toward the first rays sparkling briefly on the new snow. "Receive her now as she runs up a sun ray to you and give her the happiness and peace she never found in this life . . ."

Luci fought the grief that threatened to choke her at his simple, sincere words, but she said nothing.

Johnny Ace had let his voice trail off awkwardly as if he didn't know what else to say.

There was a long period of silence while Luci

fought against showing her agony. She did not want an enemy to see her break down. "I wish you would go away and leave me with my dead."

She thought he would object, but he only said, "Luci, I'll leave my horse for you. Don't stay long— the cold . . ."

She waved him away, her eyes stinging with tears. The soldiers were already mounting their wagon, returning to the fort. The Pawnee stayed a moment longer, then turned and followed the wagon back.

Luci stood alone on the dreary, windswept prairie, the heaped-up black gumbo dirt at her feet, so stark against the new snow. She was all alone in the world. Now she knew why lobo wolves cried to the dark sky at night. Luci fell to her knees in the snow and raised her voice in a centuries old dirge that Indian women had always wept and wailed when they put a loved one on a burial scaffold and consigned them to Heammawihio, the God who watches over all.

What she wanted to do was throw herself down on the grave and die with her mother. They had always looked out for each other. She couldn't leave Sunrise Woman out here all alone. Luci cursed the white soldier who had betrayed the innocent, trusting girl and deserted her. That would never happen to the daughter, she vowed. No, Luci was too smart for that.

The cold bit into her and she roused herself, mounted up, and started back to the fort at a slow pace. Only when she rode to the gate did she realize the Pawnee had been watching her from a distance.

She swung down and handed him the reins. "Were you afraid I'd steal your horse?" She couldn't keep the bitterness out of her voice.

He looked at her a long moment. "I wasn't worried about the horse."

"Mercy! I can look out for myself. I don't need a killer of my people to do that!" She was furious with him because she was beholden to him and he was an enemy. "I'll pay you back for every cent you've spent on me."

"No need for that." He fell in walking beside her, his long legs keeping up with her easily as he led the horse across the parade ground.

"If you think I'll let you take it out in trade—"

"Did it ever occur to you that a Pawnee warrior might have too much pride to accept the favors of a Cheyenne girl?"

She stopped and confronted him. "They've certainly raped enough of them!"

"As Cheyenne warriors have raped our women."

"*Our* women!" she raged then turned away and started walking toward the trading post again. "You're not even a *real* Pawnee, Johnny Ace. Everyone knows about the white boarding school. I hear the other Pawnee scouts don't have much to do with you."

She had hurt him with her sharp words—she saw it on his dark, stoic face. Well, she didn't care. Maybe now he would leave her alone. The trouble was she did care. It made her feel cheap and small that she had said those things. The hurt on his handsome features bothered her.

"I do not deny what you say, Star Eyes." His voice was very soft. "You, too, are a 'white man's Indian.' Have you ever been in a Cheyenne village?"

Now it was her turn to be defensive. "A few times, we visited my mother's brother, Ta Ton Ka Haska. He rides with the outlaw Dog Soldiers."

Johnny Ace frowned. "The outlaw Dog Soldiers are killers of women and children."

"The Pawnee are killers of women and children!

Now stay away from me, you wolf for the blue-coats!" She stalked into the trading post and left him standing there holding the reins of the big horse.

Johnny stood staring after the irate girl. *Why did he bother?* He ought to either forget about her or drag her into the barn and take her, whether she fought him or not. Surely after he had mated with her several times, he could get her off his mind. After all, she couldn't be that different from any other woman.

With a curse, he turned and walked toward the barn to stable his horse. The sun which had showed itself so briefly at the burial had disappeared behind gray clouds and snow began again. At least Luci would be moved to comfortable quarters. She'd ask questions, of course, but no one would tell her, he'd seen to that. He'd even bribed old Mr. Bane to throw her out of the store room if she elected to stay there. Johnny was afraid some of the men who hung around the trading post to drink and gamble might see her and decide she was too much of a temptation to resist.

The snow fell faster. He knew from looking into the ominous sky that the weather might turn into a full blizzard. At least the fiery little blue-eyed half-breed would be warm and comfortable.

The snow came down for two days and he paced his own quarters like a restless animal; Eager to be out again. What he didn't want to admit even to himself was that at night, he saw that small face in his dreams. Her arms reached out to him. Her lips were soft and moist, opening up for the thrusting of

41

his warm tongue. Neither of them cared anymore about Pawnee and Cheyenne, about old tribal hatreds.

In his dreams, he took her for the first time, very slowly and gently, and she wept against his chest. *It was so very wonderful, Johnny . . . I hadn't known it could be like this. . . .* The wind rattled the windows and he held her very close against him and stroked her hair, then kissed the tears from her small face.

Don't cry, Star Eyes. I'm here for you; I'll always be here for you. You need never be afraid or alone again. He held her against him, feeling her heart beat through her small breast. *If anyone even looks at you, I'll kill him. You're mine now — only mine. . . .*

And then she was kissing him again, arching against him eagerly. *Make love to me again, beloved enemy . . . I want you.*

He reached for her. *You're safe now, Small One, I'll look after you. Neither of us will ever be lonely again.*

She came into his arms, whispering, sighing, *Johnny . . . Johnny . . . Johnny. . . .*

He came awake with a start. Someone was really calling his name; someone was banging on his door. "Johnny! Johnny Ace, the major wants to see you!"

He sat bolt upright in bed, realizing it was dawn and some soldier was shouting to him. He had been alone as always, after all. The soft sighing had been only the wind around the buildings. "I'll be right there!"

Whatever it was that Pani Le-shar wanted, Johnny Ace would do his bidding. He looked outside. The

42

weather seemed to be clearing but the snow lay in drifts, driven by the wind. He got dressed and went to see Major North.

The officer wasted no time as he gestured Johnny to a chair. "There's a Union Pacific train stranded in a drift a few miles up the line. The army's been called upon to go rescue them."

Johnny frowned. "That's one of the hazards of traveling these plains in the spring—late storms. Why can't they just sit there until the rail crews dig them out?"

"Because that may take a while." Major North paced the office. "And there's some fairly important people on board, or so the message says. Some rich man's daughter on her way to Colorado. Her papa might raise hell with important people in Washington if his little girl freezes her tootsies while waiting for the train to be dug out."

"What kind of man would let a child travel alone in this country?" Johnny leaned back and rolled a cigarette.

North shrugged. "Something about her mother dying and her going to Denver to live with her father. The Easterners on the train are scared some war party will find the stranded train and they'll be sitting ducks."

Johnny threw back his head and laughed. "Cheyenne'll stay by their fires until this is melted off. No Indian would get out voluntarily in weather like this, even the army knows that. That's why Custer attacked them in the dead of winter down on the Washita last year."

"*You* know that and *I* know that, but no one's interested in anything but this spoiled kid being inconvenienced on a stalled train. I hate to do it, but I'll have to send a patrol out."

He already knew the answer, but he asked automatically, "You want me to scout?"

North nodded. "These plains look like a trackless white ocean right now, Johnny. No one is more aware than I am of the danger. You know my own father died in a Nebraska blizzard. But if I don't send someone who knows the country with the soldiers, they're liable to end up either in Texas or Wyoming."

That was true. But it didn't make him feel any better. With the weather breaking, he had hoped to find an excuse to see Luci again. "Can we drop these civilians off at North Platte or are we to bring them back to the fort?"

"Let them make that choice. Since most of them would be taking the train on to Cheyenne when the track is cleared, a lot of them will want to stay in town. But the little girl is to catch a stage on to Denver, so she would have been getting off the train soon anyway."

"But the stage will be delayed because of the weather."

"So we have to entertain the little girl awhile until I can free a patrol to escort the stage on."

Johnny fingered the hilt of his knife, thinking. "When they finally get that spur line to Denver finished next year, we won't have to worry about protecting stage coaches with army patrols anymore." Johnny stood up, tossed away his smoke. "Well, this is what the army pays me for. Besides Pani Le-shar, I owe you for the favor you did me about getting quarters for the girl."

Frank North's eyes were bright with curiosity but he didn't ask. "That new lieutenant needs some experience and I think you're the man to give it to him."

Johnny paused, the cigarette halfway to his lips.

44

"Osgoode? That snooty one from Boston? Major, I'd rather not—"

"Someone's got to break him in, Johnny. He hasn't had anything to do but polish his brass buttons since he arrived here, they tell me. Carter Osgoode thinks the army is all pretty uniforms and military balls. Maybe it's time he found out differently."

Johnny didn't answer. Carter Osgoode made no secret of his contempt for the Pawnee scouts and the feeling was mutual. If Johnny had ever met a man he disliked more than that handsome, arrogant son of Boston society, he wasn't sure who it was.

Major North put one hand on Johnny's big shoulder. "You're the best scout I've got. I want you to teach our brash young lieutenant enough to survive on the frontier before his inexperience gets a bunch of soldiers killed."

"According to him, he already knows everything worth knowing," Johnny griped, tossing the cigarette away.

"I'm sorry to have to send men out in this cold, Johnny. If that brat on the train didn't have a grouchy father who's already telegraphed three times—"

"I understand, sir." Johnny moved toward the door, paused with his hand on the doorknob.

"If it makes you feel any better, I hope Carter Osgoode freezes his brass buttons off!"

Johnny laughed and went to saddle up.

The ride through the drifts toward the rail line was slow going in the cold. Johnny's great black stallion, Katis, did much better than the other horses. Still it was difficult and the wind felt cold on his dark face as the sun slowly broke through the gray sky.

Lieutenant Carter Osgoode was not only arrogant but stupid, Johnny thought in disgust as he watched the handsome officer.

Osgoode's curly brown hair blew across his forehead under his hat. "This way, to the right, men," he said, pointing. "We'll go rescue that train!"

Not two miles from the fort and already the lieutenant had lost his sense of direction. But a scout could not embarrass an officer in front of his men. Johnny resisted the urge to tell the officer he was incapable of tracking a fat girl through deep snow. Instead Johnny rode up next to him. "Sir," he said softly, "didn't you mean to say, 'Column left'?"

Osgoode glared back at him with his pale-colored eyes. For a moment, Johnny saw the contempt and dislike there. But he knew even Osgoode was aware of Johnny's reputation as the best scout on the frontier. "Ye Gods! You misunderstood my order, scout. What I meant was we'll turn right here—to the left."

Johnny kept silent. But the men knew. He saw the knowing looks on their faces. No doubt Carter Osgoode had been sent to this out-of-the-way fort because of his lack of ability when he had hoped for some more romantic and important assignment.

It took several hours' riding through the crusty drifts to find the stranded train. Johnny thought it looked like a dead black snake lying helpless in the whiteness of the snow swirls.

A quick check with the crew found that they and some of the passengers had elected to stay with the train until work crews could dig it out. The few passengers who wanted to would go back with the cavalry patrol on the extra horses that had been brought along for that purpose.

Johnny followed the lieutenant into one of the passenger coaches, wondering about this child they were to bring back. He hoped the little girl could ride.

A beautiful woman in an elegant pink cloak whirled around as they entered. "Land's sake! Well, I must say, it's about time!" she seethed in a deep Southern accent. "Wait until I let everyone know how slow the army was in coming to our rescue!" She twirled a silly pink parasol.

Johnny stared at her. He had never seen such an aristocratic and haughty girl. If it hadn't been for her attitude and pouty mouth, he would have thought her a great beauty with her bright blue eyes and dark curls tied up with rose ribbons.

Carter Osgoode made a sweeping bow. "The army regrets its lack of speed, ma'am. If we'd had any idea such a beautiful lady was waiting to be rescued, we'd have come at a gallop."

That seemed to mollify her. Johnny stared at her. *Why did the girl look so familiar to him?*

"Have we met before?" he blurted out.

Lieutenant Osgoode turned on him, seething. "It isn't proper for a scout to address the passengers."

Johnny gripped the backrest of the seat, willing himself not to slug the man. There'd be big trouble if he did that.

The girl looked him over with such frank curiosity that it made Johnny uneasy.

The officer seemed suddenly to remember why the patrol had come. "We're here to take off any passengers who don't want to wait for the train to be dug out. In fact, we were actually sent to rescue some brat of a kid named—"

"Winnifred Starrett?" The girl smiled a little too

sweetly and curtsied.

Johnny couldn't control his own grin at the officer's obvious embarrassment and the girl smiled back at Johnny, seemingly amused at the joke.

"I—I didn't mean—" The Lieutenant brushed back his curly brown hair with confusion. "Ye Gods! I thought we were here for some child. They said some wealthy man in Denver was worried about his daughter—"

"And I'm sure he is," the girl replied, and smiled archly.

The lieutenant apologized again. "We've brought several horses, Miss Starrett, I do hope you can ride."

"Oh dear, my riding habit is in my trunk in the baggage car. Certainly I can't ride without a proper outfit!"

Some of the other passengers snickered. Their facial expressions indicated Miss Starrett hadn't been too popular on the train.

The officer made a gesture of embarrassment. "You won't need the riding outfit, ma'am. You see, we neglected to bring a sidesaddle."

"You expect me to ride astride?" The elegant beauty looked horrified.

Johnny spoke up. "I reckon you could stay on the train."

Lieutenant Osgoode glared at him. For a moment, his weak face mirrored an expression that made Johnny think the Bostonian was about to strike him across the face with his gloves. He'd kill him if the officer did that, no matter what the consequences. Johnny's hand went to the knife in his belt.

The lieutenant seemed to reconsider, turned back to the girl. "Miss Starrett, The army regrets the inconvenience caused by the blizzard, but we simply can't do anything about the conditions we have to deal with. I'll have the troopers get your luggage."

"There are three trunks," she said, staring with open curiosity at Johnny.

Johnny said, "The lieutenant should tell you we had a hard time even getting here and it'll be the same going back. Take the bare necessities. I doubt there'll be a cotillion while you're at the fort."

"On the contrary," Lieutenant Osgoode snapped in his arrogant Boston accent, "I just may ask General Carr to put on a small social to honor Miss Starrett."

"Land's sake, Lieutenant, how gallant you are!" She took his arm, closed the dainty parasol with a snap.

But when they went out on the rear coach platform, it was Johnny she turned to even though the lieutenant was already positioning himself to help her from the train.

She looked up at Johnny, standing very close. He could smell the scent of her expensive perfume. "You're big," she purred. "I'll let you carry me through the drift."

He hadn't expected this. Almost awkwardly, he reached for her. As he took her in his arms, Winnifred Starrett turned slightly so that her breasts brushed his arm. He almost jumped back, sure she had done it by accident. For an Indian even to look at a white woman was cause to lynch him. His face must have registered his fears, because she smiled and turned her body just enough so that her right breast was against his wide chest.

Johnny glanced around. The lieutenant was busy leaving orders. No one was looking at Johnny as he carried the girl down the steps to her mount. When he stood her on the ground by the horse, she managed to brush against him again and the way she

49

smiled let him know that none of it had been done by accident. *The lady was a tease.*

A girl like this could cause him a lot of trouble. For a long moment, he looked down at her, fighting to keep his maleness from going hard at the touch and scent of her. He had been a long time without a woman and the little Cheyenne had started a fire in him that hadn't been put out.

Winnifred Starrett looked up at him and ran the tip of her tongue along her lip. He could tell from her amused expression that she knew exactly what effect she was having.

A soldier brought her horse up. She held out her small foot to Johnny and he automatically cupped his hands, lifting her to her stirrup. Winnifred sat the regular saddle awkwardly.

"I'm sorry," he said. "If we'd known we weren't dealing with a child, we'd have brought a side-saddle."

She looked at him a long moment and took a very deep breath that made her breasts move under the pink velvet of her outfit. He tried not to look at them, knowing instinctively that she had done it for his benefit.

Johnny turned away, hoping she didn't see the hard bulge of his maleness. Behind him, she laughed softly and he realized he was being taunted . . . or being made an offer.

Lieutenant Osgoode walked briskly from the train. "The weather's warming, Miss Starrett. I trust your stay at our fort won't be too terrible."

"On the contrary, perhaps it will be interesting. I'm joining my father after many years, so I've never been west of Alabama." When the officer looked away, she caught Johnny's eye, but he pretended not to see it.

He had a terrible urge for a woman. He wasn't sure exactly how far the lovely Miss Starrett was willing to go with her teasing.

But with his need, if she wanted him to make love to her, would he be able to turn her down?

Chapter 3

Looking through the small window of her quarters, Luci watched the patrol ride across the parade ground and wondered where they were going in such weather. It must be urgent to send men out into the aftermath of this blizzard.

She stared after the handsome lieutenant from Boston and Johnny Ace on his black horse leading the patrol through the fort gates. *Big, stupid Pawnee.* She tried not to think of how he had helped her and concentrated on the fact that he rode with white soldiers against her people. In weather like this, war parties would not be out attacking trains or settlers, so where was that patrol headed?

The riders disappeared in the distance and Luci sighed, poked up her fire, and sat down to stare into the flames. Quarters were generally reserved for officers' families. Luci had asked why she had been given this nice place, but no one would tell her. Someone with influence, no doubt. Now why would any officer bother with her and what did he want in return?

Do you have to ask? she thought dejectedly. She ran through the post's officers in her mind. Only one—Carter Osgoode—had gone out of his way to speak to her and she didn't trust his motives because of the way he leered at her.

Certainly she didn't intend to make the same mistake her mother had made. On the other hand, if the handsome lieutenant had honorable intentions, it would solve her whole problem. Her only alternative seemed to be return to the Cheyenne band led by her uncle, whom she had met only a couple of times in her whole life. For all intents and purposes, Luci was a white girl in a brown skin.

Hours passed and the sun broke weakly through the clouds. Luci picked her way through the snow to deliver freshly ironed shirts to Major North. She had just started back across the parade ground when the patrol rode through the fort's gates. Riding with them were white civilians, most noticeably a beautiful girl in a rich pink velvet cloak with fur around the hood. Curious, Luci turned around and went back, joining the growing crowd coming from all directions. The patrol reined up before Major North's office and the lieutenant dismounted, turned his horse over to a soldier.

The slightly built North came out of the building, answered the salute. "You made it back all right?"

The handsome Bostonian turned and smiled at the beauty on the horse. "No problems, sir. Mission completed. And this"—he gestured—"is the young lady we were sent to rescue. Major, may I present Miss Winnifred Starrett."

The major bowed. "Glad to have you with us, Miss Starrett. Your father has been burning up the

53

wires between here and Denver about your predicament."

The elegant lady only smiled as if that were the least she could expect. "Actually, Major, I've had a delightful ride. Quite an adventure!" Her tone was honeyed and Southern. Her gaze seemed to focus on the Pawnee scout.

If Johnny Ace noticed, he gave no sign, Luci thought with annoyance and then wondered why she was annoyed.

Major North said, "We hope we can make your stay enjoyable until the snow melts and the stage to Denver is back on schedule. You might have been more comfortable at North Platte."

Miss Starrett smiled from the back of her horse as she looked around at all the men. "I think everything I'll need is right here. Staying at a fort may make for amusing dinner table conversation in Denver later."

Lieutenant Osgoode looked wistfully at the beauty, then back to the major. "I was hoping, sir, that you might prevail on General Carr to give a party in the lady's honor. We get so few important guests at Fort McPherson."

"True, true." The officer rocked slightly on his heels and tugged at his mustache. "Since tomorrow's Saturday and the weather's warming, I'm sure the general will see no reason we can't host a small celebration for officers and their guests." He seemed to consider. "The problem now is to decide where to put Miss Starrett. Our male guests can share officers' rooms, but there are no ladies' quarters available as of a couple of days ago."

The major looked directly at Luci and she realized suddenly that he had had a hand in giving her the comfortable quarters. *Mercy, who had asked him to?*

Abruptly, Luci thought of a new way out of her

54

own predicament—a better way. She pushed forward. "Major, the quarters I have would be perfect for the lady."

Miss Starrett looked down at her in obvious distaste. "Major, would I have to share them with this—this . . . girl?"

But Luci was clever and thought fast. She gave the haughty girl her most humble smile. "Won't you be needing a personal maid, Miss Starrett? No one on the post can do up your clothes as well as I can. Surely your maid generally shares your quarters?"

Put in that light, the elegant girl seemed to reconsider. "That's true. And I'm without a maid right now. Mine refused to come West—she thought savages might ravish her."

She looked directly at the big Pawnee with an amused smile.

Here was Luci's ticket out of Nebraska and her miserable life as a post laundress. "Give me a chance, Miss Starrett. I promise you'll be pleased with my work, and maybe when you leave, you'll consider taking me with you."

Luci saw Johnny Ace frown and his mouth half opened as if he would protest, then he seemed to think better of it and leaned both hands on his saddle horn.

Major North rubbed his palms together as if relieved about how to handle this problem. "Wonderful, then it's all settled! Good to meet you, Miss Starrett, and looking forward to tomorrow night. I'll send a sleigh for you at eight. Now, Lieutenant, get the lady moved into quarters. Even though it's warming, it's still cold as a mother-in-law's kiss out here!"

The lady smiled drolly as if being amused by a troop of clowns. "They do speak colorfully in the

West, don't they?"

Carter Osgoode led the beauty's horse as the little group started across the snowy parade ground. Johnny Ace dismounted and, leading both his stallion and the packhorse with all the luggage, fell in alongside Luci as she walked at the rear of the group. She decided to ignore him and looked straight ahead.

"Star Eyes, I don't like you humbling yourself that way before that uppity girl," he said softly.

"*You* don't like!" She tried to keep her voice under control so those ahead would not hear. "Do you think I give a damn what *you* like? Going to Denver as her personal maid may be the only chance I'll ever get to escape my life."

"I wouldn't like it if you went away." His tone was begrudging as if it hurt him to admit it.

"In that case, I will enjoy leaving twice as much!" Her tone came out sharper than she'd intended, but she was fighting her own attraction to the virile scout.

Luci remembered then the way Winnifred Starrett had looked at him and a burning sensation passed over her. What difference did it make to her, she thought, if the elegant beauty wanted to lower herself to toy with this enemy?

"She's a real lady!" Luci sighed, watching the pink-cloaked back on the horse ahead.

"Something familiar about her . . ." Johnny's voice trailed off.

Strange, she had thought the same thing herself when she had first seen the haughty girl, then had dismissed the idea. "Where would you have ever seen a real lady before? But she keeps looking at you as if . . ."

"As if what?" The Pawnee grinned sideways at her.

56

"You know very well what!" She marched ahead doggedly, irritated with herself that he had the same effect on her and it was galling in the extreme.

But she had a sinking feeling Johnny Ace had been right about the white girl when, later, the two women were alone together in the quarters.

Luci began to unpack Winnifred's luggage while the older girl stood before the fire. "Such lovely dresses and so many of them!" Luci said in awe, shaking the wrinkles out of a soft silk in deep cherry pink.

"Father sent them," Winnifred said. "He owed it to me, after all. Because of him, I've been raised in what is politely known as 'genteel poverty.' "

"You and your father must be very close," Luci said wistfully.

"Hardly!" The anger in the girl's tone caused Luci to pause. "Actually I haven't seen him in a long time. He deserted us and broke my mother's heart. I doubt he would have ever bothered to contact me except he's dying and suddenly his blood kin is very dear to him."

Luci wasn't quite sure what to say. "I—I'm sorry."

"Don't be." Winnifred's eyes were as cold as blue ice. "I'm going out to look after him, and in exchange, he's promised I shall be his heir. In a year or two, if I'm lucky, I shall be one of the richest women in Denver."

Luci looked away, uncomfortable with the hate and satisfaction in the other girl's voice, "I hope your stay here won't be too inconvenient. The lieutenant seems quite taken with you—"

"A fortune hunter if I ever saw one." Miss Starrett laughed, pacing up and down before the fire. "But certainly I'll need some diversion while I'm at this isolated place."

"I expect there'll be much more excitement awaiting you in Denver." Luci couldn't keep the wistfulness out of her voice as she hung up the fine dresses. They all had wide sashes designed to emphasize the white girl's trim waist. Hers wasn't as small as Luci's, but Winnifred was evidently vain about it and chose her dresses accordingly.

"There'd better be! I'd hate to think I came all this way just to watch my errant father die." Winnifred shrugged in boredom. "I can't imagine anything duller than sitting here all afternoon with no one but a squaw to talk to. Since etiquette expects me to call on the general's wife anyway and leave my calling card, I'll do that this afternoon." She reached for her cloak. "Tomorrow night, Luci, I'll wear the cherry pink; it sets off my eyes."

Luci managed to control her anger at the "squaw" insult and only nodded as she hung up the dress Winnifred spoke of. She had just been thinking the dress would enhance her own eyes. But of course she'd never get to wear anything so fine. Her own flowered cotton print was too plain to wear to a ball.

She fingered the fabric with a frown, thinking of the Pawnee. She was obligated to him and she didn't like that.

Winnifred swept out the door without so much as a polite "good-bye." Luci walked over to the window to watch the aristocratic girl crunch through the snow, nose in the air. Try as she might, Luci didn't like the girl. She had seen the scorn in the bright blue eyes. Obviously Winnifred had nothing but contempt for Indians. But she hadn't looked at Johnny Ace that way. For some reason, the thought that the older girl might be attracted to the Pawnee annoyed her. It was unthinkable that a white girl would get herself involved with a brave.

Why should she care if the scout risked trouble with the white men by flirting with the society girl? Luci returned to unpacking Miss Starrett's fine clothes.

Winnifred Starrett picked her way through the melting snow. She would be expected to call upon the general's wife, of course, and that made a good excuse to get out of that miserable room. She didn't want to have to share quarters with an Indian, even if the girl was a servant. What she'd rather have was a black maid. Too bad the War had freed the slaves.

Winnifred had reason enough to hate Indians, to hate anyone with dark skin, she thought as she slowed, then looked toward the barn. And that pretty little squaw had probably slept with a lot of white men—like Winnifred's rake of a father. Manning Starrett had always been attracted to swarthy skin. So was his daughter in spite of herself. Attracted and repelled.

Was that big scout at the barn? Winnifred picked her way across the mud and ice, went inside. It smelled like sweet hay, horses, and leather. She walked up and down the stalls, bored and annoyed.

Then she spotted him in the last stall, grooming that black stallion. She feigned surprise. "Well, hello, what a surprise to see you here!"

He stared a long moment, evidently puzzled at her appearance in the barn. He nodded to her, went back to grooming his horse.

She sauntered over, leaned against the stall door, "What a lovely animal!"

He stroked the stallion's neck with obvious affection, "I've had Katis since he was a colt. I took him in a raid against the Cheyenne."

"A warrior," she said softly. "How many men have you killed?"

He seemed taken aback by her frankness. "Miss Starrett, that's not something to be discussed with a genteel lady."

"How many?" she persisted. There was something exciting in the idea that this man had spilled blood.

"A few," he said reluctantly, and turned his back on her, returned to grooming his horse.

She stood and watched him work. The muscles under his dark skin rippled as he brushed Katis's mane. Winnifred had a sudden vision of herself in the hay naked with him, pale skin beneath dark skin, His hands would stroke and brush her own black mane of hair, loose it from its pins, and tangle his fingers in it. . . .

"Excuse me," he said softly, jarring her from her fantasy. He came out of the stall, closed the gate. "I'll have to be going now, Miss Starrett."

"Must you?" She moved closer, repelled because of her mother, attracted like her father.

"Miss Starrett . . ." He looked uncomfortable, but he couldn't back away, the stall gate was behind him. His expression told her that he knew better than she what could happen to an Indian who was caught in a compromising position with a white girl.

She felt a delicious thrill of power over this virile stallion of a man. All she had to do was scream and people would come running. All she had to do was yell that she had been molested, and he might be lynched. No, she didn't want that to happen to this handsome savage. She leaned closer, enjoying the effect her nearness seemed to be having on him, annoyed with herself that he was affecting her, too.

60

She liked teasing men into a fever pitch and then laughing and walking away, leaving them embarrassed and humiliated. It was revenge against all men, but particularly against her father, who had satisfied his appetite in a hundred careless liaisons. Manning Starrett's many infidelities had caused her dear, plain mother to weep a million tears, die an unspeakable death. For this, Winnifred would take revenge on all men.

She pressed close enough that her full breasts brushed his shirt. "Are you wanting to kiss me?" She was going to laugh in his face if he tried, laugh and run away as she had done a hundred times to a hundred fumbling, eager boys.

But Johnny Ace reached out suddenly, pulled her to him. She was too surprised to struggle, cry out. Then it was too late because his mouth covered hers as he held her with arms of steel. She couldn't scream if she wanted to. Did she want to?

She could feel his hot strength all the way down her body as he molded her against him and forced his tongue between her lips. She felt a molten heat began to build between her thighs in a rush of passion. Winnifred had meant to tease and tantalize him for her amusement. Now she strained her breasts against him and moaned low in her throat. All she wanted was for him to throw her down in the hay and take her in a rush of hot seed and abandon.

"Please," she murmured against his lips, digging her nails into his broad back. "Oh, please . . ."

But he took her shoulders in his two big hands, held her away from him. "Miss Starrett, I'm sorry you're bored at our fort, but the army doesn't pay me to entertain teasing white girls."

She looked up at him, her breath coming hard, her erect nipples straining the fabric of her expensive dress. "Lands sake! I was just tantalizing y'all."

"And you've teased dozens into a mindless frenzy," he guessed, turning away. "What makes you hate men so?"

No man had ever understood her motives so perfectly before. Winnifred felt stripped naked before him. She felt the blood rush to her face in a fury. "You're all alike," she snarled, "just like my father— taking his pleasure where he could, not caring how he hurt my poor mother."

A look of compassion crossed his face. "So that's it. Someday your little revenge may come full circle if you don't watch out."

She had an insane desire to throw herself into his arms again, let him dominate her, make love to her. It was dangerous for a white woman even to think such a thing, but on the other hand, white men and Indian girls. . . . "Oh, life is so unfair!"

He didn't say anything as her shoulders bowed, shaking with anger at the injustice of it all.

She paused and looked up at him. "In a few months or a year or two, Father will be dead and I'll be rich, and I won't have to answer to anyone. I won't care what they think!"

He stood looking down at her, that big, confident male savage. "What is it you want from me, Miss Starrett?"

"Do I have to spell it out?" she said it in a rush, not intending to demean herself this way, but the memory of his virile strength and the taste of his mouth overpowered her senses. She would buy him like a stud horse, take him to Denver. . . .

"Miss Starrett, there's a girl I care about already."

She looked up at him, not believing what she had heard. She realized that the expression on his face was pity.

"Damn you!" she raged at him, striking him with her small fists. He put his wide hands up before his face to protect it although she knew he could have killed her easily with his great brute strength. "I was only toying with you, teasing! Do you think I'd let you touch me, you — you — "

"Savage?" he said softly.

Savage. And she had wanted him to take her savagely, to rip her clothes off and force himself on her. Winnifred had a sudden vision of that big dark body sprawled on top of hers, his even white teeth pulling at her nipples while she arched herself up, wanting him to take even more of her breast in his mouth, wanting him to drive his throbbing shaft of maleness deep inside so that her body could lock onto his.

With a sob, she turned and ran out of the barn. It occurred to her suddenly that if people saw her retreat, there would be gossip. If nothing else, Winnifred Starrett was proud. That had been all that had sustained her in the years after her ne'er-do-well father had gone through her mother's small inheritance before the War and then gone off to Colorado.

Lieutenant Osgoode caught up with her before she had gone a dozen steps through the snow. "Ah, there you are, Miss Starrett. May I call you Winnie?"

She managed to pull herself together and fixed him with an aloof gaze. "Not even my mother called me Winnie. *You* may call me Miss Starrett."

Any other man might have winced at the rebuff and gone on his way, but Carter Osgoode was evidently not easily offended. "I meant no offense to a lady," he said grandly.

A lady. Five minutes ago, she had been rubbing herself up against a savage male animal with nothing more on her mind than that he should throw her down in the hay like some common slut and mount her like a dark stallion. And the Indian had spurned her. For whom? She glanced at the barn behind her. Was he watching and listening in the shadows?

"Miss Starrett, would you do me the honor of letting me be your escort to the party tomorrow night?"

She gave him a chilling look. Her father must have been very much like this young officer, when he had served in the West almost two decades ago. She hated Carter Osgoode for that. "Sorry. You heard the major say he would send a sleigh for me."

His expression was as cold, as arrogant, as she felt. "I see. A lieutenant isn't good enough for you."

"Especially not a fortune hunter," she snapped. "Take someone else, Lieutenant. I'm sure my half-breed maid would be delighted to get an invitation."

She saw him redden at the taunt. "That's unthinkable and you know it! Are you daring me?"

"You wouldn't dare, not even as a joke!" She flung the challenge at him as she turned to walk away. "Now if you'll excuse me, I must make a call on General Carr's wife."

He made a sound of rage behind her. "It'd be a joke on you if I invited her and told everyone it was your idea!"

She looked back over her shoulder, laughing at his humiliation. Behind them, the tall Pawnee had come out of the barn. She wondered how much of that conversation he had heard? *What difference did it make?* With a gesture of dismissal, she marched toward the general's quarters.

Luci straightened at the rap on the door and put down the dress she had been pressing for Miss Starrett. That couldn't be the lady back so soon. Winnifred hadn't been gone long enough to have made her social call.

She opened the door, blinking in surprise at the handsome officer from Boston. "Oh, Lieutenant. I—I'm sorry, Miss Starrett has gone out, but I'll tell her you called—"

"I didn't come to see her; I came to see you." He stood there, twisting his hat in his hands, his curly hair hanging down on his forehead.

"Me?" She touched her breast in confusion.

"I wanted to invite you to accompany me to the party tomorrow night. You're so much prettier than she is."

Luci stared at him. "Me? Mercy! You're inviting me? Lieutenant, it would be unthinkable for you to take me."

"I'll take whom I want," he declared, "and you be sure and let Miss Starrett know I invited you."

That puzzled her. She shook her head. "Even if I wanted to go, Lieutenant, I don't have anything to wear—"

"Nonsense. What you have on will be fine. Miss Starrett suggested I invite you. Be sure and tell everyone that."

A party. In all her life, Luci had never been to a real party. "Did Miss Starrett really suggest you invite me?" She felt a little guilty that she had evidently misjudged Winnifred Starrett. The beautiful white girl had a kind heart after all. "Well, in that case . . ."

"Then that settles it! You ride over with Miss Starrett in the major's sleigh tomorrow night and I'll meet you there."

She thought a gentleman always called for a lady, but who was she to question a Bostonian's manners?

She only nodded shyly. Carter Osgoode left, whistling jauntily.

What on earth had she done? Luci closed the door and leaned against it. In her eagerness to attend a real party, she was setting herself up for all sorts of trouble. She looked down at her simple dress and red, work-worn hands in despair. Even if she had a dress fine enough, she suspected the white ladies of the fort wouldn't welcome her into their midst. As badly as she wanted to go, she trembled on the brink of running after Carter and telling him she'd regained her senses and changed her mind.

An hour later, Winnifred returned. "Did you get the wrinkles out of the gown? That's the one I intend to wear to the party."

Luci nodded in breathless excitement. "I'm invited too! Lieutenant Osgoode said it was your idea and to be sure and mention it to you."

"He did, did he?" Winnifred's pretty lips curled almost into a sneer. "He'll expect you to back out at the last minute after you think about it."

Luci bit her lip, turned away. "You're right. I don't really have a ball gown. The only dress I have in this world was bought by that Pawnee when—"

"The scout?" Winnifred gave her a piercing look. "Are you his woman?"

Luci looked away, blushing furiously. "No! Why would you think that? I keep telling him I could never get involved with an enemy of my people."

"I see." There was something cold and ugly in the pretty face. "He prefers a half-breed who isn't interested, when he could have . . ."

Luci shrugged. "I'll send my regrets to the lieutenant. It was silly of me to think I could attend."

"Nonsense!" Winnifred paused with both hands on the wide satin sash of her waist. "Land's sake! We mustn't disappoint Carter Osgoode! I'll lend you a dress. You just choose one and hem it up to fit you."

"You will?" Luci clapped her hands. "Oh, Miss Starrett, you're so kind! I would be happy to be your maid for the rest of my days!"

"This party may turn out to be entertaining after all," the other girl said. "I can hardly wait to see your lieutenant's face when you show up."

She had misjudged the white girl, Luci thought as Winnifred went through her dresses, obviously enjoying helping Luci choose something for the party. Whatever doubts Luci had about attending were swept away in Winnifred's enthusiasm.

The sun came out and the snow was melting fast the next afternoon as she returned from the trading post to buy a spool of thread. The big Pawnee caught up with her.

"Go away," she flung at him, and looked straight ahead. "I have no time for you."

He grabbed her arm. "Star Eyes, we need to talk—"

"No." She shook his hand off. "I've got to finish altering a dress for the party."

"So you've been invited?" For some reason, he didn't look surprised.

"Lieutenant Osgoode invited me." She said it with satisfaction.

"Luci, you know an Indian would never be invited to an officer's party. I—I think you should reconsider."

"Just because some big, stupid Pawnee says so? No!"

He flinched and rubbed his hand across his ear. Before he could say anything else, she turned and ran through the slush of the warming day.

Winnifred couldn't have been sweeter about lending her the soft spring yellow dress and a pair of shoes, although they were too large for Luci's small feet. She even showed Luci how to sweep her long black locks up into an elaborate hairdo, braid yellow ribbons through it. When Luci looked up suddenly and caught the older girl's amused look, she felt a little uneasy. But hadn't Miss Starrett been the one who suggested to the lieutenant that he invite her?

Luci saw Johnny's Ace's dark face in her mind, its troubled expression. Could he be jealous? She had no one to turn to for advice. For a long moment, she thought about her mother. But Luci had looked after Sunrise all these years. She missed her greatly, but Sunrise had had too many problems of her own, made worse by the drinking. She had never given Luci much support or advice. Maybe this would be a step up for Luci. She certainly didn't intend to make the same mistakes her mother had made.

And now it was Saturday night and Luci actually put on the fine yellow dress and climbed into the sleigh with Winnifred Starrett. "Oh, this is the most exciting thing that's ever happened to me! I'll be forever grateful!"

Winnifred smiled as if she knew a secret joke. "Y'all are the most innocent thing I ever met. I almost wish . . ."

"Wish what?" Luci wiggled her toes in the shoes that were a trifle big. She had stuffed the toes with cotton.

But then Winnifred eyes hardened. "Nothing. Because of my father, Indians girls deserve . . ." Her voice trailed off and then she seemed to realize that Luci listened. "Deserve a little extra. Yes, all Indian girls deserve what you're going to get."

"You mean to attend a party?" Luci was almost delirious with the thrill of it. Carter would admire her beauty. The other officers would clamor to dance with her, although Winnifred had just this morning taught her how. A dozen handsome white men would want to marry her.

Winnifred smiled thinly, smoothed the wide sash of the pink dress she wore. "What a party it's going to be! I'll wager it's one neither you nor the fort will ever forget!"

The sleigh stopped before the officer's hall. Music floated faintly from inside: *Oh, Genevieve, sweet Genevieve, the days may come, the days may go, but still the hands of mem'ry weave the blissful dreams of lone ago, Oh, Genevieve, sweet Genevieve. . . .*

Johnny Ace lounged against a porch column. Luci ignored him pointedly as the driver came around and assisted both women down.

But Winnifred smiled at him. "Coming inside?"

Luci felt his gaze. Then Johnny said, "Afraid I wouldn't feel welcome. People hereabouts don't mix socially with savages."

There was some undercurrent to his words that Luci caught but didn't understand any more than she understood the look that passed between him and the white girl.

Winnifred grabbed Luci's arm. "Land's sake! Let's go in. You don't want to keep the lieutenant waiting."

The two went inside. Major North hurried to Winnifred, hesitated, and looked a little surprised at seeing Luci.

Winnifred smiled. "Lieutenant Osgoode invited her," she said by way of explanation.

The major pulled at his trim mustache, seeming ill at ease. "In that case . . ." He turned and signaled to Carter, who stood laughing with other young officers. "Lieutenant, your young lady has arrived."

Carter Osgoode's mouth sagged slowly open and the officer next to him punched him in the ribs and winked at one of the others, who glanced at Luci and laughed.

Luci smiled at him, too aware of the way people were turning slowly to stare at her.

Major North had led Winnifred to the dance floor. Carter Osgoode walked over very slowly and nodded to Luci. He turned to watch the dancers, then edged away slightly.

The small band paused between numbers, and the ladies of the post surrounded Major North and his partner and introduced themselves.

"Oh, Miss Starrett, we've been so eager to meet you! What's the news from the cities?"

Winnifred fluttered her fan. "Y'all flatter me, ladies! But in Montgomery, we hear that the new *Godey's* says the 'bustle' will be the fashion news from Paris now. The hoop is about to become passé."

"No! Really?" The women crowded around the newcomer. "And what's this we're hearing about Wyoming Territory thinking of allowing their women to vote?"

Winnifred's beautiful face frowned. "Sheer gossip, I think. I'll believe it when I see it."

The band struck up a lively Stephen Foster tune that drowned out the conversation.

De Camptown ladies sing dis song, Doo-dah! Doo-dah! De Camptown racetrack five miles long, oh, doo-dah day . . .

Luci watched the dancers and looked up appealingly at Carter.

He ran his finger around the collar of his blue uniform as if it were choking him and stared straight ahead. "Ye Gods! I—I didn't really think you'd come."

"Oh, I couldn't have, but Miss Starrett loaned me a dress and encouraged me. She said you'd be surprised."

"Did she now?" His tone was at the very least annoyed.

Luci couldn't understand why he was upset. He had invited her and she knew she looked pretty in the yellow dress with its wide sash.

He didn't say anything else, just ran his hand distractedly through his brown curly hair and watched the dancers. Winnifred swept by and waved to them both.

"Bitch!" Carter whispered under his breath so softly that Luci wasn't sure that was really the word he used. No gentleman . . . of course she had been mistaken.

Luci stood there, ill at ease. She felt people looking at her and nudging each other. Perhaps she was being too self-conscious. Surely they weren't talking about her.

Carter said, "May I get you a cup of punch, Miss Luci?"

Her throat felt so dry, she wasn't sure she could swallow. "Yes, a—a cup of punch would be nice."

Carter disappeared into the crowd toward the back. Now Luci stood there all alone. She tried to look nonchalant, but it was hard when she felt people were staring at her. Winnifred and the major danced past and Luci nodded shyly when the other girl smiled in her direction.

The music stopped and immediately, young officers crowded around Winnifred. "Oh, please, Miss Starrett, may I have the next dance?"

The elegant beauty's fan fluttered, her Southern accent became more pronounced. "Now, gentlemen, I promise to dance with y'all, but you must wait your turn."

Major North smiled, bowed, and handed Winnifred over to her bevy of admirers. Then he walked off the dance floor with one of the men from the train. "I should have known I wouldn't have her to myself. Tell me, Mr. Johnson, how are things in Washington?"

The man's heavy jowls waggled. "Lots of talk about that Suez Canal being built. Seems to me we should get that de Lesseps fella to dig us one of our own across Panama."

"But is it practical, considering the yellow fever of the Tropics?"

They brushed past Luci, lost in conversation. The music began again but no man asked Luci to dance although she felt them sneaking glances at her. *What was keeping Carter?* He had been gone a long time for that cup of punch . . . or did it just feel like forever standing here with everyone staring at her?

The music ended and another song played and then another. Still no one asked Luci to dance. However, Winnifred was besieged by eager young men. When the older girl danced past Luci, there was something almost cruel, something triumphant, in her smile.

She was imagining that, of course, Luci thought in her growing uneasiness. Miss Starrett had been so kind and helpful. Why, mercy! Luci couldn't have attended without the loan of the dress and shoes!

Where was Carter? She couldn't stand here in the same spot all evening as if roots had spouted on the bottom of her borrowed shoes. When she looked around, she thought she saw Johnny Ace's face at the window, watching the festivities. He had tried to warn her not to come. Well, she wasn't going to give him the satisfaction of saying "I told you so."

She would make her way through the crowd to the refreshment table at the back. There had obviously been a problem. Maybe they had run out of punch cups. Maybe Carter had been taken ill and had had to leave and someone had forgotten to give her his apology. Maybe . . .

Carter Osgoode stood laughing and talking with a group of young officers. His unsteady posture and loud voice told her he'd been drinking.

The men stopped talking and looked at her with curiosity. One of them nudged Carter. "I didn't know we were hosting a powwow. Did you think we were hosting a powwow, Carter? She's not wearing war paint and feathers!"

Another snickered. "Who called for a clean shirt?" They all roared with laughter.

Carter blinked, ran his finger around his collar again. "Uh, Luci? I—I thought maybe you left—"

"Good idea!" She whirled and pushed through the crowd, blinded by tears. Behind her the young officers laughed but Carter called after her, "Luci, wait!"

For what? Further humiliation? She seemed to feel every eye in the hall upon her. Though tears blinded her, she managed to keep her face expressionless as she hurried toward the door and ran out into the cool spring night.

Chapter Four

She blinked back tears as she ran down the steps. The Pawnee stepped out of the shadows. "Luci, wait!"

She walked faster, head high. Her pride would not allow her to weep in front of this enemy. She'd been shamed enough. "Go away."

He caught up then fell in step beside her. "I watched through the window."

She kept walking. "Watched what? I had a perfectly lovely evening. The lieutenant couldn't have been more charming."

He matched her short stride easily with his long legs. "Then why are you leaving early and why isn't he escorting you home?"

The tears were rising in her throat, making a hard, bitter knot that threatened to choke her. "I don't have to answer to you! Why do you keep following me?" She began to sob a little, unable to hold back her anguish any longer.

"That white bastard!" He caught her arm and she tried to pull free. People driving past in a wagon turned to look curiously.

Luci struggled to break away, crying now and furious that she was humiliating herself before him. "Let go of me or I'll scream!"

He glanced at the passing wagon. "Star Eyes, I want to talk to you." He said it quietly, but with iron determination in his voice. He didn't loosen his grip as he forced her to walk toward the barn. "Inside where no one will see us."

Inside the barn, she jerked out of his grasp, stumbled backward. "I don't see that we have anything to discuss!"

The barn was warm from the heat of the many horses' bodies and it smelled of sweet hay and leather. A horse snorted in its stall at the sound of their voices. In the moonlight, she recognized Katis pricking his ears forward at the sight of his beloved master.

"I didn't like what I saw tonight—you trying to be a white girl, and all those people humiliating you."

She choked back a sob. "You don't understand how much it hurt—"

"Don't I?" Very slowly, he rubbed his hand along his ear. "Believe me, I know. Star Eyes, we're both Indian. We can never be whites, no matter how much we try to ape them."

"No, we're not even Indians." The tears came now. "You don't fit in with your people, I'm not sure I could fit in with mine! We're white man's Indians, that's all we are! I—I was so flattered when Carter asked me to the party—"

"I tried to warn you." He stood feet wide apart, hand on the knife in his belt. "I ought to go pull that bastard out of that party and take my knife to his—"

"Stop it!" She tried to get past him and out the barn door, but he blocked her path. "Mercy! You'd say anything to keep me from going to Denver, wouldn't you? You think if I don't go with Winnifred Starrett, I'll be here for your pleasure! Stop treating me as if I were your woman! I'm not yours! I'll never be!"

"And that's what's driving me *loco*," he admitted grudgingly. He reached out, grabbed her as she tried to run past, and dragged her to him. She struggled to break free as his big arms enveloped her, pulling her hard against his wide chest. His mouth covered hers and she gasped at the sensation. As she opened her lips, his tongue forced its way inside.

He was an enemy. But she couldn't stop her body from molding itself against him all the way down their legs. His manhood throbbed hard against her belly and her nipples came erect at the touch of his chest against them.

"Star Eyes, oh, Star Eyes . . ." His mouth was hot as a comet's trail as he kissed her mouth, her cheeks, her eyes.

Without even thinking, she slipped her arms around his sinewy neck and clung to him, shaking with sobs. He was big and strong and he wanted her. He was safety and protection. More than that, her body wanted him. She could feel the sudden heat and moisture between her thighs as she pressed against his maleness.

She couldn't pull out of his arms if she tried—he held her too tightly. His tongue forced itself deeper into her mouth, teasing and tantalizing her senses. The heat and the scent and the taste of him, everything about him said "stallion." His big, wide hands stroked her back and began to pull at her dress.

She could taste her own tears as he kissed her. This could not be. She was no common whore or squaw to be thrown down on the hay of the barn. She must stop him. But instead, her breasts pressed hard against his hand as his fingers pushed the top of her dress down and closed over the nipple.

She couldn't stifle the audible sigh of pleasure when he stroked there. She found herself running the tip of her tongue along the corners of his mouth, lost in the masculine taste and feel and scent of him.

With his great strength, he lifted her up so that his mouth could close over most of her breast, the tip of his tongue running over her throbbing nipple. His mouth was hot and wet sucking there, making her tremble with desire.

In that instant, she wanted nothing more than to lie down on the soft hay, pull him on top of her, and let him tear away the yellow dress and plunge deep into her body. Would it hurt when he broke through the thin silk barrier of her virginity and made her his woman? Would it be ecstasy when his maleness throbbed deep inside her, his virile seed pumping forth from this stallion of a man?

A Pawnee stallion. Was she out of her mind? All she had to offer a future husband was the prize of her virginity, and virginity was very important to the Cheyenne; so much so that they sometimes kept chastity belts on their unmarried women. There was no future for her with an enemy male, and no Cheyenne brave would want her if she gave away the most highly prized treasure a woman could offer a man.

In that split second, as he kissed and caressed her, she saw her mother's face in her mind as Sunrise Woman must have been at Luci's age. Had she, too, succumbed to a moment's passion in some dark barn and ruined her life forever? Luci would not make the same mistake.

Breathlessly, fighting to control her passions, she broke free of him. "You damned Pawnee! Everywhere I turn, you're right there, trailing after me like a stallion trying to take a mare!"

"You want me, too, don't deny it!" He was shaking; she could see his wide shoulders trembling in the moonlight.

"Not a Pawnee! Never a Pawnee!" With a sob, she brushed past him and ran out of the barn. He called after her, but she didn't look back as she ran to her quarters. Inside, she slammed the door, slid the bolt, leaned against the door, gasping for air.

Her body was her own worst enemy. When that giant of a man took her in his arms, jerking her against his throbbing maleness, it forgot that she must use her virginity to get herself a husband who would look after her, and cherish her. She was too clever to do as her mother had done — to waste herself on some man who only wanted a female vessel to contain the seed of his lust, never mind who.

Sooner or later, if she stayed on this post, that scout was going to corner her somewhere and take her. She had seen the hunger in his dark eyes. But when she leaned against the door and thought of him, all she could remember was the taste of him, the white-hot heat of his mouth pulling at her nipple. *Or was she really afraid of her own hungers and desires?*

With a sigh, she took off the yellow dress, glanced at it to make sure it wasn't torn or soiled, then hung it up. What was she going to do? She sat on her bunk, thinking about it for the next hour. There was no other alternative — she had to leave this fort whether she went to Denver as Winnifred Starrett's maid or returned to the Cheyenne and tried to live as one of them.

She heard the jingle of the sleigh outside and then Winnifred's voice and the major's as he escorted her to her door. The white beauty came in, humming a dance tune. "My, what a perfectly delightful party!" She smiled at Luci. "So here you are. I wondered what became of you. When I looked around, you were gone."

Was that smile sympathetic or malicious?

"I—I wasn't feeling well, so I left early."

Winnifred walked over and examined the yellow dress hanging on a door hook. With a triumphant flourish, she picked a bit of straw off the hem. "Who was he?" She looked amused.

How had that bit of straw escaped her notice? She'd been so upset. . . . "Miss Starrett, I don't know what you're talking about." She got up and began to help Winnifred out of the elegant pink gown.

"I don't remember seeing Lieutenant Osgoode leave the party," Winnifred drawled, humming under her breath as she untied the wide sash.

"Not with me. He'd had a little too much to drink," Luci said without thinking as she hung up the gown.

"He's such an arrogant fool," Winnifred said, laughing. "No wonder he drank too much. He surely didn't think I'd take him up on his dare."

Luci paused, the dress in her hands. "What dare?"

Winnifred smiled again, "Never mind. It was just a little joke."

There was cruelty in the amused smile, the blue eyes as bright as Luci's own. And abruptly she saw it all with sudden clarity, remembering what Johnny Ace had hinted at. "And was I the butt of that joke?"

Winnifred shook her hair back with an annoyed gesture and took the many ribbons out. "How dare you question me? I'm the mistress here. You're only a servant!"

Luci stared at her, aghast at the realization. "You encouraged me to go to that party as a joke, laughing at me behind my back? I wouldn't have done such a cruel thing to my worst enemy!" She was so stunned, she could only stare in horror at the elegant beauty. She had a sudden urge to grab Winnifred by her beautiful black hair and give her a good shaking.

"Worst enemy? Why you Injun slut, how dare you call me on the carpet like my mother scolding a slave girl! You dark-skinned sluts lead men on, making them do things they'd never dream of doing! Bewitch them, that's what you do! Dark Jezebels!" Winnifred flung herself down on her cot in a storm of weeping.

Luci looked down at her, feeling deep pity for the girl and wondering what this fury hid. "I'm sorry for you, Winnifred, really sorry for you."

"Well, don't be!" Winnifred sat up, her red-streaked eyes blazing. "I'll not have some dark-skinned whore pitying me! I'm going to have my revenge at last, do you hear? I've waited a long time to get even with my father for what he did to my mother!"

Luci shook her head, bewildered, feeling deep pity and loathing for the beautiful girl. "If you hate him so much, why are you going to care for him?"

"Because as his only relative. I'm his heir." Winnifred smiled with grim satisfaction through her tears. "He wants me to come look after him so he won't end up in a mad house at the end."

"A madhouse? That's very admirable of you—"

"Admirable!" Winnifred sneered. "First chance I get, I'll put him away and enjoy all his lovely money! He owes it to me and Mother for everything he did! He only married her for her money, and when it was gone. . . ." She dabbed at her eyes and smirked. "With the Starrett fortune, I can do anything I want, have any man I want. I'll be the glamorous queen of Denver society!"

Luci backed away from her, slowly shaking her head. "I feel sorry for you, Winnifred. When I first saw you, I thought you were the most beautiful, the most perfect thing I'd ever seen, not realizing you're twisted inside! I think you'll regret your decision. As I said, I pity you."

"How dare you pity me!" Winnifred scrambled off her bed and stood glaring down at the shorter girl, who held her ground with spunk. "How dare a dark-skinned Jezebel pity me! I'm going to have it all, y'all hear? I'll have money and power and any man I want."

"I hope you find whatever it is you're looking for," Luci said softly, reaching for her plain cotton dress and her moccasins. "I should have listened to Johnny—"

"Is that who you were in the barn with?" The other girl's eyes flashed jealously. "He's just playing with you, you know. I've offered him a chance to work for me in Denver, and I think he's going to take it."

Luci blinked, speechless. "Johnny Ace is an enemy of my people. I don't care what he does." But inside, something hurt and burned. He was like the other men after all, saying mere words of love. How close Luci had been to making the same mistake as her foolish mother!

"And you, you Injun slut, you'll never get to lie with him again!"

Luci lost control. She slapped Winnifred Starrett so hard, the girl's head snapped back. Then clutching her clothes, Luci ran out into the night.

It was late and the fort was quiet. *Thank all the spirits for that!* Luci thought as she ran barefooted across the snowy, muddy ground. There was no one to turn and look at her curiously as she fled in her chemise.

Where to go and what to do? There wasn't a soul at the fort she could turn to for help. That damned Pawnee had acted as if he were concerned for her, but he wanted only to seduce her before he went away to Denver with Winnifred.

She must at least get dressed before someone saw her. Shivering, she slipped into the barn, and put on her dress and moccasins. Although the spring night had warmed and much of the snow had melted, still she shivered without a coat.

What was she going to do? Katis whinnied and she went over to his stall, scratched his ears, and thought about it. The horse nuzzled her hand. "Good boy! You're too good a horse to belong to some rotten Pawnee! What a good gift you would make for my uncle."

By tomorrow, the whole fort might know about the joke of the ignorant and naive Indian girl invited to the officers' party. Luci winced as she thought of people laughing at her. If nothing else, she was proud. There wasn't any future for her here at the fort. She studied her reddened hands. She'd spend the rest of her life doing laundry. Sooner or later, some soldier would force himself on her and she'd be just like her mother. Poor Sunrise. Tears started, but Luci blinked them back.

Would the big Pawnee really go to Denver with Winnifred? The white girl would probably have him drive her carriage . . . and slip into her bed at night. Johnny Ace didn't seem like the kind of man who could be kept as a pet that way. But who knew what to expect from a Pawnee?

She stroked the horse absently. What was she going to do? The horse nibbled at her fingers. A plan began to form in her mind. No, she couldn't do that, even to a hated Pawnee enemy. Then she thought of Johnny trying to seduce her while, all the time, he was making plans to go off to Denver with Winnifred. Good enough for him!

"Good boy, Katis," she crooned, "wouldn't you rather be among the Cheyenne?"

She reached for the saddle and bridle, smiling to herself as she imagined the expression on the big Pawnee's face when he came to the barn in the morning and found his horse had been stolen.

Luci thought a moment. No, not stolen. Hadn't she heard that this horse been taken in a raid from the Cheyenne? She was just going to return it, that's all.

Quickly she saddled and bridled the black stallion, smiling to herself at the image of Johnny Ace's fury when he found she taken the horse almost from under his very nose and made off with it. It was something the Cheyenne were famous for. Would he come looking for her?

The thought scared her a little. She had a feeling the big scout could be dangerous when provoked too far. Well, if she was leaving, she needed a horse and she didn't own one. And she would be safe among the Cheyenne — even Johnny Ace couldn't ride into their camp to retrieve his horse. How glad her uncle would be to see her when she brought him a gift like this!

She led Katis out of the barn. The stallion whinnied softly and nudged her with its velvet nose. "Be quiet," she admonished him. "You'll wake the whole fort."

Suppose Johnny Ace heard the horse and came to investigate? She shivered in the cool night air at the thought of facing the scout. He'd be so angry, there was no telling what he would do. If she'd had a pencil and paper, she'd have left some kind of taunting message that she was as skilled as any of her Cheyenne ancestors at stealing horses from the Pawnee.

She mounted the horse, although it was awkward in the dress. His dress. If she'd had anything else to wear, she wouldn't take this clothing that the scout had paid for. It made her feel obligated somehow. For just a moment as she rode across the parade ground, she had a twinge of conscience, thinking about everything the Pawnee had done for her.

Luci shook her head stubbornly. He hadn't done all those things out of kindness. It was all calculated to seduce her, make her let her guard down so he could use her to satisfy his lust. He deserved this.

She rode out to the fort's big gates.

"Halt! Who goes there?"

Mercy! The guard. She'd forgotten about the guard. "Uh, it's only me, Luci, you know the half-breed girl who does the laundry."

He was a very young soldier. He came over, peered up at her in the moonlight. "Where you going in the middle of the night? And ain't that Johnny Ace's horse?"

"Sure it is." Her heart pounded as she smiled down at the soldier. What would she do if he detained her? The thought of the big Pawnee's wrath scared her a little. "I—I'm on an errand to North Platte."

"In the middle of the night?"

"Actually, it has to do with a message I need to carry for Miss Starrett. Major North said it was all right and Johnny loaned me the horse."

The boy scratched his head uncertainly. "I don't

know about this. I think I should check with the major—"

"Wake him up in the middle of the night to question his orders?" She tried to look aghast, then shrugged casually and said, "Well, go ahead. If you can deal with him when he's mad."

The boy hesitated again. "I think I ought to at least check with someone."

She shrugged again and tried to look bored. "Go ahead. Miss Starrett will be madder than a hornet if her message is delayed. But I'll wait right here while you do whatever you have to do."

The boy looked even more uncertain and exasperated. "I don't really know what to do. I just got here from Rhode Island a few days ago. I know I'm supposed to keep watch for Indians and any danger from outside. No one said anything about stopping people leaving the fort, especially just an Injun girl."

"You're a good soldier. I'll tell Major North how conscientious you were. So long, see you later." She gave him a casual wave of dismissal and rode out at a slow lope. If only he knew how nervous and frightened she was. But she kept the horse to a slow pace as if she really was on a legitimate errand. What would she do if he decided to go wake Johnny Ace and check up on her story?

She trembled a little at the thought. If the young soldier thought it over, he'd wonder what kind of errand could Miss Starrett be sending her on in the middle of the night?

The only sound in the cool Nebraska night was Katis's hooves and her own heart thumping. Behind her, she expected at any second to hear shouts as the sentry alerted someone that she had ridden out. Nothing. Evidently, the boy from Rhode Island had decided he didn't want to gamble on waking anyone up to ask questions.

The whole frontier lay ahead of her, millions of virgin acres that would be wonderful for growing crops, raising beef. The whites were moving in like a great tide to take this area, every train that ran brought more of them. Even she realized that the Plains Indian's way of life was already doomed, no matter how many treaties were written. The buffalo-hunting tribes needed millions of acres to continue their way of life, those same acres that white farmers were already planning on plowing up.

Probably before her lifetime passed, the buffalo would be gone and the proud, free people sent to reservations. There was no way to stop this tidal wave of white immigration, no matter how hard the Indians fought and protested.

The thought depressed her as she rode, Did she really want to live among her uncle's people? She thought about Johnny Ace. Like him, she was a white man's Indian, belonging neither in their world nor among her own people. What other choice did she have but to try? Maybe there would be a handsome Cheyenne warrior whom she could love and who would love her. Perhaps she was too pessimistic about the chances the Plains tribes had to save their way of life. She tried to hold on to that thought as she urged Katis into a gallop and took off through the snowy darkness.

Where was she going? She had no idea where to find the Dog Soldiers. She knew only that they were somewhere to the south or west in this vast wilderness. She walked Katis awhile to cool him down before she took off again through the moonlight. Come dawn, she could look for signs of unshod ponies. It occurred to her that with no food and no weapons she could be in a lot of trouble.

Suppose she got lost out here and didn't find the Cheyenne? Maybe if she spotted a ranch, she could offer to do a little work for a meal. *White man's Indian.* Yes, that's what she was, all right. Johnny Ace's dark, brooding face came to her mind and she remembered the feel of his strong arms around her, the taste of his kiss. *White man's Indian.* They were two of a kind.

No, she shook her head. They were blood enemies. She could never be a Pawnee's woman, not when he made his living tracking down her people for the U.S. army. Her people. Just who were her people, really?

As she rode, she wondered if Johnny Ace was even now coming after her, riding in a fast fury because she had stolen his favorite horse? If so, he didn't have much of a chance of catching her; not with the way Katis traveled. But he was a skilled tracker and relentless. He'd keep looking. She imagined him overtaking her, dragging her off the horse.

Big, stupid Pawnee. She could almost feel his wide, hot hands on her back as he jerked her to him, taste the heat of his mouth. She must stop remembering that, she chided herself as she walked the horse again to cool it.

She tried to think instead of how happy she would be among the Cheyenne. Tall Bull's wife would teach Luci the Cheyenne customs, aid her with her faltering grasp of the language, and help her choose a virile warrior as a husband. But when she tried to imagine going to the marriage blankets in the darkness by a small fire, she saw her enemy's dark, brooding face.

Luci rode through the night, trying to put distance

between herself and the fort. By dawn, Johnny Ace would come looking for her and he was by reputation the best of the Pawnee wolves for the blue soldiers. Every bent blade of grass would be a map to him so that he could track her. But maybe she would be lucky and find a big camp of Cheyenne first. Even if it was not the Dog Soldier band, they would help her find her uncle.

She smiled to herself, thinking what an amusing story this would make. The Cheyenne liked to tell stories around the campfires at night, and to that tribe, a tale was a possession like a pony or blanket. No one but the owner could tell it without the owner's permission. She imagined how, generations from now, her children would still be telling the tale of how their mother outsmarted a Pawnee scout and stole his favorite horse in a way that the best Cheyenne warrior would envy.

Somewhere on the lonely prairie, a coyote howled and she shivered, wishing she had a weapon. Of course, coyotes were timid. But what if she should run across a big lobo wolf who saw her horse as dinner? Luci thought about it, then decided Katis could defend himself.

It couldn't be long until dawn, she thought with a sigh of relief. The prairie seemed so desolate and so empty. She could disappear out here, get lost, and die. It happened now and then to settlers. For the barest second, she thought about turning around and riding bark to the safety of the fort. But when she thought about facing that scout and the sneering Winnifred Starrett, Luci gave up that idea. No, she would find the Dog Soldiers and learn to be a real Cheyenne.

The wind picked up and she detected just the slightest scent of smoke. Perhaps she had only imagined it. The image came to her suddenly of a roaring prairie fire. When lightning or a smoldering campfire started such a blaze, it could roar for weeks across many miles of dry grass, consuming everything before it. Whites and Indians alike feared being trapped in such an inferno. Many was the story she'd heard of men galloping ahead of such a racing wall of fire until their horse stumbled, went down, and the scarlet flames swept over them.

The sky turned that pale lavender gray that comes just before dawn, diluted with faded pink streaks. Up ahead, she saw straggly trees which could only mean a creek in this arid country. It would be a good place to rest a minute and refill her canteen. Katis needed water. Besides, if there were a prairie fire, people had been known to survive by leading their horse out into a creek and staying there until the danger had passed.

She smelled the scent of smoke again as she rode closer. What if she stumbled on a cavalry patrol? Luci shook her head. With all this snow melting off, she didn't think there were any out right now.

Maybe it was a Cheyenne camp. Her heart beat a little faster with relief. Even if it was an Arapahoe or a Sioux hunting party, those tribes were friends of the Cheyenne and would help her.

She was close enough now to see the tiny flicker of a campfire. A pony raised its head and whinnied at the scent of Katis. Luci was hungry. She hoped there'd be some food and coffee. She could make out the barest silhouette of shapes in the shadows of the trees around the fire.

A guard called out to her but she didn't understand what he said. She spoke English and a little Cheyenne. *What was it he said?*

She tried to form an answer in Cheyenne but gave

up in disgust. He challenged her again. She'd better ride in close enough for him to see she was no Pawnee or soldier. He might fire on her before he realized it was only a girl on a very tired horse.

"It's all right," she called back in English, trying desperately to think of the Cheyenne words for "I'm a friend!"

She rode in closer to the clearing by the campfire, heaving a sigh of relief that she was finally safe and there'd be food and help. Yes, she was safe! She was . . .

The brave walked toward her, talking in a jumble of English and words she didn't understand. White man's Indian. That's all she was after all.

At the noise, other braves begin to rise up out of their blankets around the fire.

It was still too dark to make out the figures silhouetted against the cerise of the coming dawn on the far horizon. She shouted out to him in Cheyenne that she was a friend and that she'd come a long way. A prickle of fear raced down her back. There was something very wrong. She began to turn Katis.

The warrior paused, staring back at her. The hair. *Why hadn't she noticed the hair?* The traditional roached hair down the middle of the head.

Oh, mercy! With a gasp of terror, she turned Katis and made for the open prairie. Why had she been so stupid as to ride in without investigating? The hair style had revealed that she had inadvertently found deadly enemies.

Luci had stumbled onto a camp of Pawnee warriors!

Chapter Five

Crow Feather stared into the small fire and looked toward the eastern horizon. It was not quite dawn on this vast sea of grass that the white men now called "Nebraska." He looked behind him at the sentry, around at his warriors, many still asleep in their blankets.

Charish joined him and squatted by the fire. *"Wa-ti-hes ti-kot-it ti-ra-hah."*

Crow Feather did not think they would find buffalo tomorrow as the younger man said, but he only nodded. *"Tu-ra-heh.* It is good."

He stared into the fire, thinking. No, they would find no buffalo tomorrow or the day after. Already the Pawnee hunting party had ventured too far west of their village. The farther west they went, the more danger of encountering a war party of Cheyenne Dog Soldiers. "We have not many warriors in our party. Perhaps we should turn back."

Charish frowned. "Our best young men no longer behave as Pawnee warriors. They ride for the bluecoated soldiers!"

"True." Crow Feather sighed. "But only the presence of the soldiers keeps the Cheyenne and the Sioux from overrunning and destroying our people. The enemy are many, the Pawnee are few."

"You defend the scouts because one of them will be your son-in-law if your daughter has her way."

"That is not yet decided." Crow Feather regarded the scowling, younger man. His name meant "angry" and it suited him. Still Charish was the chief's wife's nephew which meant someday Charish might be Lesharo, chief of the Skidi Pawnee. He would rather his daughter marry this handsome, but sour young man. His spoiled and willful daughter, Ore-ka-raha, preferred Asataka, whom soldiers called Johnny Ace.

"Isn't it decided? You have eyes for that great black stallion Asataka rides. You hope he will give it as a bride-price."

"I want that stallion, yes," Crow Feather snapped, "but if the truth were told, I would prefer a more traditional son-in-law, one who keeps to the old ways. The one called Johnny Ace comes seldom to our village and acts more white than Pawnee."

Charish poked up the fire. "When I am finally chief, I will lead our people back to the old ways, the old customs."

Crow Feather shook his head. "I think there is no going back. Whatever future there is for the Pawnee must be ahead of us, not behind us."

"What future?" the dour man scoffed. "We are about to be engulfed by a horde of Sioux and Cheyenne. And if that were not enough, already the white farmers look hungrily at our land and talk of exiling us to the Indian Territory."

He was right, of course. This dawn, Crow Feather felt much older than his forty some winters. Gray peppered the ebony roach of hair that had once been as glossy black as his namesake. Pawnee. It meant "horned hair," an apt description of the hairstyle. "We will go back home this dawn," he decided aloud.

Charish cursed. "We are shamed to return to our village with only a few deer and rabbits. Perhaps Tira'-wa frowns on us because we have abandoned the old ways."

Crow Feather stood up, grudgingly thinking the same. "Possibly you are right. Maybe God does frown on the Pawnee now for turning their back on their traditions."

Around him, warriors were coming out of their blankets in the first gray light of dawn. The sentry yelled suddenly, "I see someone in the distance!"

Crow Feather reached for his weapons, his heart pounding. "What is it you see?"

The man craned his neck. "Only one rider, so far. With so little light, I cannot be sure!"

Charish reached for his bridle. *"Teradeda?"*

"The rider is still too far away to recognize whether he is an enemy."

"It would be better to take back an enemy scalp than to return to our village empty-handed," Crow Feather thought aloud.

The sentry yelled. "He rides a fine black horse."

Crow Feather relaxed and sighed. The biggest, blackest horse in this whole area was well known to all. "What would Asataka be doing coming here?"

Charish scowled jealously. "Perhaps he comes to offer the horse and ride back with us to claim your daughter."

"He has no way of knowing where to find us on this hunt," Crow Feather said. "Besides, he would come to the village if he has finally decided to offer

93

for Ore-ka-raha." He smiled in spite of himself. Ore-ka-raha. It meant "Deer" and was a good name for his pretty, graceful daughter. She was his only child and he spoiled her. That was why he was considering giving his grudging approval if Johnny Ace finally asked for her in marriage.

The pink twinge of dawn touched the sky as they watched the rider come closer to the grove of trees. A voice called out, a woman's voice? A boy's voice? All looked at each other in surprise.

Charish said, "Is that not Asataka's horse? Who rides it and calls out in an unknown tongue?"

A prickle of fear and surprise went down Crow Feather's back. The words were Cheyenne. *"Teradeda!* Enemies!" He gasped, "Who is this riding toward us?"

As they scrambled for weapons, the sentry questioned the rider again in the ghostly gray dawn. Crow Feather watched the rider hesitate, turn the big horse uncertainly. He saw only a slight form in the dim light. Perhaps it was a Cheyenne scout.

Crow Feather yelled a warning, sending men racing for their ponies. *"Suks-e-kitta-wit-wis-kuts!* Get on your horses quickly! *Teradeda!* Enemies!"

The slight rider turned the ebony horse at the shouts, and galloped off across the prairie.

Charish ran for his pinto. "We will catch this Cheyenne! We will take this boy back to our camp to torture for the amusement of our people!"

Crow Feather unhobbled his bay gelding, his heart singing. Yes, they would take this captive boy back to their village. They would not have to return empty-handed and shamed. Perhaps Charish was right—their people needed to return to the old ways, to the old traditions.

Around him, warriors grabbed for weapons and

unhobbled ponies. Already the great black horse was galloping away. But the dawn broke now over the hills, all pale and new, lighting the prairie beyond the straggly line of cottonwoods. He swung up on his own mount and waved his men forward. "Let us catch this enemy!"

The warriors needed no urging. With shrieks and cries of gladness, they thundered away, taking up the chase.

Crow Feather's heart sang with the old excitement as the cool dawn wind blew in his face. Once again he was a young brave on his first war party. No longer was his scalp lock graying, his bones aching in the early morning chill. One more time he galloped after an enemy as he hadn't done in many years since he had ridden with Asataka's father, Kiri-kuruks, Bear's Eyes.

Ahead of them on the flat muddy prairie, the great black horse thundered away. Here and there, melting patches of snow looked like cream on the black gumbo of the land. It was good to be alive and riding after an enemy. Tonight, this Cheyenne's scalp would hang in Crow's earthen lodge. There would be dancing and singing, and never mind that the food would be army rations furnished by the young men who rode for the soldiers.

Charish galloped at his side, waving his rifle. "I think I can bring the boy down from here!"

"No!" Crow Feather gestured in protest. "Let us capture this enemy alive so we can take him back to camp!"

"He might get away! He rides a fine horse!"

But Crow Feather shook his head. The magnificent animal was lathered and tiring—anyone could see that. No, it had already been ridden many miles. Otherwise, they would have no chance of catching it.

The breeze came up and Crow Feather took a deep breath of dawn air as he raced along. Maybe there was hope; maybe the old ways could be recaptured after all. When Charish helped bring in this enemy, maybe Deer might look on him with different eyes, and forget about that white man in a brown skin who rode for the cavalry. And if Crow Feather captured this fine black horse, he wouldn't need the one Johnny Ace owned.

He signaled his men to fan out, slowly surrounding the weary, galloping horse. Aiee! It was a magnificent animal, fleet as the wind. But it was still running strongly while the smaller ponies were beginning to fall behind. He could smell the foaming sweat of his own bay, feel it wet and hot between his thighs. Would this enemy and his valiant horse escape them yet?

The sun came up finally, bathing the scene with golden light and casting shadows across the prairie. His heart thundered in time to the pounding hooves. The blood sang in his veins like the cries and war songs of the braves who rode with him.

Then the great black horse stumbled and fell. Perhaps it had stepped in a gopher hole, its slight rider thrown to the ground. Suppose it broke its leg? But even as that thought came to Crow Feather, the horse got to its feet and stood wearily, his head hanging. The rider scrambled up off the muddy ground and tried to remount, but it was too late. They had him! They had him!

With glad cries of victory, Crow Feather's braves surrounded the horse and rider.

"A girl!" *Charish* spat dourly. "Why, all we have captured is a mere girl!"

Crow Feather's heart fell. Yes, it was only a girl, even though her stance told him she would give them a fight. "But she's Cheyenne and we still have the fine horse!"

They surrounded the spirited female, who backed against the big black animal, crouched for a fight.

One of the other warriors shook his head and spoke in Pawnee. "Do you not recognize this stallion, Crow Feather? Could there be more than one like it in the whole world?"

It was true enough. With a sigh, he slid from his lathered bay, and stared at the black mount and the girl who glared back at him defiantly. It could be no other than Johnny Ace's Katis.

In English, he said to her, "How came you by this horse?"

"I—I bought it!"

Charish approached her, struck her across the face. "You lie, Cheyenne bitch! We know this stallion! How came you by it?"

"It was given to me!" She glared back at the warrior, her pale eyes flashing although scarlet blood ran down her mouth.

Crow Feather confronted her. He spoke a few words of the enemy Cheyenne language. "Asataka would never sell or give away this horse, perhaps not even as a bride-price! No doubt he is not far behind this horse thief!"

The girl looked as if she did not understand everything he said in her tongue.

"She doesn't understand! She's not even Cheyenne," Charish sneered. "Look at the pale eyes! She's a fort Indian, a half-breed!"

"Dirty Pawnee!" she shouted in English, blood running from her mouth. "Killer and rapist of women and children!"

"Do not compare us with your outlaw Dog Soldiers!" Crow Feather retorted, losing his temper. He had hoped for a fine captive and the ownership of a good stallion. Instead he had a mere slip of a fort half-breed and Asataka's horse, which would have to be returned to him.

"A Cheyenne girl is better at stealing horses than any Pawnee," she sneered.

The girl had spirit, Crow thought, and she was pretty.

Charish said, "What shall we do with this enemy bitch? I'd like her scalp for my lodge." He spoke Pawnee, but when he put his hand on the hilt of his knife, the girl tensed as if she understood.

One of the others laughed and wondered what she would be like flat on her back, pleasing the warriors.

The girl must have guessed his words from his tone. She tried to dodge past Charish, but he grabbed her and held her while she screamed and bit and fought. He pulled her to him, laughing at her feeble attempts to protect herself while he ran his hands over her small body.

"Enough!" Crow Feather commanded. "I am still leader here! Taking a prisoner back to camp is better than returning almost empty-handed. Tie her on the horse and let us ride out."

But the girl fought as Charish tied her hands behind her, threw her and across Katis's saddle. "You filthy Pawnee make war on women!"

"It is Ta Ton Ka Haska and his Dog Soldiers who make war on women. They have raped enough of ours on their raids."

The girl looked at him, startled, and Crow Feather wondered what she knew of Tall Bull.

"Let us ride out," he gestured. "We are too far to the west and we gamble our lives that we will not cross the trail of the enemy."

One of the warriors took the reins of the exhausted Katis and led him along gently as they turned back east at a walk. Crow Feather rode in the lead with Charish. "When we get back to the village, we will have to send a message to Asataka that we have found his horse."

Charish laughed. "How do you suppose she got it away from the scout?"

Crow frowned, knowing what the younger man hinted at. He liked the dour brave less and less all the time, but he was at least a more traditional Pawnee, in sympathy with the old ways. He looked back over his shoulder at the small girl tied like a sack of trade goods across the saddle at the end of the line. She was pretty — pretty enough to take the notice of any man. His daughter would be in a fury with jealousy if she thought the scout had been keeping this half-breed enemy girl as his woman.

Had he? No, surely not even a white man's Indian like Johnny Ace would stoop to sharing his blanket with a Cheyenne girl. It was unthinkable. The two tribes had been enemies for generations, ever since the Cheyenne had carried their Sacred Medicine Arrows into battle and the clever Pawnee had managed to capture the holy symbols. The Sioux had helped finally negotiate a return of two of the arrows, but Crow wasn't sure what had happened to the other two. He thought maybe Kiri-kuruks, Bear's Eyes, had hidden them. No one would ever know, because Bear's Eyes was dead, killed more than ten years ago by a big half-breed Cheyenne named Iron Knife for killing the Cheyenne's father, War Bonnet.

Crow Feather sighed. Bear's Eyes had been horribly disfigured by a grizzly, his face almost torn away as he came face to face with it. Perhaps that was why he had been a cruel man and not much of a father to his sons. Perhaps it was not Asataka's fault that, having been dumped at the boarding school for a handful of orphan Pawnee children, he had, under the influence of stern Elvira Platt, become a white man except in skin color.

Charish interrupted his thoughts. "Do you intend to let the braves enjoy and then torture the girl when we get her to our village?"

Crow glanced back at the girl, hanging helplessly over the saddle, her black braids swinging. Even if she spoke Pawnee, she could not hear them from her place in the line. "I haven't decided what to do with her. Maybe we should just turn her over to Asataka and let him deal with her."

"Deer will be very jealous," Charish reminded him. "She, too, will wonder how the girl got the horse."

"She stole it! What other answer could there be?" Crow almost shouted at him, He had been wondering why Johnny Ace had been hesitating about making an offer of marriage for Deer, even though all knew the girl wanted him to ask her very much, Crow had thought it might be because Asataka preferred to be Johnny Ace and couldn't — or — wouldn't ever again fit into a traditional Pawnee culture.

Charish smiled. "If we are to return to the old ways, we should start with the Morning Star sacrifice. I have heard from my grandfather that times were good for the Pawnee long ago when we kept the traditions."

"The Lachikuts, the Big Knife American soldiers, don't approve," Crow said.

"They hunt down our enemy, and kill them. Why would they care if we used one to bless our spring planting of corn?"

"That is true enough." Crow slumped in his saddle. Once again, now that the thrill of the chase was over, he felt like an old man and he ached all over from the chase. He yearned to sit before his fire with grandsons playing about him while his daughter and the other women harvested corn and squash to go with the meat the hunters killed. The harvest had not been good in the last several years.

"Have you seen such a sacrifice?" Charish asked curiously.

Crow nodded. "The last time it was done, I was a boy. The Skidi clan sacrificed an Oglala Sioux maiden. The soldiers did not like it. Before that, in my grandfather's time, a young Pawnee chief, Pita-lesharo, rescued an Ietan girl just as she was about to be killed. The whites thought it so romantic, they gave him a medal. I don't think your uncle, the chief, would even consider such a thing."

"Let me deal with my uncle." Charish turned in his saddle, the leather creaking, and looked back at the trussed girl. "Tell me about it, since I have never seen it done."

"You were probably a babe at your mother's breast, it's been that long ago," Crow mused. "If you had seen it, you would never forget. She was a pretty virgin. Our people kept her for some weeks until the Morning Star would be at the right position in the sky to assure a good omen."

"According to the star chart?"

Crow nodded. The Pawnee had an ancient map of the evening sky painted on a buffalo robe by medicine men of long ago. The painting charted the stars' courses and was so old, no one remembered when it had been painted, except that it went back long before anyone had ever seen or heard of white men. They were the old, good times for the Pawnee.

"When the time was right," Crow said as they rode toward the east, "the people did elaborate ceremonies. The girl had been with us many weeks and had lost her fear because she had been treated so well. It is always a good omen if the victim shows no fear and walks up the steps to the platform of her own will."

"And?"

Crow shrugged, shifted his weight in the saddle. "She was very pretty and a virgin. The people had feasted and celebrated all night long. Just before dawn, the priests stripped the girl naked and painted her with magic symbols, then they led her out to the roaring fire where the platform had been built."

He fell silent, remembering. The Sioux girl had been very pretty, with big, dark eyes. Crow had been young and kindhearted. He whimpered to his father that they should not do this thing, but his father had shushed him sternly. The Pawnee would have good fortune as long as they kept to the old ways. The boy should always remember that.

He remembered now staring up at the lovely, naked girl as a priest led her to the steps by the fire. She hesitated only a moment, looking uneasy, but the people had been good to her for many weeks. Perhaps she could not yet comprehend that she was about to be a living offering.

He was a boy breathing the scent of the roaring fire, the dirt damp beneath his moccasins. The girl began her ascent, reached the top of the platform, and looked out at the crowd uncertainly. Her dark eyes seemed to look directly into his. The crowd had fallen silent now, the only noise the crackle of the roaring bonfire. In the predawn darkness, the red and yellow flames threw ghostly lights and shadows across the upturned faces of the crowd.

The girl looked down into his eyes and, perhaps from his expression, realized suddenly that she was in danger. With a small cry, she half turned and tried to run back down the steps. But the priests caught her, bound her, then looked toward the east. In only a moment or two, the Morning Star would be at the proper place on the eastern horizon. It shown bright as a white fire in the blackness of the night.

His father nudged him and handed him his bow. All around him, the men were taking up bows, readying arrows. Crow Feather was big enough to make his own shot, but fathers would shoot the ceremonial arrows for baby boys too young to pull a bow themselves.

The girl screamed and writhed, but a priest moved quickly to stuff something in her mouth. This was a solemn sacrifice that must not be marred by cries of the dying virgin. Even as he watched, the bow trembling in his hands, the priest tied the girl with a rope that hung out over the fire from the platform, and pushed her off.

She hung, writhing and naked over the roaring fire, a living thing being burned alive. Her tortured gaze seemed to find his again as she twisted at the end of the rope, swinging slowly over the flames.

The priest watched the Morning Star on the horizon. It was time. The girl's struggles made her swing slowly, turning. Turning. And finally she twisted so that she swung directly to face toward the star on the horizon. The priest raised his arm, The men fitted arrows to their bows, pulled back, and waited for the signal.

The boy's hands were clammy and cold with sweat and he did not want to do this thing, but it was expected of him. It was the tradition — good planting luck for the Pawnee. He would not look into her tortured face. He concentrated again on her painted, naked body, writhing at the end of the rope. She had rounded breasts and a smooth belly that made his small man's part harden a little as he stared at her nakedness. The silence echoed. There was no sound, save the crackling of the fire and the creak of bows being pulled to their limit.

Now! The priest brought his arm down at the exact moment the Morning Star was in its proper position on the horizon, the girl facing straight toward it. With a great shout, the men loosed their arrows, and they sang through the air, striking the girl with a rush of wind. She hung there, writhing still, arrows sticking out at odd angles all over her naked body, in her belly, in her breasts. At least one had caught her in the heart and she twisted no more but hung limp now over the flames as the bright blood trickled on her bare, painted skin down her smooth thighs.

The crowd set up a ceremonial song. Men put another arrow to their bows for male children too young to pull a bow by themselves. Crow's arrow had fluttered feebly and landed on the edge of the fire.

"You should do another!" his father shouted, but Crow only stood staring at the arrows sticking from the limp body, the blood making scarlet trails down her legs to drip into the fire. A blood sacrifice to ensure that the earth would now give a good harvest.

At least her eyes no longer looked at him. The dark eyes were glazed with death as the body swung a little from the impact of the second flight of arrows. As the blood ran in red rivers down her body to the fire and earth below, the people set up a great rejoicing with singing and dancing.

The ceremony would continue for some time and the boy knew it was good because the tradition had been kept; the planting would go well. But for him—

self, he went off and hid until the body was consumed by the flames because even though she was dead, the dark eyes seemed to be looking at him accusingly.

Charish said something to him and he started, coming out of his memories. "What?"

The younger man looked at him dourly as they rode back toward camp. "Was the sacrifice good for the people?"

"We had a fine harvest that year, so in spite of everything, I suppose following traditions without question is good." He sighed heavily. "Maybe that is why the Pawnee fare so badly these days. They have not done the ceremony since I was a boy." He looked back at the beautiful girl tied across the black horse. "Yes, perhaps we should prevail on the elders to try the Skidi clan's ceremony. We have a sacrifice who is pretty enough for Morning Star!"

It seemed to Luci that they rode for centuries. Perhaps not, but tied and thrown across Katis's saddle, she was so miserable, that every minute seemed like a year. What had she gotten herself into? She wished she spoke a little Pawnee so she could understand the warriors' words. They had evidently recognized the horse. Would they rape and kill her when they reached the Pawnee village, or would they send for Johnny Ace and turn her over to him?

She winced at the thought. That scout would be in a fury and they were far from the fort. Probably anything he decided to do to her would never be known, and anyway, who would care if she disappeared forever without a trace? Rape was probably the most merciful of all the things the Pawnee warriors had in store for an enemy Cheyenne girl!

Chapter Six

Johnny Ace went to the stable at dawn to feed Katis. For a long moment, he blinked in disbelief, staring at the empty stall. Could he have absently left the gate loose and his stallion had wandered?

What other answer could there be? No man at the fort would dare to ride the great stallion. He looked around outside with growing apprehension. Finally he went to see the guard who had been on duty the night before.

The soldier yawned, just heading for his bunk to sleep. "Why, that little half-breed girl took it. She said she was on an errand over to North Platte."

"Oh, of course. I—I had forgotten." Johnny tried to hide his surprised fury as he shrugged and strode away. He wasn't going to have every soldier at Fort McPherson laughing at him over the chit making a fool of him. The slight female had been nothing but trouble to him from the first moment he saw her. No man would dare take anything that belonged to Johnny Ace, but Star Eyes had done it. If he ever got his hands on that half-breed Cheyenne again . . .

He tried to think of grabbing her small shoulders

in his two big hands, shaking her until her teeth rattled. He tried to tell himself he would strike her again and again, never mind that she was a woman. First of all she was an enemy. But when he visualized her, he suddenly saw himself jerking Star Eyes into his embrace, kissing her deeply while she struggled against him. And in his mind, she stopped struggling and responded warmly, pressing her soft curves against him while he sheltered her against his body. As long as she was close to him, she would always be safe. He wanted only to hold her; make love to her. . . .

He stopped abruptly, swore white man's curses under his breath. He had been too long without a woman. That was the only reason he couldn't get the chit off his mind. He should marry Crow Feather's pretty daughter. She would produce strong Pawnee warrior sons for him, warm his blankets, and serve a man's needs. Yes, that was what he should do. Yet in his heart, he knew he was not truly Pawnee, and could never be happy in their village.

Did his brothers have the same conflicts? He hadn't seen them in years, and didn't know much about them. Johnny Ace was a man caught between two cultures whose only friend was a black horse that an enemy girl had stolen. The thought set him in a fury again and he went to see Major North for permission to ride out.

North leaned back in his office chair. "Ride where?"

"I—I need to do a little advance scouting before we go after the Dog Soldiers." Johnny stared down at his feet, which were placed wide apart, and fingered the knife in his belt.

"I see." The slight officer pulled at his mustache. "Scouting for Cheyenne?"

Johnny shrugged uneasily. "What else?"

"Or only *one* Cheyenne?"

Johnny looked Pani Le-shar in the face, and saw the knowing smile. Fort gossip. It spread word faster than the telegraph. "I should have known it would be talked about. I suppose everyone laughs at me."

"No man who values his life would dare laugh at the scout called Johnny Ace," Major North said soberly. "They all know your skill with fists and weapons. The men say that if Johnny Ace hungers for the enemy girl, he should stop playing games and take her—be done with it."

Take her. Force himself on the girl? Rape her? Terrify her? Use her to satisfy his hunger for a woman?

"I—I want no enemy girl in my blankets. I think to marry a pretty Pawnee girl in a village some miles from here. Besides, the Cheyenne wench has vanished."

"With your horse, I hear." The officer's dark eyes twinkled with amusement. "Helluva situation to be in, Johnny. You ever read a story called *Romeo and Juliet?*"

He shook his head.

"It's about two warring clans. A man and a girl from two enemy tribes fall in love even though the two sides hate each other."

Johnny pulled out his "makin's," and began to roll a smoke. "So how does the story end?"

"Unhappily. There was no way the couple could bridge that gulf between them." Pani Le-shar frowned and began to steeple his fingers absently, looking over his shoulder at the bookcase.

After rolling his smoke, Johnny stuck it between his lips, feeling his insides in turmoil. Of course that was the only way such a love could end. "I think about marrying a Pawnee girl and finally returning to my own people," he said, striking a match.

"It will never work, Johnny, you're like an apple — red on the outside, white on the inside. You won't fit in. Your enlistment's almost up. Reenlist with the cavalry."

Johnny took a deep, bitter drag on the smoke, knowing it was true. He belonged nowhere, really, and couldn't be happy in either world. He needed to build his own Eden. But every Adam must have an Eve and the gulf was too deep to cross. *Indian Romeos and Juliets.*

He shrugged with annoyance. "All I asked for was permission to track down my horse. Is it given, Major?"

The slight officer nodded and stood up. "Permission granted. If I'd lost a horse as fine as Katis, I'd be in a fury, too. However, do I need caution you the girl may be headed back to her people, if she can find them? Your horse would make a good marriage gift to some Cheyenne brave."

Johnny swore aloud, and tossed the cigarette into the spittoon. "Some damn Cheyenne riding my horse? I'd kill him first!"

"Is it the horse . . . or the small filly becoming a Dog Soldier's possession that worries you?"

He was so angry that his gut hurt because he didn't know the answer. "That little half-breed deserves to live as a squaw and be bedded by some big Cheyenne. But she won't be giving my stallion as a gift to that brave!"

North started to say something, then seemed to change his mind. "Do you want to take Cody or my brother, Luther, with you?"

Johnny shook his head and turned toward the office door. "I'm a loner, you know that. I'll travel faster that way!"

The major pulled at his mustache. "Johnny, let me give you some good advice: forget about that girl. Luci will bring you nothing but heartache. Your two tribes are too far apart."

That was true. He didn't need to be told. He started for the door, hesitated, then looked back over his shoulder. "You're right, Major. I'll take your advice. I guess I'm just in need of a woman. A good whore in North Platte will take care of that after I get Katis back."

"If you get Katis back," the major corrected.

The anger against the girl flared up and burned bright in his soul. "I'll get him back, but I'm not sure I can control what I do to her for stealing the horse!" He turned on his heel and left the office.

Johnny borrowed a chestnut cavalry mount and rode out, following Katis's trail. The fast-melting snow had made the ground muddy enough to hold a track. The black's hooves were big, compared to the average horse, and the prints he made were deep because of his weight. For a skilled tracker, it wasn't a hard trail to follow.

He rode northwest into the early morning for several hours, stopping now and then to study the tracks. The spring weather was finally turning warm, except for the occasionally chill nights. As he rode, he thought about Deer. He didn't love her, but she was pretty and agreeable, not fiery and contrary, like some girls. The bright blue eyes in the half-breed face flashed through his mind. Sassy, spirited, and Cheyenne.

Deer would make him a good wife, taking care of all his needs and producing sons for him. In his old

111

age, he would sit in his earthen lodge with the other elders of the tribe, surrounded by dark grandchildren. There would be no pale eyes and light skin among them.

That was all most of his fellow scouts hoped for. It was living among the whites that had made him think a marriage should be something more than that. But marrying old Crow Feather's daughter would make Johnny more acceptable to the tribe. Pretty, pliant, and Pawnee. She would never do something as bold and outrageous as steal a man's best horse. His head told him she was a good choice. His heart told him something else.

Johnny rode on, following the trail. In places, it grew so faint, only a skilled tracker could have followed it. Judging from the condition of the tracks and the freshness of the horse droppings, he must be gaining on her.

As he rode, he thought about a place of his own. Where did he really belong? He didn't really feel at ease among the other Pawnee scouts or in their villages. Yet as a full-blood Indian, he really didn't fit in in the white soldiers' civilization.

His secret yearning, deep in his heart that he had shared with no one, was for a small ranch out somewhere on the frontier. There would be a log home built with his own hands, a stream, and trees. He saw fat cattle grazing in tall prairie grass and fine colts sired by Katis munching hay in the red barn.

He had even designed his brand: a simple outline of a playing card, an ace, of course. Johnny Ace was good with a deck of cards and careful with his scout's pay. While the other men drank up and wasted their money, his was saved. Someday, maybe he could turn his back and ride out to build that small Eden of his own on the frontier. *What good was it all without a woman to hold in his arms on a cold winter night or without sons to leave it to?*

He brushed that thought aside, thinking of his stallion. Yes, Katis would be his herd sire . . . but first, Johnny had to reclaim the horse from that star-eyed girl.

With renewed determination and anger, Johnny rode steadily to the Northwest. He realized that the farther he rode, the better his chances of crossing a Cheyenne war party's trail. Certainly they had been seen many times lately through Nebraska as spring came and the Dog Soldiers took the war trail again. If he ran into them, he was outnumbered and stood a fair chance of losing his scalp. But he was too angry to care. The way he felt right now, he would have welcomed a good fight.

Puzzled, he studied the trail ahead that led toward a grove of trees on a creek. The horse had whirled on its hind legs and taken off at a run the other direction. From the distance between the hoofprints, he could tell that the stallion had galloped.

A feeling of dread and despair rose in him as he nudged his mount into a lope, following the churned-up trail. Luci had been pursued by other horses, also moving at a gallop. The other horses had been unshod, so they were Indian ponies, but what tribe? If the pursuers were Cheyenne, Arapaho, or Sioux, she'd be safe, since those tribes would befriend her. Or would they? Would the Dog Soldiers see Star Eyes as a half-breed white girl and use her for their pleasure?

With his heart pumping in alarm, he loped along the muddy ground that had been churned up by the galloping hooves of many horses. The hoofprints told him the story: Katis far out in the lead, then the others gaining on him as the great stallion tired. The

113

crushed dry grasses marked where the horse had stumbled and gone down.

He dismounted and squatted to read the many moccasin tracks. There were Star Eyes' tracks, all right. The slight girl had feet that would fit in his big hand. His fingers trembled as he ran them over her small print.

Luci. He saw her in his mind as she had been that night he had carried her in from the cold, the night her mother died and left her all alone. How frightened and defenseless she had seemed wrapped in nothing but a blanket, huddled on his bed. Her eyes had seemed big as blue stars, looking up at him. He forgot that he was furious with her, that she had stolen his prized horse. He forgot everything but how helpless she would be among a bunch of braves. If anyone dared hurt her . . . his hand reached for his knife.

With bile rising in his throat at the thought of what a bunch of men might have done to Luci, he strode up and down through the crushed grass, looking for clues. At any moment, he expected to find her naked and ravished body where her pursuers might have left her. If she was lucky, she might have been dead before each man took his turn, grunting and humping between the slim legs, her scalp cut away before she was even dead.

He walked the area, dreading, searching. She wasn't dead, at least not yet. He found no body. He did find Katis's big prints in a line of ponies headed back toward the east. Maybe the Indians had taken her prisoner and were carrying her back to their camp.

He mounted up with a sigh of relief, then turned his chestnut to follow the new trail. Where would her captors take her? Could they be Pawnee? Crow

Feather's village was only a few miles from here. If that was true, the braves would recognize Katis and return the horse to him.

As for the girl, she would now belong to the warrior who captured her. It would serve her right to end up spread under some dark brown brave who would use her for his pleasure. Certainly the Cavalry from Fort McPherson wouldn't care about the fate of one half-breed laundry girl and come looking for her. The warrior who owned her might even offer her to Johnny for his use when he came visiting the village. A captive had no rights, especially an enemy Cheyenne girl.

Johnny's groin ached with the thought of having her lying beneath him. But then he imagined her delicate face, so frightened and trembling, and he knew he could never force himself on Luci. The thought her captor might made Johnny's stomach tie up in a hard knot.

He dug his moccasins heels into the chestnut's flanks and took off at a gallop, following the tracks. Sure enough, they led back toward the east. He began to hope they might be leading to Crow Feather's village. The man didn't like Johnny much; he was too traditional and set in his ways. But at least Johnny had a few acquaintances in that village, even if they weren't close friends.

It was afternoon when Johnny rode into the cluster of big earthen lodges on the Loup Fork stream. Mongrel dogs ran out to bark at him as he passed. Big-eyed children and laughing women stopped their chatter and stared as he rode in. Warriors looked at him and a few nodded politely, but their attitude showed they thought of Johnny Ace as an outsider. While the Pawnees were allies of the soldiers, they were suspicious of any of their own who seemed more at home among the whites than among their own people. All because of the sanctimonious Mrs. Platt and her school.

As he rode through the village, he heard a welcoming whinny and looked to his left. Katis stood tied before a lodge. With a sigh of relief, Johnny dismounted, patted the black nose. The horse nuzzled Johnny and made soft sounds in his throat at the touch of his beloved master.

"Katis, I thought I had seen the last of you!"

Deer came out of her father's lodge, her face bright with pleasure at seeing him. "Asataka! Father was just getting ready to send a messenger to the fort to tell you we had found Katis. Father says he's the finest in this area!"

Johnny nodded to her, looking around anxiously. "That's true." He spoke Pawnee so that she could understand him, but it was a second language to him after all these years. He thought in English. "I owe your father many thanks for finding my horse." *Luci. What had they done with Luci?*

She smiled broadly. "Father has often said how much he admires the horse and what a bride gift Katis would make."

He decided to ignore the remark. There was nothing on earth that could make him part with Katis; certainly not just to marry Deer, even though she was pretty and pleasant. "What happened to the girl who rode him?"

"Why do you care?" Her dark eyes narrowed suspiciously. "Most would not ask after the fate of a horse thief, especially not a Cheyenne enemy of our people."

Shrugging, Johnny stood with feet wide apart, looking at her. Deer was taller and older than Luci. "I don't care except that since it was my horse she

116

stole, I want a hand in deciding her fate."

Her face relaxed and she put her hand on his arm, certainly a bold move for a proper unmarried girl. "Don't worry," Deer said, "she'll get what's coming to her. She's tied up in the ceremonial lodge. In the meantime, let's talk of something besides that worthless half-breed."

He heaved a sigh of relief. Luci was all right. He started to ask to see her, then realized it would anger Deer.

She caught his arm, led him inside. Johnny went reluctantly, his mind busy with Luci. Now Deer turned, slipped her arms around his neck, and pressed her full breasts against the butter-soft buckskin shift he wore. He felt his manhood harden and throb as she pressed herself against him all the way down their bodies.

"Deer, don't do that. It isn't proper. Your father would be angry with both of us if he walked in now. Crow Feather doesn't like me anyway."

"He'd learn to like you if you were his son-in-law; especially if you gave him a lodge full of strong grandsons to brighten his old age."

That was true. And hadn't he been thinking that exact thing . . . when he wasn't thinking about Luci?

She leaned against him, raising her face up to him. He could feel the nubs of her nipples through both their clothing. "Kiss me as you must have kissed white girls," she pouted.

He remembered the fleeting sweetness of Luci's lips. "Behave like a Pawnee maiden—modest and proper." He reached up and tried to break the grip of her arms locked around his neck.

"That hasn't been getting me what I want. Perhaps I should act more like the white eyes and you would want me."

Before he realized what she meant to do, Deer reached up and kissed him—a long, lingering kiss, probing with the tip of her tongue against his lips.

For a moment, he weakened and opened his mouth, pulling her against him hard. He sucked her tongue deep between his lips and ground his throbbing manhood against the vee of her thighs. She was behaving like a filly in heat, and like a stallion, he reacted, wanting to throw her down on a blanket and relieve the ache inside him

As she rubbed against him, he slipped his hand down the front of her leather shift, covering her breast with his wide hand, feeling her nipple harden against his palm. His breath came in ragged gasps as he kissed her deeply. In wild abandon, he kissed her eyes, the edges of her lips. With his eyes closed, he could pretend anything. "Luci . . ." he gasped. "Oh, Luci . . ."

"What did you say?" She stopped, looking up at him in puzzlement.

The eyes looking up into his were dark, not the color of starlight. "Nothing. I got carried away there for a moment." He wouldn't admit that he was aching inside, that he was almost in pain, he needed a woman so much. The ache that a slight Cheyenne girl had built.

Almost regretfully, he reached up and unclasped Deer's arms from around his neck. "Stop this before we both do something we'll regret."

Her full breasts heaved with gasping breaths as she looked at him. "I wouldn't regret it. If I were heavy with child, my father would have to accept you as his son-in-law."

Johnny needed a woman. He should ask for Deer. Then with no guilt, he could go ahead and use her to relieve his need. Yes, that's all it would be. His heart was with another. "Tell me where they put the captured girl."

"Luci?"

"Yes, of course Luci, I—" He stopped, realizing from the jealousy in her face that she had trapped him into admitting what she must already suspect. Behind that pretty face, the pliant Pawnee maiden was really a conniving, jealous bitch. He shrugged carelessly. "Of course I knew her name. She does laundry for the soldiers at the fort."

She whirled away from him, pacing angrily. "I don't believe you! There's something more here; something shocking between a Pawnee and a Cheyenne!"

"No, she means nothing to me. She stole my horse. I'll take her back to face the white man's justice."

"She's under Pawnee justice." Deer confronted him, arms folded, mouth grim. "My father captured her so he will be the one to decide what is done with her."

He had a mounting sense of dread. "The soldiers won't like it if they don't get the laundry girl back."

"They won't care what happens to her. She's Cheyenne, remember? The soldiers don't like Cheyenne any better than the Pawnee do and hunt for them with scouting parties all the time. You lead those parties."

He had a sudden feeling of helplessness as he stood there feet wide apart, hand on the hilt of his knife. "Crow Feather dotes on you, his only child. He will do whatever you suggest with her, Deer."

She looked smug, triumphant. "There is some talk of offering your Cheyenne bitch as a sacrifice to the Morning Star, the way your father's Skidi clan used to."

119

"The human sacrifice?" Johnny gripped his knife hilt until he felt his knuckles ache. "We haven't done that ceremony in at least a generation. Crow described it to me one time. He had seen it as a young boy."

She smiled slowly. "Some say we should return to the old ways, and the Great Spirit, Ti-ra'-wa, will smile on us again."

He managed to stop himself from grabbing her, choking her in the sheer red rage he felt. He took a deep breath and regained control. "What is it you're telling me?"

She reached out, ran her fingertips along the open neck of his shirt. "I want you, Johnny, any way I can get you. What I'm saying is: marry me and I'll save your Cheyenne bitch from the bloody Morning Star sacrifice!"

Chapter Seven

Luci stood tied inside the big earthen lodge, her wrists and feet spread-eagled and bound to a post on each side of her. She felt as helpless as a cross-tied filly, unable to move in any direction.

She took a deep, shuddering breath, smelling the scent of the musty, darkened interior, the little fire that crackled in the center of the lodge. Could she escape? Pulling at the rawhide thongs that bound her, she decided it was impossible. That the Pawnee meant to kill her, she had no doubt. But at least she hadn't been raped . . . yet.

Luci glanced down at the torn, dirty blue-flowered dress. She had never owned anything as nice as this dress that Johnny Ace had bought her, and now it was ruined. Johnny Ace. If she could only get a message to him.

You little fool, she chided herself. He's Pawnee himself; he wouldn't do anything to help you. Especially not after you stole his favorite horse.

How she wished she knew what was happening outside in the village. She had been hanging here for what seemed like centuries. She couldn't even be sure whether it was day or night, because her only light was the dim fire. If only she'd found the Cheyenne before the enemy had found her!

She heard footsteps outside. Then a big, wide-shouldered man stooped and came through the small door.

"Johnny! Thank God, I—" Luci broke off her glad cry as she saw the cold expression on the scout's face, and realized that a pretty girl had come into the lodge behind him.

He looked her up and down. "So, Luci, you steal my horse and get caught. All your tribe are thieves."

Her heart sank at his words. "I—I needed a way to return to my own people and was not sure I would be welcome without an impressive gift to give my uncle."

The other girl's lips curled with scorn and she linked her arm through Johnny's possessively. "Half-breed fort whore! But since I want no blood spilled during the celebration of our wedding, maybe father will set you free."

The smug words cut into Luci more than the rawhide thongs that bound her. Her words were as bitter as she felt. "So the big, stupid Pawnee scout takes a bride."

Johnny rubbed the back of his hand across the side of his head. "Be silent, Cheyenne wench. You are lucky to escape with your life through Deer's generosity. Don't try my patience any further."

"I seemed to have been doing that from the first time our paths crossed."

A man's voice called from somewhere outside and Deer half turned. "There's Father. I have to talk to him about the wedding, Asataka. Give me a few minutes to prepare him, then you come join us by our lodge fire so we can make plans."

She turned and left the lodge. The silence hung heavily in the air, broken only by the crackle of the fire.

Hesitantly, he approached and looked down at Luci. "I seem to spend much time doing things to protect you."

"What's that supposed to mean?" She wanted to hate him, but all she could think of was that now he would be sleeping in the other girl's arms.

He started to say something, then seemed to think better of it. "Nothing. When you get back to the fort, go with Miss Starrett to Denver. I think you'll be safe there and maybe you'll have a chance to better yourself."

"You keep bossing my life! I never asked you to look after me, to stick your nose in my business!"

He moved nearer, and stood close enough that his hand reached out and touched her cheek. "If you only knew what I've done to protect you, Star Eyes. I. . . ."

Before she realized his intent, he reached out and embraced her. Tied as she was, she could do nothing as he moved to crush her against his chest and kiss her hair.

She fought to get away from him but she was powerless against his strength. She glared up at him. "I hate you, Pawnee dog! Get your hands off me!"

"I will kiss you," he murmured. "God knows it's cost me enough!"

"I don't know what you're talking about, but—"

His lips cut off her words and he forced his tongue into her mouth, ravaging it, caressing the silken interior with thrusting strokes.

She hung helpless in his embrace while he held

her tightly against him, kissing her hotly, deeply. His hard maleness throbbed and strained against her belly and she felt his big hand fumbling with the torn front of her dress.

Luci could only gasp and shudder at the sensation of his wide, hard hand closing over her breast. She couldn't hold back the moan that built low in her throat, the way her body arched against him. She pressed against his palm, unable to control wanting his hand cupping, possessing her breast, his finger stroking the turgid nub of her nipple.

His tongue was deep in her throat, pillaging, sucking, caressing. All she could do was hang there helplessly, letting him do what he wanted to her. And she wasn't sure she wanted him to stop although, as a bound prisoner, she could do nothing except submit to his passion.

"Luci, I've dreamed of this," he whispered feverishly against her lips, "dreamed of holding you, having you so that you couldn't fight me while I make love to you."

He dropped to his knees before her and clasped her around the hips. Burying his face against the vee of her thighs, he kissed her there through the thin fabric.

His breath was hot on her velvet place, pressing his lips against her. His hands fumbled with the dress, pushing it up her hips, and then his mouth was on her flesh, his tongue caressing, probing.

"No!" she gasped, twisting and trying to pull away, but she was tied in place. There was nothing she could do to keep him from kissing her most intimate spot and his mouth was warm and wet and wonderful. She found herself pushing against his lips, wanting his mouth to taste there, shuddering as wave after wave of sensation swept over her. The feelings he brought out were unfamiliar. She had never felt anything like them before, and it frightened her that this enemy stallion had such power over her body.

"Stop it, you worthless dog!" She managed to get her emotions under control. "No!"

He looked up at her, still on his knees before her. "You are a captive and have no right to deny me this one last homage to the virginity I never took from you. And now I guess I never will!"

He stood up suddenly and took her in his arms. As he kissed her gently, she tasted her own essence on his lips.

He had ravaged her with his mouth and she had liked it, no, ached for it! She felt furious with herself and him as he kissed her. In her helpless rage, she struck out in the only way she could—she bit his mouth.

With an oath, he stumbled backward. His fist came up and she winced, realizing how strong and powerful the man was. He could kill her with one blow. But instead, his hand slowly cupped her chin and she had never seen such sadness in a face. He looked down at her a long moment, scarlet blood running from his lip.

"Star Eyes, if you only knew to what lengths I was willing to go to save you . . ." He broke off uncertainly. "I won't forget you. I don't want you to ever forget me."

Before she could react, he reached out, tore the front of her dress savagely, and bent his mouth to her bare breasts, kissing and smearing them with his warm, red blood.

She looked down at his mouth on her nipple, trembled at the feel of his sucking her body, saw the red smears shining there, reflected in the firelight. She could not hold back her sob of betrayal and rage. "Your bride would hate you if she knew!"

"My bride owes me at least this," he murmured, and then he kissed Luci very gently, leaving the coppery taste of his blood on her mouth. "Blood is symbolic, Star Eyes. When you think of me, remember forever that I never got to take your virginity, but I smeared you with the blood pulsing from the beat of my heart. And damn you for it, that's where I'll always keep your memory!"

With a shuddering sigh, he turned and strode from the lodge.

She stared after him as he left. After a long moment, her legs collapsed under her so that she hung from her wrists, her head drooping to her chest so that she saw his blood on her breasts.

Without thinking, she ran the tip of her tongue along her lip, tasting the saltiness of his blood smeared there. "I'll never forget you either," she whispered, and then hated him and herself for it.

There was a burning in her eyes, a misery in her heart. She told herself it was hate, but it felt like jealousy.

Damn the big, stupid Pawnee to hell! She concentrated on her own fate, on her anger, not wanting to think that he would marry that smug, pretty girl. In spite of everything, images came to her mind of the two of them locked in mating, straining and wrapped about each other. His mouth on that girl's breasts as he pumped his seed deep within her so that she might give him a Pawnee son. He had no need of and would not want a son with Cheyenne blood. Damn him for making Luci want him, then marrying Deer!

She fought against her ropes, weeping at the thought.

Johnny sat cross-legged before Crow Feather's fire and tried to follow the conversation between Crow and his daughter. His face furrowed into a frown. He was in love with an enemy girl and marrying another to save her from Deer's vengeance. There was no future with the Cheyenne anyway. She hated him too much and the trouble between the tribes went back too far. He thought about Major North and Romeo and Juliet. How did that story end? Unhappily, Pani Le-shar had said.

Crow Feather cleared his throat, bringing Johnny back to the present. "I will not pretend you were my first choice, Asataka, but I can deny my daughter nothing; I spoil her because she is an only child."

Deer smiled as she went over, got the ceremonial pipe, and handed it to her father. He raised it to the spirits for a blessing, then solemnly filled it with tobacco, lit it, and took a puff.

Deer said, "Asataka will prove to you, Father, that he can live like a Pawnee. He will leave the scouts and return to live in our village, isn't that right, Asataka?"

Johnny sighed. He had truly thought of leaving the scouts because he wearied of the killing. But living as a traditional Pawnee depressed him. He thought of the small ranch he had yearned to build somewhere on the frontier. "If it pleases Deer, I suppose that is what I will do. Now about the captive—"

"We are here to talk of wedding plans," Deer interrupted with a slight warning shake of her head. Her eyes told him she remembered what she had promised. She was right, Johnny thought. Crow would be offended if he heard of the bargain the two had made. But of course Deer would keep her end of the bargain. She had given her word.

Crow Feather took several puffs then passed the pipe to Johnny. He inhaled the pungent smoke, wishing he had a cigarette. It might offend the traditional Pawnee to pull out his makin's and begin to roll a smoke.

Johnny looked at Deer, but thought of Luci. "It is right that a man finally take a wife to look after his needs and give him sons."

Crow nodded with a smile. "Perhaps you are more traditional than I thought. Yes, I want my daughter to be happy and I long for grandsons playing about me. It will be good to have a strong hunter to bring meat to my lodge."

He paused and looked troubled. "Perhaps my medicine has gone bad. We have just returned from a hunt and brought in very little meat. The tribe will have to depend greatly on our harvest of corn and squash, so the planting will be most important."

"I am a good hunter." Johnny handed back the pipe. "This lodge will not lack for food when I am your son-in-law. And I am as virile as my stallion. I will give you a new grandson every year."

He thought about lying between Deer's brown thighs, doing stud service so that Crow Feather would have grandsons. But when he pictured himself pumping his seed deep into a woman's velvet place and kissing her breasts, he saw Luci's face in his mind. If his sons had been Luci's, would any of them have her blue eyes?

"See, Father?" Deer's eyes shone. "He will be a better choice than Charish, I know it!"

Well, why not? Johnny thought with a shrug. He needed a wife sooner or later. Deer was pretty, wide

128

enough through the hips for childbearing, and her father was an important man. Maybe Johnny could learn to be a traditional Pawnee. But returning to the past did not appeal to him.

Crow Feather said, "The marriage will have to be postponed until there is enough food for a feast." He looked shame-faced. "As I said, the hunt was poor."

"But Father, Asataka is a great hunter." Deer put her hand on Johnny's shoulder. "I'm sure he will be happy to lead a hunting party to bring in proper food for this celebration. Wouldn't you?"

Johnny nodded. "Of course! I will lead the hunt. We can have the marriage when I return. You need not be ashamed of no meat for the feast. There will be plenty!"

Deer beamed at him and Crow stood up slowly. "Perhaps my daughter is right, perhaps I have misjudged you. I will go tell the others and ask some of the young men to join you on this hunt."

Johnny started to ask about Luci again, then decided against it. He dared not anger Crow, who had captured her and therefore could decide her fate, although he might turn that over to the chiefs and priests. It was better for Johnny to be gone from the camp when Luci was freed and sent away. He didn't want to have to see her again, see her riding out of his life forever.

But when Crow had left, he turned to Deer. "Remember you promised that you would see he freed the captive."

"Can you think of nothing else but that small wench?" Deer's dark eyes blazed. "She's too slight and too small-breasted to give a man much pleasure!"

Johnny closed his eyes, remembering the feel of

129

that tiny waist between his two big hands, the taste of those small, firm breasts.

He looked at Deer and saw the jealousy there. He must not anger her because she could influence Crow to set Luci free. "You are right," he answered carelessly. "The star-eyed one is too small to take all of a man's maleness, and her breasts would not give the rich milk to sons as yours would."

He reached for her, pulling her to him. Closing his eyes, he kissed her, stroked her big breasts. When they were swollen with milk, they would sag like a cow's and she would grow fat as she produced children.

Her hand reached to stroke his maleness. "In the long run, you will be glad you chose one of your own kind, and returned to your people. Like my father, I cling to the old ways."

"All things change, Deer. The Indians will either adapt to the white man's way or finally be destroyed. Perhaps I was too long among them to ever really live like the Pawnee, but I can give up my dreams and try."

"But our people are friends of the whites. I see no reason we cannot always live as we do now here in our beloved land."

Johnny shook his head. "Do not count on that, Deer. All that keeps the mighty Sioux and Cheyenne from sweeping down and wiping our small group out is the soldiers. Someday that may make a good excuse to send us where they have sent the other tribes, to the Indian Territory. White farmers already speak with resentment about how much wheat and corn they could grow here. I have heard them in the stores and streets of North Platte."

He paused. "I will keep my word if you keep yours. Talk to your father while I am gone. I do not want to ever lay eyes on the half-breed girl again. Give her a horse and send her back to the fort or to her people."

Deer nodded. "I promise. While you are gone, Father will turn the captive loose."

"As long as you keep your word, Deer, I am bound by mine." He sighed heavily and stood up. "Now I make ready to leave on the hunt. In a week's time, I will be back with enough meat for the biggest feast any bride ever had. You father will be pleased and proud."

Johnny went outside, glancing over at the lodge where Luci was tied. He had a terrible urge to run in there, cut Luci free, throw her up on his horse, and gallop away with her. He reconsidered. To do so would cut his last ties with the Pawnee. He would no longer be welcome in their village, and he was so alone already. If he could have Star Eyes, that wouldn't matter to him, but the girl hated him. The minute she made it to safety, she'd slap his face and walk away.

No, he'd leave it to Deer to set her free. Perhaps he should stay and make sure Deer kept her word. He decided against it. For one thing, he didn't want to gaze into those pale, star-colored eyes again, knowing he was seeing her for the very last time. Indians did not break their word. To do that was unthinkable.

He gathered up a small hunting party, looked wistfully one last time toward the lodge where Luci was tied, and rode out of the village.

Deer stood watching the hunting party ride out. She knew she should be happy that she would finally be Asataka's wife, but joy eluded her. What

131

boiled up in her throat was bitter anger and jealousy. He might marry her, but his heart belonged to that half-breed Cheyenne. It was unthinkable that such a thing would happen. It could never work. Such a union would make each of them outcasts among their own people.

Deer scuffed her moccasin in the dust, thinking. She had loved the Pawnee scout for a long time, although she saw him seldom. He was different from the other Pawnee braves, probably from the years in the white man's school and whatever he had endured there. The difference made a gulf between him and the others of the tribe. Well, she would start at once to change him, make him more like the traditional Pawnee sitting by the lodge fires. Deer liked an orderly, traditional world. She liked life as it was, as it had always been. All she needed to make her world complete was to be Asataka's wife, and to bear his children.

What should she do about the Cheyenne girl? She had given the scout her word that the girl would be given a horse and set free. But he loved the Cheyenne bitch. As long as that pale-eyed one lived, Deer would always worry that someday he would return to his old life at the fort, return to that girl. Deer would never feel secure as long as the girl lived.

She had given her word. Deer shrugged and turned back to her lodge. What did that matter? If she could figure out a way to get rid of the half-breed, she could be assured that Asataka would never leave her.

When she went outside, she saw Charish. "You didn't go on the hunt?"

"For a feast to celebrate your marrying another man — one I hate?" His lip curled jealously.

Because he cared for her, Charish would consent—she knew that. "I want your help."

He frowned at her. "Why should I help you when I wanted you myself?"

Deer considered a long moment. She had no qualms about doing whatever it took to get what she wanted. Behind her pleasant, pliant face lived a very determined woman. "What would it take to get your help?"

He put his hands on her shoulders, breathing heavily. "You know what it is I want."

She loved Asataka, but she needed Charish's help. "Is my virginity a fine enough gift for you?"

He looked shocked. "You must want something very bad to give me that which should be given to your husband."

She smiled. "You will like my idea. It is traditional, something from the old way. If you will help me, I will meet you tonight and let you enjoy me, if it means that much to you. Perhaps I can fake enough on my wedding night that Asataka need never know his wife is not a virgin."

She told him what she wanted, and as she knew, he was enthused and delighted. Charish was as ambitious as she was herself and as unscrupulous. She had no intentions of giving him her virginity, but after he became part of her plot, what could he do about it? It was a dangerous game, and she knew it.

But to her father, she said, "I don't want blood spilled before my marriage, that's a bad omen. Why don't we give the chit a horse and send her back to the fort?"

Crow smiled at her fondly. "You are a fine daughter, kind and soft-hearted as a woman should be. I regretted killing the girl, but didn't know what

133

to do about her."

"Trust me." She patted his shoulders "Tomorrow Charish will take the chit part of the way and turn her loose before Asataka gets back with the hunting party. Then we will have the wedding."

Late that night, after her father was asleep, Deer slipped from the lodge to meet Charish out in a grove of trees by the river.

He stepped out of the shadows, a little unsteady on his feet. She could smell the white man's whiskey on him. "I did not think you would come," he said. "I thought you would change your mind. Here, try this magic drink."

She smiled and took a big gulp to humor him. Deer had never tasted whiskey before. She liked the warm feeling as it went down. She took another drink. "Maybe it is magic, the way it makes me feel."

"I'd never have believed you would meet me, Deer." He took a big drink of the liquor and she watched it drip down the sides of his mouth.

"Didn't I tell you I'd come?" She reached for the bottle. Once he did what she asked, she'd stall him, then tell Asataka the man lied about everything, and had approached her. No doubt the scout would kill him for the insult. Even if Charish told anyone it was her idea, all she had to do was deny it. Who would believe him? Her own daring scared her a little and she took another drink.

Charish stood looking at her beauty. To think that she would become Asataka's wife upset him. But what a joke it would be on that scout if

Charish had taken his bride's virginity. "Drink some more," he urged her. "We celebrate returning to the old ways!"

He wondered suddenly if he couldn't blackmail Deer with his silence. Yes, that was what he would do. He would threaten to tell Asataka about this meeting unless Deer met him regularly in the darkness. He smiled, thinking. What a joke it would be on the scout if Deer gave him a child by Charish.

He knew her well enough to suspect a trick. Everyone thought her a simple girl, but underneath, he had long ago recognized her cunning and ambition. He would be chief someday; she should be marrying him.

Charish reached out and took her in his arms. Her breasts were full and warm, her skin soft to the touch of his fingers. He brought her close and kissed her face. His manhood went hard as stone, so hard his groin ached with the wanting of her. "I love you, Deer."

She looked up at him, laughing drunkenly. "I have to go back. Let's stop this nonsense and I'll tell you what I want you to do."

He both hated and wanted her. It was bitter in his heart that she cared nothing for him. If he had not agreed to do her bidding, she would have offered herself to some other warrior. The others would have been afraid of Asataka, but Charish was a brave man . . . and he wanted Deer, had always wanted her.

If he raped her, who would she dare complain to? She'd have to explain what she was doing meeting him in the middle of the night. No, she wouldn't tell.

He grabbed her roughly, clapped his hand over her mouth, and dragged her over to the shadow of the trees, where he had spread a buffalo robe in anticipation. "This time, my love, you have out-foxed yourself!"

She struggled and tried to bite his hand, but he was past caring about anything but possessing her ripe body. Charish pulled away his loincloth and fell on her, his mouth savage on her breasts. She whimpered in pain.

"This is the way it is done for pay, the soldiers tell me," he said grimly, reaching to touch between her thighs. She was dry and unready. He would hurt her, but he was so angry, he didn't care any-more. He wanted only to mate her, to unload this ache between his loins, to know that he had been the one to take her virginity, no matter whose wife she became.

He pressed his maleness against the opening of her body. She recoiled, trembling, protesting against his hand but the sound was muted. No one would hear her. "If you're going to act the whore, expect to be treated like one — no tenderness, nothing but animals coupling in the moonlight."

He wanted to hurt her for her cold, conniving plotting. He was built big and she was a virgin and unready. Even as he made ready to enter her, he kept his hand over her mouth as she fought him. Her breasts beneath his hands were full and large. Later he would suck them into raw peaks, but now, he could not wait a second longer to relieve this ache in his groin.

He came up on his knees, forced her thighs wider apart, and rammed into her hard. She screamed against his hand and arched up, struggling to get away from the dagger that impaled her. Charish felt his throbbing maleness break through her virgin sheath as he pinned her against the ground with his manhood. He drew back, saw the smear of blood on his flesh, and that drove him to a frenzy.

He rammed hard into her again while she writhed under him and struggled to escape. He rode her now, savagely, roughly, and she whimpered against his hand. Once he would have cared, but no more. She had teased and played him for a fool once too often. Possessing her was all that mattered.

Deer felt her lower body burn like fire. She struggled to get out from under him, clawed at his face, tried to tell him to stop. But he was strong and his hand never left her mouth. In all her plotting, she had never expected this.

His fingers squeezed her breasts hard and he drove into her like a molten lance. In spite of herself, the tears came. But he did not stop moving up and down on her, grunting deep in his throat. His mouth sucked her nipples into raw, red peaks while his free hand pawed at her. Her lower body felt as if it were on fire as he throbbed deep within her. Then he shuddered, drove deep one more time, and collapsed on her as though dead.

She was afraid to move, and could not anyway because of his weight on her. The whole thing would be hard to explain if people came running. And when he realized what he had done, he might kill her to keep her quiet.

Finally he rose up on his elbows, and looked down at her. "I've thought of nothing but this moment for years. Now don't scream and I'll take my hand away! I know you won't; you wouldn't want to explain what you were doing meeting me in the dark." Very slowly, he moved back.

She swore and struck out at him. "You coyote! You hurt me!"

"Have another drink." He forced the neck of the

bottle between her lips and she swallowed to keep from choking. "I've got plenty more where this came from and you can have all you want. We've got a long night ahead of us!"

She was furious, but she liked the way the white man's drink made her feel. She reached for the bottle. It tasted like liquid fire in her throat and belly, but it spread a warm dizziness through her that she liked. No wonder braves craved the white man's drink. She took a gulp and felt it spread though her body.

This time, when Charish forced her onto her back and took her again, she was past caring.

Charish took her a half-dozen times before he was sated and pulled her to her feet, smiling with satisfaction. Her blood smeared them both. She looked down at it and cursed him, swayed a little on her feet. "It's cost me enough, you'd better keep your end of the bargain."

"You were good, Deer. White men would pay good money, give you all the whiskey you wanted as the price of lying between your thighs. Tell me again what you expect." He paused on the edged of the river.

"You take the girl out as if you were setting her free. The people won't like it, but they listen to my father." She looked toward the water, more than a little drunk. Her body reeked of the big Pawnee's seed. She'd have to wash off before she went back to her lodge.

"And then I take her instead to the Skidi village?"

Deer nodded. It was worth it to be rid of the girl, no matter what it cost. And she liked the taste of whiskey. "Tell them you bring them a gift, a captive to insure their planting and harvest of corn."

138

"Aren't you afraid Asataka will hear of it from someone?"

"It might be years before he does, and who's to say we didn't set her free and the Skidi captured her on her way back to the fort? How can he blame us . . . unless you tell."

"It would be worth my life to tell. I'll keep silent . . . as long as you keep meeting me in the moonlight."

Once this deed was done, what she'd really like to do was figure out a way to silence Charish forever. She'd have to give some thought to how to do that. "I agreed to meet you just this one time, Charish."

He pulled her against him, kissing her roughly. "We're two of a kind, Deer. Neither of us will tell what we know. You may marry him, but I intend to have you now and then."

She pulled away from him, wiped his kiss from her mouth with the back of her hand, and reached for the bottle. She hadn't realized she would like whiskey so much. Maybe Charish was right—maybe she would like being a white man's whore. It was easier than curing hides and drying meat. Some of the men who hung around the fort made their women whore to buy the men whiskey. But, of course, the scout would never stand for that.

"You play a dangerous game, Charish. Asataka would kill us both if he caught us."

He smiled slowly and began to dress. "I want you enough to take the chance. What really should worry you is what the big scout will do if he ever finds out who plotted to send the girl to the Skidi village—if he finds out you sent the girl to be used in a Morning Star sacrifice!"

Chapter Eight

It was dawn. Luci could tell from the dim light outside the earthen lodge that filtered in where she still stood tied to the posts on each side.

What was going to happen to her? No doubt the Pawnee intended to kill her although Johnny had sworn she would be safe. Johnny Ace. She thought of him with conflicting emotions.

There was a noise outside and Luci jerked up, half hoping to see the big Pawnee stoop and come through the door. Instead, that pretty girl, Deer, and her father came in to confront her.

The girl sneered. "I hope you had a nice night."

Luci raised her head proudly. "Could one sleep in a stinking Pawnee village? The Cheyenne move theirs often so as to always have clean surroundings."

Bright spots of anger mottled the other girl's cheeks. "What do you know of *real* Cheyenne? You're just a fort whore, that's all."

"Don't call me your own name!" Luci snapped, spitting at her.

140

For a moment, she thought the girl would attack her with both fists but the man caught his daughter's arm. "There is no need for this," he said in halting English. "We come to set you free."

Luci raised her eyebrows in surprise. "This I did not expect."

Deer wiped the spittle from her face. "It is a marriage gift." I do not want blood shed just before my wedding. It might be a bad omen."

"So I owe Johnny Ace my life?" She didn't like feeling obligated to him. She owed him so much already.

"No, you owe *me*," the Pawnee girl said. "Asataka said to do anything I wanted with you, he didn't care. So I choose not to kill you."

Was she telling the truth? What difference did it make?

"Where is Johnny?"

"Gone with a hunting party to bring back meat for the feasting. The chief's nephew, Charish, has offered to escort you partway back to the fort and safety." The girl pulled out a small knife and cut Luci's bonds.

Luci suppressed a groan as she rubbed her raw wrists. She was too proud to have these enemies see how much pain she had borne. "I don't need an escort. If you'll give me a horse, I can get back to the fort by myself."

But the father shook his head. "No. Deer insists on an escort to ensure your safety. She doesn't want blood spilled right before her wedding." He turned to his daughter. "Perhaps I should send more warriors with her, my dear, just in case—"

"No," Deer interrupted. "Charish will manage fine. He'll just take her a few miles out, head her

141

toward the fort, and good riddance!"

Luci flexed her aching shoulders as Deer cut the last of the bounds on her ankles. "I'll be happy to have seen the last of any Pawnee and especially that wolf for the bluecoats!"

The three of them went outside. The daylight was almost blinding after the dim interior of the lodge. She was half-naked and dirty, and her muscles ached from being tied in one position all night. In front of the lodge, three horses waited, and mounted on the pinto was that tall Pawnee with the traditional roached hair and the sour expression.

He glared down at her. "So this is the whelp I'm to take to safety. Better we should turn her over to our warriors to enjoy as a spoil of war."

The old man shook his head, looking from the mounted Pawnee to Luci. "You owe your life to my kind-hearted daughter," he said in halting English. "Don't ever come near our village again or, next time, Deer might not be so generous."

She wasn't going to argue. If they were turning her loose, she wanted to get out of here before they changed their minds. Luci swung up on the dun horse they offered.

Deer said, "The village isn't too happy about setting an enemy free."

A small, hostile group had gathered to watch them ride out. Luci knew by the angry expressions that some of the Pawnee were disappointed. Evidently, they had been looking forward to the pleasure of killing her and were only forgoing it because Crow Feather was popular.

When they rode out, Luci was almost afraid to look back, but no one tried to stop her from

142

leaving. Charish rode next to her. She wondered with nervousness how far he intended to escort her?

They rode out of sight of the camp.

Luci said, "This is far enough. I think I could find my way back to the fort now. Let me ride on alone."

"No, I have my orders." Luci felt sudden uneasiness at his tone. They kept riding.

They covered several more miles before the sour man reined in. "Here is where we turn off to the left."

"Are you sure? I would have sworn the fort lay straight ahead." Before she could move, he reached out and grabbed her reins.

Terrified, Luci tried to kick the horse into a gallop and break away, but now he was off his horse, pulling her down to tie her wrists behind her and put a gag in her mouth.

"You Cheyenne bitch!" he snarled as he threw her across her saddle. "I'd rape you if you didn't need to be a virgin for the ceremony!"

Ceremony. What ceremony? Luci hadn't volunteered to take part in any ceremony. *Johnny Ace would kill you for this!* she wanted to scream. She saw his dark, brooding face in her mind, the way his eyes had caressed her. Beloved enemy. Johnny, where are you? I need you. I need you so.

It seemed like forever that she and Charish rode because Luci was so miserable trussed up with a rag stuffed in her mouth, but it was only dusk when they rode into another Pawnee village and she was pulled from her horse.

Immediately, a crowd of Pawnee gathered around to stare at her. Some of the tribal elders came out and conversed with Charish. The crowd grew more excited as they talked. Then they dragged Luci into an earthen lodge. She was tied helplessly between two poles again, and this time, Charish stripped her completely naked so that the chiefs could inspect her. She closed her eyes so she could not see the hungry look on some of the faces. Luci flushed with shame.

She didn't have to speak Pawnee to realize from their expressions that they were pleased about something and happy to have Charish in their village.

An old woman came forward, ran her fingers up into Luci's velvet place, and nodded approvingly while Luci's face burned with humiliation. The wrinkled crone turned to the men, jabbering something.

Charish laughed. "So you are a virgin! I thought you had been warming Asataka's blankets at the fort."

"I share no Pawnee's bed," Luci snapped back, but Johnny's image came to her mind and she wanted more than anything to see his tall frame stoop and come through the lodge door. He would stop all these indignities, cover her nakedness with one of his shirts, and take her away from here.

The elders talked for a few minutes among themselves. Then they went out, leaving only Charish and the old woman.

Luci took a deep breath of relief and struggled to pull free of her bounds. "What do they intend to do with me?"

Charish smiled as if he knew a good joke.

"They needed a virgin for a ritual to ensure a good crop."

"Why me?"

"It has to be someone outside the tribe. All they are going to do is feed you well, dress you up, make you take part in the ceremony, and then they'll turn you loose."

Luci hardly dared to hope. "And is that all?"

"Didn't Deer promise to set you free? Otherwise, she said Asataka wouldn't have agreed to marry—"

He stopped suddenly as if he had said something he hadn't intended to say. "Anyway, if you'll go through the ceremony, I can promise on my honor that tomorrow you won't have any worries."

So Johnny had agreed to marry Deer to save Luci's life. She wanted so badly to believe that. And Deer and Charish had both given their word, which was sacred to an Indian. "All right, I'll go through this ceremony, to humor them."

"Good. The old crone will bathe and paint you with ceremonial paint and feed you well. There will be singing and dancing all night, but your part isn't 'til morning."

He turned and went out. Luci was still scared and suspicious, but there was nothing she could do about all this anyway, tied up as she was. She saw Johnny's dark face in her mind and wished he were here to ensure her safety. She realized suddenly that she had come very much to depend on the enemy scout. Enemy. Beloved enemy. She might as well admit it.

What was that remark that Charish had let slip? Had Johnny Ace agreed to marry Deer to ensure Luci's safety? Did he really care so much? Of course that was all wrong. He was marrying Deer because she had a ripe body and would give him Pawnee sons. Luci thought of the two sharing marriage blankets and it made a knot in her chest that hurt.

Outside, the beat of drums began along with the chanting and singing of dancers. The old crone came back with water and soft rags to wash Luci's body, then she brought a heaped platter of roast deer and the best of food. Since the whites supplied much of the Pawnees' provisions, there was even coffee with plenty of sugar in it, an unexpected luxury.

The old woman helped her wash her naked body, and gave her a clean blanket. "You sleep now," she said in broken English. "I come for you just before dawn."

Luci wanted to ask more, but the old woman indicated she spoke little English, shook her head, and left.

Maybe it would be all right after all. Luci sighed with relief as she ate the heaped-up plate of food and wrapped herself in her blanket. At least they hadn't tied her up tonight. Not that she would have much chance of escaping anyhow. And she was weary to the bone. The drums beat a steady rhythm. What should she do now? What could she do? Luci lay down beside the small fire lulled by the steady beat of the drums. But the last thought in her mind as she dropped off to sleep was the image of Johnny Ace's face.

Johnny sat in his blankets and stared up at the night sky. It had been a good afternoon's hunt and the men were tired. All around him, they lay

146

wrapped in their blankets near the campfire. Only he was still awake.

Luci. He couldn't get her off his mind. He wondered if she was thinking of him at this moment, too. With a sigh, he took out his makin's and began to roll a cigarette. In love with one girl and planning to marry another. Love. He had finally admitted what he had tried to deny, even to himself.

What a helluva note. It could never work out, not with an enemy girl. He'd be better off married to one of his own. Tomorrow the hunting party would ride back. There'd be dancing and celebrating, then the wedding ceremony. Luci would be sent on her way to the fort.

Luci. She seemed to be calling him. Was she in some kind of trouble? He considered a long moment, shook his head. No, Deer had given her word and such a vow was sacred among the Indians. He took a deep puff and looked up at the sky. *Lucero.* Morning Star. At dawn, the sacred Morning Star would hang over the eastern horizon. His feeling of uneasiness grew.

Johnny threw the smoke in the fire and shook one of the other warriors awake. "Something's come up. My medicine tells me to return to the village. You return in the morning with the meat."

The warrior yawned sleepily. "Do you need us?"

Johnny shook his head and stood up. "See you in camp."

In moments, he saddled Katis, and headed back at a gallop.

It was the middle of the night when he made it

147

back to the village. He rode to the lodge where Luci had been imprisoned and ran inside. Empty.

His heart skipped a beat as he went to Deer's lodge.

She and her father sat up suddenly as Johnny ran in. The old man looked bewildered. "What are your doing back?"

Johnny ignored him, grabbed Deer by the shoulders, and hauled her to her feet. "All right. Where is she?"

"I — we let her go early," Deer stammered, but she didn't look at him.

"That's right," Crow said, and yawned. "Deer persuaded me to let the Cheyenne girl leave. Charish escorted her part of the way back to the fort — "

"Is he back yet?" Johnny demanded.

The guilt was evident on Deer's face. "Well, I don't know. He said something about going hunting after he saw her off. But we did release her — "

"I warn you, if anything's happened to her, if you broke your word, Deer, consider our deal off!"

Crow Feather blinked. "What goes on here?"

"Ask your daughter." Johnny strode from the lodge. The guilt on the girl's face was evidence enough that something was not as it was supposed to be. Johnny had decided to give Luci safe escort back to the fort himself. It didn't make any sense for Deer to be so concerned about the girl that she would give her an escort. And Charish?

He mounted and took off at a gallop through the moonlight. On the edge of the camp, he picked up the fresh trail of two horses. He followed it. A couple of miles out, they headed east.

148

That wasn't the direction of the fort. Now why would Charish take Luci east? There was nothing in that direction except his father's old Skidi village. Johnny had not been in that village since he was a small boy. There were too many memories attached to that place—unhappy memories. His father had been cruel, even to his own sons. They had all scattered like windblown leaves as soon as they were old enough to fend for themselves—except for Johnny, who was too young and was placed unwillingly in the white man's boarding school.

Was that where Charish and Luci were heading, and if so, why? Johnny nudged Katis into a gallop. Even riding fast, it would be dawn before he arrived.

The old woman awakened Luci less than an hour before dawn. The drums still echoed outside and Luci heard rhythmic chanting. Obviously some kind of ceremony had been going on most of the night.

Luci looked at her. "What is it you want?" she asked in English.

The withered hag struggled for words. "Ceremony," she said finally. "You must get ready."

Luci tried to ask her more about the ritual but gave up with a shrug when the old woman could not understand. She knew nothing about Pawnee custom—except that they revered the Morning Star that showed on the eastern horizon just before the sun rose.

Luci started to refuse then reconsidered. Deer had said she was going to free Luci. And she had given her word. If Luci took part in this ritual, whatever it was, then they would set her free. She was too afraid to think of any other possibilities.

The old crone brought in ceremonial paints and indicated she would paint Luci.

Mercy! What was this about? Not that she had any choice. If she refused, no doubt the old lady would bring in someone to help her tie Luci up and paint her anyway. Luci didn't seem to have much choice. With growing doubt and more than a little fear, Luci submitted to having her naked body smeared with red and black paint. Outside, the chanting and drums seemed to be growing in intensity as dawn neared.

Now the old woman threw her a buffalo robe to wrap herself in, and indicated they were to go outside. Without any clothes? She tried to argue, but the old crone ignored her. What else could she do but go with her? Maybe once outside, she could break and run for a horse, then escape. But she wasn't even wearing moccasins. The ground felt damp and cool beneath her bare feet as she followed the old woman out into the darkness.

Any thoughts she had for escape were lost when she found herself suddenly surrounded by some kind of honor guard, which escorted her across the village toward a giant fire burning in the center of the camp circle. *Now what?*

The people pressed forward around the big fire, chanting and dancing. As Luci and her escort neared, they fell back and made room for them to pass. The drums beat so loudly that they sounded like thunder in Luci's ears . . . or was that the beating of her own frightened heart?

What to do? She walked toward the blazing fire,

150

holding the robe close about her naked, painted body. She was all alone with no one to help her in this enemy camp.

Johnny. Johnny Ace, where are you? And then she chided herself. He was an enemy, too, about to marry that Pawnee girl. He wouldn't help her; why had she grown to think of him as a refuge in time of trouble?

All the men seemed to be armed with bows. She wondered if there was to be a hunt this morning. It wasn't long until dawn, Luci noted, glancing toward the eastern sky. Already the Morning Star hung over the far horizon with the first gray light breaking behind it.

She recognized Charish standing near the bonfire as she approached. He smiled at her. She looked back at him suspiciously, pulling the robe tighter around her small, naked frame.

She spoke English to him, "What is this? Why are these people gathered?"

He smiled disarmingly. "It is nothing. The people are gathered to see you off."

"Such a ceremony for a mere captive?" She blinked in surprise, knowing there was something terribly wrong here. Now she saw that there was a stairway with a platform next to the fire and at the top of the platform were several old, important-looking, Pawnee priests, all garbed in ceremonial dress. They stood staring down at her as the drums beats louder and the people broke into frenzied chanting and swaying.

Charish spoke loudly. "It is a good omen if you take part in our ceremony; if you walk to the top of the platform unassisted and greet the priests."

151

She swallowed hard, looking around for an escape through the hundreds of people. The crackle and heat of the giant fire were warm on her face. "Suppose I refuse?"

Charish grinned and shrugged. "Then you will anger the people. Perhaps they won't release you."

She wanted to ask a million questions, but all she thought of was that the sour man was right—she could easily be dragged up the platform if she wouldn't walk. If she angered them, maybe the Pawnee wouldn't set her free. For whatever reason, she would humor them and take part in their curious ceremony.

All eyes seemed to be upon her. Luci took a deep breath for bravery, squared her small shoulders, and walked to the foot of the steps. The people set up a roar of approval, nodding and chanting. The priests at the top of the platform smiled encouragingly at her. She put one small, bare foot on the first step and the Pawnee shouted again.

Of course it was the right thing to do—not that she had any choice in the matter. She must not make them angry. What kind of a ceremony was this anyway? She took another step upward and the people chanted louder. Her knees shook so, she was having a hard time climbing the steps up to the platform next to the fire, but she went halfway up. For the first time now, she noted a wooden beam out over the fire. Curious. *What was that for?*

She paused uncertainly and looked behind her, back at Charish standing at the foot of the platform. He smiled encouragingly at her, then followed her up, taking her arm.

"Do you need help?" he asked in English and then half led, half carried her up the rest of the steps to the top of the platform.

From the top, Luci stared out at the sea of dark faces looking up at her expectantly. *What was it they wanted? What was it they had come to see?* She half turned as if to run back down the steps, but Charish held her arm.

He said to her, "It is a good omen for our people that you walk to the top willingly and bravely."

The old priests were obviously happy about it, too, smiling and nodding to her. Her heart pounded so hard, it threatened to burst through her chest. She didn't like the way the people were pressing in closer to the fire, looking up at her, the way their eyes gleamed in the firelight.

She took a deep breath and smelled the smoke of the big fire, felt the heat of it as the flames crackled in the pit below the platform.

The chanting and singing began all over again. Now a grizzled old priest held up one gnarled hand and the drumming and the singing ceased so suddenly, the silence echoed through the darkness. The only sound was the crackle of the flames and her own gasping breath. She was scared, so scared that she didn't think her legs would support her if she made a run for it, but of course she couldn't since Charish still held her arm. Beneath the robe, she felt perspiration on her naked skin begin to smear the scarlet and ebony ceremonial paint.

The old priest turned and looked at the Morning Star, seemingly suspended on the eastern horizon at this moment. He nodded toward Charish.

The dour warrior said to Luci, "Take off the robe. The people must see you naked and painted with the ceremonial paint."

"Naked? Before all these people? No! I—"

But he reached out and jerked the robe away, and she stood there, naked and ashamed, her beautiful, petite body bared for all to see.

Luci cried out in protest and tried to cover herself with her hands while the people roared their approval at the perfection of her virgin body.

"Let them see you!" Charish commanded, and he grabbed her arms, twisted them behind her, and tied them while she struggled. Then he turned her slowly so that the crowd below could gaze on her lovely, nude body.

There was nothing she could do except close her eyes so that she could not see the hunger in the warriors' faces looking up at her in the glow of the firelight. She brought her head up proudly and stood there, enduring the stares. She would show them the pride and dignity of the Cheyenne to these cowardly Pawnee!

If only Johnny Ace were here. What would he do? She thought bitterly. *Nothing.* Maybe he had known about this. Even if he hadn't, he wouldn't bring down the wrath of his people on his own head by helping her.

When she opened her eyes, the priests were shouting instructions to each other and the people. She stood there on the platform, naked and proud, staring down into the hundreds of eyes. The men seemed to be fitting arrows to their bows. A priest pointed to the Morning Star on the horizon. Of course. The Morning Star ceremony. She had only heard it whispered about around the

154

forts. She was going to be sacrificed. Why hadn't she realized that?

She couldn't escape. Very well, she would show them how a Cheyenne died. To Charish, she said, "Even a Cheyenne girl has more bravery than a Pawnee dog!"

His cruel eyes gleamed with admiration. "What a waste to sacrifice a female like you! What a waste that some Pawnee doesn't get to enjoy that virginity!"

Wasted virginity. She thought of Johnny Ace, regretted the chances she had missed to let him make love to her. Now she would never experience that coupling between a man and a woman that led to such ecstasy. Then she chided herself. He was an enemy. His people were about to murder her and all she thought of was the taste of his mouth, the way his strong arms had sheltered her against his chest. How ironic that in the seconds before her death, all she could think of was an enemy warrior.

The priests came forward and began to tie her. She glanced up at the beam out over the fire. She knew now what was to happen. They were going to hang her out over that fire and at the precise moment she swung to face the Morning Star, there would be hundreds of arrows loosed to pierce her naked, painted body. Her scarlet blood would drip into the fire to ensure a good planting and harvest.

She would show them how a Cheyenne could die. These cowardly Pawnee would be impressed with her bravery and dignity. For only an instant as they bound her, she wondered if she would feel the flames or if the shower of arrows would kill

155

her quickly so that she need never feel the heat on her defenseless skin.

She was so afraid, she could not swallow and her heart pounded as loudly as the drums. Tears tried to well up in her eyes and she blinked them back. She would not let the enemy see her fear. She closed her eyes, hoping it would be over quickly, wondering what part Johnny Ace had played in this, then shook her head. She could not believe it of him. From the first moment she had seen him, he had protected her, looked after her. Was it his revenge because she had spurned him when he wanted her?

It didn't matter now. She saw his strong dark face in her mind and it comforted her. As she died, she would think of him, remember the taste of his mouth, the strength of his arms around her.

Vaguely in the distance, she heard a horse whinny, and she half opened her eyes. Was that Johnny coming in at a gallop? She felt a deep, burning disappointment. So he was arriving just in time to see the enemy Cheyenne girl sacrificed. She wouldn't have believed it of him. And in spite of it all, deep in her heart, she loved him still.

Johnny rode at a gallop into the Skidi village and turned Katis toward the crowd gathered around the roaring fire in the center of the open area. *What the hell was going on?*

He reined in, almost unnoticed in the darkness by the milling, chanting people. He looked up in horror at the platform with the ceremonial-garbed priests, Charish standing next to a small, bound woman.

Her naked, painted body was beautiful and she looked out at the crowd bravely while the priests conferred. Her tragic eyes were full of dignity as if she knew she was to die and would show them how to meet death with her chin raised high. Blue eyes. Eyes the color of a starry sky.

With a strangled cry, he recognized Luci even as Katis whinnied. The sacrifice to the Morning Star. In that split second, he realized he would have to make a choice between his heritage and the girl.

If he tried to stop this ceremony, he would be forever an outcast and an outlaw among his own people. What a price to pay in a vain attempt to save a girl who hated him, had spat at him, fought him. *Enemy. Beloved enemy.*

He looked up at her. She looked back at him. In the length of a heartbeat, he made his decision. There was no chance to save her against all these hundreds of his people, but he would die trying. At least he would fight his way up that platform and they would die together as he tried to defend her. If he could just hold her one more time, he didn't care if they killed him.

"We'll die together, Star Eyes!" With a curse, he slashed the startled Katis with his reins and crashed through the crowd at a gallop.

Chapter Nine

With eyes closed, Luci stood prepared to die. She didn't want to see the arrows flying through the air in the split second before they found their target. Perhaps one would pierce her heart and she would die instantly before she felt the flames burning her alive.

She heard noise, shouts, confusion. She blinked. Katis galloped through the crowd, scattering people. They scrambled to get out of the path of the stallion's big hooves. The reflected firelight gleamed on Johnny's knife as he rode to the foot of the platform, swung down, and raced up the steps.

So he was the one chosen to administer the fatal thrust before the rest of the ceremony took place. In that split second as he mounted the steps, fast and fleet as a mountain cat, she was both saddened and relieved. No one could handle a blade like Johnny Ace. He would kill her skillfully, painlessly. And yet she had thought he cared for her. Perhaps it was revenge on his part against an enemy girl who had vexed him so.

The next split second was a blur of babbling, shouts, and shoving.

Almost in a daze, she watched Charish throw up a protesting hand, and scream out a challenge as he reached for his own knife.

Quick as a heart beat, Johnny stabbed the big warrior and shoved him aside, grabbing for Luci. "Star Eyes, will I never stop saving you?"

Even as she blinked in disbelief, his blade slashed her bounds. She collapsed into his strong arms. "Johnny, you came for me! I thought—"

"No time for that now, Small One! We either escape or die together!" With that, he swung her up against his wide chest and turned back toward the steps even as the stunned crowd stared at him in disbelief.

A priest shouted a protest, but Johnny shoved him aside and ran down the steps. All Luci could do was cling to him as he carried her and fought his way down the steps. They would never make it, she thought, but they would die together. Somehow, that was enough for her.

But she hadn't counted on how fast Johnny could move or how stunned the crowd was. Even as he threw her up on the black horse and swung up behind her, the crowd still stood as if paralyzed—as if they could not quite believe what was happening: that a Pawnee would defy his priests and make enemies of his own people to save a mere enemy girl.

"Hang on, Star Eyes, we haven't got a chance, but we're gonna try!"

She nodded, clinging to his big body as he urged the stallion to wheel and run. Behind them, the priests yelled at people to stop the pair.

The night air felt cool against Luci's perspiring face. Johnny turned the horse through the crowd and people ran to escape the great drumming hooves. Behind them, people milled in confusion, but the riders had gained the edge of the circle now and were galloping away from the village.

"Oh, Johnny, we won't make it!" She clung to him as they raced through the night.

"Then we'll die together, Star Eyes, I won't let them have you!" So saying, he held her against the shelter of his wide chest and the big horse thundered away.

There was nothing she could do but hang on to him as the horse ran. She was helpless and naked, his big body her only protection. Behind them, a hundred warriors loosed a flight of arrows or fired shots after the fleeing pair. But the big horse could run, and he ran as if all the devils were pursuing them.

Luci closed her eyes and lay her face against the soft buckskin of Johnny's shirt while the prairie disappeared beneath the stallion's drumming hooves. She felt the heat of his big hands on her bare skin as he cradled her, but nothing mattered any more except making it to safety . . . and that he had cared enough to come for her.

They rode for a long time after dawn broke until Katis was stumbling and lathered. Then Johnny dismounted and led the horse to cool him out while Luci sat the saddle, still naked and painted.

She looked down at his wide back as he led the horse. "You've made an outcast of yourself among your own people to save me."

He didn't look back. "You think I don't know that?"

"What about Deer? I thought you wanted to marry her. She won't want you now."

"What about her? I was only agreeing to marry the conniving little bitch to save your life."

"To save me?" So it was true.

He looked back over his shoulder. "I know it's *loco* to give up everything to save an enemy girl."

She wanted to ask why he had done it; but she wasn't sure she wanted to know the answer. "*Hahoo,*" she said finally. "Thank you."

After a few minutes, he mounted up behind her and they rode at a slow pace with Johnny's hands warm on her bare waist. Luci was suddenly aware of her nakedness and the heat of his hands on her skin. "I—I wish I had some clothes."

He chuckled. "When we stop again, I'll get you one of my shirts from my saddlebags. Right now, there's no one to see you but me, and if you'll remember, I've seen everything you've got to offer."

She felt her face burn but she didn't say anything. After all, modesty wasn't as important now as escaping.

He finally stopped, pulled a buckskin shirt from his saddlebags, and gave it to her. The sun climbed in the sky as they kept moving across the prairie. At times, Johnny would walk the big horse to cool it out. Then he would climb back up behind her in the saddle and push Katis into a slow lope.

Once in sheer exhaustion, she slumped back against him and he held her tightly a long moment, brushed his lips across the back of her neck, then seemed to remember himself and straightened up. But she felt his manhood swell and throb against the back of her hips.

His body wanted her. She knew he had always wanted her. And she had denied the fact that she yearned to couple with him because she was saving her precious virginity for a Cheyenne husband. But she was obliged to Johnny Ace. He had saved her life and she owed him something. She was too proud to owe an enemy. How could she pay him?

It was almost dark before Johnny crossed a small creek with a few sheltering cottonwoods and reined in. "I think we can camp here for the night."

He must have felt her unasked question because he looked back over his shoulder. "If they haven't come after us and caught us up by now, maybe they aren't going to try. They may be thinking about how mad the Long Knives, the Lachikuts, would be if they heard about the sacrifice. They know I ride for the cavalry. They may figure I've made it all the way to the fort and General Carr will send his troops out in retaliation."

He dismounted and reached up his hands to her. Luci hesitated, then slid off into his arms. His hands were hot, almost spanning her small waist.

He looked down at her then hesitated. For a long moment, she thought he would kiss her. But instead, he took a deep, shuddering breath and pushed her away. "I've got a little dried meat in my saddlebags. While I make camp, you can wash up and get that damned paint off!"

She owed him a great obligation and now she knew how she would repay him. Luci went to the creek, took off his shirt, and washed off the paint. When she looked up, he stood on the creek bank staring at her. "I had forgotten how beautiful you were," he said softly. "Did they hurt you? Did that damned Charish—"

"No, no man touched me," she said quickly, her face burning as she realized what he was asking.

"Of course, the sacrifice is supposed to be a virgin." He seemed to think aloud. "If I had taken you myself back at the fort, you might not have been in any danger."

She didn't say anything as she slipped the shirt over her head, very much aware that he watched her as she did so. "I seem to spend a lot of time wearing your clothes," she tried to smile brightly, but he didn't smile.

They walked back to where Katis grazed. Johnny spread a blanket, gesturing for her to sit. The shirt was so big, she had to push up the sleeves to accept the smoked meat he handed her.

It was good; smoky and salty. She dug her small teeth into it with relish. "Are we in any danger stopping to rest here?"

He shrugged as he ate. "Katis needs rest. So do we. Somehow, I think they may be regretting getting caught up in this sacrifice thing. They'll be afraid I'll bring the soldiers back to attack them."

"You've made an outcast of yourself among your own people."

He paused in eating. "I don't fit in anyway, never have. I suppose I belong with the whites."

"But you aren't white, you're Pawnee."

"Am I?" He laughed coldly as he finished his meat and began to roll a cigarette. "Star Eyes, there are times I don't know what the hell I am.

I'm not white, I'm not Indian. I really belong nowhere and no one cares what I do or where I go."

She started to say that she cared, but she reconsidered. Nothing could overcome the wide chasm between them. But she owed him and she was proud.

The sun set all purple and gold as he finished his cigarette. Johnny stretched and yawned. "I'm going to wash up and we'll rest a few hours here in the cover of these trees. Before dawn, we'll ride on into the fort."

The fort. She didn't even want to think about what lay ahead tomorrow. She still didn't know what she was going to do. Maybe she should swallow her pride and go to Denver with Winnifred Starrett.

Johnny went off down to the creek in the growing twilight. While she heard him splashing, she made her decision. She owed the scout. She knew what pay he'd want.

When he came back from the creek, barechested, the water glistening on his wet, dark skin, Luci had stripped off the buckskin shirt and sat naked on the blanket.

His eyes widened in surprise. "What the hell you think you're doing?"

"Sometimes you sound more like a smart-alec cowboy than an Indian," she said, standing up.

His gaze swept from her feet up to the top of her head, lingering on the dark vee of her thighs, on her small, firm breasts. Luci didn't flinch. She stood there, letting him look her up and down, almost feeling heat from his dark eyes staring at her nude body.

"You didn't answer me," He sounded tense. "I don't know what your game is, Star Eyes, but—"

"No game," she said softly. "I owe you. I owe you for everything you've done for me from the start. And I only have one way to pay." She held out her arms.

He swore softly under his breath. "A whore. You're gonna whore for it?"

She flinched at the anger in his tone but she didn't lower her arms. "I'm a virgin, Johnny. You want me, I know you want me. I'm offering all I've got to thank you."

With almost a growl in his throat, he came to her, pulled her into his embrace. His naked skin still dripped water but his bare flesh burned like a fever against her.

His passion scared her as he held her, covered her mouth with his, and put his big hands on her small, bare bottom. His big body seemed to envelop hers so completely, she could scarcely breath. She felt his hard arousal through the blue cavalry pants he wore. He was built like a stallion, and it terrified her.

He seemed to sense her woodenness, stopped kissing her, and looked down into her face. "What's the matter? You don't want me?"

She tried to smile up at him bravely. "I—I owe you. I pay my debts."

He took her face between his two big hands, then smiled with no mirth. "So that's how it's to be? No tenderness, no wanting—just like a white whore in North Platte?"

"If you say so." She was so afraid of the experi-

165

ence, of the fervor of his passion, that she trembled in his grasp. Would it be sheer agony when this Pawnee stud rammed into her and tore her virgin sheath?

"Then if you're going to play the whore, Luci, let's not make any pretenses about it." He sounded disappointed and shoved her roughly to the blanket. "If you can be so cold about this, I'll treat you like a paid slut. Do you hate paying a debt to a Pawnee that bad?"

She didn't hate him at all . . . or did she? She didn't know what she thought or felt. Woodenly, she lay down on the blanket on her back.

"Now spread your legs." He began taking off his pants, tossing two silver dollars on her bare belly. "I don't know how much you figure you owe me, but I don't want you to come up short on this deal."

Would he leave her no dignity? She lay there in the almost darkness of the coming night, looking up at him. The silver dollars felt cold and heavy on her bare skin. Luci dutifully spread her thighs and looked up at him.

He was naked now and even bigger than she had thought. She could never take the size of him without tearing and bleeding. She tried to stop herself from trembling as he came down on his knees between her thighs. His expression and his voice were cold as steel. "The best whores don't just lie there, Star Eyes, they pretend they want the man, too. You'll get a bigger tip that way and the customer will come back again."

"I—I don't know what to do. You'll have to show me." She kept her voice matter-of-fact although a torrent of fear and emotion was raging

166

inside her.

"You're right, you know, I've wanted you from the first time I saw you. I keep trying to forget you're an enemy, that we could never make a go of it." His voice became a ragged, reluctant whisper as he leaned over and took her small breasts in his two big hands. "Maybe once I've had you, and smeared my seed all over you, the hunger will be gone and I can forget you."

And he sprawled on top of her, his manhood hot and throbbing against her bare thigh. His hands squeezed and stroked her breasts while his burning mouth covered hers and his tongue plunged deep between her lips.

His skin was still wet and his nakedness was like a flame against her body. Part of her wanted what he had to give, but she was afraid and trembled violently.

He rose up on his elbows, looking down at her in puzzlement. "Are you that afraid of me?"

She tried to deny it, gasped, and began to cry. "I—I pay my debts and I owe you!"

He cursed and sat up. "You damned little bitch! I've got pride, too. You think I'd take you, knowing—"

"You said you wanted me, and I owe you for saving my life, and—"

"Will you stop saying that?" His eyes were so full of fury, she thought he would strike her and shied away.

He sighed heavily and stood up. "I've never raped a woman and damned if I'll start with some Cheyenne chit who'll make me feel guilty about it forever!"

He went over to his saddlebags, got his makin's

and rolled a cigarette while she rose up on one elbow and watched his magnificent body gleam in the moonlight.

"Mercy! Did I do something wrong?" She couldn't understand why he was so angry.

"No, you didn't do anything wrong—except be yourself. I'm angry with myself." He lit the cigarette and leaned against a tree.

"Why?"

"Dammit, Star Eyes, do I have to spell it out for you? I never had a virgin before, I didn't know they were so—" He seemed to struggle for a word, then gave up with an exasperated sigh.

She didn't know what he expected her to do now so she kept silent, watching his magnificent naked body while he smoked.

"I want you, yes, and I guess I'm crazy. I want *you* to want *me*." He acted embarrassed, chagrined to say the words. "It's all I can do to keep from climbing on you, shoving my rod as deep into you as I can get. It's the stallion in me, I suppose. All I can think of is how I'd like to explode within you, put my baby in that smooth little belly. Nine months from now, I'd like to see those small breasts swollen with milk for my son . . . and for me!"

"You don't need to make me think you care about me. Don't feel guilty about taking what I offer," she whispered softly. "We both know it could never work out. Not unless we turned our backs on the rest of the world and went off together, just the two of us."

"Like Adam and Eve in the book they made us read in the boarding school." He shook his head, and threw the cigarette away. "You're right. All you've got to give is your virginity and I know how the Cheyenne prize that among their women. That's all you've got to give, Small One, and I'm either too noble or too stupid to take it."

She looked at him, not sure whether she was relieved . . . or disappointed.

"When we get back to the fort, I guess I'll try to help you get back to your tribe. Maybe that's where you belong, with some big Cheyenne buck between your thighs, putting his son in your belly. You'd have a place of honor in his tipi then. Let's get some sleep," he muttered, going over to the saddlebags. "We have to get started before dawn."

He got himself a blanket and moved across from her. "Roll up in the one you've got, Luci. You've got my word I won't bother you. Your precious virginity is safe. You can iron some clothes for me if you still feel beholden when we get back to the fort."

He had rejected what she offered. Either that or he wanted something more that she didn't know how to give. Without a word, she wrapped up in her blanket. He did the same. After a while, she heard his soft, even breathing as he slept, but she couldn't sleep.

She lay there for hours, staring up at the stars. Her mind went again and again to the memory of his hot, wet skin against hers, the taste of his mouth. In her mind, his big hands covered her breasts and kneaded her nipples. She felt the dewy wetness of wanting a man deep in her velvet place.

The night had turned chill and she had only the one blanket. Her oversized shirt lay thrown carelessly across the grass a few feet away. She knew that if she moved to get it, Johnny would awaken.

Somewhere a coyote howled and Katis raised his great head briefly and then went back to munching grass.

Luci shivered again and looked over at Johnny, remembering the heat of his skin against hers, remembering the security and shelter of his warm embrace.

The coyote howled again, closer this time. Even though she knew the cowardly little animal wouldn't dare move in close enough to bother her, she was scared. She was also cold. For a long time she lay there until she was so chilled, her teeth were almost chattering. Finally, taking a deep breath for courage, she gathered up her blanket and crawled across the intervening space between them.

Johnny exploded out of his blankets as she reached him. She couldn't move or even cry out as he grabbed her, and held his blade against her throat.

Then he seemed to recognize her, relaxed, and swore softly. "Dammit, Star Eyes, don't ever do that again. I might have cut your throat before I realized you weren't an enemy brave sneaking up on me. What is it you want?"

She looked up at him. "I—I'm cold."

He shrugged. "I only got one blanket, but if you want it—"

"We'd be warmer if we spread both of them over the two of us."

He shrugged. "I'm not cold,"

"I am."

He sighed heavily, and threw up his hands as if in defeat, "You push me to the limit, Star Eyes, you know that? After everything that's happened,

170

you expect to cuddle up next to me and just *sleep?*
I have to keep reminding myself that I've sworn
not to rape you."

"I'm not worried."

"Damnit, you oughta be!"

She crawled in next to him and spread the two
blankets over both of them. The heat from his big
body spread though her and she put her head on
his shoulder. He lay stiff, as if afraid to relax.

She wanted him, she knew it deep inside. She
wanted him and it had nothing to do with owing
him. She turned over and faced him, pressing
tightly against him.

"Luci, don't do that."

"Make love to me."

"You don't owe me, you hear?"

"Make love to me anyway."

He groaned aloud. "Your little Cheyenne chit.
You've brought me nothing but trouble. I can't
sleep for thinking of you. My body actually aches
from wanting you, I—"

Her lips cut off his words and he paused as if
surprised at her action. "No, Luci—"

But she flickered her tongue along his lips and
pressed her breasts against him so hard that they
flattened against his hard chest.

"Luci, I'm warning you . . ."

"I—I want to be taught whatever I need to
know."

He rose up on one elbow, looking at her in the
moonlight, his eyes dark with pent-up emotion.
"Taught by a Pawnee?"

"I—that doesn't matter,"

"Your eyes, your expression, tell me it does."

His gaze burned into her and she looked away.

171

"I only know that at this moment, I want you, Johnny, and I don't care about anything else."

He seemed to be fighting some kind of battle with himself. "Tomorrow you'll regret giving your virginity to an enemy."

"Maybe. I—I don't know." She slipped her arms around his neck, and kissed him.

With a shudder, he pulled her against him and kissed her hotly, sucking the tip of her tongue deep between his lips while his hands stroked and explored her body. She started to protest, stiffening in a momentary fear as his big hands stroked her bare thighs and probed inside her. "I'll go slow," he whispered, "I'll—"

She cut off his words with her mouth as she pushed her body against his hand, trembling with the touch of his fingers stroking and teasing there. She felt his manhood big and hard as a stallion's against her thigh and the wetness of his virile seed leaving a trail on her belly as he tilted her head back and kissed her deeply, filling her throat with his tongue as she surrendered to his domination. But still he did not enter her.

His hot mouth covered her breast, sucking her nipple until it was sensitive and tender before he moved to the other one. Suddenly she wished that she was carrying his child in her belly, that her breasts were swollen with milk for his eager mouth to share with a small son.

Her hand went down to stroke his maleness and came away—wet with his virile seed. He took her hand in his. "Taste it," he commanded, and bent her fingers to touch her own lips. "That's what makes a man a man. I want to smear you with it, mark you as mine, feel you kiss me there."

172

For a moment, she wavered, shocked at the idea. It was the ultimate female surrender to male dominance. She slid down in the blanket so that her mouth covered his throbbing hardness. His seed was hot to her mouth and it excited her to hold his throbbing staff between her lips, and run her tongue along it.

Before she could stop him, he had gathered her up in his arms, moving her so that his mouth was on her private, most tender place. She stiffened and almost protested, but his tongue was probing between her thighs and it felt too good to stop him.

"Don't, Luci," he commanded softly. "You're mine! Surrender yourself to me."

With a shudder, she let her thighs fall apart, felt the heat of his mouth kissing her there, his tongue running down the tiny ridge of flesh before he slipped it deep inside her. "No," she moaned, "you shouldn't . . ."

"Surrender, Luci," he commanded, and his breath was hot against the ridge of flesh as his hands spread her thighs. "By the time I get through, you'll want me too much for it to hurt."

She didn't care anymore if he hurt her if he would only stop this hungry throbbing of her own body. She thought then he would take her but he only kept stabbing relentlessly with his tongue until she couldn't stop herself from opening her thighs like a night-blooming flower spreading its petals, wanting the kiss of the moth's wings as it takes the flower's nectar.

Shudders began to sweep over her, shudders she couldn't control. "Johnny. . . ."

"Easy, Luci, let it happen, don't fight. It's all

right. Let it happen. . . ."

She could do nothing else as his tongue probed her and the shudders began to build deep in her soul. For a moment, she was terrified of what was happening to her, and tried to fight it. But Johnny's hands and mouth were everywhere and there was no escaping from the black unconsciousness that swept her out of control.

When her eyes flickered open again, she was sobbing in his arms and he kissed her hair. "Johnny, I—I don't understand . . ."

"I'm not finished with you," he whispered, and now his fingers probed between her thighs, stroking and teasing.

The feeling began to build in her again like a wave that begins far out at sea and rises bigger and bigger until it crashes against the shoreline. "Johnny, no, I—"

Then she couldn't say anything more because his fingers had started a throbbing in her that seemed to be cresting like a wild wave and she didn't want it to end. She wrapped her slim thighs around his hand so he couldn't take it away while his free one stroked and teased her taut nipples. The darkness came again, sweeping her up in shuddering ripples and he could do anything to her as long as he didn't take his hand away.

This time, when her eyes opened in the moonlight, he held her against him tightly, his lips caressing her hair. His body felt as tense as a steel spring and she felt his maleness hard as stone against her. "Johnny . . . you want me?"

"You know I do, but you don't owe me."

She felt wet and warm but still she craved more. "Let me do it," she whispered.

174

He rolled over on his back and she saw how very big and hard he was. It would be like a man's fist shoving up into her to the elbow and she was afraid. "I — I'm ready."

But he only lay on his back, looking up at her as she paused there on her knees beside him. "I'm not going to force myself on you, Star Eyes. I don't want you to have regrets; to ever say that you were raped by a Pawnee."

"I'm not going to say that; not ever." She put one knee on each side of his body, and looked down at his maleness. He was big, all right, and she was a virgin. "Will it hurt?"

"I can't tell you it won't." There was tension in his voice as if it was all he could do to keep from grabbing her, rolling her over, and ramming deep inside her. "You don't owe me, Star Eyes."

She came up on her knees, settled herself on the tip of his manhood, and hesitated. Then very slowly, she slid down on him until he throbbed against the silk of her virginity. She was about to give that precious jewel to an enemy. A beloved enemy.

Very slowly she slid down on him, biting her lip to hold back her cry as he broke through her virginity. "Now, Johnny, I — help me . . . I don't know what I'm supposed to do!"

With a strangled cry, he grasped her small waist in his two big hands, and forced her all the way down on his throbbing rod. He held her there, bucking under her, ramming up into her, lifting her up off the ground from the sheer strength of his sinewy muscles, fueled by his need of her.

It was pain and it was pleasure. It was fear and it was ecstasy. His hammer-hard dagger pushed up

175

under her ribs, impaling her while he held her with his strong hands so that she could not move off him. She felt every inch of him deep inside, throbbing in her very depths with the rich seed he had to give. She was powerless to do anything with her small body impaled on his burning sword. Then he cried out and began to convulse within her.

She felt the throbbing, the swell of his rod as it began to surge and spill its hot liquid fire within her velvet depths. Then her own body seemed to catch fire and respond, clasping his throbbing member tightly as if afraid he might leave before her womb had squeezed from this stallion what it hungered for.

With a strangled cry, she pitched forward into his arms as he exploded beneath her and her body convulsed, too. They locked and meshed and strained together in the age-old mystery of mating while time stood suspended in the moonlight.

Then he rolled her over and rode her savagely, pushing her ankles up over his shoulders so that he could put all his power behind his drive as he tilted her small hips up for his thrust.

It felt as if his hot fist were being forced up to the elbow deep between her defenseless thighs. She couldn't cry out because his tongue was in her mouth and her body wanted him too badly to whimper as he rode her in a frenzy. A molten steel bar rammed up under her ribs, setting fire to her insides, making her convulse under him again and again while he strained to give her every drop of seed within him.

Finally they both lay locked together and sated, skin shining with a slight sheen of perspiration.

He moved off her and she saw the scarlet stain of her virginity on his manhood. It occurred to her now that she had ruined her chances of getting a respectable husband. No Cheyenne brave would want a wanton woman who had lain with an enemy.

"Beloved enemy," she whispered, and pulled him against her again, seeking the shelter of his arms.

He kissed her face. "Now where do we go from here?"

Where indeed? Now that the rush of passion was over and dawn was new and pale lavender on the eastern horizon, she felt a sense of loss and despair. He was right. Nothing could come of this. How could she love a man who hunted down her people for the bluecoats? They could not live among her people or his.

"Regrets, Star Eyes?" He stroked her face, looking sadly at her as if he saw deep into her soul.

She had been grateful to him for saving her life and she had paid him. That's all it was—she had paid him with what he wanted most. She couldn't love an enemy. She didn't look him in the face as she disengaged herself from his body and he stood up. Her scarlet blood smeared him. A woman can give that most precious gift but once and she had given it to a killer of her people.

The romantic night had fled and daylight with its hard reality was slowly dawning. Now she had regrets. But when she closed her eyes and remembered his embrace, the taste of his mouth, the feel of him throbbing deep within her, she would have done it again.

When she didn't answer, he sighed heavily and turned away to pick up his clothes. Then he disap-

177

peared down to the creek to clean up.

Luci took a deep breath and smelled the scent of his male seed all over her body. She was no better than a bitch in heat, wanting to couple with a stud in the moonlight. She didn't look at him when he returned.

She had nothing to wear but his shirt. Mercy! Why did she always seem to end up in his damned shirt? She picked it up, clasped it against her bare body to hide herself, then went down to the creek and washed off. After a moment's hesitation, she slipped the butter-soft shirt oven her head. She always forgot how big he was until she wore his shirts. The sleeves came down over her fingertips. The leather was warm and soft as it slid down her breasts, down her naked skin. It reminded her again of how he had felt spread out on top of her, covering her, dominating her.

They ate a bit of smoked jerky in the silent dawn. Then he mounted and held out his hand. "Luci, I'm sorry."

"Nothing to be sorry for." She avoided his eyes. "I owed you and I paid, that's all."

For a split second, she thought the offered hand would pull back and strike her, there was such a fury in his face. "That's all I can expect from a Cheyenne chit, I guess," he said coldly. "You were good, Small One, good enough to compete with the best of them. Maybe you should get a job at one of those whorehouses in North Platte."

She felt the blood rush to her face but she wouldn't let the tears come. "Maybe I will. A whore who'll bed a dirty Pawnee can't be too choosy."

He caught her hand and jerked her up on the

178

stallion before him. "Don't push me, Luci. I'll dump you out here on the prairie and let you fend for yourself."

Despite the cold fury and hurt in his voice, she didn't think he was capable of that, but she wasn't sure. His body felt rigid with anger against hers.

She had given herself willingly to an enemy Pawnee scout in the magic of the moonlight. Now what?

Without a word, he nudged the horse and Katis broke into a slow lope. Neither of them said another word all the way back to Fort McPherson.

Chapter Ten

It was a big mistake to return to Fort McPherson. Luci realized that as she and Johnny rode through the gates on the big stallion.

Johnny helped her dismount before a gathering crowd of settlers and soldiers, their eyes bright with curiosity. She looked down at her bare feet, acutely aware that she wore nothing but Johnny's long buckskin shirt. She felt her face burn under the frank scrutiny of the gawkers.

But the Pawnee said loudly, "Next time you decide to go berry picking, Miss Luci, you need to take someone else along so you won't get lost and the major won't have to send out a search party."

Winnifred Starrett stood on the edge of the crowd, twirling her pink lace parasol. She made a skeptical, sniffing motion. "Land's sake! And to think I considered taking that girl to Denver as my maid!"

"We both know that's not what's really bothering you!" Luci shot back, and immediately regretted it. Winnifred had been her only chance to escape this hopeless existence.

"Humph!" Winnifred put her nose in the air, snapped the parasol shut, and walked off with such a stiff, fast gait that her hair ribbon and wide sashes blew out behind her.

Johnny actually grinned, but Luci pretended not to notice. She had other things to regret as well. Now in the cold reality of daylight, it seemed incredible to her that she had lost her reason and had given way to passionate abandon under a star-filled sky.

The crowd, easily bored and seeing no excitement in the return of a girl lost while picking berries, drifted off.

She stood there, twisting her work-worn hands together. "I suppose I forgot to thank you for saving my life. Do we tell anyone what really happened?"

"About what?" He stood with feet wide apart, his hand on the hilt of his knife. His dark eyes seemed to be staring straight into her soul.

Her face burned with the memory that she knew crossed his mind, too — of them locked and straining together, both smeared with his virile seed and her virgin blood.

His mouth. She looked at his mouth and remembered the sweet taste of it, the way it had burned into hers, then caressed her body like a fire brand. "About the Pawnee sacrifice."

He shrugged. "It would only cause trouble and I doubt they'll ever report it, knowing the army would be upset. I don't think they'll ever do it again."

She averted her eyes, uncomfortable with the

way he was looking at her. Yet she saw uneasiness in his expression, too, as if he knew it could never work out. "You've lost your bride, killed Charish, and become an outcast among your people. Even the scouts may treat you differently, once they've heard—"

"I already was an outcast, Star Eyes." He played with the reins in his hand. "I'm not white, but I'm not really Pawnee anymore either. I keep hoping maybe someday. . . ."

She waited for him to finish, but he only looked off toward the horizon and the vast frontier beyond. She followed his gaze. All she had ever seen was the prairie around some of the Kansas and Nebraska forts. There was no future for her in these states. She allowed herself the luxury of dreaming of a fresh start somewhere out there in the wilderness.

There would be a cozy ranch house with a fireplace and children snuggled down in their beds. She'd be waiting on the porch for her man to ride in from rounding up stray cattle from their own fine herd. But even as she saw the vision, the man riding into the corral in her dreams rode a big, black horse. When he dismounted and came toward her with his arms outstretched, it was Johnny Ace.

"No," she said aloud, denying the vision with a shake of her head. "Not an enemy, no."

He looked at her as if he had read her thoughts. "Luci, if you're with child—"

"Oh, God, I never even thought of that!" She shook her head violently and ran into the trading post.

Johnny stared after her. Well, she had given him her answer. It had been a *loco* thought anyway. Who ever heard of a Pawnee cowboy? He thought about his dream, about the money tucked away in his things, so carefully saved from his pay, from his skill at poker.

For just a moment, his thoughts had seemed in tune with the girl's. He had imagined himself riding Katis into the corral at his ranch—their ranch. A woman stood on the porch in the twilight waiting for him, and in his mind, she was a small, slight girl with dark hair and bright blue eyes. Over the corral gate hung a sign with their brand: The Ace High Star. The fat cattle he'd just rounded up carried a brand on their hips, an ace and a star.

What a fool he had been to think she might care for him, that love could bridge such chasms as the bitter hatred between their people. He'd had her virginity, but she wouldn't give him her love. With a sigh, he remembered the horror in her face when he had tried to tell her that he wanted her, would be ready to marry her anytime, so that she need not worry if she carried a child.

He turned and walked away to the barn to groom Katis and put him away. What had he done? There was no more to regret than the fact that Luci didn't care about him. He knew the Cheyenne set such value on virginity that they often put chastity belts on their unmarried women. If she returned to her people now, she might not have much of a future unless she was skillful enough to fool some brave. And she was too innocent for that.

He fed his horse and crossed the parade ground to report to Pani Le-shar, his mind busy with thoughts of the night before. Though he felt guilty for what he'd done, he didn't regret it. He'd had his love in his arms for one unforgettable night. Now that she had regained her senses and spurned him, that memory would have to last a lifetime.

Major North grinned and stood up to shake hands as Johnny entered. "So you tracked her down and brought her back?"

Johnny stood feet wide apart, not looking at the major. "Does it show so much then?"

Frank North cleared his throat slowly as if hesitant to say more, then sat down in his chair behind his desk. "I don't like to stick my nose in my men's business, Johnny."

"Then don't." He took out his makin's and began to roll a cigarette.

"With all the hatred between the two tribes, this can't work out. I told you about Romeo and Juliet, didn't I?"

"Don't preach to me, Pani Le-shar," Johnny said sharply, lighting the cigarette.

"I wouldn't take that from just anyone, Johnny."

"I'm sorry, Major. I didn't mean anything—she's got me *loco,* that's all."

"I understand." He leaned back in his chair, steepled his fingers, and stared at them as if seeing them for the first time. "There's something more, isn't there, Johnny? Something you haven't told me."

He'd tried not to think about it. It could only complicate things. He rolled the cigarette over and over in his brown fingers. "Her uncle is Ta Ton Ka Haska."

184

"Good God!" The major's chair came down on all fours with a bang. "The bloodiest Dog Soldier of them all and my top scout is mixed up with his niece? If he finally learns his sister is dead, he may try to reclaim Luci."

Johnny smoked and watched the tip glow. It was bad enough to get mixed up with a Cheyenne girl, but blood kin to Tall Bull. . . . "You think even if we try to make a life together, he might come after her someday?"

"Do you think the chief of the Dog Soldiers would allow his niece to live with a Pawnee scout?"

The answer was too obvious to bother. The girl on the porch of the ranch house suddenly faded into smoke and he stood in the twilight alone—always alone. "We've both known from the first we can't work it out. She was trying to get back to her people when she stole my horse."

The major looked at him thoughtfully. "You want to tell me what happened out there?"

What had happened? He'd fallen madly in love with the niece of the bloodiest killer raiding the frontier, saved her life, and spent one night of ecstasy in her arms.

"No. Not much happened." He puffed his cigarette, avoiding the major's gaze.

"If you say so, Johnny." Frank North stood up. "Has it occurred to you she might be a spy, trying to report on our troop movements and scouting expeditions to her uncle?"

And he was the Fifth Cavalry's most important Pawnee scout, responsible for the Fifth's best-kept secrets. He felt a little sick—betrayed. Had that been where she was going when the Pawnee had caught her? To tell the Dog Soldiers the strength of the fort, how many soldiers there were? When the campaign might move against them? A laundry girl picked up a lot of gossip on her rounds.

"Major, I don't think I want to talk about this." With an annoyed gesture, he pitched the cigarette into the spittoon.

"Johnny, she's probably just a little half-breed girl trying to survive." He chewed his lip a long moment as if choosing his words carefully. "But think twice about what you tell her."

"I will." He had to fight a terrible impulse to run out the door, find Luci, and choke the truth out of her. Had she coldly let him make love to her to bring his guard down? Would she yet try to learn more about the Cavalry's coming offensive and then ride out and report it to her uncle?

North interrupted his troubled thoughts. "We'll be finally moving in full force in a couple of weeks. I'm sending Lieutenant Osgoode, my brother, and a scout into Denver to see about coordinating a full-fledged offensive by including troops from Colorado Territory. I don't suppose you'd like to be that scout?"

Johnny hesitated. "Ride all the way to Denver with that Boston bastard?"

The major chuckled. "I hear you two have been at loggerheads over that girl."

"Amazing how fast gossip travels," Johnny said wryly. "It's better than the telegraph."

"Which reminds me, that's why I'm sending men to Denver instead of just wiring." North paced up and down. "The Dog Soldiers have learned how important the telegraph is to us. They keep cutting the lines and then tying them back together with

186

rawhide so it's hard to spot the break. I'll send Cody, then."

"Are you sending Miss Starrett with them? She's a pain in the—"

"No, I'll want the messengers to travel fast and Miss Starrett has enough boxes and baggage to fill a caravan. I'll be glad when things settle down enough that the stage will begin to run again and take her on to Denver. At least with the telegraph down, her rich papa isn't wiring me continually with instructions and inquiries."

Johnny had a sixth sense about things. "Why are you really sending Luther to Denver?"

The major sat down on the edge of his desk. "If I didn't trust you so much, I wouldn't tell you, considering the Cheyenne girl—"

He couldn't control his temper. "Don't call her a spy, Major! You have no proof!"

The major looked at him without blinking. "We go a long way back, don't we, Johnny? You saved my life. I'm thinking about that now when I should be throwing you in the guardhouse for insubordination."

Johnny didn't answer. It was true. In the heat of battle, North's horse had stumbled, throwing him. As he lay there unconscious, his men had rallied around his limp form. Ten of them had held off over a hundred Cheyenne until he regained his senses rather than desert him to certain death at the hands of the enemy. "Pani Le-shar, I'm sorry. Like I said, I can't think anymore because of her."

"As to why Luther's going to Denver—Washington suspects some white might be trading with the renegades."

Johnny stared at him, thunderstruck. "You

mean, providing guns and supplies to be used against other white people? That's so lowdown, I can't believe it!"

The major shrugged, and stood up. "Just a suspicion. The hostiles seem too well armed to just be picking up an occasional weapon in a raid."

"So besides being outnumbered and ill-equipped, we may be going up against savages better armed than we are?"

"It sure looks that way. Congress always wants to cut the army's budget at the end of a war, and that's what's happened. You've seen the old castoff guns and ammo they've issued us. I don't know whether Luci knows how badly we'd fare against the Cheyenne right now or not."

"She's innocent, Major." *Was she?*

"For your sake, I hope so. That's why I don't just lock her up." He pulled at his mustache. "So why has she suddenly been trying to rejoin the Dog Soldiers?"

"To get away from me, I think," he answered with a sheepish shake of his head.

"There really is more to it than just wanting to take her a few times?"

Johnny fiddled with the hilt of his knife, looking all the while at the floor.

"A man who's that crazy about a woman doesn't think straight, Johnny. Be careful."

Johnny stared at his moccasins. "You don't trust me, Major?"

The slightly built officer smiled. "Let's say I don't trust the judgment of a man who's so taken by a woman that he'd risk his career, his life, and maybe the lives of his comrades over her."

Was Luci trying to get information from him to

take to her uncle? Would she do that? "Is that all, sir?"

North nodded and Johnny snapped him a sharp salute, turned, and strode out.

He stood looking up at the stars, deeply troubled. Morning Star. Niece to a bloody killer whom the cavalry hunted. Johnny walked slowly through the twilight, past the quarters.

A woman called behind him. "Johnny?"

He turned. Winnifred Starrett stood in her doorway, smiling at him. "Oh, hello, Miss Starrett." He nodded, then turned as if to go.

"You might come in a minute, we've things to discuss."

He studied her in the light from the room behind her. She was beautiful in her expensive sunrise pink dress with a wide sash that accentuated her slim waist, her dark hair tied up in ribbon. Something about her face made him wonder why she looked so familiar to him, then he decided it was only his imagination.

Winnifred smiled at him invitingly. "Do come in."

He started to refuse, but she was already stepping back to allow him to enter. Johnny followed her into the room, watching as she closed the door behind her. "Your reputation will be ruined if I'm found in here with the door closed."

She smiled cooly. "I'm not worried," she drawled.

"What was it you wanted, Miss Starrett?"

"Land's sake! Don't act so coy, Johnny. We're both adults." She came over and slipped her arms around his neck.

He looked down at her, slightly amused. "What

happened to the shy, Southern belle act?"

"You make me forget I'm a genteel lady; maybe it's the swarthy skin." Her small, white teeth nipped his lips as she pressed her full breasts against his chest.

He felt his manhood surge as she molded her curves against the hard planes of his body. Very slowly, her hands reached to undo the laces on his shirt. Her fingers ran over his bare chest, with slow, stroking movements. When the tips brushed his nipples, he caught her hand. "Don't play games, miss. I'm a man, not a boy to be teased."

"I know. That's what I like about you. You're a dark-skinned, primitive savage. I'll bet you wouldn't take no for an answer like the simpering fops I've known." She kept stroking his nipples while she pressed up against him.

He could feel the hard rosettes of her breasts though her sheer dress as evidence that she wore no camisole or maybe anything else beneath it.

She bent her head as she pushed his shirt open and ran the hot tip of her tongue across his dark nipple. "Go to Denver with me, Johnny."

He took a deep breath, his groin aching at her touch. She wore some wonderfully expensive perfume. He smelled it on her hot skin. "You're supposed to be a lady. I'm trying to remember that." He grabbed her wrist.

"But you make me feel like a tart. That's what I like about you. No woman can tame you; you're all man."

Winnifred's fingertips still stroked his chest in a teasing way that drove him crazy and made him want a woman—any woman. No, that wasn't true. He saw Luci's face in his mind and cursed her for

190

her hold on him.

Winnifred smiled coyly at him. "Come to Denver with me, Johnny."

"And do what?" He was almost hypnotized by the way her little pink tongue licked her lips so slowly.

"Anything that needs doing, I reckon." She reached up and kissed along his high cheekbone.

"In a town like Denver, I could get gelded and lynched for messing with a white girl." He let go of her wrist, his pulse beating faster. Johnny was too much man not to be affected by her nearness, her perfume.

"Who'll know?" she drawled. "I'll have a husband Father's chosen for me. As long as I'm discreet. . . ."

Looking down into her bright blue eyes, he suddenly saw another pair of eyes. *Luci*. Why did Winnifred's face make him think of the little half-breed?

He turned toward the door.

"You aren't leaving?"

"Watch me!" Johnny strode out, feeling a little cleaner as he reached the open air outside. He went back to his quarters and lay sleepless on his cot, thinking what a fool he was not to take advantage of the situation. Winnifred was beautiful and rich. She wanted a dark stud; he ought to be willing to service her. But he had a feeling that every time he tried to take her, he'd see that other pair of bright blue eyes and wouldn't be able to complete the act. Helluva note!

It was a nice morning for late spring, Luci

decided as she shook out a wet shirt and hung it on the line. Although she'd had a few curious stares, all the soldiers seemed to be going out of their way to be polite to her. Somehow she suspected that might be the Pawnee scout's doing, but she couldn't be sure.

He hadn't spoken to her in the several days since that night under the stars when she'd lost both her reason and her virginity. In fact, she'd been avoiding him, not quite sure where they went from here.

As far as Johnny Ace himself, she had seen him riding out the big gates this morning on patrol, and when he saw her, he stared at her long and hard as if to fathom what was inside her head. But he said nothing, only nodding curtly.

No doubt he regretted it as did she. But he didn't have to worry about being pregnant. If that happened, what in God's name would she do? She decided not to borrow trouble by worrying about that now. For that matter, what was she going to do with the rest of her life? She saw herself suddenly as a gnarled, gray-haired laundry lady, still on suds row doing soldiers' shirts with red, wrinkled hands.

She mused over the possibilities of returning to her uncle as she stuck a clothespin in her mouth and reached for another shirt. That would be better that this—unless she came up with a Pawnee baby. She couldn't expect some Dog Soldier to raise an enemy's child.

What about the possibility of marrying some soldier? It would be a gamble like the one her mother had taken and lost. A soldier was more apt to use her and throw her aside when his hitch was up—unless he really cared for her. Stranger things than that had happened. After all, she was considered pretty and the chaplain's wife at Fort Leavenworth had educated her and taught her some of the niceties of white women.

Lieutenant Osgoode rode by, turned his dun gelding, came over, and touched the brim of his hat. "Why, Miss Luci, how nice to see you again!"

"I was just thinking the same about you!" She smiled prettily at him, thinking how handsome he was, how elegant and well bred.

He looked embarrassed, fumbled with his hat, and took it off. The brown curls fell across his forehead. "I—I had been meaning to look you up and apologize for what happened at the party the other night. When men have had too much to drink, they do foolish things."

"Think no more of it, Lieutenant. It was my fault for rushing in somewhere that I obviously didn't belong."

He looked at her a long moment as if really seeing her for the first time. "You are a real beauty, you know that? I think not only did I act the fool, I must have been blind."

"You're too gallant—such a perfect Boston gentleman." She went on hanging up shirts, uncomfortably aware of his ardent gaze.

He fumbled with his hat. "I'm embarrassing you. How awkward of me."

"It's all right, really," she said. "I don't think a man need apologize for being gallant."

"Spoken like a real lady," he said softly. "Miss Luci, I know I've behaved badly, but can I hope you might somehow forgive me; give me another chance?"

Luci hesitated, her emotions in turmoil. The well-bred Bostonian might be her ticket out of here—a remote chance, true, but a chance. Why then did she see herself suddenly on the porch of that imaginary ranch house with Johnny Ace dismounting to take her in his arms?

She smiled prettily. "There's nothing to forgive."

"I've got to leave tomorrow to go to Denver, but I'd love to take you picnicking today."

"Denver?" It now seemed as far away as the moon to her. "I suppose you're finally escorting Miss Starrett to meet her father?"

He laughed. "Hardly. Army business. Miss Starrett will have to cool her heels here at the fort until the raids die down and the stage begins to run again. Major North can hardly spare a whole patrol to escort a spoiled lady."

"You're going alone, then?"

"No, I'm going with Luther North and Cody. What about that picnic?"

"Let me think on it." She was actually enjoying flirting with the handsome man. "You're the only one who's approached me the last couple of days. I feel like the most unlovely frump on the post."

"Ye Gods! Then you don't know?" His face sobered.

"Know what?"

"That Pawnee scout has passed the word to stay away from you. A man could get his ears cut off, the camp gossip says, for even looking at you."

She felt terrible indignation. "He doesn't own me!"

"He seems to think he does." Carter grinned. "But I'm not afraid of him. What about that picnic, Miss Luci?"

She felt carefree and reckless. "Why not?"

"I'll bring a buggy around to the front of the trading post in about an hour. You pack a lunch. See you then!" He put his hat back on, touched the brim with two fingers, and rode away.

What had she done? She didn't really want to go on a picnic with Carter Osgoode. But she'd show that Pawnee scout! Without giving herself too much time to think, she ran inside, put on a cheap cotton dress she had already done a mountain of laundry to pay for, and recombed her hair, putting it up on her head the way white women did.

She packed homemade pie and pickles, then made some sandwiches and lemonade. True to his word, when she went out on the porch, Carter Osgoode was in front of the trading post in a light buggy.

He stepped down, bowing gallantly. "It's a lovely day for a picnic with a beautiful girl."

"You have such nice manners, Carter. Such a model gentleman." She blushed with pleasure, letting him assist her up into the buggy. As they passed the major's quarters, she thought she saw his troubled face looking out at her. Carter clucked to the horse and they drove at a fast clip through the gates.

It was only a couple of miles to a shady spot by a small creek, and it was there Carter reined in and helped Luci from the buggy.

"This reminds me of my college days before the

war," he said, spreading a blanket and reaching for the picnic basket. "My younger sisters had a school friend I was rather sweet on, Summer Van Schuyler. We all went picnicing a few times with the Shaw boys and some of the others. Her twin is that new medic here at the fort."

She thought a minute. "Oh, yes, the blond, sensitive one who paints pictures." He had been kind to her.

"Yes, that's him, David Van Schuyler. We went to Harvard together, but he dropped out."

Could she ever forget Carter's blue-blooded background? What was she doing out with this perfect gentleman from Boston? She didn't have to answer that. She'd done it to get back at Johnny Ace.

Well, she was here now. She smiled at Carter while she unpacked the lunch. "What happened to Summer? Did she marry someone else?"

He scowled in memory. "Ran away to the Indians, if you can believe that," he snapped. "Caused quite a ripple of scandal in staid Boston, I can tell you. Imagine, with all the men to choose from, she ran away with an Injun buck!"

His angry tone made Luci uncomfortable. "Love makes people do crazy things sometimes." She took a sandwich and some of her homemade apple pie and filled a plate for Carter, her mind busy with thoughts of her mother and her own foolish behavior with Johnny Ace.

The food was good and the weather pleasant under the shade of the cottonwoods. Luci ate with enjoyment, pouring some cold lemonade for the two of them. Carter talked about himself, his life in Boston, how his family had lost much of their fortune during the war with bad investments.

"Unless I marry well," he said, "I suppose I'm stuck in this hellhole with the army. Terrible place for a man with my upbringing."

She wondered then if he was making it plain that he couldn't take her seriously. As she finished eating, she looked up and caught Carter staring at her.

"You are beautiful," he said softly. "You could make this outpost almost livable."

She looked at him a long moment, holding her breath. Was he proposing already? "I don't quite know what to say."

"Say yes, Luci." He reached out and caught her hand. "I know I shouldn't rush you, but I've been stuck out here in this hellhole for weeks. I — I've got a — a man's needs. You're alone, trying to survive."

Even though he was her ticket out, she hesitated, seeing the big scout in her mind, tasting his lips in her memory. "Mercy! Maybe we shouldn't rush into anything, Carter. After all, marriage is a big step, and —"

"Marriage?" He blinked at her and she felt suddenly sick at the astonished expression on the gentleman's face, realizing that hadn't been what he'd meant at all.

Luci winced, imagining her mother's face as she must have looked less than twenty years ago with another young officer making perhaps the same offer to Sunrise. Had it happened on a blanket during a picnic?

She jerked her hand from his, shaking with rage. "You cad! You rotten bastard! Why was I so stupid to think — never mind!"

She got up and began to gather the picnic items.

Carter caught her arm. "There's no reason to hurry back; we've got all afternoon."

She pulled away from him, not looking at him as she finished packing the basket then walked over to put it in the back of the buggy. "I've got laundry to do."

He caught her, pulled her to him, and turned her face up to his although she struggled to break free. "Don't act so indignant, you little half-breed. You've probably let that scout mount you, so why turn up your nose at a white man?"

"You rotten—!" She tried to slap him, but he caught her hand, pinned it between them while they struggled. His mouth came down to cover hers, his hand pulling at her bodice, fumbling with the buttons so he could slide his hand down the front to cup her breast.

She had forgotten how small she was until she tried to fight her way out of his embrace. He kissed her so hard, his teeth cut her lip, smearing them both with her blood. "You little bitch! I've tried to behave like a gentleman, but I mean to have you here and now! But if you want to fight, I can deal with that!"

"Johnny'll kill you for this!" She struggled, but he had her hands pinned to her sides while he pulled her bodice down.

"I'm not scared of that buck!" Carter sneered. "If you belong to him, what are you doing out here with me?"

"Good question," a man's voice said behind them and Carter whirled in surprise.

Luci blinked, then staggered as she tried to

198

regain her balance.

Johnny Ace stood behind them in the shadows of the cottonwoods. "I put the word out that no man was to touch her." His voice was almost a whisper, but the tone was as hard as his dark eyes.

Carter laughed. "I'm not afraid of you, Injun! I'm an officer. Officers get first choice!"

"Not with my woman, they don't!" She saw him move even as he spoke, throwing all his sinewy strength and muscle behind the blow.

His fist caught Carter in the nose and sent him stumbling backward, blood dripping down his blue uniform. And then Johnny was on him.

Horrified, Luci watched them fight. They meshed and struggled, blows flying. "You two stop it! You'll both be in trouble!" she yelled.

But neither man said anything or even acknowledged that they heard her. Carter stumbled to his feet, swung and missed. Like a graceful cougar, Johnny was on him again, smashing his fist into the aristocratic face.

They rolled over and over in the dirt, under the hooves of the buggy horse, which snorted and stepped sideways while the men scrambled and clashed.

There was nothing Luci could do but watch.

Now Carter managed to get in a blow, connecting with Johnny's chin. The sound seemed loud in the meadow's stillness as Johnny stumbled and went down. Carter landed on top of him, striking him with both fists in the face.

Luci couldn't control herself anymore. "Stop that, Carter!" She ran over and began beating him on the back with her small fists.

But quick as a cat, Johnny scrambled out from

under the other man. They lunged at each other again like fighting, rearing stallions, fists cracking on bone, blood flying.

Finally, Johnny's fist connected solidly with Carter's chin and the other man went down like a crashing tree and lay still. The Pawnee stood up slowly, wiping the blood from his mouth.

She didn't quite know what to say. "Johnny. . . ."

"Forget it!" he snapped, brushing the dirt from his clothes. "Get in the buggy, I'll take you back."

She looked over at the officer, now struggling to sit up, still groggy. "What about him?"

"Let him walk . . . if he's able."

Johnny didn't even glance at the man as he took Luci's arm and propelled her toward the buggy. "You're lucky I was out on patrol and stopped to water Katis at the creek or I wouldn't have been here to help."

She let him help her into the buggy, annoyed by the possessive way he gripped her arm. "I look after myself."

"And you were doing such a good job of it!" His tone was sarcastic as he tied Katis on behind the buggy and climbed up beside her. "If I hadn't happened along, you'd have gotten raped." He slapped the horse with the reins and the buggy started off.

"It's not as if I had any innocence to lose," she snapped back, and then was immediately sorry as she saw the hurt in his dark eyes.

"I told you that night you might regret it, and now I see you do."

"No, I—I—what happened that night was as much my fault as yours."

"I don't have regrets. I'm sorry you do, Luci." He looked straight ahead as he drove back to the fort.

She wasn't sure whether she had regrets. Finally she said, "You'll probably get in trouble over this."

"It was worth it." Johnny smiled with satisfaction, rubbing his skinned knuckles, his discolored, bruised face. "He'll stay out of my way."

Luci sighed. "You won't have to worry about crossing his path for a while. The major's sending him to Denver."

He looked at her sharply. "You seem to know a lot about the army's business."

His tone hinted at something she couldn't quite understand. "Mercy! I don't know what you're driving at. We just talked, that's all. You know how men will talk to impress a girl."

She couldn't read his expression. "Luci," he said, "just whose idea was this picnic anyway?"

Now she was totally bewildered. "What difference does it make? You're opposed to picnics?"

Johnny frowned. "Never mind. Things are beginning to look clearer to me now. The major said . . ."

She waited for him to continue, but his voice trailed off and he didn't speak to her the rest of the way back to the fort.

Chapter Eleven

Manning Starrett glared with disgust at his housekeeper and threw his napkin into his supper plate. "Slop! Just slop!" he drawled. "I want to see steak and fried green tomatoes and corn pone on this table! What good is it to be the richest man in Denver if I can't eat what I like?"

The tall, bony woman bustled to move his plate, fear on her lined features. "Tomatoes are a little hard to come by this early in Denver," she said apologetically, "and I was trying to follow your doctor's orders, sir, he said with arthritis, a simple diet—"

"Simple? I'll tell you who's simple, my doctor!" He reached for his cane and struggled to his feet. "Goddamn it to hell! He doesn't pay your salary, Mrs. Polinski, I do! Remember that or you'll be looking for a new position, not easy to find for a stupid immigrant!"

"Yes, sir." Properly humbled, she took the plate, her hand shaking.

Manning lit one of the big, black cigars he loved. "Billy send a message?"

"Yes, sir. Mr. Reno said he'd see you at the office. Sir, you know what your doctor said about getting more rest and smoking cigars—"

"God damn it to hell! I'll have plenty of time to rest when I'm dead! If that doctor's so smart, why isn't he rich like me? Tell Josh to bring my carriage around!"

Leaning on his cane, he hobbled out of the ornate dining room. If his daughter would only arrive to take charge of things, Manning thought, avoiding looking in the ornate hall tree mirror. Once he had been the handsomest man in Mobile with his black, wavy hair and bright blue eyes. Now he was fifty and looked seventy. If only his doting mama could know what had become of her youngest child.

Arthritis! Manning snorted at the doctor's stupidity. Why, back in Alabama, the man wouldn't be allowed to doctor a horse! He couldn't figure out what was killing the most prominent man in the Colorado Territory, but Manning knew. A trip to a top clinic back East some years ago had confirmed what, deep in his heart, Manning had already guessed. He reached in his pocket for the mercury capsules, and swallowed one. Not that the damned stuff seemed to be doing him any good.

He took a defiant puff of the cigar smoke then hobbled to the etched glass door. *No cure.* The words echoed and reechoed in his mind. He had known it was coming because of Clara's death. But he didn't want to die that way, screaming out his life in an asylum. He wouldn't think about that. His daughter was coming any day now and she'd look after him as the disease progressed.

Josh came to open the door of the grand Victorian house for him and helped him out to the carriage. When the black driver was clumsy as he assisted him, Manning rapped him sharply across the shins with his cane. "Be careful, nigger, if you value your job! I'm surrounded by fools and thieves and idiots!"

"Sorry, Mr. Starrett, suh." He saw the ill-disguised hatred and fear in the black's eyes before he closed the door and the carriage moved away from the curb.

Manning leaned back with a sigh and enjoyed the taste of his cigar. He was undoubtedly the richest man in Denver and therefore the most powerful. He was also the most hated. He didn't care. He grinned, thinking about it. There were only two people in the world he cared about: Bill Reno and Lily. He'd wait to pass judgment on Winnifred when she finally got here from Fort McPherson. After all, he hadn't seen her since just before the war began, when he'd gone back to sign the papers committing Clara.

Billy came out to help him from his carriage, gently assisting him inside. "How do you feel today, Manning?"

"How do I feel every day?" Manning drawled grumpily. "Like hell, that's what!"

"I understand," Billy soothed, helping him to a comfortable chair. "Arthritis must be a terrible thing to bear."

He hadn't even told Billy, afraid the young man would withdraw from him in horror. He liked Billy even if he was a Yankee. More than that, he needed Billy. When he looked at the dapper, charming protégé, he saw himself as he had been at that age. It was almost like looking in a mirror. Billy had even started to wear the same type of suits and ties Manning wore. If he'd just do something about his bottom teeth. But still . . .

Looking Billy over, he grunted in approval. "I hope my daughter likes you. We could be just one big, happy family. Right now, it's pretty lonely rattling around in that big empty place."

Billy patted his arm. "I hope she likes me, too, Manning. Since she's your daughter, I'm bound to like her."

Manning beamed at him as Billy went over to the sideboard, poured a bourbon, and brought it back to him.

"A Southern gentleman's drink," Manning drawled. "In the old days, a slave would bring me one in the evening on the veranda after I'd be looking over the cotton planting. Why, I recollect one time—" He paused. "Have I told you the story before?"

"No, and I'd just love to hear it," the man said smoothly, pouring himself a drink. "You're the most interesting person I ever met."

Manning beamed at him and sipped his whiskey. "For a damned Yankee from Ohio, you're not too far from being a real gentleman—charming, our Southern gals would say."

"You eat?"

"Paw! Slop! That idiot doctor—"

"I'll send Josh for something." He stood up and went quickly to the door.

"Never mind." Manning grinned expansively. "I'm going to Lily's later. But I like the way you try to look out for me."

"What are friends for?" Billy said, and smiled carefully, the way he always did, self-conscious over the gap where he was missing his two lower front teeth.

He must see about getting Billy to a dentist back East who might make him some false bridgework or even those implants dentists were trying to do. Winnifred might not cotton to a man with missing teeth.

"Yes, sir," Manning said expansively, now thinking aloud. "You'll make a hellava son-in-law, Billy. My daughter better think so, too, or I'll cut her out of the will."

"Aw, don't even think about that." Billy blushed. "Winnifred might not like me any better'n Lily does."

"I been meanin' to say something to Lily about that." It was embarrassing to him that his mistress made no bones about how much she disliked his protégé. "Maybe it would be better, though, if I sent you back East and got your teeth fixed. Women sometimes don't understand about men behavin' like men — fistfighting and all that."

"I was younger and hot-tempered in those days —"

"Goddamn it to hell, Billy, don't make any apologies to me for being a man's man. I was that kind myself in my younger days. Might have gotten higher than captain in the army if I hadn't been such a hell-raiser!" He chuckled, enjoying the memory.

"I never did quite understand what a Southerner was doin' in the Union army." Billy ran his tongue around the gap in his teeth.

"Got in long before the war just to get away

from a naggin' wife." Manning leaned on his cane. "Then when I saw there was gonna be war, I decided which side was most likely to win." He winked. "Good business man wants to be on the winnin' side."

"You're a smart one, all right. I'll never be the man you was, Manning, but maybe you can teach me a little of your smarts." He fingered the diamond stickpin in his tie.

"Hell, boy! Stick with me, and I'll make you rich. You remind me of myself at your age."

Billy blushed, then shrugged. "I'm willin' to learn anything you can teach this poor Yankee, Manning. But I'll never be as successful nor as good-lookin'. I'll bet you was a devil with the ladies. Cigar?"

"Yep, I was. And don't I always want a cigar?" He took one from the box Billy offered, and let the younger man light it for him. "I trust you, Billy. Matter of fact, you and Lily, y'all are the only two in the world I trust." Manning smoked, thinking about his dark, sultry mistress.

He had always had a weakness for women—dark women. Clara, of course, had been homely, blond—and an heiress. After he'd gone through his doting mama's fortune, he'd looked around for more. Manning had gradually gone through everything Clara owned after the wedding, except the plantation and it wasn't worth enough to sell. The land was worn out from cotton.

"I'm mighty proud to be your friend, sir, and I hope someday to be just like you." Billy grinned. "I wish Lily and me could at least get in the same room without a fuss; it makes it hard on you, always havin' to referee."

"It is touchy," Manning admitted, sipping his whiskey. "I wish you never had to go to her place at all, but with you handling so much of my business and havin' to check her books, you'll just have to try to keep peace with her."

Billy made a face. "I don't know what you see in her, honest I don't." He shook his head, running his tongue through the gap in his teeth.

"Now, boy, she ain't but half a dozen years older than you. For almost forty, Lily is still a very pretty woman."

"If you say so, boss. Of course, women like you better than me. Sometime you need to give me some pointers."

"I was always a lady's man." Manning leaned back in his chair and grinned. "You're handsome, Billy, maybe you just need a few hints on how to be charming to ladies."

"If every woman in the world was crazy about me, Lily would still hate my guts, but I try to keep peace with her for your sake, Manning."

Lady's man. How many had there been? Hundreds. And somewhere down the line, one of them had given him this death warrant. Manning had known he had it when he first began sleeping with Lily. But he didn't care enough about her to deny himself her body. He wondered if he had passed it on to his mistress.

"I trust you, Billy. In fact, just got through putting your name down to have power of attorney so you can take better care of my business without havin' to bother me about so many details on days I'm not feelin' well."

Billy looked worried. "I wish you hadn't done that, boss. Lily won't like it and maybe your

208

daughter won't either—"

"I'm still not so sick yet that I'm not in charge of my own empire," Manning snapped, and banged his cane for emphasis. "Those two better keep their mouths shut. I'll do what I damn well please and I pride myself on being a good judge of men and horses. You're just like me—more like me than a son, if I had one. I trust you to look after my business!"

"Which brings me to the latest news." Billy looked around as if afraid the walls might hear and leaned closer. "The shipment's in."

"Good!" Manning sipped his drink. "Did I tell you I had to get a partner, Banker Peabody in Boston, to help on this?"

"As rich as you are?"

"It'd look suspicious if I pulled a lot of money out of local banks. Besides, old Peabody is the one who had the connections back East to get us this deal to begin with."

"You're smart, Manning," Billy said with admiration. "I always say you're the smartest man I ever met."

"No, I just have the knack for picking loyal employees who look out for my interests."

"I'm more than that, I hope. I'm your friend, Manning."

"And maybe sometime soon, my son-in-law. I can't last forever, the shape I'm in—"

"Now let's not talk about that," Billy soothed. "People with arthritis live to die of old age."

He was tempted then to tell Billy the truth; then decided against it. People were always terrified of catching this disease, although it wasn't very contagious in its late stages. *Wild oats,* he thought. *A man sows wild oats and comes up with weeds.*

Instead, he said, "Tell me about the shipment. Good as last time?"

Bill grinned, his eyes sparkling with greed. "Brand new Winchester repeaters. Three big wagon loads of them. They came in packed under flour, salt, and calico."

Manning laughed and banged his cane against the floor. "We make double on this deal! Starrett Freight Lines can charge more for flour because the Injun scare has most of the supply lines shut down and we sneak in guns to sell to the Injuns who keep the lines shut down!"

"Not so loud," Billy cautioned him with a raised hand. "If we're caught with those, remember you have permission to provide a few hunting rifles to the Pawnee, and the other friendlies."

"We must keep up appearances. You meeting them at the usual place?" He smiled with satisfaction at the younger man. Yes sir, Billy Reno was just like himself—sly, clever. The perfect choice for his daughter's hand.

"Yep. And then later, the Dog Soldiers come get the rest. You know, Manning, we might not have been having all this trouble with the tribes if you had really fulfilled those government food contracts you had for them."

Manning snorted with glee. "The flour the tribes didn't get, I can sell for double or triple because the outbreak keeps supples low in Denver. Then I turn around and sell guns to the Injuns, who are on the war path because they didn't get the supplies. Clever, huh?"

"Clever, Manning. No wonder you're rich."

Manning felt his stomach rumble. "You hungry?"

"You wanta go to Lily's place?"

"She'll at least have a steak for me and maybe corn pone and fried green tomatoes. Damned doctors!"

He stood up and immediately the younger man hurried to take his arm. "Let me help you out to the carriage."

Manning leaned on his cane. He seemed to be having more trouble with his gait these days. If everyone who knew him only realized . . . "You want to go with me?"

"Naw, you know Lily and I don't like each other! I only put up with her because she's your woman."

"She isn't so bad, Billy. I wish you two could learn to get along without arguing."

"I'll try a little harder, boss, just because you want me to, but you know I only go in her place when I have to check on the receipts, and see how business is going."

They went out to the carriage, Manning hobbling feebly.

Billy patted his arm as he helped him in the carriage. "I respect you, Manning. You're smart as a whip and you know how to make money."

"And I'm gonna teach you." He nodded with satisfaction as he leaned in the carriage. "You're my good right arm, Bill. You'll be rewarded for this."

"Your friendship and a job with you are reward enough," the younger man said, "but being your son-in-law is a dream come true. Suppose she wants to choose her own husband?"

"Winnifred has used up what little I didn't get

of her mother's. The war made the plantation pretty worthless, you know. I'm sure that's the only reason she's consented to come out here; she has no money and, therefore, not much choice. She'll do as I tell her. Keep me up on details."

"Sure!" Billy slammed the door. The younger man was cut out of the same pattern he was, Manning thought with smug satisfaction as the carriage pulled away.

The carriage stopped in front of the Gilded Lily, one of the finest establishments on Holladay Street, that busy street of saloons and bordellos just off the main street of Laramer. Before it had been built, the site had been occupied by another elegant place called the Duchess' Palace. But that had burned down. Manning smiled, remembering the Palace's owner. She had been pretty and dark, too. Manning liked his women with dusky skin.

He was ushered through a discreet side door into the elegant red velvet interior. Lily was waiting for him in her rooms, a sultry, mature beauty of almost forty, dressed as always, in scarlet. He'd found her years ago on a business trip to New Orleans.

"Hello, sweet, I was wondering if you'd come tonight," her voice purred, soft and Southern.

"I come when I feel good, Lil, which ain't often these days." It was a liability to love a woman — bad business. He'd liked it better when he'd just used them and tossed them aside. Manning regretted now that he'd probably signed Lily's death warrant, too. But he didn't regret it enough that he'd have denied himself her body if it were all to do over again.

"And I always look forward to it, sweet." She brushed her lips across his cheek. "Let me get you a drink."

"Do better than that. Tell the cook I want a steak and a pan full of greasy fried potatoes, real crusty and brown, with corn pone." He looked up at her wistfully. "I don't suppose it's time yet for green tomatoes?"

"Knowing how you like them, I had the cook hunt some down." She smiled triumphantly and patted his shoulder. "I'll go tell her to rustle something up."

She went out and he leaned back in a red velvet chair with a sigh. Dark-skinned women. If he had one weakness, it was sultry, dusky-skinned women. There'd been a hundred, no, more like a thousand in all these years, but he and Lily Thibodeaux had been a pair longer than he usually kept a woman. He'd found her working as a whore, brought her here, and bought this place for her to run. Lily was a beautiful mixture of Seminole Indian and French Cajun.

How was he going to keep Winnifred from finding out about Lily? He'd have to be more discreet. But then Winnifred didn't know. At least in this stage, the doctor said he wasn't very contagious, so the chances he'd give the disease to his own daughter were slight.

His only daughter. No, that wasn't quite right. Actually, somewhere there was another, but it would only be borrowing trouble to track her down, although it wouldn't be that hard. Over the years, he'd heard mother and child were drifting around the West, looking for him. He didn't need

213

that pair, so why bother? Winnifred and Billy were going to look after him. Yes, he had it all worked out. He sipped his drink, listening to the music floating up the stairs.

"Oh, Genevieve, sweet Genevieve, the days may come, the days may go, but still. . . ."

There had been many women in his life—dark, passionate women. So many, he'd lost count of them. He thought about it now. Funny, only one virgin in the bunch, a special girl, but pure Injun, so he didn't take her seriously.

Women. His mind ran through the many faces, wondering which one had given him this deadly surprise. Not the Cheyenne girl. No, she was a virgin. It was one of those who came later.

Lily came back in. "Food'll be here in a minute." She paused, looking at her fingernails a little too casually. "Heard when she's coming in?"

"God damn it to hell! Don't mention my daughter, you hear? I intend to keep her from ever finding out about you. As far as she's concerned, I'm a respectable widower—Denver's most respectable citizen."

"I won't get to meet her? It hurts that you're ashamed of me, you hypocrite."

"Lily, I'm warning you—"

"All right." She went to the window, stood staring out. "I reckon you think you can keep hiding me forever then. Denver ain't that big a place."

He glared at her. "She's hardly likely to come into a whorehouse, now is she? Why an innocent, high-class girl like Winnifred would be shocked—"

"Would she be shocked to know her daddy owns it?" She whirled around. "Along with half the other sin spots in this town?"

"That's enough!" He stood up, raising his cane threateningly. "Don't push me, Lily. Just because I'm fond of you doesn't mean I'll tolerate uppityness! No wonder Billy doesn't like—"

"Don't mention that young bastard's name to me!"

"Now Lily, I wish you two would get along. It would make things so much easier. He's probably going to end up as my son-in-law."

She laughed, pulling the red filmy thing around her. "I feel sorry for your poor daughter then! If she knew that, she probably wouldn't come. I wouldn't sleep with that snaggle-tooth bastard to be able to inherit all your money!"

"Billy would be handsome if it weren't for those two bottom teeth. I'm going to send him back East and see what they can do to fix them. If he weren't all man, he wouldn't have been in so many fist fights, and gotten them knocked out."

"He's just a lowdown saloon brawler!"

"He's my right hand and I depend on him, so you might as well get used to the idea he'll be around a long time!"

"I wish you would keep him out of my place," she pouted. "He's always wanting to take my best girls to bed."

Manning laughed. "Like I said, he's a lot like I was in my younger days. At least he's probably the one man in town who doesn't want you! Is that what's bothering you, Lily? Billy's the only man in town who doesn't lust after Manning Starrett's mistress?"

She came over and slipped her arms around his neck. "I love you, Manning. Don't let's argue. You know I never look at anyone else; I know when I got a good thing going."

"And don't you ever forget it! Get me another drink and let's eat."

The food was good and he ate with gusto. Being from the South herself, she understood his tastes. It had been a smart move to take her out of that bordello in New Orleans and bring her here, let her run this place for him.

Once his belly was full, Manning settled back in his chair, sipping the bourbon she poured him. "You look good to me tonight, Lily. It's been weeks since the last time."

"You sure you're up to it? I worry about your health, sweet, maybe we'd better not—"

"God damn it to hell! I like women who do what they're told. Y'all are only good for one thing—besides naggin' a man to death."

She bit her lip, then began to strip slowly. When she stood naked, she turned around slowly for his inspection.

He liked to see her naked, although it was hard for him to service her anymore. Sometimes it was so frustrating to see her long dark legs, her fine dusky belly and breasts, and not be able to cover her as expertly as he once had, that he lost his temper and beat her bare buttocks with his cane. That was almost as satisfying—to watch her cringe and cry while he put red marks on that rounded bottom.

He watched her parade up and down, posing for him as if she were a slave on an auction block and he was trying to decide whether to bid on her or not. It was a game he liked to play. Lily was a beautiful woman. He motioned her to come over to him so he could feel her breasts and stroke her dusky thighs.

"Manning, I wish you wouldn't humiliate me like this."

He laughed. "What are you talking about, Lily? When I found you in that dive in New Orleans, it was the kind of place a man could buy anything — for a price. I took you out of there. You should be grateful to me."

"I am, Manning. You know how much I care about you."

"Then do all those things that only you know how to do," he said softly, reaching for the buttons on his pants.

"Here, let me do that, sweet." Immediately, she was on her knees, naked between his legs while she unbuttoned his pants and shirt. "What do you want to play tonight?"

He took the pins from her hair then watched it fall around her naked shoulders. "I'm in a good mood," he said expansively, watching her dark skin catch the lamplight. "Let's play slave and master."

She hesitated as if to argue, then seemed to decide it was useless. She went to the wardrobe, and took out chains and a small whip. "At least it's better than the cane."

"Put on some of the tokens, too."

She reached in a drawer, took out several strings of small brass tokens with a lily on them, draped them around her waist and wrists, and strung a necklace of them around her neck so that they hung down on her full breasts.

"Now parade on the auction block like a slave girl on the docks at New Orleans. Make me want to buy you."

He leaned on his cane, watching her walk up

and down, posing for him. It was one of the games he liked best because he felt powerful when she posed naked before him, her wrists and slim ankles draped with chains, the brass tokens strung around her neck and slender waist.

Manning motioned for her to come over and let him feel her expertly, as he had done so often at slave auctions in the past, before the war ruined everything. He and some of the others used to frequent the auctions whether they intended to buy or not. It was a perfect excuse to handle dark, naked girls. Manning stroked Lily's breasts, her dusky thighs. "You've been a bad girl, Lily. You know what happens to bad slave girls?" He reached for the whip.

Finally Manning tired of the game and had Lily call for his carriage. He went back to his ornate, empty Victorian mansion, took his mercury capsule, and lay in bed staring at the ceiling. Dark women. He couldn't get enough of them. Only one of them had been a virgin. That Cheyenne girl he found eighteen or twenty years ago during an army hitch. There'd been many, black and brown, in the time since. One of them had given him this deadly gift, which he took home to his ugly, cold wife who kept the plantation running and looked after their child. Winnifred had been a beauty, inheriting his looks instead of her mother's.

He wondered disinterestedly whatever became of the Indian beauty and the little girl she had produced. What difference did it make? With a legitimate daughter, he didn't need the Injun one. Now if he could just get Winnifred out of that damned fort and over here to Denver to marry his trusted protégé, Billy, Manning would have someone to look after him if he finally went insane. He didn't want to end up in a horrible asylum like the one he'd put Clara in.

He drifted off to sleep, dreaming of Lily with her warm, wet mouth and fine breasts. Lily, who knew how to please a man. The only fly in the ointment was that she and Billy couldn't stand each other. Maybe things would eventually get better between them. At least he didn't have to worry about Lily cheating on him. He didn't think she would, but if it ever crossed her mind, she'd know better, knowing Billy would report back to his employer at once.

Billy. The young man was just like him. And he was loyal. That made Manning rest a little better. He yawned and drifted off to sleep.

Lily Thibodeaux poured herself a gin and sank down on the settee, wincing because of the welts across her hips. Damn that bastard! She'd never hated a man as much as she hated Manning Starrett. She'd kill him if she could get away with it. It made her skin creep for his hands to touch her. How much longer would she have to submit to his sexual pleasures? Not much longer, her lover said. When everything was right, they'd finally be together. Until then, she'd have to pretend to be the loving mistress.

Mistress. Lily laughed and pulled her silk dressing gown closer around herself. Most of the time Manning couldn't perform anymore, which suited her fine.

She heard a slight rap at the door. Her heart beat hard with anticipation. "Who is it?"

"You know who it is," whispered the Yankee twang.

"I thought you wouldn't come tonight." Lily ran to the door, unlocked it, and flung it open.

They went into each other's arms and he came in, closing the door behind him. "I had to come when I was sure he'd left. I get sick, thinking of that old bastard pawing you. I'd kill him if I could get away with it!"

"Let's not waste this precious time talking about the richest, stupidest man in Denver!" She looked up at him, straightening the diamond stick pin in his tie. He'd be so handsome—once he got his lower teeth fixed. "Sweet, make love to me."

His hands slipped inside her scarlet silk gown. "Does he suspect anything?"

"No, Billy," she whispered as she kissed him, "not at all!"

Chapter Twelve

He came into her arms and Lily kissed him again. Billy was a good lover, not perverted like Manning. He swung her up in his arms and whirled her about. "I get tired of all this sneaking around."

"I do, too," she sighed, "but we can't just let all this money get past us, Bill. He looks so sick, I keep thinking he'll die and then maybe we'll get it—"

"I doubt anyone ever died of arthritis."

"I suppose not," she admitted.

But later after they had made love and Billy was asleep, she lay looking at the ceiling, wondering privately if that was all that was really wrong with Manning. Could she have given him the disease? She wouldn't care if she had. Of course, she herself was cured. Lily remembered when she had first had all the symptoms, several years back— sores on her genitals, followed by a red rash.

She'd gone to an old granny herb doctor and

been given a potion that was guaranteed to kill the disease. All the symptoms had gone away, so the herbs had evidently worked. Some of the girls who worked here thought it wasn't curable. Fat lot they knew! Not wanting to scare anyone, Lily kept it all a secret.

Lily wondered idly if she had infected Manning. Maybe he hadn't recognized the signs and hadn't had treatment. She smiled, thinking about Manning dying. It would serve the scoundrel right! But where had she gotten it? Had her lover given it to her? Lily hoped she lived to dance on Manning Starrett's grave or see him locked away in a mad house.

It was quiet now. The piano had finally stopped playing; most of the girls had sent away the last customers. She and her love could sleep tonight without fear of discovery. But the next time . . .

Later in the night, Billy awoke and wanted her again. Then they lay talking in the dark while he smoked a cigar.

"What are you going to do about his daughter?" Lily asked.

"What do you mean, what am I going to do? If the ugly little broad ever gets here from Fort McPherson, I think Manning is going to pressure me to marry her."

She felt her heart sink. He was good-looking, charming, and weak. But she loved him.

"Don't worry, baby." A grin lit his handsome face. "That way, I can control everything when he finally dies and then I can dump her. We'll have everything her stupid papa's worked so hard to build up. That is, unless a better opportunity presents itself."

"If it does, I'd like to close the door on all of it, the two of us run away to California."

"But otherwise, we're stuck here." Billy rubbed his chin. "We might have to spend the rest of our lives being the old goat's henchman."

"He trusts you, Billy." She kissed his cheek again. "Just think, if you hadn't trailed me here from New Orleans, he wouldn't have met you on the street and hired you."

"Yeah, he trusts me." Billy grinned. "He says I'm just like him, the son he never had."

"I think the randy old goat's left a trail of bastards behind him."

He hugged her. She winced in pain as he squeezed her. "That bastard!" Billy said. "Was it the whip this time, or—"

"Don't ask, Billy. It doesn't matter. I consider it an investment . . . for us."

He held her very close and kissed her lingeringly.

"Billy, if you—if you have to marry his daughter, will you still love me?"

He patted her absently. "Suppose she isn't ugly? Her old man must have been good-looking in his day before he got sick. I didn't know arthritis could make a man that sick."

Lily shrugged. "How would I know?"

Did Billy suspect anything? She was cured, she couldn't give it to her lover, and she didn't care about Manning. The rich bastard deserved to die a slow and horrible death. "I wish we could be together all the time, Billy, and not have to sneak around."

"Me, too, baby." He raised up on his elbow and looked down into her eyes. She was a lot older than he was, but that didn't matter to him. It tore him apart that Manning used her with no more thought than he'd use any of his other possessions. Manning liked his women dark and sultry. If Billy could find his boss another woman with the same qualities, would Manning leave Lily alone? It was worth some thought.

He lay back with a sigh, wondering if there was any chance that he had given her the pox . . . or had she given it to him? If so, where had she picked it up? It wasn't something a man would discuss with a woman.

Then he dismissed that idea. Lily looked perfectly healthy, but Billy himself hadn't been too careful about some of the women he had bedded — and there had been many to succumb to his easy banter and boyish charm.

Last time Manning had sent him back East on business, he'd seen a doctor, who had listened to him describe his symptoms: a sore on his genitals, then a rash. The doctor had given Billy an expensive medication of herbs mixed with mercury and pronounced him cured. Well, he must be. Certainly the symptoms had gone away, and he didn't want to borrow trouble by worrying about it.

On the other hand, he'd heard that sometimes the symptoms disappeared for years and then reappeared, leading finally to death, blindness, or even madness.

He wouldn't borrow trouble or scare Lily by bringing it up. He kissed her full breasts. "You're beautiful, baby. I'm sure Manning's daughter can't hold a candle to you."

Lily put her arms around his neck. "I love you."

He put his face against her breasts, enjoying her Louisiana Cajun accent like purring velvet. "It

224

tears me up, thinkin' about him pawin' you all the time. I'm gonna look around, see if I can find a girl he'll like better."

"I'd be much obliged for that," Lily sighed with relief. She laid her hand lightly between his thighs and he felt his body react immediately. "Billy, make love to me."

He kissed her, running his hand down her body, feeling her wince at his touch when he brushed against a fresh bruise. "That old bastard! Someday, baby, someday . . ."

"Let's not think about a future that maybe will never happen," she whispered. "Let's just think about tonight." She opened the scarlet negligee.

He cupped one creamy mound while she unbuttoned his shirt. Her breath and tongue were hot and wet on his nipple.

He must be gentle with her after what Manning had done. Billy closed his eyes so he wouldn't have to look at the purple and green bruises under the scarlet dressing gown. He spread her thighs, then took her gently while she wrapped her long, dark legs around his waist.

Afterward, she wept in his arms and he held her and kissed her hair. "Someday, baby, someday . . ."

The next day, Billy still had fond thoughts of Lily as he drove the wagon load of supplies out to meet the Pawnees.

Absently, he ran his tongue through the gap where his teeth were gone and laughed. Even Lily thought they'd been knocked out in one of many fist fights. What no one knew was that Billy was a coward, afraid of the sight of blood, especially his

225

own.

When the war had begun, they tried to draft the husky Ohio farm boy. He was working like a slave himself on his stepfather's farm, and didn't feel any obligation to go die to free black people.

The draft was so unpopular, there were riots over it, buildings burned, and people killed. A lot of poor immigrants didn't want to fight and die to free blacks from slavery. Especially when rich men were allowed to pay a substitute to go in their places.

The boy decided sacrificing his front bottom teeth was better than catching a mini ball in the belly or amputation in a bloody field hospital with nothing but a little chloroform and sometimes not even that. No, he didn't regret the small sacrifice of his teeth. Better a live hound than a dead lion.

Yep, he was a coward, all right, he thought sheepishly now, remembering. The morning he was supposed to go into the army, he got very drunk. Then he took a rock and knocked out his two lower front teeth.

The army's old Enfield rifles used cartridges with paper tabs that had to be bitten off before the bullet could be fired. The army didn't accept any man who didn't have at least one bottom and upper front tooth that met so he could bite those tabs off. Bill had literally knocked himself out of combat.

Finally, he had drifted down to New Orleans and met Lily. But he didn't have the money to take her out of that bordello. Then he heard that some rich Denver businessman, Manning Starrett, had fallen for Lily and was taking her back to the Colorado Territory with him. Billy had trailed her to Denver. There he worked in the mines or anything else he could do to stay close to her. He used to watch her pass in Starrett's elegant carriage.

Finally he and Lily had arranged a chance meeting with the rich man, and Billy's charm ingratiated him with Manning.

It broke his heart now that she still slept with Manning occasionally when the old goat was up to it. But there was nothing Billy could do until he got more money except bide his time. Again the idea crossed his mind that if only Billy could find a similar girl to take Lily's place, maybe Manning would keep his hands off Lily.

He saw the Pawnees camped up ahead, drove the wagon in, and reined to a halt. "Hello, Crow Feather! I'm here with your allotment of sugar and coffee and guns."

The Pawnee leader and some of his braves came over, frowning as they peered at the small load stacked under a tarp in the back of the wagon. "Why does the Great White Father in Washington send us less and less each time? How can we feed our people with so little?"

Billy shrugged as he jumped down from the wagon seat. "Times are hard because of the big war several years ago. The Congress has even cut back on supplies and weapons for our own bluecoats. I'm not responsible for the fact that my red brothers get less and less each year."

In truth, Billy wasn't. It was Manning Starrett, whose greed couldn't resist cutting the supplies back each time. It worried Billy. He had a tiny bit of conscience left about such things, but more than that, he was afraid that sooner or later,

Starrett Freight and Shipping Company might be in trouble if the army ever investigated its tie with that crooked Indian agent.

If only the Pawnee knew their legal guns and supplies were being diverted to their old enemies, the Cheyenne. Billy got out some cigars and passed them around with a flourish. There was no reason to think these peaceful tribes would ever know, and even if they did, they would be almost powerless to stop it. Who in Washington would listen to an Indian?

The Pawnee gathered around and he supervised the unloading of the supplies, tossing the tarp carelessly back into the wagon bed.

Crow Feather was in a better mood as he hefted a new rifle in his hands. "We talk, eat and drink some, Reno."

Billy nodded. "You bet." It was dusk and the warriors were roasting meat on a big bonfire and drinking whiskey. Bill had conveniently brought many bottles to pass around.

For the first time, he noticed the pretty Pawnee girl looking him over from behind a tree.

Crow Feather's gaze followed his. "My daughter, Deer."

"Very pretty." Billy looked away quickly. He didn't want to risk the warrior's wrath by looking at the girl too long, but he was struck by her beauty. He thought immediately of Manning Starrett, who liked his women dark and sultry. If he could hand this one over to the randy old goat, maybe it would divert his attention from Lily.

Crow said, "Someday Deer will wed a Pawnee brave. She wanted one that I didn't approve of, but all that has changed now."

The talk bored Billy. "Let us sit together by the

fire, Crow." He gestured toward the center of the circle. "We will drink whiskey and eat, tell tales, and smoke cigars."

The brave smiled and nodded. "That is good, Reno. Yes, the warriors will do this thing."

They sat down cross-legged by the fire with the others. The drums began a steady rhythm. Women served roasted meat and big hunks of bread and beans while the whiskey made its way around the circle. Later the dancing began.

Billy watched them, feeling no pain as he sipped yet another glass of whiskey. Crow had joined the dancing. Deer slipped through the shadows and squatted next to Billy by the fire, taking the glass from his hand and draining it. "Once I wanted to cling to tradition, to fight change. But I know now that it is foolish. Besides, having tasted the whiteman's firewater, I can see why they like it so much!"

Without a word, Billy reached for a fresh bottle and handed it to her. She was attractive and very young.

"Be careful," he cautioned the girl, "the bottle contains powerful magic that does strange and wonderful things."

"I've found that out for myself," she said, and laughed, obviously flirting with him.

She was very pretty and had a good body. Bill looked her over critically. No, he shook his head. He might as well forget it. There was no way to take her back to Manning as a gift or as a new whore to work in the Gilded Lily. It wasn't worth infuriating Crow Feather over.

Bill watched her as she turned the bottle up again. He could see the nubs of her nipples under the leather dress she wore. She was dark and probably not more than nineteen or twenty years old. Yes, Manning would like her. "If you ever come to Denver," he said softly, "I know a rich man with horses and much whiskey who would like to meet you."

The last seemed to interest her. "Plenty of whiskey?"

"Barrels of it!"

She studied him, wiping her mouth. "If I ever get to Denver, I'll remember that."

She got up and walked away, a little wobbly on her feet. Bill laughed under his breath. Injuns and firewater. The two didn't mix. He reached for another piece of meat and another drink.

The Pawnees had the boxes of rifles open now, and were passing them out. As they danced, the braves waved the rifles, shouting in defiance as the firelight flickered off the brass breeches.

It was sometime in the middle of the night before Billy finally left the Indians dancing and drinking and went over to crawl under the wagon and get himself some sleep.

At dawn, he had a splitting headache when he was awakened by confusion. "What the hell's happened?"

Crow's face was lined with worry. "Deer is gone. She disappeared during the night."

Billy sat up, groaned aloud and put his head in his hands. "Have the women make some strong coffee. I feel bad myself, but I'll help you look."

When it got right down to it, all the clues they had were that she was missing and so was a horse. Billy sipped a tin cup of strong coffee. "Where would she have gone?"

The Pawnee shook his head. "I don't know. She has been unhappy since the man she wanted declined to marry her, and the man I chose was killed. I never understood it all."

"Simple," Billy said. "She's gone looking for the man."

"But why now?"

"Does any man understand women?" Bill said, lighting a cigar.

"I will send a message to the fort, asking if that scout has seen her or if she went back to our village. What I fear is that she might run across a Cheyenne war party while riding alone. In that case, she might disappear without a trace."

All Billy could think of was the waste of her beauty. Manning might have liked her, and at least she would have brought a lot of miners and soldiers into the Gilded Lily. "I'm sorry about all this, Crow Feather, but I must be getting back."

The father looked at him anxiously. "She has no reason to ride that direction, but if you should see or hear anything of her, will you send word?"

"Sure, sure," Billy said. He hadn't any interest in what happened to the little tart. If she ended up serving the lust of a Cheyenne war party, she deserved it.

Crow Feather said, "I don't think we will leave the area just yet—in case she tries to come back or if anyone should hear something. We will camp in the area of the Great Balanced Rock for the cycle of a moon. We can hunt and camp there. Do you know the place?"

"Castle Rock? Sure." Billy nodded. "Everyone does." It was a landmark south of Denver, a landmark even whites held in awe because it seemed to draw lightning and thunder out of the front range of the Rockies.

He got some meat and more coffee, then climbed up on the wagon seat as the sun beat down on his throbbing head. "I'm sorry about your daughter, Crow Feather. I'll be on the watch, and if I hear or see anything, I'll send word to your camp grounds."

The Pawnee nodded, his shoulders slumped with worry. His expression said he didn't believe he would see her again, not if she had crossed the trail of a Cheyenne war party.

Too bad, Bill thought with disgust, too bad to waste that lovely, hot little bitch on a bunch of savages when Billy could have given her as a gift to Manning.

He watched warriors riding out again to search. One group headed back along the trail to their village and another rode along the creek. Stupid girl! Billy thought in disgust, fingering his diamond stickpin. She hadn't a chance out there on that desolate prairie alone. Probably she had been drunk when she rode out and hadn't been thinking straight.

He nodded good-bye to Crow Feather, clucked to the mule and started back over the trail to Denver.

An hour passed and he began to feel a little better. At least this part of it was done. Soon he'd have to deliver the other guns to the Cheyenne Dog Soldiers. When he made that delivery, he'd take some of the other boys along with him. The Dog Soldiers were a mean bunch and Billy had always been afraid of them. Delivering guns to renegade savages was no job for a coward, and yet it had become his job.

He heard a noise in the back of the wagon and

turned in the seat.

Deer popped up from under the tarp. "Are we to Denver yet?"

He reined in, his mouth falling open. "What the hell are you doing here? Your father's riding over half of Colorado Territory, searching for you."

She smiled and scampered up to sit next to him on the seat. "I didn't think anyone would remember to look in the wagon, not when I took my horse out on the prairie and turned it loose."

"Well I'll be damned!" He was speechless. "You decided to take me up on my offer?"

She nodded. "First I want some whiskey. Then I want you to take me to this place called Denver. I can't have the man I want, so I don't want a traditional life either."

Billy reached under the seat and handed her a bottle. "There's plenty more where that came from. You aren't worried about your father?"

She shook her head and took a big swig. "He'd just make me go back to our village. I'd rather go with you, as long as you buy me pretty things and give me all the whiskey I want."

"Baby," he replied, and grinned, clucking to the mule and making it trot, "I promise you are going to get all the whiskey you can drink. All you got to do is make men happy, and I'll bet you already know how to do that!"

She was already a little drunk. "As long as I don't have to work hard. I'm tired of planting squash and harvesting corn."

Billy clucked to the mule, hurrying it a little. Yep, Manning would be willing to teach her. With Deer's looks, she could be a real drawing card at the parlor house.

He presented her to Manning that night in a private room at the Lily. The older man's eyes shone. "Billy, you've done good—real good. I won't forget you for this."

Lily had seen to it that Deer had been cleaned up and dressed in gaudy yellow satin that set off her dark skin.

Billy handed her a drink. "Deer, this is the rich white man who will give you pretty things, and all the whiskey you want. All you have to do is be nice to him."

She came over, sat down on the sofa next to him, and put her hand on his thigh. "I can be very nice."

He heard Manning's sudden intake of breath. "She's younger than Lily. I wonder if she's as talented."

Billy winced. But he only shrugged. "Obviously I wouldn't know about that."

Starrett laughed. "God damn it to hell, Billy! I keep forgettin' how much you two dislike each other."

He kept his face immobile. "Will your French slut care if you take up with this Injun gal?"

Manning leaned on his cane, admiring Deer. "What if she does? I'll get back to her eventually when I've had my fill of this sweet little bitch. And then maybe you can think of some way to make her a real drawing card for the establishment."

Billy frowned. "That's Lily's department. Remember I just look after the books and the business angles."

Manning leaned over, put his hand on Deer's thigh, and stroked the yellow satin. "Yes, she's one sweet little brown bitch."

"Don't let her drink too much, boss. She's got a hollow leg. You do want her conscious, don't you?"

Manning laughed. "Not necessarily. Call one of the maids in, and have Deer undressed and put in a bed for me."

Billy stood up and turned to go.

"There's enough of this little brown gal for both of us. Why don't we go three in a bed?"

The thought made Billy a little sick. What sort of things did Lily endure that she never told him? Once again, he wished he had enough money to take her away somewhere. "No, thanks, boss, I'll send a maid to get Deer ready. Enjoy yourself."

Manning's blue eyes were bright with lust. "I intend to! She's young, isn't she? I had a Cheyenne girl about this age I kept for a few months back when I was in the army, eighteen or nineteen years ago. It sure brings back memories."

Billy looked over at Deer. She was very drunk and didn't object as Manning reached over and fumbled with the front of her yellow satin bodice. He pulled it off her big breasts. "Maybe I don't need a maid to do anything," he said thickly. "Just tell them I'm not to be disturbed."

Billy's heart began to beat hard. "I hear you."

He watched Manning cradle the girl's head in his lap, and reach to unbutton his pants. "She looks like she's got a talented, hot mouth. You sure you don't want to stay? We could have some fun, the two of us."

The perverted old bastard. "No, I'll be going. Maybe if I'm lucky, I won't have to run into your French whore as I leave."

Manning didn't even answer. He had one trembling hand on the girl's full breasts. He took the whiskey from her hands and she complained softly.

"Little Injun gal," he said, "you do what I want with that warm little mouth, then I'll give the liquor back to you."

Her smile said she'd do anything to get that whiskey bottle returned, that she understood what it was Manning wanted.

She wouldn't live very long if she kept drinking like that, Billy thought as he closed the door softly and went out. Who the hell cared? Injun girls were a dime a dozen. While her father searched the prairie for her, she could entertain Manning, maybe make a little money for the establishment if Lily could think of something exotic to do with her.

He walked softly to Lily's door and rapped. She opened it, and came silently into his arms. "You're taking a big chance, Billy. Isn't he down the hall?"

He put his finger to his lips for silence, went into her room, and closed the door. "I just brought him a new toy, a pretty, dark girl that should keep him entertained for at least a few days."

She sighed with relief. "That means that we—"

"Yeah, baby." He cut off her words with his lips as he took her in his arms. While Manning Starrett rutted like some old stag over a drunken Pawnee girl in a room down the hall, Billy Reno could enjoy the old man's mistress with safety. He swung Lily up in his arms and carried her to the bedroom. "I haven't thought about anything but this moment all day."

She opened her scarlet dressing gown and freed her breasts for his mouth. "Be my baby," she whispered. "They're aching for you. Nurse

236

me . . ."

He needed no urging. Tonight she was his. "I'm your baby tonight," he murmured, pulling her breasts down to his mouth. "Feed me, sweet. Feed me . . ."

Chapter Thirteen

Major Frank North leaned back in his office chair and looked at the three men sitting on the other side of his desk. Cody was a handsome devil, but at this moment, the others . . .

He studied Johnny's bruised face, Carter Osgoode's black eye and cut lip. "What happened to you two?"

They both fidgeted, avoiding his direct gaze.

"Are you two deaf?"

Johnny Ace studied his moccasins. "I—I fell off a horse."

"Fell off a horse? You're the best rider on this post!" No answer. In the silence, a fly buzzed through the open window. North sighed audibly, and turned his attention to the uppity young snob from Boston. "What about you?"

"I fell down some stairs."

"Looks like you rolled under the feet of the whole outfit," North snorted, then steepled his fingers, considering. So they weren't going to tell him. He would have been surprised if they had. Could it have been over that half-breed girl, Luci? Of course it had to be.

He glared at both of them. "I have enough trouble with hostiles without my men trying to kill each other."

Still no sound, save for Osgoode, shifting his weight nervously, glancing over at the Pawnee. He must be scared spitless of Johnny. North didn't blame him. He looked at the big knife in Johnny's belt.

Cody shook back his shoulder-length hair. "Major, I don't mean to be impudent, but I don't see how one man falling off a horse and another falling down some stairs is of any importance—"

"Do I look stupid enough to believe those stories?" North shouted as he lost his temper, and was immediately sorry. The stress of this Plains war was beginning to get to him. It wasn't anything to him personally if these two young stallions wanted to fight over some pretty girl—as long as it didn't affect the Fifth Cavalry.

Cody looked carefully out the window. Obviously the chief scout knew what had happened, and was hoping North didn't.

"I ought to turn this matter over to General Carr," North grumbled, knowing he wouldn't. They were his men; he'd deal with it. But now he was afraid to send Johnny and Osgoode on a mission together. What the hell was he supposed to do? "The Dog Soldiers seem to be better armed than we are lately. A patrol out of Fort Sedgewick was ambushed a couple of days ago. Hostiles were armed with new repeating rifles."

The three of them looked thunderstruck.

He nodded. "I'm afraid it's true. We need to find out where those rifles are coming from."

Johnny rolled a cigarette. "What kind of bastard white man would sell them rifles, knowing soldiers were their targets?"

"Someone who cares more about money than conscience," Major North said, and shrugged.

Cody's handsome face furrowed. "Any clues at all, Major?"

"I don't know what to make of these," North replied, reaching in his top drawer and throwing the brass coins out on his desk.

Johnny leaned over, picked one up, and stared at the hole punched in it. "These look like—"

"They are," North said. "Brass whorehouse tokens. We found these on a Dead Dog Soldier. He had used them to decorate his hair."

The three handed the coins around, looking as puzzled as North felt. In some bordellos, the customers bought tokens from the madame and paid the girls with them. That way the madame handled all the money herself. It kept girls from cheating the house or the customer.

Johnny turned one of the small brass coins over in his hand. "That's what it is, all right. He tossed it back to the major, who caught it. "It stands to reason no Cheyenne warrior was buying entertainment at a whorehouse. Probably he took them off a dead prospector."

Osgoode held out his hand. "Let me look again."

The major tossed it to him. The lieutenant studied it. "Isn't this a flower on one side? Looks like a lily."

Cody grinned. "Seems I recall an elegant place in Denver called the Gilded Lily, but Johnny's right—no warrior would be welcome in an elegant Denver whorehouse. Not much of a clue, Major." He

ACCEPT YOUR **FREE GIFT** AND EXPERIENCE MORE OF THE PASSION AND ADVENTURE YOU LIKE IN A HISTORICAL ROMANCE

Zebra Romances are the finest novels of their kind and are written with the adult woman in mind. All of our books are written by authors who really know how to weave tales of romantic adventure in the historical settings you love.

Because our readers tell us these books sell out very fast in the stores, Zebra has made arrangements for you to receive at home the four newest titles published each month. You'll never miss a title and home delivery is so convenient. With your first shipment we'll even send you a FREE Zebra Historical Romance as our gift just for trying our home subscription service. No obligation.

BIG SAVINGS AND **FREE** HOME DELIVERY

Each month, the Zebra Home Subscription Service will send you the four newest titles as soon as they are published. (We ship these books to our subscribers even before we send them to the stores.) You may preview them *Free* for 10 days. If you like them as much as we think you will, you'll pay just $3.50 each and *save $1.80 each month* off the cover price. *AND you'll also get FREE HOME DELIVERY.* There is never a charge for shipping, handling or postage and there is no minimum you must buy. If you decide not to keep any shipment, simply return it within 10 days, no questions asked, and owe nothing.

Get a Free
Zebra
Historical
Romance

*a $3.95
value*

Affix
stamp
here

flipped it back to North.

"Not much, but all I've got at the moment," North admitted, studying the trio. "The Dog Soldiers seem to know a lot about troop movements, or if not, they're awfully lucky to be at the right spot at the right time."

"Major"—Johnny paused, a match halfway to his cigarette—"who do you think would stoop to spying—?"

"Ye Gods! Come to think of it"—the Lieutenant rubbed his chin thoughtfully—"that little Luci did ask me a lot of questions when I took her picnicking—"

"Why, you rotten—!" Johnny came up out of his chair, grabbed him by the front of his uniform, lifted the smaller man off the floor, and gave him a good shaking.

"Dammit, Johnny!" North barked. "Scout! Sit down!"

Johnny let go slowly, flopped back down in his chair, and tossed the cigarette away dejectedly.

North glared at both of them. "Scout, how dare you cause a disturbance in my office!"

Johnny didn't look at him, but sat clenching and unclenching his fists. Osgoode smirked in a way that made the major wanted to shake him like a terrier with a rag. "And Lieutenant Osgoode, wipe that smile off your face!"

Silence again. So that was what it was about. Osgoode had taken the girl on a picnic. For the first time, he wondered if Luci might be slipping information to the Dog Soldiers. How much would officers tell her if she smiled prettily when she returned their laundry? He dismissed the idea. She wouldn't know that much, and wouldn't have any way of getting the information out of the fort anyway. Somehow, he suspected whatever help the Dog Soldiers were getting came from outside and higher up.

The handsome chief scout cleared his throat, bringing North back to the present. "Cody, I'm sending my brother to Denver. He'll need a scout, so you go along. Take Osgoode with you."

The lieutenant brightened. "May I inquire if we are escorting Miss Starrett to her father? I'll be so delighted—"

"No, Miss Starrett is staying right here until it's safe enough for the stages to run again. For one thing, I'd have to send a whole patrol to ensure her safety and deal with all her bags and trunks, and I can't spare the extra men." North paused. "Besides, I want this mission carried out as quietly and with as little notice as possible. A big cavalry patrol escorting a beautiful, prominent girl would let the whole of Denver know you were in town!"

Cody nodded. "You're right, Major. A trio of men could move a lot faster than a patrol escorting a buggy."

North looked at Johnny glowering and saying nothing. His handsome face was purple with bruises, but Osgoode looked worse. Damn the two of them! Getting the snotty young officer off the post for a few days might cool things down.

"Pani Le-shar,"—Johnny leaned forward in his chair—"I'd like to go—"

"Request denied," North snapped, "Dismissed!"

All three jumped to their feet, saluted at the curt command, and turned to go. Even though North knew the Pawnee had personal reasons for hating the Cheyenne because of his father, there were important scouting duties here.

North reached out and handed the tokens to

Osgoode. "Take these with you, although I'm not sure what good they'll do. Dismissed!"

The trio started to leave. "One more thing," North said, "I don't want anyone else falling down stairs or off horses. If any man wants to fight, I can guarantee he's about to be belly-deep in hostiles this summer!"

The three saluted again and left his office. He leaned on the door post and watched them scatter out across the parade ground. The Fifth Cavalry was outmanned, outgunned, and the Indians had better horses. These brass tokens weren't really clues. The brave had taken them off a dead miner or settler as Johnny suggested. It was bound to be a wild-goose chase unless they overheard some gossip around Denver. One thing he did know for sure. This was going to be a helluva summer already without those two fighting over the favors of a woman.

Out of the corner of his eye, he saw Luci come out of the back of the trading post, lugging wet laundry to hang on the line. He felt bad about the way she had been treated the night of the party, but had been powerless to help her. He wondered whose idea of a cruel joke it had been to invite her in the first place.

Johnny Ace couldn't sleep. He lay staring at the ceiling, stripped as usual to his loincloth. But on a hot night like tonight, it didn't help much.

He thought about the meeting in Pani Le-shar's office two days ago. Why hadn't North let Johnny be one of the ones going to Denver? Did his beloved commander no longer trust him? North had made it plain that he might suspect Luci of

243

leaking information, which was ridiculous. Or was it? Did North fear that Johnny, bedazzled by Luci, might leak to her what little he knew of the Fifth's plans?

Johnny had gone on a couple of scouting trips since those three had left for Denver, but he didn't find anything the cavalry didn't already know. The Cheyenne Dog Soldiers were roaming the whole of Kansas and Nebraska, and when the Fifth hit the campaign trail again, there were going to be a lot of women wailing in empty lodges and tipis, a lot of blood watering the buffalo grass.

The Pawnee scouts thirsted for revenge because of all the killings by the more numerous Cheyenne. And the Dog Soldiers would rather die fighting than be forced back onto reservations. He couldn't blame them.

Cheyenne. Luci. He felt a strong stirring in his groin as he always did at the thought of her. Restlessly, he rolled over on his belly, ground his hard tool against the cot, and imaged her spread beneath him, her body and her soft lips open to him, wanting him, too.

He swore in sheer frustration. What the hell had she been doing out picnicking with Osgoode? What was it that officer had hinted at? Johnny hadn't seen much of her since that fight. She seemed to be avoiding him. Was she afraid he might ask questions she didn't want to answer?

He rolled back over, clasping his hands behind his head. His manhood was still hot and swollen big under the skimpy loincloth. When she had let him make love to her, had it been because she cared for him, because she'd wanted him, too? Or had she been trying to wheedle information out of him? Try as he might, he couldn't remember whether he might have told her anything important. In her arms, all he could think of was her Cheyenne caress, her pliant body as he entered her, the hot warmth of her open mouth accepting his tongue.

Damn! He had to know! Getting out of bed, he slipped into his blue cavalry pants and moccasins, and padded quiet as a cat to the trading post. Cautiously, he threw a small pebble against her window, then another.

Her small face appeared at the glass. He gestured in the moonlight for her to come out. Her expression told him she might not. He gestured again. She hesitated, then disappeared. In a couple of minutes, she stood before him with only a thin wrapper pulled over her sheer night dress. "What is it you want, Pawnee?"

You, he thought, feeling his manhood throb, his groin ache. "I need to talk to you."

"In the middle of the night?" She sounded outraged.

"Don't talk so loud, you'll wake someone." He put his finger to his lips in a cautioning gesture.

"Wake someone?" Her whisper was loud. "You throw rocks at my window and then worry about waking someone? I ought to start screaming and get the whole post up. You'd end up in the guardhouse!"

"If you do, I'll tell them we had a prearranged meeting, you got mad, and decided to get me in trouble."

"Why, you worthless Pawnee dog!" She turned as if to leave, but he reached out and put his hand on her small shoulder. The cloth was so thin, he could feel the heat of her under his fingers. He fought a terrible urge to reach out with both hands, push her nightdress down her shoulders to her waist, and then pull her hot, naked breasts against his bare chest.

"Let go of me, Johnny." Her voice sounded tense, her half open mouth looked shiny wet.

He had to fight himself to keep from dragging her to him, covering that mouth with his.

"Let go of me, Johnny. I'm going back inside."

"Not 'til we've talked." Then he couldn't control his impulse, jerked her nightgown off her shoulders, pulled her hard against him even as his mouth covered hers.

She struggled but he only held her against him more tightly, feeling her small nipples harden like two points of fire, burning into his broad chest. He pressed his throbbing manhood against her belly, grinding it into her while he probed his tongue deep into her mouth, forcing her head back. She struggled only a moment, then she trembled and clung to him, letting him ravage her mouth.

"I've missed you, Star Eyes," he stroked her hair.

"I—I should go back in." Her voice was shaky. Could she not dare admit she might have missed him, wanted him, too? Or had it all been an act? Had she played up to him and Osgoode both for any information she might get to help the Dog Soldiers?

"Don't go in—yet." Two could play this game, he thought grimly. He knew what made her weak and breathless. If she had any secrets, could he get them from her while they were in the throes of passion?

"There's no future in this, Johnny. It was loco from the first." But she gasped breathlessly against his mouth when he ran the tip of his tongue along her bottom lip, kissing the corners.

"Let's not think about that. I want you. You want me. Can we only think of that and let tomorrow take care of itself?"

"That's the attitude that got my mother in trouble," she whispered, but she kept clinging to him, rubbing herself against his pulsating hardness.

He nuzzled the lobe of her ear, kissed his way down her neck, then swung her up in his arms so that he could bend his head to suck her nipples.

She made a soft cry and wrapped her arms around his neck, holding his face against her breast.

He had her now, he thought coldly, grimly. He looked around for a place to take her. Off behind the trading post was a row of giant lilac bushes, just going out of bloom. A lavender bloom still clung here and there, radiating heady scent into the warm night air. In the dark sky, the giant star that she had been named for now hung over the eastern horizon. It was almost morning.

He carried her there and stood her on her feet.

"I — I don't think . . ." She looked around wildly as if she might bolt and run for the building. In answer, he reached out and savagely ripped the nightdress from her, leaving her standing naked in the shadowy moonlight.

"I'll have you now if I have to rape you! And don't pretend you don't want me, too!"

In answer, she fell to her knees before him, clasped him around the thighs, and kissing his swollen manhood submissively through the cloth.

He reached down, unbuckled his belt, let his pants slide down so that her hot, sweet mouth caressed his hardness. For a moment, as her tongue kissed there, he forgot about where her loyalties

247

were, or that she might have lured Osgoode just as she was driving him crazy now. All that mattered at this moment was this agonizing ache in his groin that only she could satisfy.

He pulled her away long enough to get his pants and moccasins off and spread her torn nightdress under the lilacs. Now she was on her knees, naked and submissive before him, her ebony hair hanging loose so that it half-covered her small, firm breasts.

"Anyway you want me, Johnny. Anything you want!"

He ought to humiliate her, force her to submit to anything he could devise. But she was small and defenseless and he loved her. Yes, he couldn't deny it. He loved this Cheyenne girl, no matter what, and the vulnerability of his situation drove him to anger.

His fury made him rough as he grabbed her and threw her down on her back. "You were playing the whore for the lieutenant," he raged. "Now show me all your tricks!"

Tears came to her eyes. "I don't know what you're talking about!"

"Don't you, Cheyenne slut?" He cupped her breasts in his hands as he knelt between her thighs. "Were you offering him what you had given me and if so, why?"

She began to cry, covering her face with her hands. "I don't understand you! I don't know what it is you want!"

All his angry resolve melted at her tears. He couldn't bear to see her cry. Johnny lay down between her thighs, slipped his arms under her shoulders, and kissed her tears away. "I'm a jealous fool, Star Eyes. I hate the idea of any man touching you but me."

She put her face against his broad chest, weeping softly. "It was silly for me to go with Carter. He only wanted one thing and I wouldn't give it to him."

"You drive men crazy until they can think of only one thing, Luci." He began to kiss the tears off her small face. She pressed turgid nipples against his bare chest. He caught her small wrists and pinned them above her head on the ground with one big hand so that her back arched, offering her breasts up to his mouth and free hand.

She slipped her legs around his waist, holding him tightly against her body. "Neither of us can escape now," she said, and smiled up at him.

"Who wants to?" And he bent his head and sucked as much of her breast into his mouth as possible. He had a terrible, driving need to put his seed deep in her belly, plant his son there.

No, that could never be. She was Cheyenne and possibly a spy. But it didn't matter tonight. All that mattered was that they were in each other's arms. He moved down her body, fired by the woman scent of her. He moved to kiss between her thighs, stroked her throbbing wetness with his fingers. He would satisfy her several times this way and then force his sword into her velvet softness.

But he couldn't control his urge to ride her and he thrust into her, tilting her hips up so she could take him deeply. He was swept along the edge of some kind of dark wave, like being whirled up and caught in one of the tornados that he had seen swirling across the isolated plains. Then nothing mattered to him but emptying himself into her; and her slight body convulsed, locked onto his as if determined to take every drop he had to give.

When he dimly realized where he was again, they were wrapped in each other's arm, weary and spent under the bushes. Fragrant lilac petals floated down and fell on them.

He brushed them off her delicate face. "I didn't mean to hurry it," he whispered against her ear. "I was going to take you a dozen times tonight. I couldn't help myself. We seem so right together."

He hesitated, wanting to tell her about the dream, about the woman on the porch of the ranch house in the twilight and how she ran out to meet him as he dismounted from his horse. She might laugh. She might tell him again there was no future for them. He already knew that. It was enough for now to hold her tightly against him, to kiss her hair. It had to be enough; this was all it ever could be.

"I ought to go in," she whispered, but she didn't move.

"You're right. It'll be dawn soon and we wouldn't want people to see us." But he only held her against him more tightly. She was his for the moment anyway. *Romeo and Juliet.*

"You'll be riding out against my people soon, won't you?"

Immediately, his guard went up. "You know that. Why do you ask?"

She ran her finger along his cheekbone. "Do you suppose we could forget about Cheyenne and Pawnee, just turn our backs on all of it and ride away?"

"Together?"

"Of course together. I wish . . ."

She didn't finish though he waited.

"Luci, my enlistment isn't up until about the middle of July."

Her eyes were two deep pools, looking up at him. "Will you reenlist?"

He shrugged. "I—I don't know. I don't have any other plans."

She moved out from under him, her body suddenly wooden. "So for at least a few more weeks, you'll be out killing my people?"

"That's what they pay me for."

"Even if I asked you not to?"

"So that's it!" He sat up, suddenly disappointed and a more than a little angry. "What a cheap trick! Luci, the Fifth has other scouts. They'd still go after the Cheyenne even if I didn't scout for them."

"But at least you wouldn't have their blood on your hands! How can you expect to make love to me at night and kill my people in the daytime?"

With fury in her voice, she grabbed up her torn nightdress, wrapped it around her, and ran into the building while he called after her, "Luci, wait!"

But she didn't wait and she didn't look back.

Chapter Fourteen

Carter Osgoode looked over at Luther North and Cody as they rode down the brightly lit street. "So this is Denver! Doesn't anyone ever go to bed around here?"

Cody laughed. "Not to sleep!"

Even though it was getting on toward midnight as they rode in, weary and coated with trail dust, the streets seemed full of men and horses. Loud, off-key piano music floated from two different directions as they rode in and dismounted at the livery stable, waking a sleepy hand to put away their horses. The street they stood in seemed to be mostly saloons and bordellos with bright lights and men coming and going. Somewhere a woman sang a plaintive ballad that had been popular during the war: "*. . . we loved each other then, Lorena, more than we ever dared to tell; and what we might have been, Lorena, had but our loving prospered well . . .*"

"Let's find a hotel," Luther said, and they began to walk past the saloon from where the drunken woman's voice drifted: *"It matters little now, Lorena, the past is in the eternal Past, our heads will soon lie low, Lorena, life's tide is ebbing out so fast . . ."*

The song saddened Carter, making him think of the beautiful girl back in Boston, David Van Schuyler's twin sister, who had never noticed Carter and, in the end, had run away to the Indians.

A man cursed and his words echoed, "Sing something happy, you stupid wench!" followed by crashing glass.

Immediately, the voice broke into: *"Oh, Susanna, oh don't you cry for me . . ."*

A body flew through the bat-wing doors of a saloon as they walked past and they dodged. From inside, the sounds of a fight echoed.

Carter craned his neck to look around at the raw boomtown. "We must be crazy to stay in the cavalry when there's gold around here."

Luther laughed. "There's more gold in fleecing miners," he said as they walked toward the hotel. They had a bad meal at an all-night place and went to their rooms.

Carter didn't want to go to bed, but he washed up in the cracked bowl and pitcher on the wash stand, lay down, and stared at the wall. On the yellowed paper hung a typical Victorian print of a young man saying good-bye to his true love while she hung on to his arm, evidently begging him not to go. *Women!*

He sat up in bed, went to the window, and looked down on the rowdy street scene. Even if the trio was dog tired, Carter had been stuck at that isolated post for months now and he didn't intend to spend his first night in a wide-open place like Denver going to bed early—at least not by himself.

Maybe he could do a little early investigating. He took the tokens, got dressed, strapped on his pistol, and slipped out of the hotel. Now what? These tokens might not mean anything. They might not even be from a bordello in Denver. But they were all he had.

Carter walked down the board sidewalk, tossing a token up in the air and catching it. A pair of bearded miners stumbled past him. On impulse, he reached out and caught one of them by a dirty sleeve. "A friend told me I could have a good time at this place, but I can't remember the name of it. Something like a flower. Maybe Rose's Place, or—"

"Lily, the Gilded Lily," the miner said, peering drunkenly at the coin in Carter's palm.

The other one looked and nodded in agreement. "Yep, it's from the Lily, all right. But that's a bad place, mister. Purty gals, yes, but they'll cheat you at the card table and anywhere else they can."

"But purty gals." The other grinned, hooking his thumbs in his vest. "Got a new attraction—a punch bowl full of delectable stuff!"

The other laughed and licked his lips suggestively.

Ye Gods! What idiot would be impressed by a punch bowl? It didn't sound like much to Carter, but then maybe these poor, backwoods hicks had never seen a silver punch bowl such as Carter's mother had used for her parties—before they lost all their money.

He got directions and walked rapidly to the Gilded Lily. He'd have a drink or two, enjoy a girl, and get back before Luther and Cody ever knew he was gone. If he solved this mystery about the contraband guns, he'd be a hero with maybe an advancement. Captain Carter Osgoode.

The Lily was an elegant saloon by anyone's standard, Carter thought as he walked in. Certainly it drew a higher-class clientele than the others to its big, scarlet-papered room where men leaned on a carved, mahogany bar. Pretty girls danced in skimpy costumes on the stage at one end. It had a three-piece orchestra, too, rather than just a piano.

". . . *He'd fly through the air with the greatest of ease,*" the crowd sang along as the girls danced, "*the daring young man on the flying trapeze; his movements were graceful, all the girls he could please, and my love he has stolen away. . . .*"

Carter went to the bar, ordered whiskey, and sipped it, impressed. The glass looked clean and the whiskey tasted good enough to be shipped from back East, not the local home-brewed stuff with rattlesnake heads and red pepper.

"They're getting ready to fill the punch bowl," said the man next to him, jostling him a little as he turned.

Curious, Carter turned, too. The dancing girls had cleared the stage and a tough-looking bouncer carried the biggest crystal punch bowl Carter had ever seen out to the edge of the stage, and set it down.

A buzz of excitement ran through the crowd with men elbowing each other to get closer. The bartender carried a case of bottles up by the bowl.

"Okay, Gents," announced the burly bartender, "you've been waiting for the mysterious princess of Egypt and here she is!" The men set up cheers and applause. From the side of the stage entered a tawny, beautiful girl with her hair done up elaborately on her head. She wore nothing but elegant shoes. Carter could only press forward himself and stare. It was considered daring for a girl to dance

255

in a skimpy costume in public in these times, no matter what went on in the private rooms. The girl had a magnificent figure, beautiful breasts, small waist. And suddenly Carter realized there wasn't a hair on her beautiful, sleek body except for the elaborate ebony locks done up on her head.

Carter felt his breath quicken, his groin ache as he looked at her, pushing through the appreciative crowd of men. The girl walked slowly, teasingly, across the stage, smiling invitingly at the men. Kicking off her shoes, she sat down in the punch bowl, reached for a bottle of wine, and opened it.

As Carter watched, spellbound, she slowly poured the red wine down her breasts, where it trickled across her belly and into the bowl, then she reached for another bottle.

In the sudden silence as the men watched, Carter was close enough to see the burgundy running across her satin skin, dripping off her nipples. She smiled at the crowd. "Come on, fellas," she purred, "doesn't anybody want a drink?"

That broke the spell. As the girl kept pouring wine over herself, men jabbered to each other, pushing and shoving to grab a punch cup and elbow their way to the bowl.

Carter had forgotten to breathe. He took a sudden breath, aware of how hot the room suddenly seemed to be. He pushed his way through the crowd, watching the men dip their glasses between her thighs into the punch, drinking it greedily.

He got through the crowd somehow and stood looking at her. She paused in reaching for a bottle, eyed him, and ran her tongue along her lips in invitation. "Want to pour, soldier?"

He couldn't stop his hand from shaking as he opened the wine bottle, then hesitated.

She indicated one magnificent breast. "Pour it over this." He did as he was told, mesmerized by the scarlet wine dripping off her dark nipples as men pushed each other to get their glasses under that stream.

He thought he'd seen some wild times in staid Boston, but there had been nothing like this. This was Sodom and Gomorrah with faro tables.

"Soldier, don't you want a drink?" She smiled again.

He forgot he didn't care for red wine. Like the others, it seemed the most erotic drink in the world. Carter dipped his glass between her thighs, and drank. The thought of this liquor touching her beautiful, naked body was so arousing to him, his groin ached. Quickly, he gulped the wine and dipped in again.

He couldn't take his gaze off her as he filled his glass again. "If we drink it dry, does the last man get the cherry in the drink?"

"Maybe." She smiled at him. "I get to choose which one gets me."

"Then I'm going to stay right here until it's all gone," he said, swaying a little on his feet. He had another drink, then urged other men to crowd around and drink up. When the wine was gone, maybe she would choose him.

The evening became a blur to him as he stood there, helping lower the level of the punch bowl. "How can the management afford to do this for free?"

She shrugged one bare shoulder, gleaming wetly with red wine. "It's cheap stuff. Besides, once fifty men have tried to drink it dry, they have a tendency to spend more at the card tables and upstairs."

"Can *I* take *you* upstairs?"

"You're a bold one, ain't you? I like your style, soldier." She grinned, held out her arms. "Here, help me out. I'll get my robe and—"

"Ye Gods! You don't need a robe!" He reached to lift her out, but didn't put her down. She clung to him wetly, staining his uniform with wine. "I'll take you just the way you are!" He started for the stairs with the men cheering him on.

They went down a shadowy hall. "Which room?"

"You're in a helluva hurry, ain't you, Soldier?" She indicated a room with a nod.

Carter went through the door, kicked it shut with his foot, dumped her on the bed, and began to peel off his clothes.

"Don't rush, Lieutenant. I can show you a way to make it more fun."

He hesitated as he took off his clothes. All he wanted to do was fall between her wet thighs and get rid of this ache as fast as possible. There was something he liked to do to women, but most wouldn't let him. Still maybe this strangely beautiful girl could teach him new delights.

Carter finished undressing, took the brass token, and laid it on her naked belly.

She lay there, red wine from her body staining the white sheets, and looked down at the token with a smile. "Uh-uh,"—she shook her head—"you'll have to put something extra in this deal for the Girl in the Punch Bowl to satisfy that craving you got."

He hesitated, took out some silver dollars, and tossed them with a clink on her belly. "Is that enough?"

If it wasn't, he was going to rape her before anyone could get in here to stop him. There was something about this girl that reminded him of the half-breed girl back at the fort. And then suddenly, he knew what it was. "Dark Egyptian princess, my foot! You're just an Injun!"

She laughed, not moving except to gather up the coins. "Pawnee. In my old life, I was called Deer."

"Well, Deer, get ready because its rutting season and you've found yourself a stag!"

He fell across her, kissing the red wine off her wet breasts, and running his hands all over her.

She reached for a bottle, and rose up on her elbow to take a long drink. "And now some for you," she whispered, and she poured a small pool in the hollow of her belly.

It had to be the most wildly erotic thing he had ever done, licking the wine from her satin skin. He realized she was more than a little drunk herself. "I thought girls weren't supposed to drink when they worked."

"I'm not." She smiled at him and reached for the bottle again. "But I don't think the boss knows so far." She ran the tip of her tongue along her lower lip invitingly. "I'll make you happy enough not to tell either."

"Damn right you won't!" He was suddenly afraid of completing the act with this girl. She looked experienced. Carter was always concerned that women would laugh because his maleness was small. Carter licked her slowly, savoring the taste of the wine on her skin.

"I'm ready for you, soldier." She spread her thighs wide and closed her eyes.

"Uh-uh, we do it my way!" Before she could realize what was happening, he grabbed her arm, rolled her over on her belly, and fell on her. She struggled but he had one hand over her mouth and the other under her, squeezing her breast. He knew how to make a woman feel he was built big. He thrust hard into her from behind. Women always fought him when he did that to them, but it felt good and tight to a small man. She fought him, too, and tried to scream. But he had his hand over her mouth, and when she struggled, he jerked back on her head, and squeezed her breast. Hard.

"Lay still, little Injun bitch! Not many men take you this way, do they? You're getting what I didn't give another little Injun gal, but that's okay, too!"

He must be hurting her, ramming into her this way, but he didn't care about anything but the throb in his groin. At least she wouldn't have to worry about getting a baby.

Carter laughed at the thought, ramming into her savagely. She still struggled, but she was helpless with his weight on her back, and he knew it. "Stop fighting, bitch! It'll make it easier on you!"

He jerked back harder on her head, squeezing her breast as he rode her from behind. She stopped fighting abruptly. Good! That made it a little easier to enjoy her. Probably she was passed out drunk, but Carter didn't care. He had no objections to using an unconscious woman.

With a sigh, he rammed into her limp body one last time and gave himself up to ecstasy. He lay on her a long moment, reaching under to stroke her breasts. No, there was nothing like her in Boston. He'd have to come back first chance he got.

Finally, he stood up and began to dress. "Deer?"

No answer. *Dead drunk.* He snorted in disgust, looking at the naked brown beauty sprawled on her belly. Deer might complain to her boss when she finally came to—if she could remember what happened. But he had a feeling Indian girls were expendable; the management could always find another pretty one to pass off as an Egyptian Princess — especially when this one had a drinking problem.

He picked up the token and went out into the hall. Somehow, he had a feeling someone around here knew how that token got on a dead brave. Maybe he should go back and get Cody and Luther . . . or wait until morning.

Carter shook his head and checked his Colt again as if to reassure himself it was loaded. The wine and the rape had made him feel reckless, potent. He wasn't going to share the credits. He'd investigate this all by himself.

When he ran across a girl in the hallway, he winked at her. "Direct me to your boss, honey."

She led him down another hallway and pointed to a door. Carter hesitated. Maybe he should go back and get the others. He didn't feel quite so brave now that he was sobering up, and realized that if he disappeared without a trace, the pair back at the hotel would never really know for sure what happened to him. Downstairs, the noise and laughter had subsided. Even gamblers and whores finally go to bed, he thought, as he rapped.

"Who is it?" A woman's voice.

"Lieutenant Carter Osgoode."

"Who the hell is Carter Osgoode?"

She might decide against opening the door.

"A handsome, daring devil who needs to talk to you about business and money."

She laughed. "Business and money always interest me!"

There were sounds of discussion, a man's voice. Obviously he didn't want her to open the door.

After a moment, the lock turned and a woman

261

in a scarlet negligee opened the door. She was a very beautiful, dark woman whose expression said she had lived hard. It showed in her face. "Okay, handsome, daring devil, what is it you want to talk about?" She leaned against the door, ready to swing it shut on him.

He smiled to disarm her. "This is hardly to be discussed out here in the hall." Actually, he was bluffing, fishing for information.

She frowned at him. "Look, kid, if you need a woman, you go find one of my girls, I don't—"

"It's about Indians and running guns." Carter reached out to stop her from shutting the door.

She hesitated. "So what's that to me?" But her purring voice went tense and her dark eyes widened, betraying she lied.

"A cavalry patrol killed a warrior the other day. One of the dead braves had a necklace of these." He reached into his coat and pulled out the brass tokens.

"So I still say what's that to me?"

He gave her a long look, pretending he knew more than he did. "Do you want to talk about it with me or do you want to face the authorities?"

She hesitated, looking behind her. "Come in."

He followed her into her room, watched her close the door. The room was overdone in the height of Victorian decoration—burgundy horsehair furniture, big cabbage roses on the wallpaper, knickknacks and trinkets everywhere. It smelled like old perfume and cigar smoke.

Carter looked around. A cigar still smoldered in an ashtray on the ornate walnut table near the sofa. "Who else is here?"

"Nobody." The dark beauty pulled the filmy thing around her full breasts and settled into one

262

of the burgundy chairs. "I don't know anything about tokens taken off some Cheyenne."

He didn't sit down, and he kept his gaze on a closed door—bedroom, probably. "I didn't say he was Cheyenne. How did you know that?"

She looked confused. "I—I don't know. They're the ones on the war path, aren't they?"

Carter put his hand on the butt of his pistol uncertainly. He was a poor shot. Now he wished he had practiced more, or waited and brought the others with him. "Tell your cigar-smoking friend to come out."

She hesitated, looking from him to the door. "Billy, come out."

The door swung open suddenly, and before Carter could react, he found himself staring into the muzzle of a double-barreled shotgun held by a handsome man in his middle thirties. "Okay, sport, now what the hell is it you want?"

Carter backed away, making sure he made no sudden moves. "I—I was bluffing. I don't know anything."

The man came out into the lamp light. His front two lower teeth were missing, and a diamond stick-pin reflected the light. The man gestured toward the sofa with the shotgun. "Sit down, Lieutenant."

Carter stumbled in backing toward the sofa. He was so scared, he was afraid he would wet his pants and then what would the beauty think? "I-I'm not the only one who knows. The army knows a lot. If anything happens to me—"

"Now, what ever gave you that idea, sport?" The man grinned. "We just need to talk, that's all. If I blow you in half, Lily here will say she did it to protect herself against a drunken soldier who tried to break into her room."

He was so afraid, his voice shook. "I'm not drunk."

"Who'll know that when she finishes pouring liquor all over your body? Lily is an institution in this town, soldier. They couldn't find a jury who would find her guilty of anything except running the best parlor house this side of the Mississippi." He laughed, reached for his cigar, and rested the shotgun on his knees.

"I—I don't really know anything, I was just bluffing, that's all." Carter brushed back his brown curls. He felt bathed in cold sweat.

"There isn't anything to know," Billy said soothingly. "A string of tokens don't mean anything."

"Billy," the woman scolded, "I told you it was stupid to give that Injun—"

"Shut up, Lily!"

"For all the army knows," Carter said, "the Injun took the tokens off dead miners' bodies."

Billy sat smoking his cigar and looking at him. "Why did you come alone?"

Maybe he could yet work a deal. "I—I thought maybe we could do a little business. I hate the army. I'd like to make a little money and clear out of here."

"Did, huh?" Billy relaxed a little. "Then maybe you're my kind of man. I like a man who knows what he wants and goes after it!"

Carter sighed with relief. The woman smiled at him, her negligee falling off one tawny shoulder in a teasing manner. "Drink, soldier?" Her voice almost reached out and stroked his body. He nodded.

She went over, poured him a whiskey while Billy put the shotgun to one side, and offered him a cigar.

Carter leaned back in his chair, drink in one hand, an expensive cigar in the other. "I might even be able to help you in this."

Billy laughed. "I doubt we need it. There's bigtime money and connections from back East involved. They only lose if the Indian trouble is over and the hostiles go back to the reservation."

Carter blinked in disbelief. "They'd sell the guns to kill our own men?"

"You are naive, aren't you?" Billy smiled. "Someone always makes money in a war." He reached for the brass tokens and stared at them.

"Well, I want my share." Carter sipped his drink.

Billy shrugged, running his tongue around his gapped teeth. "There's enough to go around. You talk to anyone around here, let them know why you came?"

Carter thought fast. He needed an alibi so they'd know he couldn't just disappear without a trace, They'd think twice before they double-crossed him and murdered him. "Sure," he lied, "that girl in the punch bowl knows everything. I ended up in her bed; told her why I had come, and for her to let the army and the sheriff know I was going to Lily's room to investigate if I should turn up missing."

Billy's eyes widened. "Aw, you didn't really think you were in any danger, did you? Hell, I can use a smart man in this deal. Maybe you could go to work for me full-time after you get out of the army. There's plenty of easy money, whiskey, anything you want."

"Anything?" He looked over at Lily, sitting with her negligee half open, revealing beautiful breasts. He had a sudden vision of himself mounting her from behind, riding her like a dark, wild filly.

"Anything, right, Lily?" Billy looked at the woman.

She got up, came over, and sat on the arm of Carter's chair. "I like soldiers," she purred, running her hand through his hair, brushing the brown curls off his forehead.

"Matter of fact," Billy said, "I'm riding out in less than a hour to make a delivery to the Cheyenne. I need a man I can trust to go with me. You got a horse?"

Carter nodded, his senses reeling from the scent of Lily's perfume. He had a terrible urge to pull her into his lap and bury his face between her breasts. He imagined her beautiful bare bottom bent over the chair arm while he grasped her narrow waist. . . .

"Swell, sport!" Billy said. "Now you go get your horse and don't let anyone follow you. Meet me behind the Lily in less than an hour. We've got to be well on our way before dawn."

Carter stood up slowly and Lily stood up with him, holding on to his arm, pressing her breast against his sleeve. Money. He'd have money. And maybe the services of this sultry, tawny woman. "Sure."

Billy stood up. "Remember, don't tell anyone. See you behind the place here."

"You can trust me," Carter grinned happily, turned, and left. He'd found his own gold mine, he thought as he went through the hall and down the stairs. And he wouldn't have to work to get it. After all, he didn't have any friends in the Fifth. Why shouldn't he help arm the hostiles with new rifles? Maybe he could eventually figure out how to double-cross Billy and end up with the whole business and the woman besides.

Hurrying through the darkness, he went to the livery stable to saddle his horse.

Billy stood holding the brass tokens, staring after the soldier.

Lily looked at him, "So what you gonna do?"

He signaled her to keep quiet until they heard the lieutenant's footsteps on the stairs. Then he stuffed the tokens in his vest and began to curse. "Of all the damned bad luck! I only had you let him in in the first place because I thought he might have heard my voice and was one of Manning's men,"

"So now what? He could ruin everything. Looks like the kind who would brag around, tell everything he knew!"

"He's dumb as a box of rocks, anyone can see that! So he goes with me to meet the Injuns—and never comes back. Who's to know what happened if he disappears without a trace?"

"But if lots of people saw him down at the bar—"

"Lily, lots of men come in here, have a drink. You can say you saw him leave with a suspicious-looking character. Nobody can prove nothing."

She wrapped her arms around herself and paced the floor. "Don't forget, Billy, he said he told Deer everything!"

"I forgot that drunk Injun bitch!" Billy rubbed his unshaven face with annoyed agitation. "With a couple of drinks in her, she'd tell anything!"

"She's already a big problem," Lily complained. "The other girls are talking about how sloppy drunk she get at night. She's fast becoming a real liability."

He fingered his diamond stickpin. "Let me talk to her. I'll think of something."

She came over and slipped her arms around his neck. "I love you, Billy. I keep hopin' maybe we can go away together. I almost puke every time Manning touches me."

"Be patient a little longer, baby. We need to get our hands in his money. You wouldn't want to run off to California dead broke." Billy kissed her forehead. He did care about her and was glad that doctor had cured his problem. He wouldn't want to give it to Lily. Curses on the bitch who had given it to him!

"But what about Deer—?"

"Let me handle everything, Lil." He stood up and pulled away from her. "You go on to bed and I'll take care of things. You don't know nothin' about nothin', if anything comes up."

She nodded and kissed him. Then quietly, he left her room. The parlor house had finally settled down for the night. Billy tiptoed to Deer's door and tapped lightly. No answer. A light shown dimly under the door.

"Deer? Are you in there?"

No answer. Very cautiously, he opened the door. Deer lay sprawled naked on her belly on the rumpled bed. "Deer?"

She didn't move. *Drunk again,* he thought with a sigh. He wished he'd never brought the Pawnee girl here. True, her punch bowl act drew crowds, but so would any pretty girl nude in a punch bowl. He hadn't told Lily he'd heard complaints about Deer's taste for liquor, too. Billy knew from experience that drunks always had loose mouths. Whatever that green officer had told Deer, he didn't want her telling the whole world.

268

"Deer?"

No answer. Billy went over to the bed. The lamp threw shadows on the wallpaper, on her beautiful naked body. Just what was he going to do about the girl? Ship her out of town? Sell her to some Comanchero off to the South who might have use for a pretty Pawnee? Billy had no stomach for killing, never had. Deep in his heart, Billy wasn't the street brawler everyone believed he was. If there was fighting or killing to be done, Billy paid to have it done.

"Deer?" The first thing he'd have to do was sober her up. He reached out to shake her, then jerked back when he touched her flesh. It felt like cold brown marble.

Oh, my God. Deer was dead.

Chapter Fifteen

Oh, my God! Gingerly, Billy reached out and touched her again. Ice cold. Only then did he notice the odd angle of her head. Although he hated to touch her cold flesh, Billy moved her head and decided her neck was broken. Who in the hell would do something like this? The lieutenant? A man would hardly kill a girl, then come sauntering to Lily's room to talk business. More than that, what was Billy going to do now?

Billy paced up and down a long moment, rubbing his chin. If he just left her, letting one of the girls find her in the morning, there'd be a murder investigation. Had Carter Osgoode been the killer? Billy sure didn't need the sheriff looking for Osgoode, asking him lots of questions.

What a shame she hadn't died accidentally in a way that no one would question—like maybe drinking herself to death. The police would investigate, sure, but not much.

What a helluva note! Billy ran his tongue around

the gap in his teeth. How ironic! He needed to get rid of the lieutenant, but he couldn't just turn him over to the authorities; he might talk too much. For right now, Billy had to save the officer's hide.

Suicide. He stopped to think. *If he shot her, put the gun in her hand* . . . No, that would bring everyone running before Billy could clear out.

What about throwing her down the stairs so it would look like she tripped? Again he might not be able to get away before girls stuck their heads out the doors and saw him in the hall. If only the damned broad had drunk herself to death or drowned in that punch bowl. Nobody would think much of that. Certainly she'd tried to drink the Gilded Lily dry in the few days she'd been here.

The punch bowl. Billy went to the door and peered up and down the hall. Even the whores were asleep now. He went to the bed, and took a deep breath, and picked up the naked corpse, already stiffening in death. All he needed to do was get caught carrying a naked body down the hall. He'd be the one hanged for murder and maybe even Manning's money wouldn't help. Besides, then he'd have to explain to Manning what he was doing here in the middle of the night. The old sonovabitch could be meaner than a stepped-on rattlesnake.

Floor boards creaked under his feet as he carried the body down the hall. It seemed a million miles down those dark stairs.

A dim light shone behind the bar, but the place was deserted. He saw the silhouette of the big punch bowl still setting on the stage.

His pulse pounding with apprehension, Billy carried Deer over to the stage, then gently lowered her so that her naked upper torso was in the half-filled punch bowl. He pushed her face down in the red wine and put a cup in her hand. "Little Injun gal, looks like you finally get all you want!"

The authorities would look in to it, sure; but not much when the other girls talked about how Deer liked liquor. It would look as if she tried to drink the punch bowl dry all by herself. And anyway, who would get excited about a dead Injun girl? Wasn't the army killing them every day? Not Pawnees, of course, but most whites didn't know one Injun from another.

He took one last look, satisfied that this was the best answer. He wouldn't warn Lily; that way she could be noticeably shocked when the girl was found. Now he had to do something about the lieutenant.

As Billy met his men and readied the wagons, he wondered if he could use Deer's death and simply blackmail Osgoode into keeping his mouth shut. But suppose he was innocent of that or, worse, got scared and told the police about the gun running?

He turned to his three tough henchmen. "We'll have someone else riding with us tonight; someone I don't trust, so watch what you say around him. He's going, but he's not coming back, if you get what I mean."

The three laughed and nodded. They had been with him a long time and could be trusted—as much as one crook can ever trust another. But greed made them partners. There was money to be made.

He sent them to load out, using Starrett Freight Line wagons. The arms were hidden in one of Manning's warehouses on the outskirts of town.

Then he went back to meet Osgoode.

The lieutenant grinned. "I was afraid you weren't coming."

You stupid sonovabitch, Billy thought, *women are to be enjoyed, not killed.* But what he said was, "Something came up and delayed me. Let's go."

They rode in silence, joined the shadowy three with the wagons and drove east out of town. There was a prearranged meeting place a couple of hours out of Denver and they would meet Tall Bull and his Dog Soldiers there.

Billy felt for the brass tokens in his pocket. He shouldn't have panicked. There was no real evidence.

He and Osgoode followed the wagons through the darkness to the rendezvous.

Tall Bull sat his Appaloosa pony on the little rise, watching for the wagons. In the last hours before darkness chased away the dawn, his war party waited silently around him. Finally the three wagons came into view, creeping along the ribbon of road in the moonlight toward the straggly cottonwoods on the creek bank below.

Snake grunted and motioned. "Ta Ton Ka Haska, why do we do business with these whites? Why don't we just kill them and take the guns?"

The chief of the outlaw Dog Soldiers shook his head. "Much as I would like to," he answered in the soft, musical words of the Cheyenne, "we need these coyotes! If we hang their scalps on our belts, who would bring us the next load of guns?"

"True," the ugly warrior said, "but someday when we think they can no longer be of any use to us, can we kill them?"

"Of course! Men who would sell out their own kind for profit have forfeited the right to live." He shifted his weight on the Appaloosa and watched the men pull the wagons into the shadows of the trees. "There is one more man than usual. I see the gleam of brass buttons in the moonlight."

"Maybe it is a trap," Snake said, straining to see. "Oh, Great Chief, let me be the one to accept the danger of riding in to see."

"We will all go." He nodded approvingly at Snake.

"Bear Cub? What is it you do?" He looked over at the crippled boy who rode with them, the sketch book in his hands.

Snake made a noise of derision. "What do you think? What he always does! He sits his horse and draws pictures."

"I—I didn't think you would mind," the boy apologized. "The moonlight was bright enough and I thought the scenery beautiful."

"Beautiful!" Snake laughed. "Spoken like a squaw admiring a string of beads!"

"It is no matter," Tall Bull said. Bear Cub was not a warrior, because of his crippled leg, but he was good with horses. The leader had brought the boy along only in case they stole some ponies and the herd boy could help with them.

They watched the men below them. When Tall Bull was sure there were no other soldiers with them but the one, he led his war party cautiously down the rise and surrounded the group of whites.

"Ah, Tall Bull, good to see you!" The white with the missing teeth came forward and held out his hand. Tall Bull brushed it aside, ignoring him while he confronted the one in horse soldier blue.

"Who is this *veho?*"

"He's all right," the one called Billy Reno said. "We will drink some whiskey and then talk business."

"We will talk business and *then* we will drink whiskey." Tall Bull glared at him. "When the whiskey comes first, the white men always get the best of the trade." He looked the whites over. All five scalps would look good hanging on his lodge pole, but he needed the men too much to enjoy that pleasure.

The soldier looked so frightened, Tall Bull wondered if he would dirty his clothes like a papoose.

"Do not be afraid, *veho*." He smiled. "We will have some food and smoke." He turned to look. Already his men were building a council fire. The man called Billy Reno and his crew were getting out food and tobacco.

"Come see what we bring to trade," Reno called. Tall Bull went over, watched them break open a crate, and nodded with satisfaction. The brass on the breeches of the new rifles gleamed dully in the moonlight.

The gap-toothed one said, "These are Winchester sixty-sixes. The whites call them Old Yellows because of the brass on them."

Tall Bull took the one the white held out, inspected it. "These are good," Tall Bull grunted. "Yes, these are *very* good."

The other man grinned. "I have fifty of these fine guns, one for each of your men. Now let us see what you bring to trade."

Tall Bull motioned to Snake who brought the bundles from the pack horses. "The settlers don't have much, but some of the covered wagons passing through had more."

They unrolled the bundles. There were many

trinkets that Reno shook his head at, but he took the gleaming coins and the packets of yellow dust the Dog Soldiers had taken from dead miners. There was a little jewelry, a few of the big ticking things that told white men the time of day. Tall Bull thought that if a man was too stupid to look up at the sun and know the time, he might be too stupid to understand the magic markings on the face of the thing, but that was not his concern.

The young soldier made an exclamation of dismay as he looked at the things. His face look pale as a fish belly in the moonlight.

He was a coward, Tall Bull decided, and he had no use for cowards. "What's the matter, soldier? Have not you seen white men lay out the plunder taken from slain Indians? Is this so different then?"

The man acted as if he didn't know what to say, and Tall Bull looked around at his war-painted braves and shook his head contemptuously. The Dog Soldiers were the bravest of all the Cheyenne warrior societies. But now most of the Dog Soldiers were renegades, unable or unwilling to accept being forced onto reservations because a few chiefs like Black Kettle had trusted the white man's word. That had cost Black Kettle his life.

In that month of the Freezing Moon the Cheyenne called Hikomini, and the whites called November, little more than half a year ago, the bluecoat officer called Yellow Hair had struck Black Kettle's camp on the Washita River in the Indian Territory. That chief and many Cheyenne were dead.

They finished the trading. Reno gathered up the

things he seemed to think valuable although Tall Bull had never decided what men saw of worth in the yellow dust that had sent thousands of them invading the Shining Mountains they called the Rockies.

He set a guard because he did not trust the whites not to try to take advantage of them if the braves got too drunk. The whites had brought coffee with lots of sugar, beef, and whiskey. The beef was not as tasty to the Indian tongue as buffalo, but already the buffalo were beginning to thin out and sometimes the Cheyenne went hungry. The hunters who came with the great steel horse that rode two iron tracks had seen to that.

Much dancing and singing began. Tall Bull and Snake did not drink much. Later Tall Bull would enjoy the whiskey the whites had brought, but he had not lived this long without being crafty as an old bear.

The young soldier, now that he had a belly full of firewater, took off his pistol, danced, and sang with wild abandon. Tall Bull looked over at Snake and registered his disgust. If this was the best the army offered, no wonder the Dog Soldiers had been able to hit them hard. Often the only thing that had kept them from defeating the soldiers were the wily Pawnee scouts who rode with the bluecoats.

Reno sat down next to Tall Bull in the fire light, drinking coffee. He offered Tall Bull and Snake cigars, then lit theirs and one for himself. "It has been a good trade," he said, "but soon we must go. It will be daylight."

Tall Bull enjoyed the taste of the smoke and looked toward the eastern horizon. Already the bright Morning Star hung there. "It is true, Reno.

And we have soldiers to kill. We think the cavalry will come looking for us any time. We have seen wagons of supplies arriving at that fort on the river."

"McPherson?" Reno said thoughtfully. "The Fifth's there with all their Pawnee. You'll do well to avoid them."

"We have run out of room to roam," Tall Bull said, sipping the whiskey from a tin cup. "They try to send us back to the Indian Territory. Those of us who love the cool plains of the north do not want to go."

"They say you break the treaty signed in '67."

"Treaty?" he snorted with contempt. "I signed no treaty! Tall Bull feels no need to go where I do not want because some white man's bootlicker made a mark on paper he could not even read!"

"In the end, they will send you back anyway," Reno said.

Tall Bull shrugged and stared into the fire. "Not the Dog Soldiers. They will not pen up Dog Soldiers like cattle. They can only overrun us with many, many soldiers and kill us. But before they do, we will take a life for every one they take, we will rape a woman for every one of ours they rape. The Dog Soldiers are the bravest of the brave!"

Reno nodded and leaned closer. "I want to make you a gift you will like."

Tall Bull grunted noncommittally. "I do not trust white men who offer gifts for no reason."

"Your men will like this." Reno fingered his glittering stickpin. "I make you a gift of the soldier, to do with as you please."

Tall Bull stared at him in surprise, the cup of whiskey halfway to his lips. "You betray one of your own men?"

"It—it has to do with a woman."

Tall Bull laughed. "White women have loose morals, everyone knows this. They do not even wear the *nihpihist*, the chastity belt that protects them. How does a white man know when his woman is virgin?" The Cheyenne were very protective of the chastity of their women.

"Besides that," Reno said, "you see how he is when he drinks? I worry that he might betray us to the army."

"We will not let him leave with you then," Tall Bull said, already thinking what punishment should be meted out to a man because of a woman.

"One more thing," Reno said. "My path crossed that of some Pawnees only a few suns ago."

"Pawnee?" Tall Bull leaned closer. No Cheyenne could pass up a chance to kill Pawnee. They had been enemies for many generations because years ago, the Pawnee had stolen the Cheyenne's Sacred Medicine arrows. As a result, the Cheyenne had had bad luck ever since, and only lately, the other sacred object, Tssiwun, the buffalo hat, had been defiled by a Cheyenne woman.

"They are heading back east to their village," Reno said, blowing smoke, "but first, they are headed south to that place we call Castle Rock to hunt and camp awhile."

Tall Bull frowned and shook his head. "The place of the Great Balanced Rock is a holy place—home to the thunder and lightning. We may not spill blood there."

"Not even Pawnee blood?" Snake asked.

"It is a temptation," Tall Bull admitted. Would some great bad luck come their way if they killed enemies in the magic place?

He smoked and considered Snake. Though not

279

well-favored so that maidens smiled at him, he was a brave man. If Tall Bull had a daughter the right age, he would give her as wife to Snake. He wondered suddenly what had happened to his sister, Sunrise Woman. She had a daughter about the right age. The girl was only a half-breed, true enough, but she was blood kin.

Bear Cub limped past on his twisted leg. The boy had been one of those children wounded at Sand Creek. Yes, the Cheyenne had many wrongs to avenge. Tall Bull thought he must remember to tell Bear Cub of some of the other battles the Dog Soldiers had fought in. It was good to have scenes of bravery put on paper to remember.

Reno stood slowly and signaled his three men. They got up and began moving toward the empty wagons. Reno gathered the bundle of coins and jewelry then turned toward his horse. Tall Bull watched the soldier. He was so drunk, he hadn't even noticed the other white men moving away from the fire as he drank and danced and sang.

Tall Bull motioned Snake to pick up the soldier's abandoned pistol, and some of the others to move between the bluecoat and his horse. The others were ready to pull out and still the soldier hadn't noticed.

The Dog Soldiers had noticed. One by one, they stopped dancing and moved where Snake signaled them to go. Now only the soldier still danced around the fire, so drunk he could hardly stand.

In the sudden silence, the soldier stopped uncertainly, looked around. His befuddled gaze went to Reno sitting on his horse. "Billy? Is it time to leave?"

"Time for *us* to leave." Reno leaned on his saddlehorn and the other white men exchanged knowing smiles.

The soldier stumbled toward them. "Then I'll get my horse and. . . ."

He seemed to realize for the first time that a line of war-painted warriors blocked his path. He looked appealingly over at Reno. "Billy, tell them. They don't understand."

Reno rubbed his chin and looked over at Tall Bull. "He's all yours!"

"No, Billy! Wait!" The soldier shouted even as braves grabbed him and Snake moved in with his knife. "Wait, Billy! Ye Gods! There's some mistake! They don't understand! What is he going to do—?"

His words ended with a scream as Snake cut open the blue pants as the warriors held the soldier. It wouldn't be hard to do, Tall Bull grunted with satisfaction. Snake had gelded stallions before.

Snake laughed. "He is built small for a man— more like a yearling!"

"Please!" The soldier wept and begged, "Oh, God, please!"

"You will mount no more women ever, so you have no use for your small manhood!" Snake's knife blade flashed in the firelight.

The soldier shrieked as the warrior cut him. Then the braves dragged him over to a level place, stripped his clothes away, and staked him out flat on his back.

With a sneer, the brave flung the bloody flesh in the soldier's face.

"Don't kill me!" the soldier wept. "Oh, please don't kill me!"

Tall Bull turned to Reno and the other whites now ready to leave with their wagons. "He will beg for death before the ants and the hot sun finally

281

finish!"

The one called Reno looked a little sick. "Why don't you just kill the poor devil?"

Tall Bull shook his head. "It is not our way. Good-bye, Reno. We will see you here again at the appointed time next autumn."

The four white men looked toward the naked man tied down by the fire, then at each other. Reno started to say something again, then he shrugged and touched the brim of his hat with two fingers. The whites turned and went back up the trail.

Tall Bull crossed his arms over his chest and watched the empty wagons pull away, the man called Reno riding in front of the line. Over by the fire, the soldier wept and screamed like a woman giving birth, not anything like a warrior.

Tall Bull had not much stomach for this anymore. He went back to the fire as the dawn turned the color of pale wild flowers in the east. He poured himself another cup of coffee and reached for more roasted beef as Snake and his men packed up the shiny new weapons so they could ride out. There was only one last trophy they wanted. With his knife, Snake took the curly brown scalp while the soldier whimpered and wept in babbling terror.

Soon the soldier would beg to die, but there would be no one to hear him. The ugly brave came back to the fire, the hair hanging from his belt. He wiped his bloody hands on the dry grass and reached for some whiskey. "I put one of those shiny coins on his belly so the bluecoats will know this is payment for the Dog Soldier they killed when they surprised our scouts a few days ago."

Tall Bull nodded. "It is just."

Snake grinned. "Have you decided whether we

may attack the holy place of the thunder and lightning?"

Tall Bull drank the steaming coffee and considered, ignoring the writhing, screaming white man. No one knew why, but at the edge of the Shining Mountains, there was a great rock balanced high on a hill. Storms blew out of these mountains more frequently than any other place he knew, and when that happened, lightning and thunder danced continually around the big rock as if God himself, Heammawihio, sat on that rock and directed it.

He could not pass up the chance to kill Pawnee. The Balanced Rock might be holy, but Tall Bull was willing to chance it.

"Yes." he nodded and stood up. "We will attack the Pawnee camp. After that, we will have a scalp dance before we divide our forces."

They both turned to watch the soldier writhing by the fire, but he was no longer of much interest to them. A man was judged on his valor, even in death, and the soldier could not even die well. Reno had been right not to trust him.

Snake turned back. "What is your plan, great chief?"

Tall Bull said, "When we divide into two war parties, I will take half to the south to attack settlements and the tracks of the Iron Horse. You will attack up along the river east of here."

"Near that fort?"

Tall Bull nodded and walked toward his horse. "But first, there are Pawnee dogs waiting to be killed!"

They rode out into the early dawn at a gallop. Behind them, the staked-out, naked man still screamed and wept like a woman.

Chapter Sixteen

This was an impossible situation, Luci told herself again. She had to get away from Johnny Ace. But where else could she get a job? Was she desperate enough to try to find work in the squalid little settlement of North Platte a few miles away?

Luci hesitated for the same reasons she hadn't considered the rough town before as an alternative. As a railway stop, North Platte was a small, brawling place — dangerous for a woman alone.

But she wanted to get away from Johnny. Luci gathered up her small bundle of belongings, caught a ride on the back of a supply wagon, and set out to find work. No one wanted to hire a half-breed maid or give her a job in any of the shops. Finally she got a job serving drinks in a tough, low-class saloon.

Although she was a little scared, she decided maybe she could take care of herself. But she did check her squalid little room to make sure there was a lock on the door. Maybe she could save up enough money to leave this area forever. She wouldn't let herself think any farther ahead than that.

That afternoon she managed all right. Business would be slow until dark, the sweaty-jowled bartender had told her. Then it would be hell with the lid off because it was payday for the track crews who kept the trains running.

Mercy! He was right, Luci thought as night came on and the place began to fill up. By dark, the saloon was full of soldiers, trappers, railroad men, renegades, and drifters. The faro tables were busy, the off-key piano loud, the beer flowing. She pushed her way through the crowd to deliver mugs to a table of rough-looking men playing cards in the early summer heat.

"Hey, girlie!" A brawny man in a dirty plaid shirt and heavy beard reached out and caught her arm as she passed his table.

"I've got work to do," she said, and tried to pull out of his hairy-armed grasp.

He laughed, let her go, and she carried the beer to the table behind him, set it down, and wiped her perspiring face. "Honey," said a lout at that table, taking a big gulp and wiping his mouth on his sleeve, "you ain't hardly big enough to carry that!" He slapped her on the rump as she passed.

Over at the piano, a blowsy, painted whore began to sing: *"De Camptown ladies sing dis song, Doo-dah! Doo-dah! De Camptown racetrack, five miles long, oh, doo-dah day . . ."*

With a weary sigh, Luci turned, went back to the bar, and picked up another heavy tray of drinks. "Where do these go?"

The barkeep wiped the shiny sweat off his jowls. "The bearded gorilla's table."

She hesitated, "Him?" She looked toward the big man in the dirty plaid shirt. He grinned back at her, apparently waiting for her to come to the table.

The bartender pushed the tray at her. "Don't make such a big thing of it. Let him handle you a little. He'll tip good."

She started to ask if the bartender would carry it, but knew by his expression that he wouldn't.

It was heavy. She balanced it, took a deep breath, and pushed through the laughing, jostling crowd. After setting it on the table, she tried to move away fast. She wasn't fast enough.

The giant track layer reached out and caught her arm again. "Now, girlie, you got time to set and talk awhile with Nick!" He jerked her down on his lap.

She took a deep breath and recoiled as she tried to pull back. He stank.

"I've got work to do." She tried to break his grip. "You let me go, and maybe I'll come back to your table later."

"What's wrong with now?" Before she could stop him, he pulled her against him and covered her mouth with his. His beard was wet with chewing tobacco. Luci shuddered and tried to pull away.

When she struck out at him, he caught her arm and twisted it until she whimpered in pain. "See, Squaw? Be nice to Nick! You got a room we can go to?"

Helplessly, she looked at the men around the table and those standing nearby. Some of them laughed sheepishly; others averted their eyes. Even the bartender got suddenly very busy wiping the bar and didn't look up.

She tried again to pull free. Nick laughed and held on to her easily, one big dirty hand going down inside her dress to fondle her breast. Fear made her reckless, and she fought him, but he only laughed. "You got spunk, girlie! That's how I like 'em. Any you fellas want to share her with me?"

But suddenly all the men seemed to be looking toward the door. Conversation gradually ceased, and even the piano stopped playing.

Nick looked up. "What's going on, keep that music going! I want . . ."

But there was only silence.

With a sob, Luci's gaze followed Nick's toward the front door.

Johnny Ace stood there, feet wide apart, hand on the hilt of the big knife in his belt.

The silence hung heavily over the suddenly silent room. Men begin to back away, clearing a path between the two.

"Mister," Johnny said so softly, it was almost a whisper, "that's mine. Let her up and let her up quick!"

"Injun, you got more grit than brains to come into a white man's saloon." The man leered back at him, slightly drunk. "If this little blue-eyed squaw is wearing your brand, I ain't seen it!" Defiantly, he pulled her even tighter into his grip, but his hand reached for an iron railroad spike in his belt and laid it on the table.

Johnny advanced slowly, his hand still on the big knife. "Maybe you don't hear good. I said, let her go!"

The crowd formed a ring now, an excited buzz going up and rising. *Fight!* they whispered. *Fight!*

Luci struggled to move again, knowing the railroad man was big, maybe even bigger than Johnny Ace, and that spike could be as formidable a weapon as Johnny's knife.

No matter what happened to her, she didn't want Johnny hurt. "Mercy, Johnny; it's — it's okay. I sat down here of my own free will." She tried to laugh. "Figure the tips would be better!"

But as he advanced, his dark face never changed from its mask of cold, killing fury. "Railroader, maybe you don't hear so good!"

She felt the man's muscles bunching under her and shouted a warning as he pushed her to one side and came up out of his chair, armed with the spike swinging wildly. "Okay, Injun bastard! Let's see you eat Nick's steel!"

An excited roar went up in the crowd that circled the two as they faced each other warily. "I bet on Nick!"

"No, that Injun looks like he can use that knife! Fifty dollars on the redskin!"

Nick hefted the spike in his hand. "Come on, Injun — " he gestured Johnny toward him — "come on and let me smash your head flat and then I'll ram this spike up your — "

But Johnny moved, quick as a cat. Three steps and he closed in on the man, skillfully dodging Nick's wild swing. Then he reached under Nick's guard and cut him across his hairy belly, exposing it through the dirty plaid shirt.

Then Johnny dodged backward.

Nick stood dripping blood, mouthing obscenities as he put his hand down, brought it up, and stared at the wet, scarlet trickle.

"Johnny, no!" Luci took a deep breath of the scent of blood, saw the look in Johnny's dark eyes, and knew he meant to kill the railroader.

"I'm not hurt! Let him go!"

Johnny shook his head, but he never took his gaze off the man's face as he advanced again. "No man puts his hands on my woman!"

"The hell I don't!" Nick snarled. "After I kill you, Injun, I mean to do more than handle her a little. While you're dying, I want you to see me lay her across a card table, and me and the boys—"

"You filthy bastard!" Johnny moved, fast as a rattlesnake's strike, up under Nick's arm, and slammed him back against the wall. The spike flew from the beefy hand. Nick stumbled, and went down. Like a hawk on a wounded rabbit, Johnny was on him, knife drawn back.

Luci caught his arm. "Enough, Johnny! You kill him and you'll face the law! Don't! I—I'll go with you!"

Her words seemed to work some kind of soothing magic. He hesitated and stood up slowly, looking down at the sobbing hulk cowering under his feet. He looked around. "Anybody else want to handle her?"

The crowd backed away, all shaking their heads, keeping their hands out where Johnny could see them.

Now he turned to Luci. "Sometimes I think you're almost more trouble than you're worth, Star Eyes."

"Then why don't you just stay away from me, and leave me alone?"

"Because you're mine," he said firmly. He reached out, took her in his arms, and carried her easily out the swinging doors into the night.

"I was trying to earn some money," she explained as he put her up on his horse then mounted behind her.

"You were trying to get away from me," he said against her hair. "I'll look after you, Luci. You can move into my quarters." He turned the horse around.

"In exchange for what?"

He looked down at her, one of his big hands hot on her thigh. "However you want it to be."

She felt confused by her mixed feelings. "I'm not a whore."

"No, you're not. I'd kill the man who called you that. Let's just say I can't seem to get along without you; I'm not sure I ever can."

She looked up at him. "I thought we agreed this can't work."

He flinched. "We'll take each day as it comes and not worry about the future."

I'll bet that's what my mother did, she thought miserably as he nudged Katis into a lope.

They rode in silence back to the fort. As late as it was, nothing stirred but the sentry, who challenged them then waved them on through when he recognized Johnny. They rode to the stable, where Johnny turned over his horse to a sleepy stable boy to bed down. Then he swung her up in his arms and started for his quarters.

"I can walk," she protested.

"I know that, but I like carrying you."

There was nothing else to do but relax against his wide chest and let him carry her to his quarters. Once inside, he let her slide to the floor and stood looking at her.

She didn't like the heat of his gaze in the flickering lamp light. "I'm going back to the trading post."

"No, you aren't. I want to know I can finally sleep at night without worrying about some man raping you."

"Except you, of course?" She took another step, but he turned and locked the door behind him.

"I've never done that and you know it." He advanced.

"No," she said, "you just put your hands on me, and make me lose all my reason and forget about the consequences." She put her face in her hands and began to sob.

He came over, lifted her chin with his hand, and kissed the tears away. "Luci . . . Luci . . . you're the one driving me *loco!*" He pulled her to him and kissed the corners of her mouth, kissed her cheeks, kissed her tears away.

With a sob, she threw her arms around his neck. "This is crazy!"

"I know it. God, how I know it!" He pulled her against him, patting her back and shoulders the way one does a child. She nestled her face in the hollow of his shoulder, feeling his manhood throbbing hard against her belly.

He was big enough to throw her across his bed and mount her anytime he wanted to, and she knew it. "How can you almost kill a man and then be so gentle with me?"

"You know. Why do you ask?" He kissed along her jawline, running his hands down the backs of her arms as his tongue found her ear and kissed there.

And she wanted him to. It made her weep to think she had so little control over her own body. He went to his knees, his arms clasped tightly around her hips, and buried his face against the soft vee of her thighs.

Hesitantly, she reached down and slid her long skirt up, knowing she wore nothing underneath but wanting his hot breath, his lips, touching her there.

With a groan, he buried his face against her naked body, kissing her there, running the tip of his tongue over the throbbing ridge of flesh. She couldn't stop herself from grasping his head, pressing him harder against her body. His hand pushed up under her dress, holding her small bottom against him as he kissed and caressed her with his tongue. "Johnny . . . Johnny . . ."

She wasn't sure she could keep standing as he teased her with his mouth; her legs were threatening to give way beneath her.

Just as she thought she would faint, he stood up, reached behind her to unbutton her dress, and pulled it off her shoulders. It fell at her feet.

"Luci, you're so very beautiful!" He swung her up in his arms and carried her to the bed.

In the flickering lamp light, he pulled off his buckskin shirt, his boots, and stepped out of his pants. She hadn't known a man's body could be beautiful—even one scarred by old wounds. His skin was deep brown and his manhood was big, erect, and throbbing.

She had forgotten how big he was. For a moment, she hesitated, her legs tightly closed.

"Luci, submit to me," he commanded in an urgent whisper. "You want this and you know it; surrender to me!"

Very slowly, she opened herself up like a flower to a bee. He tasted nectar there. She opened herself up even wider, arching up so his thrusting tongue could go even deeper as his lips caressed her velvet ridge.

"Oh, please, Johnny. . . ." She pulled him on top of her. He lay there a long moment before he slipped his body slowly, tantalizing inside hers. Then he rolled her over on top and reached to pull her breasts down to his lips. Luci sat up on him, grinding herself down on his iron bar of flesh. It felt as if she were being rammed up under her breasts every time she came down on him.

His hands gripped her waist and now he began to buck under her. When she leaned over, he caught her nipple between his teeth and laved the tip with his tongue. They were locked together as he shuddered and exploded within her.

Her body began to convulse. Then the bucking stopped and she rode him hard. The last thing she remembered was whispering, "I surrender, beloved enemy, take me . . . take me!"

Winnifred Starrett had had enough! It wasn't bad enough that she had been stuck at this miserable fort for several weeks because of the stage line shutting down over the Indian trouble; even the one man she found appealing, that Pawnee scout, was more interested in that half-breed laundry girl!

She'd seen them together last night, riding in mounted double on his horse. As she spied on them, he had swung Luci up in his arms and carried her to his quarters. What had happened after that, she could only guess. She went to bed by herself, lying sleepless and restless all night, thinking of what he must be doing to that girl. In a jealous rage, she imagined his hands and mouth all over that half-breed girl, doing to her what no one had ever done to Winnifred and what she wanted done so badly. Because of her father's women, she hated dark skin, but she had too much of his blood in her not to lust after it.

She lay there, twisting on the hot sheets, trying to decide what to do. Probably she ought to get on the train, go on up to Wyoming, and catch a stage to Denver from there. But suppose the stage from there wasn't running either? Would Winnifred be any better off stranded in some miserable collection of log huts in the wilds of Wyoming? It didn't seem any better than what she had.

She could go stay in the tiny town of North Platte just across the river from the fort, but that was an awful place, too. Tomorrow she'd inquire and see if the major knew when the stage to Denver might be running again.

When Winnifred finally dropped off to sleep, she dreamed she had a handsome Indian between her thighs, with another waiting to take his place. They were hung as big as stud bulls, and when they took turns thrusting into her, the throb in her insides finally ceased.

The next morning, Winnifred made a decision to use her father's power and money to get some action. After all, her father was rich, important, and knew many people in Washington.

Pulling her ebony hair up into a mass of curls on the back of her neck, Winnifred tied the wide cerise sash of her pale pink dress, admired her own trim waist in the mirror again, then picked up her lacy pink parasol, and set off to Major North's office to find out about the stage.

His window was open in the heat of the day and she heard voices from his office. She was not too honorable to eavesdrop.

"Luther, are you sure he deserted?" The major's voice.

"No, Frank, I'm not. Like I told you, Cody and I woke up in the hotel room and he was gone. He left this note."

Intrigued, she peeked over the windowsill to see Major North reading that note while his brother, Captain North, stood by his desk. The handsome scout with the long curls, Cody, sat with one booted foot crossed over his knee.

The major shook his head, then grunted. "I knew Osgoode didn't like the army—he was too much of a spoiled weakling for it—but I never thought he'd desert."

Cody tipped his hat back. "Still, he's gone without a trace except for this note."

The major pulled at his mustache. "Maybe he stumbled onto something and someone killed him for it."

Luther shrugged. "There's no evidence of that. Maybe this is a trick to confuse us while he goes over the hill to California."

"Find out anything about the tokens?"

Cody shook his head. "We went to that place, but they acted like they didn't know what we were talking about. Maybe that dead Injun did take them off some miners."

"Besides," Luther broke in, "it was hard to get anyone to talk to us because of all the excitement with the sheriff and all; it seems one of the whores had fallen into a punch bowl and drowned."

North's eyebrows went up. "What?"

Cody shook his head. "No big thing. You know how those whores drink. She tried to drink it dry,

I suppose, and fell into it before she got to the bottom."

North sighed, leaned back in his chair, and put his feet up on his desk. "Didn't you learn anything?"

Luther gestured with frustration. "You have to understand, Frank, Denver is a wild boomtown. There's lots of men on the run from the law and nobody sticks his nose in anyone else's business. If anyone knew anything, they weren't talkin'."

The major steepled his fingers as he thought. "Maybe Osgoode did desert, and headed for parts unknown. Maybe he left that message to throw you off the trail."

"Reckon we may never know if he doesn't turn himself in." Luther sighed. "Anything happen while we were gone?"

"No, thank God for small favors! We haven't heard any reports about the Dog Soldiers in days. Maybe they've headed back to the reservation, or at least cleared out of this area."

"Don't count on it." Cody looked grim.

"The stage company is willing to gamble on it. They've lost a lot of money with their routes shut down. Now that we've finally found and fixed the cut telegraph line, the stages must be going to run again. At least, we've gotten a wire there's a special one coming through to Denver this afternoon."

"They'll think 'special' if they run into a war party!" Luther snorted. "Must be someone or something important on it to take that chance!"

The major shrugged. "Donno. Probably some bigwig stuck somewhere and getting impatient to get where he's going; although he might think twice when it comes time to go."

Winnifred turned away, already bored with her eavesdropping. It didn't concern her, so she didn't find it interesting except for the part about the stage coming through this afternoon. She'd send her father a wire that she was on her way so he could meet her. In fact, maybe Father had arranged this stage just for her; but no, if he had done that, surely he would have wired her here at the fort. As far as Carter Osgoode was concerned, what if that fortune hunter had deserted? That didn't surprise her a bit.

On her way back from sending the telegraph, she saw Johnny Ace ride by. She tried not to look at him, but she couldn't help it, wondering what he looked like naked. She envisioned him again, dark against her fair skin. In a rush of heat, she imagined herself with fair legs wrapped around a dark-skinned body. She bit her lip, chagrined. She must be just like her father after all.

Winnifred remembered little of Manning Starrett. Her father had been gone from her life a long time. But she did remember the night of the big argument.

Father had been serving in the army and was home again. How long ago had it been? A dozen years? More? Less? Winnifred couldn't be sure. She only remembered she was young and it was before the war, because they still had slaves on the plantation her mother had inherited.

Her parents had sent her to bed. She was awakened by loud, querulous voices and tiptoed to peek around the door of her mother's bedroom.

". . . damn you, Manning, you've given me the pox! How could you bring your whores' diseases home to me?" Her mother's plain, homely face was red from weeping.

Her handsome father only yawned. "Oh, get your doctor to give you some mercury capsules; that's what I've been taking. As to my women, you've known about them a long time, Clara."

"They say it's incurable!" More weeping. "They say—"

"Oh, shut up, you'll wake Winnifred!" He stood there half-dressed, and annoyed.

"You don't care about her any more than you do me! Admit it! You married me for my money!" She collapsed on the edge of the bed, sobbing. The small girl wanted to run to her, comfort her, but she stayed where she was.

"Okay, I married you for your money, you knew that. Why else would anyone marry a homely thing like you?"

"And now that you've about gone through that, I suppose you'll finally leave me—"

"Why do you think I joined up?" His tone was scathing. "It gave me a perfectly honorable way of escaping for months at a time. Yes, I'm leaving for good. My hitch is about up and there's rumors of gold in Colorado—"

"You don't seem like the type to sweat over a pick and shovel." Her mother's tone was bitter as she glared back.

"There's easier ways than that." Father laughed. "Lonely rich women like yourself—"

"And dark ones—the kind you really like!"

"You'll never really forget about catching me in your maid's bed, will you?"

"I sold her down the river, but I couldn't do anything about you!"

"All right! I like them with dark skin—niggers, Injuns, mixed bloods. And do you know why, my dear wife?" He went over, put his face close to

298

hers. "Because they have hot, passionate natures, that's why! Because, unlike you who lie there like a thin wooden board and submit, those dark ones are all mouth and claws and tits, and—"

"Stop it! Stop it!" She was screaming now, hands over her ears to keep from hearing him. "Get out! Get out!"

"With pleasure, my ugly, cold wife." Manning grinned cruelly as he reached for his shirt. "As you said, the money's about gone anyway from my gambling and wild ways. You and Winnifred may be able to survive on what's left."

"What about Winnifred? Don't you care about your own daughter?" More hysterical weeping.

"I'm afraid she's too much like you, Clara." He turned and was gone forever.

No, not forever. He had returned one more time to commit her mother to an asylum. The disease he had given her had progressed to gradually destroy her mind. And now he was ailing. Revenge was going to be sweet, Winnifred thought with a determined shake of her beribboned head as she walked across the fort grounds to the telegraph office. He thought she was coming to Colorado to be a nurse maid.

Instead, first chance she got, Winnifred intended to put him in an asylum as he had done her mother, and take control of his fortune!

Chapter Seventeen

Winnifred thought of his final words as she returned to her quarters to pack. No, she wasn't like her mother at all. Manning Starrett's blood ran hot in her veins. In the next few years as her young body matured, she found herself drawn to the black and brown and cream-colored slaves of her mother's plantation.

She began to spy on the slaves when they swam naked in the creek; when they made love in the barn, in the fields. Winnifred was fascinated by the rippling dark muscles, the intertwined bare legs and arms. So that was how it was done.

She began to have dreams, fantasies about dark-skinned males doing those things to her. She would lie in bed at night, aching with desire, and imagine some handsome swarthy stallion humping between her thighs. Yes, she was very much like her father after all. The fact terrified her because she wanted to be more like her saintly mother. Not that she ever acted on her lusts. The results, if she got caught, would be too terrifying. On the next plantation, such a thing had happened. The master had forced his beautiful young wife watch him geld her dark lover and then had killed them both.

The war began and things were terrible for everyone in the South. She could only be glad her mother was going insane and couldn't know her whole civilization was crumbling into ruin around her. But it cost money to keep Clara in that place. In the last few months, there hadn't been any and the slaves had all been freed so it was almost impossible to keep the plantation running.

The war ended and Clara died, insane and screaming. Manning Starrett had written to Winnifred right after her mother's death. Yes, she would go out to Colorado Territory, pretend to be the loving, caring daughter—until she could seize control of his assets and dump him in the worst madhouse she could find.

Money was power. Once she had his, she would finally choose a man to take her virginity, a man like that scout, bronzed and virile. Her dreams would finally become reality. Maybe she would have more than one man. With money, she could have a whole harem of dark-skinned studs and thumb her nose at convention. Yes, when she was in control, she'd come back here and offer Johnny so much money to be her business manager or butler that he'd come to Denver and forget about that little half-breed girl.

Winnifred hurried back to her quarters and began to pack. She had her trunks ready and sitting on the porch of the trading post when the stage pulled in. As the driver and guard loaded her luggage in the boot of the stage, Major North came out of his office, frowned when he saw her, and came over.

"Miss Starrett, I didn't realize you had decided to leave—"

She decided to ignore the disapproval in his eyes. "I've already telegraphed my father I'm on my way."

"Just because the stage is running again doesn't necessarily mean it's safe to take it. If you'd stay a little longer, maybe I'll get orders to begin sending an army escort with the civilian—"

"That's hardly necessary," she replied in her most snobbish tone. "I'm quite weary, Major, of your miserable little fort. Besides, I'm sure it will be perfectly safe."

"You notice no one else is taking the stage?"

Winnifred looked around. There weren't any other passengers. Maybe they would pick up some along the way. "Major, my mind is quite made up. My father will be expecting me in Denver."

And to preclude other discussion, she snapped her pink parasol shut with a flourish and let the driver assist her into the stage. She sat down with a flounce of blossom pink skirts, hair ribbons, and wide silk sashes.

The major gestured helplessly. "Miss Starrett, I won't be held responsible by your father if—"

"Land's sake! I didn't ask you to!" She leaned out the window. "Driver, aren't we scheduled to leave?"

The mustachioed driver tipped his hat to her. "Beggin' yore pardon, ma'am, if I was you, I'd listen to the major—"

"I have a bonafide ticket, do I not?" Her tone was scathing.

"Yes, ma'am." At this point, the driver gave the officer a resigned look, sighed, shrugged, and climbed back up to the seat of the stage along with the shotgun-wielding guard.

Johnny Ace rode by just then but didn't even see her as he passed. She had a sudden vision of herself lying naked beneath this virile, noble savage. He was thrusting between her thighs, driving deep into her virginity. . . .

Major North looked in the window. "Miss Starrett, does your father know you're doing this? Do you have his permission?"

"Of course!" she lied. Actually she'd sent a wire for him to meet the stage, and wasn't waiting for a reply. He might tell her to wait until the latest outbreak was settled. Winnifred didn't want to spend one more night here, knowing that Johnny Ace was mounting that little chit of a half-breed when he was so welcome in Winnifred's bed.

"Well, then . . ." The major looked undecided as to what he should do.

"Are you prepared to drag me off this stage bodily, Major?"

He backed down. "No, of course not, only—"

"Thank you for your hospitality," she drawled. "You must come to call on my father and me if you should ever be in Denver."

Major North sighed and nodded, stepping away from the coach. Evidently he had decided not to cross her and bring her wealthy father's wrath down on the post. She didn't look back as the stage pulled away.

They didn't pick up any passengers at the next stage stop or the one after that. What they got instead were dire warnings of Indian signs and smoke signals.

The second day, she wished she had listened to Major North. The stage pulled into the station—what was left of it. The driver swore as it lumbered to a stop and Winnifred stuck her head out the window to see what he had upset him.

Smoldering ruins. The station and all its buildings were heaps of blackened rubble. Here and there, a wisp of smoke still drifted into the still air.

The driver and the guard climbed down, poking about in the wreckage. Impatiently, Winnifred jerked open her door and climbed out, too.

Both men carried guns as they walked about, looking. Winnifred stood by the stage, not quite sure what to do. "Maybe someone dropped a kerosene lantern," she suggested, "and the fire spread."

The driver looked back over his shoulder at her. "Then the people would still be around, wouldn't they? If I was you, miss, I'd stay in the coach."

She didn't like being told what to do. Besides, she needed desperately to relieve herself. She spotted the outhouse still standing, went over, and yanked open the door. She stumbled back, screaming.

The body was pinned against the inside of the door with a feathered lance. Evidently the man had been surprised just as he began to pull up his pants to come out.

The two men came running.

"Is it Hank?" the driver said.

"Yep," said the guard, "or what's left of him. "I'll bet we find his helpers off in the brush somehow."

The driver pulled an arrow out of the body. It

had striped feathers on it.

The guard nodded, and looked toward the wooden crates tied on top of the stage. "We need ammunition, and they're shipping Bibles from Boston!"

"Maybe if they attack us, we can quote Scripture to them." The driver spat a stream of tobacco juice.

Winnifred blinked. Sure enough, the wooden crates on top of the stage were plainly marked: BOSTON BIBLE SOCIETY.

It was all so ridiculous. She began to laugh. Then suddenly the sights and smells overcame Winnifred and she stumbled off into the brush to be sick. It was there she found the helpers—or what was left of them.

This time, she couldn't even scream. She could only sob and run back to the coach. This couldn't be happening to her. No one would dare frighten or inconvenience the daughter of the richest, most powerful man in Denver—would they? Money and power bought everything.

The driver strode over to where she had run from. She heard him cursing. Then he came over and leaned in the window. "Miss, you stay with the coach. Hank and I'll bury them."

She was sobbing now and afraid—very much afraid. "Land's sake! Let's leave right this minute! Right this minute, y'all hear me?" She clutched her parasol to her. It seemed the only evidence she had at the moment that somewhere out there was an orderly, civilized society that cared about such niceties.

The guard leaned on his shotgun. "We can't just go off and leave them, miss. It may be days before a cavalry patrol comes by here."

She had not been this terrified through the entire war. She sat there trembling while the pair dug a hasty, shallow grave for the tortured remains.

The guard said, "Maybe we should go back to the fort and get an escort."

"And suppose them Injuns are between us and the fort? All the sign looks like they rode out here east. Besides, remember there seemed to be some reason this stage had to get to Denver. Remember how the man stressed that point?"

There were no fresh horses. The Indians had stolen them all. So they went on with the tired team they came in with, but much slower now.

Winnifred began to calm down. If the stage was stopped by Indians, she would hurry to tell them she was Manning Starrett's daughter. Surely even the Indians had heard of him. When they heard that, they would not only let her go unharmed, they might even give her an escort to Denver.

On the other hand . . . As the coach bumped along through the swirling dust of the hot day, she envisioned being captured by a handsome Noble Savage who looked a lot like Johnny Ace. No, he wouldn't just be a warrior; he would be an important chief. He would fall in love with her, and mesmerized by her beauty, he would kidnap her and have his way with her.

She leaned back in the seat and fanatisized about his skillful lovemaking that brought her to unbelievable heights of ecstasy. He would pledge his undying love and they would cavort naked like true children of nature. Finally she would go on to Denver, but Handsome Chief would come there often and climb her trellis in the darkness to couple with her again and again.

Oh, if only the real thing turned out to be half

as good as she imagined when it finally happened! Winnifred's pulse pounded with excitement and desire as she replayed the Noble Savage Carries White Girl Off fantasy in her head.

Winnifred wished she could have a bath. The heat of early summer settled over her like the dust churned up by the stage. The wide sash of her pink dress was smudged and dirty, her hair ribbons hung limply, and her hair was falling down her neck as her hair pins loosened. The lace parasol had been tossed on the opposite seat as useless.

She would not think of how miserable this trip had turned out to be. It would soon be over. When she finally reached Denver, there would be money and excitement. She intended to make her father pay dearly for what he had done to her mother. But in the meantime, it would be wonderful to be part of wealthy Denver society.

She imagined being the center of attention at a ball. "Tell me, Miss Starrett, is it true you came through hostile territory on the stage?"

She would wave her fan airily, flirting with the handsome men who clustered around her. "It was nothing, really. Some of the Indians rode right up to the stage and stopped it."

The women stared wide-eyed. "Weren't you petrified?"

"Land's sake, no!" She would flutter her fan. "What y'all don't understand is that these Indians are just like simple children—Noble Savages. A handsome chief fell in love with me and begged me to come live in his tipi. But I told him, of course, that I had to get to Denver to attend this ball, so he let me go."

Even the men listened with admiration. "Miss

Winnifred, you are so beautiful and so very brave!"

She liked that daydream so much, she relived it a dozen times as the stage swayed along. *Well, it could happen.* Somewhere between here and Denver, the stage might stop to rest the horses. Winnifred would find a stream to bath in. She would look up to find a handsome, virile Cheyenne chief watching her from the stream bank. He would look just like the idealized paintings in her poetry books.

When she started to scream, he would say to her in excellent English, "Don't scream, Beautiful One. I've been following your coach all these miles. I want to be your first man and teach you to enjoy love!"

And he would grab her, tie her up, and kiss her tenderly all over as he carried her over beneath a tree and made passionate, tender love to her. Maybe he would tie her up. After all, a lady couldn't be blamed for letting a brown stud make love to her if she was helpless and at his mercy. She couldn't stop him because she was a captive— nor did she want to.

He would be so handsome and virile and so wonderful when he finally entered her, his dark body straining against her pale one. His name would be something like Flying Hawk, or Running Horse. He would beg her to go with him and live in the woods, where they would make love continuously and eat roasted deer and berries. At night, they could lie in a tipi and listen to the rain outside while they made love.

Finally after Flying Hawk had taught her all the delights of love, he let her go back to her stage coach. He would pledge undying devotion and wave good-bye. He would fade into the distance with all his braves as they rode off into the sunset.

But no, she hadn't seen the last of him. The Noble Savage would then sneak into Denver in the night, climb the trellis outside her window, and make love to her. If she resisted, he would tie her up so she was helpless while his hands and mouth touched every inch of her naked body. She would be unable to do anything to resist him while he taught her all the forbidden delights of love.

Yes, she liked this daydream. She could have it all that way—her father's money (after she threw him in a madhouse as he had done her mother) and a dark Noble Savage who made love to her night after night as he crawled up the trellis. Some nights, she would tie him up and do things to him that made him gasp with delight.

Abruptly, she was startled out of her daydream by the driver's shout and the sudden crack of his whip. Immediately, the stage jerked forward and began to move at a fast clip.

Winnifred, annoyed at having her reverie disrupted, stuck her head out the window to scold him.

That's when she saw the riders in the distance. Oh, thank God, they were going to get a cavalry escort. They were going to—

Land's sake, Indians! Her heart almost stopped as she recognized the mounted, almost naked men galloping after the stage.

"Cheyenne!" the driver shouted. "Get back in, miss!"

But she was too mesmerized to do anything but

stare at the riders now rapidly gaining on the coach. There must have been at least fifty of them, all war-painted, dark-skinned, and almost naked. Somehow none of them looked like the handsome chief of her dreams. They all seemed to be armed with shiny new rifles that reflected the sunlight like mirrors.

She was both terrified and excited. Of course there was no danger, she thought, pulling back inside as the guard fired at the riders. If the Indians stopped the coach, she would explain who she was.

Her ears rang with the firing of the guns above her, the echo as the Indians returned the fire. Dust whirled up from the trail, choking her, clinging to her pale dress and hair and skin.

Terror began to take over—mindless terror. She would not think of that. She would think of her Noble Savage. He would be both handsome and gallant—begging her to go with him, kissing her fingertips when she insisted she really must be going on to Denver. Winnifred closed her eyes as the stage bounced along. Somehow the bronzed man looked a lot like Johnny Ace.

When she opened her eyes, naked riders galloped along on both sides of the coach, grinning in at her. *I must not be afraid,* she told herself, her heart pounding uncertainly. When they knew who she was, they would let her go.

A shot, a scream, and the driver fell past her window to the dirt. She stuck her head out. Already braves had jumped from their horses and were pulling out their knifes and . . .

Oh, no! Land's sake, this wasn't the way the daydream went at all! Sheer terror took over, and she felt the sudden, warm wetness as she wet her drawers. How humiliating. This wasn't the way it was supposed to happen at all.

The stage faltered and began to slow. Indians jumped up on the still-moving coach and climbed in her doors.

This couldn't be happening to her. In her shaking terror, she squeezed her eyes shut.

Yes, she was at the ball. Do tell us again of your narrow escape, Miss Winnifred.

Her fan fluttered at the cluster of elegant people. Just as the savages were about to . . . well, you know, the Handsome Chief galloped up on his magnificent black stallion, and forbade them to touch me. . . .

The stage stopped with a lurch. Slowly Winnifred opened her eyes to look into an ugly, paint-smeared face. His skin was dark, all right, but he looked greasy and grimy and she could smell him from here. What had happened to the Indian of her dreams?

She must not show fear. Indians respected bravery. It took her two tries to speak. "I—I am Winnifred Starrett," she said primly, forcing herself to smile. "My—my father—"

"Me, Snake." the Indian grinned back, exposing a mouthful of dirty, bad teeth.

At least this Simple Savage spoke English. Hope began to build in her quaking soul. "I am Winnifred Starrett of Denver. I—I am in sympathy with your people and all Noble Savages everywhere. Now if you will get a message to my father, who is a friend of the Great White Chief in Washington—"

He struck her then, slamming her back against the seat, "Shut up, white squaw!"

Pressing her palm against her stinging cheek,

311

she looked down, horrified at the crimson trickling down the front of the blossom pink batiste and across the dainty rosebuds of her wide sash. "You don't understand. My father—"

He grabbed her arm and dragged her out of the coach. She fought for control so that she would not give way to hysteria. *She must remember not to show fear.* Indians respected bravery. Out of the corner of her eye, she saw a brave opening and closing her parasol with wonder in his eyes. Others cut the lathered horses loose and dug in the wooden crates.

One of them held up a Bible and yelled a question in his language. The ugly Snake shrugged and motioned him away. *Bibles. Three crates of Bibles from Boston.* Somehow it seemed almost funny. She had to struggle with herself not to laugh and laugh over it.

Don't show fear. Keenly aware of her wet drawers, Winnifred stood there, trembling and looking around as the Cheyenne Dog Soldiers crowded closer. None of them looked handsome to her behind the dirt and gaudy war paint. All of them smelled like sweat and grease and the smoke of a thousand campfires.

Frantically, she looked around the circle for the Handsome Chief of her daydreams. None of these were any better-looking than the ugly Snake, and the way he was looking at her terrified her.

What had happened to the driver and guard? Winnifred turned to look back at the limp bodies. Knife blades and hands gleamed wetly scarlet as the braves took the scalps. One of them brought them to Snake.

He grunted with satisfaction as he examined them and hung them from his belt. Then he turned back to her and put his hand on her sleeve. His brown fingers left red smears.

Winnifred's heart pounded so hard, she was sure he could hear it. Backing slowly away, she knew she must try again. "I—I am Winnifred Starrett. My father is *the* Manning Starrett of Denver. No doubt you have heard of him? I am very much in sympathy with the noble Red Man—"

Snake reached out with his knife and cut her dress down the front as the others crowded closer.

"Are you crazy! This is an expensive gown!" She pulled the front together with her hands.

But he laughed, reaching out as the others yelped encouragement like a hungry wolf pack. Snake grabbed the torn front of the expensive dress and ripped it away.

She had been as brave as she could be. With a cry, Winnifred tried to turn and run, but he caught her and tore the rest of the dress from her struggling body.

"Oh, no, please!" Y'all don't understand!" She tried to cover her dainty lace underwear with her hands. *Where was the handsome chief, the dark-skinned brave who would claim her for his own, save her from these filthy, smelly wretches?*

Winnifred began to run. The Indians behind her laughed and jeered. Obviously they were playing some kind of game with her.

She kept running. The sun felt hot on her half-naked body. Up there ahead were some small trees, maybe she could lose herself in them.

Behind her, the Indians took up the chase, running her a few yards. Then seemingly tiring of the game, Snake caught her, ripped away the rest of her clothes, and pulled her to him.

This wasn't how she had pictured it at all. In

sheer horror, Winnifred screamed and fought. He signaled to the others. They came running with scraps of her white petticoat, her silk sash. Even as she fought, he reached to pull the ribbons from her hair,

"No, you don't understand! I am Winnifred Starrett, a rich girl from Denver—"

"Shut up, white girl!" He hit her across the face hard enough to stun her and let her fall to the ground. Someone was spreading her out on her back, spread-eagling her. The ground was hot beneath her naked skin.

Winnifred struggled, but a warrior took her wrists, tied them together with her dainty rosebud sash, staked them down above her head.

She flayed wildly with her legs, screaming while she did so. They stuffed the bit of petticoat in her mouth, almost choking her. Her bright hair ribbons were looped around her trim ankles, spread apart, and staked down.

She lay helpless.

Now the ugly leader pulled aside his loincloth. His aroused manhood looked as big as the stud bull's on her mother's plantation—bigger than any of the male slaves humping a dark girl in a cotton patch.

This couldn't be happening to her. Any moment, she would wake up safe in her own bed back home. Either that, or the handsome chief would ride to her rescue, make them free her, swing her up on his stallion, and carry her to safety.

She struggled against her bounds, tried to cry out in protest, but she could barely breath with the gag.

All the fifty had their loincloths pulled aside now, coming toward her. She hadn't saved her virginity all this time to let some filthy savage with bad teeth take it. Any moment, she would wake up from this fantasy gone awry. Any moment . . .

The leader knelt between her thighs, holding his swollen manhood in his hand and leering down at her. The fresh blood had dried on his hands. He leaned over and put his bloody, filthy hands on her white breasts.

She tried to protest, to tell him who she was. But he paid no attention to her muted sounds. He ran his bloody hands over her creamy thighs. Grinning with pleasure, he rammed into her like a rifle stock, tearing her apart. He rose up, grunting with satisfaction at the scarlet stain on his throbbing flesh. Then he came into her again, putting all his power and muscle behind his thrust, This time, he went all the way up into her protesting body.

Winnifred screamed in pain but couldn't get the sound past the gag in her mouth, Her insides seemed to be on fire, the savage grunting like an animal as he rode her, thrusting deep into her, his dirty hands squeezing her breasts. In seconds, he shuddered and she felt his hot seed spewing into her torn flesh.

He stood up, indicating her blood on him, evidently pleased to have taken her virginity. The others were coming at her now, fifty of them, all waiting for their turn. Winnifred Starrett, daughter of the richest man in Denver, was about to get more dark men between her thighs than she had ever dreamed of.

Chapter Eighteen

Johnny Ace leaned against the door post inside Major North's office, rolling a cigarette as the officer opened the folded message Johnny had just carried over from the telegrapher.

The officer's face furrowed darkly.

"Pani Le-shar, is there something wrong?"

North crumpled the message and threw it against the wall with a gesture of frustration. "Orders from General Carr. That stage never made it to Denver!"

With mounting dread, Johnny hesitated, then finished rolling the smoke and stuck it in his mouth. "Maybe it just lost a wheel somewhere along the way and is delayed at a stage station."

The slightly built officer gave him a long look. "Do you really believe that?"

Johnny paused with a match halfway to his lips. "No." He shook out the match in disgust. *Cheyenne Dog Soldiers*. He thought of the arrogant beautiful girl who had ridden that stage. "Boots and saddles?"

"Boots and saddles in twenty minutes!" North stood up. "Osgoode ever turn up?"

"No." Johnny shook his head and tossed away the unlit cigarette.

They strode out the door together, but North signaled a sergeant and his bugler, and stopped to give orders while Johnny ran toward the barn.

Before he made it past the trading post, the loud, clear notes of the bugle calling men to saddle up echoed through the fort.

Luci stood in the heat hanging clothes. She turned at the signal of the bugle, her face showing that, like everyone else on the post, she knew something big had happened. "Boots and saddles? Johnny, what is it?"

He paused. "That stage didn't make it to Denver."

"Mercy! The one Winnifred took?"

He nodded and turned to go. "We'll be riding out to see."

"Anything could have happened."

He looked down into her tense face, wanting to reach and out and touch her, but forcing himself to keep his hands at his sides. "Anything could have, but both of us know what's most likely."

"You don't know that it was Cheyenne."

"Luci, what else could it be?"

She looked away, conflict and indecision in her eyes. Around them, troopers ran in all directions as the cavalry made ready to ride out on short notice. "You'll be leading soldiers out there to kill my people."

There was no point in pussyfooting about it.

317

"Most likely. That's my job, Luci. The army has to protect citizens."

"You Pawnee would grab at any excuse to kill Cheyenne!" Her voice rose.

"Look, Luci, I've got to go. We'll talk about this when I get back."

"No, we'll talk right now!" Her bright blue eyes blazed at him. "You'll come back with scalps hanging from your belt, Cheyenne blood on your hands, and want to sleep with me as though nothing had happened!"

"We both knew it would come to this."

"You're damned right!" She pulled away from him. "If you go out on this patrol, Johnny Ace, I—I'll be out of your quarters when you get back."

"Don't do this to me, Star Eyes!" He grabbed her by the shoulders and shook her. "Don't make me choose between love and duty! You can't expect me to refuse to go!"

"You'll have to choose between me and your beloved major." Her voice turned cold.

"If Pani Le-shar goes out without a top scout, his troops might get ambushed or led into a trap. I can't do that to him. You shouldn't ask me!"

"Then don't come to my bed when you get back with blood on your hands!"

He hesitated, seeing by her expression that she meant it. He loved her as he had never loved a woman, but he could not—would not—shirk his duty. "I'm a man, Luci, and I don't bow to ultimatums."

The bugle blew again. Johnny reached out, jerked her into his arms, and kissed her. Her lips almost opened in surrender, her body began to melt against his, then she turned stiff and wooden in his embrace. "Get your hands off me, Pawnee!"

With an oath, he turned and strode away toward the barn. When the troops rode out, she wasn't standing with the other women, waving good-bye. Probably right now, he thought bitterly, she was getting her things out of his quarters. They had both known from the first that this could never work, and yet, they had been irresistibly drawn to each other.

He didn't look back as the troop headed out the big gates. His enlistment would be up in July. This time, he decided, he was going to leave the army, and put as much distance as possible between him and the half-breed girl.

Several days out from Fort McPherson, Johnny spotted a tiny wisp of smoke in the distance. At first, he hoped it might be a campfire or a small prairie fire set by lightning, but in his heart, he knew better.

The major sent him up ahead to scout it out, thinking they might have run onto a war party. But when Johnny topped a small rise and saw the wrecked stage coach abandoned on the road, his worst fears were realized. He rode back at a gallop to report in. The troop rode forward, weapons ready in case of ambush. In the middle of the trail before they reached the wrecked and burned stage, they found the guard—or what was left of him.

Johnny's stomach churned and he looked away as the flies rose in a noisy cloud. Even holding his breath didn't dim the stench. He must be getting soft. Once the sight of death had not bothered him. Warriors were raised to die in battle. He had always expected to go that way himself. Now life seemed very precious to him; any life lost seemed like such a tragic waste. That star-eyed girl was ruining him as a soldier.

What was left of the driver lay charred in the half-burned wreckage of the stage. The major yelled for a burial detail and rode up next to Johnny. "Was it Cheyenne?"

Johnny nodded, pointing to a striped feather arrow. "Turkey feathers. Their favorites."

Another scout galloped up to Johnny, asking the same in Pawnee. Johnny nodded and made the hand sign for that tribe, running his right forefinger across his left: *Cheyenne*.

North cursed. "Well, that's the driver and guard. I guess they've carried off the girl."

Behind them, Luther North yelled, "Frank, shall we try to do anything about the stage?"

The major shook his head. "Is there anything of value on it, Lute?"

Captain Luther North dismounted and looked around. "Three wooden crates, only slightly damaged. Looks like the braves opened them to see if there was anything of value."

North leaned on his saddle horn. "Is there?"

Luther dug in the top of one of the boxes and shook his head as he held up a half-burned book. "Bibles. Looks like three crates of Bibles from the Peabody Bank in Boston."

The major snorted in derision. "One of those donations from some rich liberal back East, no doubt! He should come out and see for himself what we're dealing with, then he might ask Congress to send us guns!"

Luther stood up. "Shall I get a burial detail?" His brother nodded.

Johnny sat his horse, looking around. *What had happened to Winnifred?* Probably they had taken her with them to satisfy the warriors' physical needs for a while, before selling her to the Comanchero, who would sell her south of the border for use in a whorehouse. At least she must be still alive. He'd been expecting to find her raped and tortured body near the driver's. When a war party was setting a fast pace, often they didn't want to be slowed down by a captive.

He turned Katis, riding slowly along the brush, looking for clues. A slight movement in the undergrowth caught his eye and he pulled his pistol. "Come out, damn you!"

Only another rustle in the brush. His heart beating hard, his gun cocked, Johnny rode closer to investigate.

It was then he saw the girl. For a long moment, he did not recognize this naked mad woman crouching in the brush, her skin burned dark, her blue eyes crazed and vacant, her magnificent hair wild and tangled. "Winnifred?"

They stared at each other, as much horror on her face as he felt. Then she screamed and turned to run through the brush.

"Winnifred!" Johnny shouted. "Come back! We're here to help you!"

But even shouting at her in English did not stop her flight. Major North galloped over. "What's happened?"

Johnny had already dismounted and ran through the brush after the fleeing girl. He caught her in a few steps, whirled her around, but she fought him

321

like a wild animal.

"Miss Starrett, it's me, Johnny Ace! You're all right now!"

She looked up into his face, screamed in terror, and fought him.

Johnny struggled with her, yelling over his shoulder, "Major, I need help! She's out of her mind!"

North dismounted and ran over. He stared, mouth half-open in horror. "Good Lord, is that Winnifred Starrett?"

Johnny pulled her to him, twisting her hands behind her back to control her. When he took a breath, he could smell the scent of men's seed on her. "What's left of her!"

The officer returned to his horse, got a poncho, and brought it back to cover her. When she saw the blue uniform, she seemed to calm somewhat, although her eyes still looked vacant.

The major cursed softly. "What on earth did they — ?"

"Guess!" Johnny said bitterly.

Major North touched her arm soothingly. "Miss Starrett," he said softly as if talking to a scared child, "you're safe now."

Winnifred Starrett looked at Johnny, her face still etched with terror. She flung herself at the officer, screaming in hysterics.

Major North put his arms around her and patted her hair while signaling for David Van Schyler, the medic. "No offense, Johnny, but your dark face seems to be scaring her."

Johnny nodded and stepped away from her. "I imagine she's seen enough dark faces to do her a lifetime."

The sensitive blond medic came running with a canteen, took the girl's arm, and led her away.

Johnny leaned against a tree and closed his eyes, heartsick. He had seen raped women before, but he would never get used to the haunted look of their eyes, the effects of violence that was more humiliating to the soul than dying. Some of them recovered—to a point. Some of them never did. He'd heard too many stories of women going insane or committing suicide. Among Indian women, it was taken as a matter of course that they would be raped by the victors. Who knew what happened to those brown victims eventually?

He had his job to do. Pulling himself together, Johnny scouted around quickly, assessing the scene. The Dog Soldiers had evidently split into two parties—maybe more. Tracks led off to the south and west. If they hadn't bothered to take the girl, they were traveling fast and light. That could mean only one thing. They meant to make some lightning-fast raids then get out before the cavalry could arrive. A shiny object glittered in the sun. He bent to pick it up and swore as he recognized it.

Johnny went back to the stage, knowing he'd have to find something to clothe Winnifred. She couldn't travel all the way back to the fort in nothing but the major's poncho. Most of her luggage and personal things were scattered around the landscape. When he found one dress, the elegant gown she had worn the night of the party, he quit looking and carried it to the medic.

When Winnifred saw his face, she began to scream. Johnny handed Van Schyler the dress and strode back to the major.

North pulled at his mustache. "This ends the mission. We'll go back to the fort."

Johnny looked over at the half-crazed girl again and heard the angry mutter of the troopers. "The men are in a mood to look for Dog Soldiers and kill them."

The officer shook his head. "We've done what General Carr told me to do—find the stage. Besides, we can't drag her along with us and we might be outnumbered. How many warriors do you think they have?"

"At least fifty. Maybe more than that. They'll keep building their strength as others ride in to join them on these raids."

"Then we need reinforcements, more ammunition before we take in after them again," the major said.

Johnny held out the object he'd picked up and handed it to the officer.

Frank North whistled low and began to curse. "New Winchester shells! I don't think I saw the guard and driver armed with these—"

"But I'll bet the Dog Soldiers were," Johnny said.

North looked at the shell a long moment then put it in his pocket. "We've suspected gun running for a long time, those dirty—! Too bad those swine couldn't be the ones the Dog Soldiers ambushed!" He looked over at Winnifred. "I dread telling her father what's happened."

They returned to Fort McPherson. It was an ordeal riding with Winnifred. She wept continuously, and no one with a dark complexion dared get near her for fear of sending her into hysterical screams.

Someone from the fort had evidently seen the patrol from a distance because little groups of people had gathered to watch them ride in. Luci stood in front of the trading post alone.

Johnny saw her and felt an overpowering anger with her because she was Cheyenne, and with himself because he loved her in spite of it. He couldn't stop himself from shouting at her, "Take a good look at what your damned Dog Soldiers have done!"

He saw the horror reflected in her eyes as Winnifred rode past with the medic. At the sight of her shocked face, he was abruptly weary and sorry at his outburst.

Luci looked up at him, both horrified and angry at his unjustified attack. "Was that Winnifred Starrett?"

He sighed, leaning on his saddle horn. "What's left of her."

"I must help the poor girl!" But as Luci ran forward and Winnifred saw her, the white girl began to scream and babble.

David Van Schyler winced and gestured Luci away. "Sorry. Anyone with dark skin . . . well, you understand."

Luci looked up at him and nodded dumbly. She really didn't know the young man except that he had a reputation for being kind and caring. She knew he was an artist. Once she had seen him with his paints out sketching landscapes. And everyone knew about his sister.

Winnifred continued to scream. Two officers' wives rushed up in a rustle of petticoats, glared at Luci, muttered something about "Dirty Cheyennes," and rushed to help Winnifred.

Johnny dismounted, caught Luci's arm, and pulled her aside. "You see? It's already started. Walk with me to put my horse away."

He had such an iron grip on her wrist, she couldn't do anything else. Behind her, Winnifred's high-pitched screams were enough to tear at even the hardest heart.

"What—what happened?" she asked.

"You know what happened." He kept walking, dragging her along into the barn. "Have you moved your things out?"

She stood in the shadows, stroking Katis's neck with her free hand, avoiding Johnny's gaze. "I told you I was going to. How can I sleep with a man who kills my people?"

"You'd claim a people that does that?" He gestured toward the parade ground, where Winnifred's screams still echoed.

Immediately she felt defensive. "The Cheyenne have had their women raped, their people killed, too."

"They aren't *your* people, Luci. You've never really lived among them. You owe them no loyalty."

"I owe them the loyalty of blood kin."

"So when it gets down to it, blood really is thicker than water, isn't it?" he challenged her, his swarthy face hard as dark granite. He stood looking down at her, still clasping her wrist. "I ought to treat you like a captured female enemy!"

His lips were slightly parted and she had to

326

fight an insane urge to throw her arms around his neck and kiss him. "What is it you want from me, Johnny Ace? You've had my body! Would you feel better if you raped me? Do you want to shame and humiliate me?"

"I—I don't know what I want, but I want you!" His grip on her wrist tightened. "Move back in with me. We won't discuss anything about Cheyenne and Pawnees. We'll pretend that subject doesn't exist!"

She loved him; she couldn't help herself. But she couldn't ignore what he was—a wolf for the blue soldiers, paid to hunt down and help kill her people. She shook her head, trying to pull out of his iron grip without success. "It wouldn't work. I know that as soon as the troop can be resupplied, you'll be going out again. I've been closing my eyes too long, knowing the chasm between us is too deep and wide to ever bridge."

"Then damn you, don't call what we have 'love.' Let me *pay* you to sleep with me. I need you, Luci!" Before she could react, he pulled her against him, kissing her while she fought him. The big Pawnee held her easily while she struggled in his arms. He forced his tongue between her lips, grinding his body against hers. Her pulse began to race and she felt herself wanting him, wanting to mold herself against him, put her head against his chest, and tell him how much she had missed him, how glad she was that he was back.

But when he freed her, she slapped him. "How dare you say that! I'm no whore!"

"I'd killed men for less than that," he said softly, rubbing his face where she had struck him.

"Then kill me, big, stupid Pawnee!" she taunted

him in a frustrated rage. "Kill me, you paid wolf for the army!" Then she turned and ran out of the barn.

Major North sat at his desk, staring out the window, ignoring for a long moment the red-faced sergeant waiting patiently in front of the desk.

His body ached from today's long ride back to the fort and he had just returned from a meeting with General Carr. Somewhere a baby cried and the sound drifted through his open window in the early summer heat. *Or was it that hapless Starrett girl?*

The sergeant cleared his throat as a gentle reminder in case the major had forgotten he had sent for him.

"Oh, yes, Sergeant. Send a wire warning other forts. We've got something here worth looking into." He stared at the shiny, telltale cartridge in his hand. What kind of men would arm the Dog Soldiers against their own kind? Men to whom money was everything. As in every war, the only ones who won were the arms dealers. He hoped whoever this sonovabitch was, he got what he deserved someday.

The sergeant cleared his throat. "Anything else, sir?"

"Yet another request for more horses, better arms." He smiled wryly. "Although we won't get them."

He rolled the Winchester cartridge around in his palm. The Cheyenne were well armed and had nothing to lose. They had already lost many of those dear to them at Sand Creek in '64, and again last fall when Custer attacked Black Kettle's camp on the Washita one cold November dawn. Knowing that when the army finally defeated them, they would be sent back to reservations, the Cheyenne could not win but they would not quit. And he was up against the Dog Soldiers, the bravest of the brave, the best of the warrior societies.

"Sergeant, you ever see a *hotamtsit?*"

"Sir?" He looked bewildered.

"It's a Cheyenne honor—a long strip of decorated rawhide. A Dog Soldier who wears one is pledged to sacrifice his life, if need be, to win a battle. That's what we're up against if any of them ride with this band—a suicide unit."

"What did you call it, sir?" The sergeant scratched his red face in bewilderment.

"*Hotamtsit.* I saw one once." North steepled his fingers, remembering. "Only the bravest of the brave win one—a ceremonial, decorated band looped around the body."

"But I don't see how—"

"There's a red wooden stake tied to the end. If the position is overrun by the enemy, the wearer is pledged to drive that stake into the ground so he's literally tied to that spot to fight to the death."

"Good Lord!"

He closed his fist over the cartridge. "So that's what we may be up against, and better armed than we are. Did you know the Dog Soldiers always brought up the rear when the tribe was on the move for that same reason? To protect a retreat if necessary?"

The sergeant made a whistle of grudging admiration. "Tough people!"

"And we're going out after them just as soon as we can get fresh horses, and get reequipped."

"Begging the major's pardon, but I doubt we'll get much, no matter what kind of telegram you send. Congress hasn't quite gotten over the cost of the war; they're terribly tight-fisted with the army right now."

North shrugged. "Happens after every war. We relax, let down our defenses, spend the money on other stuff. Then we're unprepared when the next war starts."

He thought about the Cheyenne and had a fleeting sense of admiration for them. They couldn't win, but they wouldn't quit. Didn't they have a right to live as they had always lived, wild and free and uncivilized?

Somewhere in the quiet, he heard screaming drifting on the hot air, and recognized it as Winnifred's voice.

On the other hand, didn't the small groups of Pawnees and other Indians have a right to live without being harried off the face of the earth by the Cheyenne and their allies? And what of the settlers? They were starving immigrants or refugees from crowded big cities, trying to make a home for themselves on the rich farm land that now only buffalo and Indians roamed. He was glad he didn't have to make any moral decisions in this. Major Frank North and his men would follow orders and do their duty—whatever that was.

"Major, was there something else?" The sergeant shifted his weight restlessly.

Of course there was. North had been stalling, unsure how to word the other telegram he had to send. *How did you tell a man something like this?*

"Send another wire to Manning Starrett in Denver. Tell him . . ."

Tell him what? Not the truth. No man should hear such a truth in a telegraph message.

Dear Mr. Starrett. Stop. Your elegant daughter raped and tortured by fifty savages. Stop. The fort doctor is not sure if she will ever regain her sanity. Stop. Just in case, look into the possibility of an asylum for the insane in Denver. Stop.

The sergeant cleared his throat, shifting his weight from one foot to the other while North hesitated.

She was screaming again. He hoped the doctor would be able to sedate Winnifred soon so she wouldn't keep the whole fort awake tonight. He got up, went over, and closed the window, even though the early summer night was hot.

North looked down at the shiny cartridge in his hand. Somewhere there was a white man who had caused Winnifred's terror. He hoped God would even the score somehow.

"Okay, Sergeant, send him this wire: Dear Mr. Starrett. Stop. There has been an unfortunate incident. Stop. Stage waylaid and wrecked near state line. Stop. But your daughter is alive. Stop."

Too bad, North thought. Too bad she's alive.

"If you can get a stage to bring you here," he continued, "do come get Winnifred. Stop. She needs love, reassurance, and a personal escort back to Denver. Stop."

"Is that all, sir?"

Should he add that if Mr. Starrett had any household help with dark skin, he'd better fire them because Winnifred screamed when she saw anyone who remotely favored an Indian? "That's all, Sergeant. Send it."

The man saluted and left. North sat back down and turned to stare at the books on the shelf behind him. Sometimes he wished real life could be like fiction, where everything worked out right at the end, where the bad were punished, and the boy and girl found true love.

He frowned, thinking of Johnny Ace and Luci. Life was more apt to be like Romeo and Juliet, where there was no way things could work out and the lovers died in the end.

Try as they might to keep it quiet, the gossip about what had happened to Winnifred would finally get to Denver and she would be an outcast. No white man would marry a girl who had been raped by a whole war party—even if she regained her sanity, which Major North doubted. And suppose she was pregnant by one of those braves? He didn't even want to think about it.

With a melancholy sigh, he buried his face in his hands and devoutly hoped that Manning Starrett was a kind, compassionate man who would be understanding and supportive.

Manning Starrett screamed one last time at his housekeeper and limped in to sit in the elegant parlor of his Victorian mansion. He ought to fire her but she was the only one in a long line of help who would put up with his temper. Mrs. Polinski was a widow, the sole support of younger sisters and brothers in an orphans' home somewhere, so she couldn't afford to quit, no matter how badly he treated her. Money was power. Manning liked both.

What in the goddamn hell was holding up that overdue stage? He'd withdrawn a large sum he kept in the Peabody Bank in Boston to finance this arms deal. Manning prided himself on not ever putting all his eggs in one basket. Besides, people might be curious if he withdrew that large a sum from his local bank.

The front door bell rang, making him start. He heard the housekeeper answer it, and a little of her friendly conversation with Billy Reno.

"Billy! Get in here! Don't stand out there jawin' with my hired help!"

Billy came into the dining room, rubbing his chin. "News of the stage, Manning. Bad, I'm afraid."

Manning began to swear, reached for his cane, and got to his feet with difficulty. "I knew it! God damn it to hell! I just knew it! And all that gold—"

"Manning, have you forgotten your daughter is supposed to be on that stage, too?" Billy looked reproachful.

He really had forgotten. Still compared to a large gold shipment, any man would worry about the money first—wouldn't he? "Oh, yes," he grunted, "Winnifred. Have you heard anything?"

"That's why I'm here. I just came from the office. This wire came in just a little while ago from Major North at the fort."

"Did he say anything about money? Did they find it?"

"Sometimes even I'm surprised by you, Manning." He leaned against an ornate dining chair. "Couldn't you have asked about your daughter first? The Cheyenne hit that stage, probably with rifles we supplied them."

Manning swore. "I suppose that's poetic justice, isn't it? Don't look so upset, Billy. You developing a conscience in your old age? And here I thought you were just exactly like me."

"I must be." Billy went over to the sideboard, poured himself a whiskey, and looked out the window at the darkness, "Or I wouldn't have gotten mixed up in this latest deal. Selling weapons to hostiles is the lowest of the low."

"But profitable." Manning grinned. "Now read me the wire."

Billy read it to him.

"They must not have found the money," he mused.

"He wouldn't mention that, not knowing it's yours." Billy sounded exasperated.

Maybe Billy wasn't like him after all; maybe he was a little too soft and decent to fill Manning's shoes. "Anyway, Billy, she's okay. You were worrying for nothing."

"So you're going to Fort McPherson?"

Manning had not felt so annoyed and put out in a long time. "Can't they just send her later when the stage begins to run again?"

Leaning against the sideboard, Billy sipped his drink. "You aren't too popular in Denver. It would look better to everyone if you went after her."

Manning yawned. "Why don't you go, Billy? You're supposed to marry her."

"But nobody knows that yet, Manning. I haven't even met the girl."

Manning laughed. "You're right, Billy. It would look good in the papers if I went. *The Rocky Mountain News* has been after me on their editorial page; they'd have to back off if all the citizens sympathized with me because my poor daughter had survived an Indian raid. Then later they can do a story entitled: 'Rescued Heiress Weds Prominent Young Businessman.' "

Billy shook his head. "You have an angle for everything, don't you?"

"That's how I became so rich, my boy, and as my protégé, I'm going to teach you how it's done. Now I'll hire a private coach and take shortcuts to reach that fort."

"And what am I supposed to do?" Billy sipped his whiskey.

"You ride out, find the wrecked stage, and save that hidden money for us."

"Me?" Billy's voice rose in sheer disbelief. "Why me? That's hostile country out there!"

"Because you are the only one I trust, that's why." He fiddled with the carved head of his cane. "Before someone else finds it, you take a wagon, go out to that site, and bring the money back for safekeeping. A tough saloon brawler like you shouldn't be afraid of a few Indians!"

"I—I don't even know where it wrecked or how you hid the money—"

"God damn it to hell, sometimes I wonder if you really are like me! Think!" He tapped the side of his head. "Didn't you hear what the man said? The state line! Just follow the route. And the money's in three big crates, packed under a layer of Bibles."

"Bibles?"

Manning shrugged irritably. "Doesn't the Bible say something about laying up treasure in heaven?"

"I don't think you got it right—"

335

"What the goddamn hell difference does it make?" Manning roared, waving his cane. "I may be gone awhile Billy, and business'll have to go on as usual."

"It can't without you, Manning." He took his drink back to the table and sat down.

"Sure it can, my boy." He reached out with one frail hand and patted Billy's sleeve. "You and Lily can keep this all running while I'm gone."

Billy rubbed his chin. "Thought you said, 'Never trust a woman.'"

"I don't; but I trust *you.*"

"Smart, boss! Since we hate each other so much, each of us would be happy to tattle on the other." Billy grinned, sipping his drink. "I'd love to catch the bitch doing something wrong, so maybe you'd dump her—"

"Sorry to disappoint you, Billy, knowing how much you hate her." Manning smiled with satisfaction. "But after all, she's just a woman, and brainless like the rest. She serves my needs, so I'll keep her—at least 'til one comes along to replace that stupid whore who drowned in the bowl!"

Billy ran his tongue around his gapped teeth. "Don't say I didn't warn you, Manning. The French slut's not to be trusted."

"No woman is. But Lily knows which side of her bread is buttered. And you'll make sure she toes the line." He looked at the lion on the head of his cane. "Billy, you're more like me than my own son would be if I had one; all I've got is two daughters—that I know of." He winked at Billy.

"Two? You never told me about the other one—"

"Doesn't matter." Manning stood up, leaning on

his cane. "She didn't count anyway — just a pup by one of my Injun gals. Now you make the arrangements and I'll leave for Fort McPherson. But first, you let the newspapers know about the distracted father and his beautiful daughter who escaped death —"

"Maybe you should wait until you know —"

"Know what, God damn it to hell! I need a few kind stories about me so the crusaders will back off screaming about how I run Denver! Call my stupid housekeeper to pack my bag and see if Owens can get the coach ready —"

"I mentioned it to him on my way in. He's afraid to go, boss, what with five children —"

"Then go fire the cowardly bastard and hire me a private coach!" Manning banged his cane on the floor. "And Billy, you get out to that wrecked stage and save that money for us!"

Chapter Nineteen

Luci knew that the people of the fort held her partly to blame for what had happened to Winnifred Starrett because Luci was Cheyenne.

Women of the fort gave her withering glances when she passed by, then gathered in little groups to whisper and make sneering remarks. Many of the soldiers now switched to another laundress, despite the fact that Luci had a reputation for turning out the most crisply washed and ironed shirt of any girl on the post.

She began to wonder if she was going to be able to make enough to live on. Since she was back at the trading post for want of anywhere else to go, old Mr. Bane began charging her rent on that miserable room for the first time. When Johnny tried to talk to her, she carefully ignored him and went on her way.

Worst of all, when she ran into poor Winnifred crossing the parade grounds, that unfortunate girl took one look at Luci's dark face and broke into screams that brought everyone running.

Luci was too proud to go to Johnny Ace for help or to even tell him how people were treating her. She didn't see that much of him anyway. He seemed to be busy conferring with the officers about equipment and poring over maps as the Fifth Cavalry made plans for its campaign against the Dog Soldiers.

Late May settled over Nebraska with its heat, wild flowers, and ripening sand plums and choke cherries. Word came every few days of more killings. The Dog Soldiers were on the move, striking random settlements, raiding ranches, stealing the stock, and murdering the inhabitants. The Fifth could do nothing but swear vengeance as it waited for reinforcements and better guns and equipment to arrive.

Luci became desperate, wondering what she was going to do. With the soldiers giving their laundry to other girls on Suds Row, she was not sure she would even be able to buy enough food. She began to see how hungry Indian women gradually gave up the precarious fight to exist and became some soldier's squaw. She thought then of her beloved mother and wondered about the handsome officer who had deserted Sunrise Woman.

What was it her mother had said at the last? *You named for your father . . . he name sound like Morning Star.* Well, of course that was ridiculous, Luci thought with a shake of her head. White men didn't have names like that; they had names like Brown or Jones.

When Johnny rode past her on patrol, she stared after him wistfully, wishing she could forget he was an enemy. She thought of the white man's saying: Blood is thicker than water. In the long run, that fact was something that maybe love wasn't strong enough to overcome. The only thing for her to do was forget him.

Mercy, how to do that? Every time she saw him riding past, once again, she remembered being in his bed with his dark body ramming between her thighs. There was only one way to keep from seeing him constantly—she had to leave. Move on to another fort or go back to her people.

But how would she find them? The Dog Soldiers were raiding closer now, emboldened by the army's lack of retaliation. Every day, new reports came in of a ranch burned, a settlement attacked. It had been less than a week since Winnifred had been brought in, but with her unhappiness and the hostility of the post toward her, it seemed like centuries to Luci.

Maybe she wouldn't have to find *them*. Maybe they would find *her*. If she rode out across this prairie, with the Dog Soldiers riding in a dozen small raiding parties all over Nebraska, Kansas, and Colorado Territory, maybe their paths would cross—if they just didn't kill her before she could explain who she was.

Very carefully she laid out her plans. One day, she talked David Van Schuyler into loaning her a roan horse so she could go berry picking. Along with the horse, she got a lecture on waiting until someone had time to accompany her. With the Indian trouble, it was loco to venture even a few hundred yards from the fort alone.

She nodded obediently, but rode out almost immediately at a leisurely pace. When she was certain she wasn't being followed, she turned and galloped off to the southwest.

How she would find the Cheyenne in this vast wilderness, she couldn't be sure; she'd have to hope they found her. One thing was for certain: anything was better than remaining at Fort McPherson. Not only did the whites treat her badly, but she had to see that Pawnee scout and yearn after him, knowing how hopeless it was.

She hid out for the rest of the day in the first grove of trees she found, knowing how visible she would be against the flat, open prairie. After dark, she continued on her way.

The hours passed as she rode. Luci was beginning to have doubts now. Suppose she didn't cross the trail of the Dog Soldiers? Suppose her food and water gave out before she found them? To make her food last long enough and conserve her water, she would have to search out ranches where she could earn a meal cooking and cleaning. Even that could be risky. Luci wasn't too sure any white ranchers would be glad to see her Indian face. With all the tension, some of them might shoot first and ask questions later.

It was just after dawn when she stumbled onto the burned-out ranch house. The wreckage still smoldered and the family sprawled dead and scalped, striped feather arrows sticking out of the bodies like strange pin cushions. Luci went off into the bushes and got very sick. Mercy! Could her people have done this terrible thing? Maybe white renegades or enemy tribes had done this, using Cheyenne arrows to misdirect the blame. On the other hand, the Dog Soldiers were desperate and fighting for their very existence. Men fought, and women and children on both sides died.

She found a shovel in the ruins of the barn and set out to bury the man, woman, old grandmother, and young boy. Her back ached and she had blisters on her small, work-worn hands by midmorning. It occurred to her that she should ride on and let the cavalry or whoever happened on the scene bury the family, but it seemed indecent to just ride off and leave them exposed to the flies and weather. It took a long time, but she did it.

The roan had been munching grass in the yard all this time and Luci watered it well at the pump, then filled her canteen. In the burned house, she found a little corn bread and a hunk of smoked bacon that she could take with her.

She rode off again toward the southwest, watching for pony tracks, an occasional broken blade of grass, or anything else that might give her a clue.

When she found tracks of unshod ponies farther south, she knew Indians had been there lately. Finally she began to have a feeling of being watched, but when she stood up in her stirrups and looked around, she saw nothing. Still the feeling persisted.

It was two days later that she came up over a sudden rise and found herself face to face with a large war party, all painted and armed with shiny new rifles.

She had found her mother's people at last — or had they found her? Looking into the solemn, scowling faces, she reined in her horse. At that instant, Luci didn't know whether to feel happy —

or terrified.

The warriors rode out to meet her. She held up her hand in greeting, trying to remember the little bit of Cheyenne language she knew. *"Pave-voona o.* Good day. I am Morning Star, niece to Ta Ton Ha Haska."

There had to be twenty-five or thirty of them. She was too nervous to count as the war-painted braves rode slowly to surround her and stare at her. One of them was a boy with a crippled leg, not more than fifteen winters old.

The ugly leader scowled at her. "You have blue eyes," he said in halting English. "I think you are only a white man's pup, a fort Indian."

She drew herself up haughtily. "Does a white man's Indian speak Cheyenne? Has not Tall Bull spoken of his sister, Sunrise Woman, who became a bluecoat's woman and so disgraced herself? Take me to my uncle, who will tell you."

There was a ripple of excited discussion among the braves. Yes, some remembered seeing her in camp with her mother many years ago.

The ugly one nodded finally. "Yes, now I remember Sunrise Woman, as do some of these others. I am called Snake. We ride now to join your uncle and raid the white settlements between here and the Indian Territory."

Suddenly, Luci wanted to be anywhere but riding with these war-painted braves, especially the ugly leader. She had found her people whom she had not seen in many years, and should be happy and relieved, but she wasn't. Maybe she didn't belong with the Cheyenne either.

She brushed that thought aside as she fell in beside Snake and the war party broke into a lope.

"We are going to Kansas?"

He looked over at her, puzzled. Obviously the word meant nothing to him. "We ride to join Tall Bull to the south." He gestured that direction. "Many Cheyenne have escaped from the Indian Territory in defiance of the treaty. The Dog Soldiers gather strength. Soon we will run the white men out of our country!"

She started to tell him it was a foolish goal—that there were too many white men with a sophisticated civilization that the simple Indians couldn't even fathom—but she kept silent. These Cheyenne braves had no idea of what they were up against. It was both sad and futile.

Now that she had joined them, she realized that she belonged with them no more than she did the whites. Luci was tempted to leave them, then had a sinking feeling that it wouldn't be that easy. If she tried to ride away, she suspected they would stop her. She had wanted to find Tall Bull; they were going to see that she did.

The sun beat down on the rolling prairie as the war party rode south. In the heat, the crimson and ochre war paint on the dark faces mingled with sweat and smeared. Many of the braves carried war shields painted with sacred symbols. The barrels of the new rifles glinted in the light as did the lance points and arrowheads. *Where had they gotten the repeating rifles?*

"Snake," she asked, "your men are well armed. Where did they get the new guns?"

He laughed softly. "Some white men sell out their own kind for silver coins and trinkets."

"Where do you get silver coins and trinkets?"

He glanced over at her as if she were a stupid

child, then gestured to the fresh scalp swinging from his pony's bridle. "By raiding white farms and settlements and stagecoaches, of course!"

For the first time, she noticed a pink lace parasol tied to a brave's saddle. Winnifred Starrett. This war party had hit that stage.

Luci felt sick at the pit of her stomach. She didn't belong with these primitive people. It had been a crazy dream. *How could she escape?*

Snake seemed to take her silence for awed respect. "We also attacked a Pawnee camp lately at the holy place of the balanced rock."

Luci felt her eyes widen in horror. "You dared spill blood at Castle Rock? Even I know that is taboo!"

The other warriors had caught some of her words as they rode along. The crippled boy said, "I am called Bear Cub. You are right, niece of Tall Bull. Many of the men are worried about angering the *mistai,* the ghosts, by spilling blood at the holy place of the lightning and thunder. They think it will bring us bad luck."

Snake struck at him with his lance, but the boy dodged his white pony away. "Crippled, worthless one! How dare you question my leadership! Besides, we killed many Pawnee there. It is never bad luck to kill our old enemies!"

Some of the men must have agreed with him, for she saw a few heads nod. But others looked troubled.

It was only then Luci noticed the curly brown scalp dangling from Snake's lance as he shook it at Bear Cub. There was something familiar about it. . . .

"Yes, it belonged to a white officer." Snake

345

grinned proudly. "When we made the deal for the guns, he rode with the whites."

That couldn't be Carter Osgoode, she thought dazedly, and yet, there was something about that curly hair. . . . "A bluecoat officer rode with the white gun runners?"

"He must have done something wrong, because they turned him over to us before they left, with him begging and screaming for them not to leave them. We made him beg and shriek a lot more!"

Snake smiled in satisfaction and the other braves laughed as they remembered, except for Bear Cub, who looked sick and uneasy.

Luci reined in. Immediately the others did, too. She had to get away from this primitive savages. What had ever made her think she might belong among them?

Snake frowned. "What is the matter?"

"I—I've decided I don't want to ride the war trail," she said. "I think maybe I'll go looking for a peaceful camp of Cheyenne farther north." she gestured vaguely behind her.

"I think you will not," Snake said. "For all I know, you will tell the bluecoats where we are and they will send soldiers to hunt us down."

"I would never do that to my mother's people!"

"This is not for me to decide." Snake rubbed his ugly face thoughtfully. "You will ride with us for now. Tall Bull can make the final decision about what to do with you!"

There was nothing she could do but ride south with them. Now that she had realized she could never be a real Cheyenne, they were not going to let her go.

Perhaps she could reason with them. "You

346

should all go peacefully back to the reservation," she told Snake as they stopped to rest at a small creek. "In the long run, you can't win against the whites. They are as many as the snowflakes in the winter."

"Your cowardly words make me wonder if you are really a niece of Tall Bull's!" Snake's lip curled in disdain. "We will not return to the Indian Territory, even if they kill us to the last man. You know the reputation of the Dog Soldiers. We are the bravest of the brave, the best of the warrior societies, and would rather die in battle than be white man's Indians on a reservation!"

For that she couldn't blame them, Luci thought. There was no dignity in sitting day after day with nothing to do but eat the white man's free food. No, it wasn't free. Letting the government care for them made them trade their dignity and their most cherished possession, their freedom, for the rations.

Luci said, "So what will you do?"

Snake shrugged. "We will raid and kill as we have been doing, of course! It is all we can do."

"In the long run, the white soldiers will hunt you down and kill you."

"We know that." He looked at her a little sadly. "But we would rather live a few brief months as warriors than live many, many years like cowards on our knees, begging before the Great White Father in that place called Washington!"

There was no reasoning with them, no solution, and maybe even no right or wrong, Luci thought sadly. No matter how well intended anyone was or how many treaties were signed, Plains Indians and white farmers would not be able to live peacefully side by side. The warriors would soon forget what they had signed and be back killing and raiding as they had always done. If there were no enemy tribes to attack, the Plains warriors would raid the white farmers and ranchers.

"Where do you suppose my uncle will want to lead us?" she asked as they mounted up and took off south again.

Snake said, "After a few raids, maybe back up to that place in the rolling hills east of the Shining Mountains. The grass is tall and green there, the spring clear and cold." He called it by its Indian Name.

Summit Springs, east of the Rockies. She remembered the place vaguely. Once when she was small, she and her mother had ridden to that place in northeastern Colorado Territory to visit her uncle.

Snake looked her over admiringly as they rode. "You are very pretty, even if you are only half Cheyenne. Do you have a man?"

How should she answer? She didn't like the way Snake looked at her as if he could already imagine her in his blankets. Yet she dare not say that she had been the woman of a hated Pawnee scout. "I—I am only seventeen winter counts old. My mother had not made any promises for me when she died suddenly."

"Plenty of Cheyenne girls your age are already married." Snake smiled at her.

She felt cold chills go down her back at the hint in his words. Luci dropped back and rode with the crippled boy for the next few miles.

"I am Morning Star," she said to him as they finally dismounted again to eat and rest.

He looked at her shyly, holding fast to a ledger book. "I am called Bear Cub. I have watched you. I think you are the prettiest girl I have ever seen."

Luci laughed. "I am not so pretty. What is this you carry?"

He hesitated a long moment before offering the ledger for her inspection. "I draw the battles I have seen for our people to remember, since I will never be much good as a warrior."

She took the ledger, watching with pity and admiration as he hobbled about on his bent, twisted leg. When Luci opened it, she gasped with admiration. "Why, Bear Cub, these are wonderful!"

There was page after page of drawings. They were crude, but showed a great deal of talent. By beginning at the front of the book and turning the pages, she could follow many of the battles the Cheyennes had fought over the past several years. Here for all to see was the Kidder Massacre, the fight at Beecher's Island last September, where a handful of Forsythe's scouts had held off a large group of Cheyenne for nine days until a rescue party had arrived to save the soldiers.

Bear Cub watched her expression. "It was at that fight that we lost the great war leader, Roman Nose, because his spirit medicine had been broken."

Luci nodded, remembering what she'd heard from the white soldiers. That battle, too, had happened in eastern Colorado Territory.

"We outnumbered them," Bear Cub said, "but because they had repeating rifles, we could not defeat and overrun them. So now we have the new rifles, too."

"You have a great talent, Bear Cub," she said as she handed the book back to him. She thought of David Van Schuyler at the fort, the medic who painted as a hobby. David seemed like a sympathetic and deeply caring person. "I know a white man who is an artist, too. Perhaps he would help you sell your work, find you good teachers back East—"

Bear Cub shook his head. "I cannot leave my people. Even I can do a little—guard the horse herds, make records of their fights. I am lucky to be alive, after the whites shot me at Sand Creek and left me in the snow to die."

"In the long run, if the Cheyenne insist on fighting, you will all die."

He looked at her solemnly. "In the end, all people die, Morning Star. But maybe some of us will make our death count. We will show our bravery and be remembered. No warrior can hope for more than that."

She had forgotten this was the outlook of the Dog Soldier, the bravest of the brave. This crippled boy could never be a great warrior because of his leg, but he could help his people a little against the whites. He wanted nothing more.

Snake walked up just then. "Useless pictures! As useless to his people as the crippled boy who draws them! If he were not my second wife's little brother, I would not take him along! When his leg was shattered, he should have been left to die in the snow!"

The boy flushed and looked away in humiliation.

Luci's heart went out to him. "His pictures are good," she declared. "A hundred years from now,

350

maybe people will still look at them and think of the one who put history on paper so all could remember what happened these few short months."

"No, he and his silly pictures will soon be forgotten," Snake sneered, and turned to walk away. "Deeds like mine, like your uncle's, will be remembered."

Luci and Bear Cub both watched Snake's retreating back as he walked away to see to the setting up of camp.

Bear Cub sighed. "He is right. I am of no use to the tribe."

"That's not true," Luci patted his hand. "I believe that *Heammawihio* has some grand design and that we all play our parts in it, important, even if small. You will play some part, too. Just be patient."

He looked down at her hand on his. "Morning Star, how old are you?"

"Seventeen." She felt much older with all she had seen and experienced.

He bit his lip. "I—I am fifteen. That's not much difference. Has a warrior spoken for you?"

She could see where this conversation was headed and she did not want to hurt this shy, sensitive boy. "I have not even thought about things like that, Bear Cub. I wanted to live among my mother's people awhile, get to know them, and learn their customs. Then there will be time enough to think of marriage."

"I saw Snake staring at you. I think he will make an offer to your uncle." Bear Cub looked at her earnestly. "He is a rich man of many ponies."

The thought made her shudder. "Doesn't he have two wives already?"

"Yes, but the first is nursing a child and my sister is expecting one any day."

She nodded in understanding. It was forbidden to have relations with a nursing mother because to impregnate her would stop her milk and the baby would starve. She knew from things her mother had said that a Cheyenne wife nursed a baby three years. No wonder Snake might be wanting a new wife in his blankets.

Mercy! How had she gotten herself into this mess and how could she get herself out? She had a horrible vision of herself spread out on a buffalo robe with Snake's ugly face kissing her breasts as he rammed his manhood deep inside her, riding her roughly and brutally until his seed spilled into her womb.

It was all so sad and futile that she put her face in her hands a long moment, willing herself not to weep in sheer frustration. Any day now, the Fifth Cavalry would be departing Fort McPherson in an offensive against her people. No, not her people. She didn't have a people. Like Johnny Ace, she was caught between two worlds and belonged nowhere. Johnny Ace. Beloved enemy. As a scout, he would be riding out in front of those troops when they came up against the Cheyenne. He might be killed. Bear Cub might be killed.

And yet, all she could think of at this moment was how she might end up as Snake's woman with his body between her thighs as he enjoyed her and gave her his child.

Chapter Twenty

Major North wiped the sweat from his face and studied the man limping into his office. Once the man might have been a handsome rake, but dissolute living showed in his ravaged face.

"Major North, I believe you sent for me. I'm Manning Starrett."

"Have a chair, Mr. Starrett." North pulled one up for the man and tried to smile, although he somehow already didn't like the man. He certainly looked like Winnifred, but strange how the Denver man made him think of someone else. But who? "Hot, isn't it?"

"Let's get right to the point." The man leaned on his cane and glared at him with bright blue eyes. "I didn't spend my valuable time coming all the way from Denver just to discuss the goddamned weather! I'm a busy man, Major."

"And of course I'm not!" Immediately he regretted his sarcasm. He needed to be compassionate, knowing what this father faced. "I'm sorry, Mr. Starrett. Here at the fort, we've all been under a strain because of the Indian trouble." He needed to prepare Starrett. The man didn't look as if he was in good enough health to take much stress. "Have you seen your daughter yet?"

"Hell, no! I just got in! I don't know what this is all about, Major, but it appears for an important taxpayer, the army could take the time to send my daughter to Denver with a patrol and save me this trip."

"We feel all the taxpayers are important," the Major said gently, sitting down behind his desk. He hadn't even asked about Winnifred, North thought with a sinking heart. Somehow he had hoped that the arrival of her father would help the pitiful girl. She had improved very little since she'd been rescued. But now that he had met Starrett . . .

"Goddamn it to hell! I had to leave a lot of urgent business in the hands of my associate," Starrett grumbled, fingering his cane, "and since the stage isn't running, I had a helluva time getting a private coach that wasn't scared of Injuns."

"I'm sorry to inconvenience you, but it seemed necessary, under the circumstances." North held his temper but just barely. If he threw this rich man out of his office, no doubt the Fifth Cavalry would get even fewer supplies than they were now getting. Since Grant had just become President, maybe that old general would do better by the army.

"That's what I'm complaining about," Starrett said, "Nobody's told me what in the goddamned hell happened!"

Was there an easy way to tell a man his daughter had been raped and tortured by fifty savages and, as a result, seemed to be insane?

North steepled his fingers and studied them. "The stage your daughter was on was attacked by a party of Dog Soldiers armed with repeating Winchesters."

He reached into his desk drawer, took out one of the shiny cartridges, and tossed it to the other man, who automatically caught it and stared at it. For a moment, he seemed almost speechless, rolling the cartridge about in his palm. "Ironic," he whispered, "ironic!" He tossed it back. "Where's the stage itself? The troop bring it in?"

It seemed like a strange question to North, but he had already decided Manning Starrett was a strange man. "No, it was too wrecked. We just left it to lie out there beside the trail." He waited a long moment, growing more and more agitated. "Mr. North, aren't you going to ask about your daughter?"

The other man shrugged. "She's alive, didn't your telegram say that?"

"Well, yes, but —"

"Then what else in the goddamned hell is there to know?"

The obvious had not even occurred to him, North thought suddenly, and then felt both dislike and pity for the man. "Mr. Starrett, I—I don't know how to tell you this, but Winnifred may need a lot of tender, gentle care to ever be what she was before. She's been through a terrible ordeal."

He glared back with steely blue eyes. "Meaning what?"

He was not sure he could bring himself to say it, although he was a tough, professional army man. To say it brought back the ghastly memories of finding her. "She—she's . . . been outraged."

"Outraged?" Starrett looked blank for a long moment. Then the horror of what North meant seemed to slowly dawn on him. The blue eyes widened and he gasped audibly. "You—you don't mean to tell me those savages had the gall to take the daughter of the richest, most important man in Denver, and—"

"Probably all fifty of them," North interrupted. He couldn't stand to hear the word said. The sight and smell and terror of the girl were too recent.

Starrett opened and closed his mouth several times like a fish out of water fighting for air. "How dare they!" he seethed. "Wait until I complain to friends in Washington about what a rotten job the army is doing in protecting taxpayers!"

"And while you're at it," North fired back, "tell them we're trying to protect a gigantic prairie with a few troops against thousands of warriors from most of the Plains tribes! And we're doing it with the remnants of Civil War weapons while the hostiles have better arms than we do!"

Oh, my God, what had he done? The other man looked as if he might go into shock, and die right here in front of him.

"Mr. Starrett, let me get you a drink." He dug around in the desk drawer, sure that there might be a bottle in it. There was. He handed it over and watched the man's hand shake as he took a gulp. "Do you want to see her now?"

Manning Starrett looked as if no words were registering. "How dare they? And with Winchesters I . . ." His voice trailed off. Obviously he was taking it as a personal insult.

North waited for the other man to show concern for the girl herself, but he only said again, "How dare they!"

Getting up, North went to the door and told an orderly to have one of the medics bring Winnifred over. "I've sent for her. She'll need a lot of care if she's ever to recover from this ordeal—"

"Recover? Was she shot?"

"Well, no, but—"

"Then what in the Goddamned hell is this about 'care' and 'recover'? Poppycock!" Starrett banged his cane on the floor, seemingly recovered from the shock. "Do I look like someone in good enough shape to care for some invalid? I need a live-in nurse myself, Major. That's why Winnifred is coming to live with me!"

North pulled at his mustache. What he needed to tell him was even worse, if possible, than the fact that she had been raped. But how?

Staring past Starrett's shoulder out the window, North saw David Van Schyler leading Winnifred gently across the parade ground toward the office. Bless David's sensitive, caring heart!

The girl was still a great beauty, her ebony hair pulled up with ribbons, her soft batiste dress of sunrise pink tied with a wide sash of deeper rose-colored silk.

"Mr. Starrett," he said softly, "I'm not sure— Winnifred will ever be able to care for anyone in

357

the shape she's in, but maybe with time, she'll improve."

He could tell by the other man's face that he didn't have the slightest idea what North was hinting at. He only look annoyed that his well-laid plans had been thwarted. "I had everything worked out," he grumbled. "Now Billy probably won't want to marry her. No self-respecting white man would take dirty Injuns' leavings!"

North winced. He had to tell him the rest, since Winnifred was almost at the office. Now he regretted deeply that he had sent for her. But would it have been any better dealing with the cranky rich man an hour or a day or a week from now? "There's something else. Winnifred's been through a terrible ordeal and is reacting to the shock by withdrawing into herself. I've seen men behave like this after surviving a battle. Sometimes they eventually get better, sometimes they don't."

"What in the goddamned hell is that supposed to mean?" Starrett exploded. "Are you telling me she's as crazy as her mother was? Of all the rotten luck! I send for a daughter to look after me and now she turns out to be a' liability! Her mother died in a madhouse, you know that?"

Of course he hadn't known, but it didn't matter. He watched Winnifred come to his door. The medic gave her a reassuring pat on the arm, knocked, and walked away.

North stood up. "I'm afraid, Mr. Starrett, that instead of your daughter assuming the burden of care for you, it's going to have to be the other way around."

"I didn't bargain for that. I didn't agree to it!"

358

North lost his temper. "Winnifred didn't bargain for what she got, either!" He went over and opened the door. "Hello, Winnifred," he said softly. "Come in. Your father's here. Everything will be all right now."

The other man stood up with difficulty. He stared at the girl as North led her in. "Winnifred?"

The girl's vacant blue eyes brightened a moment and she acted as if she was not quite sure what she was expected to do. She looked from one to the other.

Major North led her to a chair. "Winnifred, your father has come all the way from Denver to take you home with him. You'll be safe there."

"Home?" she said softly. "Home is Alabama. I want to go back to my mother. The Yankees will be invading soon. I've got to make sure she's all right; hide the silver . . ."

Starrett stared at her in horror. "The war was over four years ago, girl, and your mother's dead!"

"No," Winnifred said in a little girl's voice, her eyes vacant, "they keep telling me she's dead, but she isn't; she's crazy." She seemed to be talking to herself. "They locked her up in a madhouse. Daddy came back from the army when I was a little girl and gave her a disease. She's insane. I hate him for that. . . ."

Manning Starrett groaned aloud and buried his face in his hands. "I didn't know she knew. Clara hanged herself in that madhouse."

Syphilis? Frank North looked at him in horror. Was that was what was wrong with Manning Starrett? Had he contacted that unspeakable, incurable sexual disease and taken it home to his innocent wife? In the last stages of syphilis, the afflicted often went insane. No wonder Starrett wanted someone to look after him in the future—someone he thought he could trust.

The major hadn't realized how loud silence could be. In the seconds that passed, he heard the clock on the wall ticking away loudly, the sound of an army unit drilling on the parade grounds. A bumble bee buzzed in and then out of the open window in the summer heat.

And now Winnifred had been driven over the edge by her horrible experience. *Why hadn't the Indians killed her?* North thought with a sigh. It would have solved so many problems. Then he felt guilty at the thought.

Winnifred stared out the window, humming tunelessly.

Starrett cleared his throat, then looked at North. "So what in the hell am I supposed to do with her? I hadn't planned on this! All Denver will gossip—"

"You might start by thinking of her, and having a little compassion for her." North watched Winnifred play with the ends of the wide sash of her dress. "But I don't know what to tell you, Mr. Starrett."

"I had planned a big coming-out party for her in Denver society." The wealthy man seemed to be talking to himself, becoming more and more agitated. "Then an engagement to my business partner. I can't ask him to marry Winnifred now!"

At the sound of her name, she looked at him

blankly. "What's the matter? The Yankees are coming, that's what's wrong, isn't it?" She stood up.

"Wrong!" Starrett roared. "I'll tell you what's wrong! Any self-respecting white woman kills herself in a case like this! How can I face the humiliation of everyone knowing? They already hate me! They'll laugh, do you hear? You're ruined! You hear? Ruined!"

North jumped to his feet, came around the desk, grabbed the man, and shook him. "Stop it! Starrett! Stop this!"

Winnifred seemed to pull herself together. Head high in the air, she got up and walked out of the office.

North almost stopped her, then decided she'd be better off not to hear the tongue-lashing he was about to give her father. He went to the window and watched her walk proudly toward her quarters. He decided he would send the doctor over to her in a few minutes, as soon as he got Starrett out of his office.

And then he couldn't do it. He stared down at the sick man who had everything and nothing. There were many things money couldn't buy after all.

Starrett looked up at him, anger and frustration in his bright blue eyes. "So what do I do now?"

"I'm sorry for your problems," North said gently. "The only thing I can suggest is to take Winnifred back to Denver and give her a lot of care and kindness. Maybe eventually . . ."

"But you don't really believe that, do you?" The blue eyes looked so directly into North's that he

361

found he could not lie.

"I'm sorry," he said again, shaking his head.

"I had already promised her in marriage," Starrett said. "I was going to throw a wedding that would set Denver society back on its heels!"

"Even if she should recover, I think it may be years before Winnifred will let a man touch her . . . in that way." He hunted in the desk for tumblers and poured them each a drink.

"Sounds like every respectable woman I ever knew," Starrett snorted, accepting the drink. "None of them want to give a man his rights to her bed. That's why men go looking for the other kind."

The kind that give him disease, North thought, studying the other, but he only sipped his whiskey. As soon as Starrett left, he'd go see about Winnifred himself. He couldn't help feeling guilty about how relieved he'd be to get the pair away from the fort.

"Starrett, don't you have anyone else to turn to? Another relative, perhaps?"

The other laughed softly, staring into his glass. "There might have been other children, who knows? I was pretty randy in my younger days; had a thing for dark-skinned women. But I only knew of one for sure."

North's sympathy turned to disgust and dislike again. "What happened to him?"

"Oh, it was just a daughter, not a son." He shrugged as if a girl child was of little consequence. "If it had been a son, I might have claimed my bastard."

"But you never did," North guessed. "Didn't you know where to find her?"

"Of course I knew where to find her! I got reports for years about them hanging around the forts, hoping I'd return." He slammed the glass down on the desk top and stood up. "But I didn't need them, so why bother? I already had a white family!"

It looked like Manning Starrett was going to get what he deserved—to be alone and unloved in his final, desperate days, North thought as he stood up. He could only pity Winnifred who would be in the same predicament. "Come, Mr. Starrett, I'll see you to your quarters. Tomorrow, you can decide what you're going to do."

Johnny Ace walked toward his quarters from the barn. He was one of the few on the post who knew that the Fifth Cavalry would be leaving tomorrow or the next day on a long campaign designed to either destroy the Cheyenne Dog Soldiers or put them back on the reservation.

For the first time, he was not looking forward to battle, smearing his knife with enemy blood. When he thought of Cheyenne now, he saw Luci's small face looking up at him. In his mind, he saw the ranch house again with the Ace High-Star brand hanging over the gate. As he dismounted his horse in the ranch yard, chubby children toddled toward him as he took their mother in his arms. As he kissed her, she reached up to touch his face. *Pawnee passion. Cheyenne caress*. No, the two could never bring anything but trouble and heartache.

It was just as well that she had again run away

363

back to her people. This time he wouldn't pursue her. Luci had done what she thought she must do. Maybe she would finally find a little happiness in the arms of some Dog Soldier, although the thought of her in another man's arms caused his chest to tighten so that he couldn't breathe.

Head down, deep in thought, he bumped into someone as he rounded a building. "Oh, excuse me, I—"

Then she began to scream. He stared down into Winnifred's horrified eyes as she backed away from him.

"Winnifred, I mean you no harm."

But when he reached out to her, she seemed to see only his dark, Indian face, and she turned and ran away. He started to go after her then decided against it. That would only terrify the crazed girl more. He wondered for a long moment why she was out alone, where she was going. Had she just come from Pani Le-shar's office? He turned to look at her, but she had fled in the direction of her quarters. Maybe he should check with the major about her. He got almost to the major's door, heard voices from inside, and realized he had a visitor. Johnny had better not disturb him.

Instead, he hunted up the doctor, who checked on Winnifred, put her to bed, and gave her a sedative that he said would put her to sleep for many hours.

Finally, the whole post settled down for the night.

Winnifred slept fitfully. Screaming, dark savages

chased after her in her dream. She came awake and sat bolt upright in bed, hands clasped over her mouth to hold back a shriek. Screams would bring people running and she didn't like the way they looked at her these days and shook their heads.

Her sheer lace nightdress clung to her perspiring body in the hot night air. With a sigh, she got out of bed and padded barefoot to the window. The fort was quiet in the middle of the night. In the moonlight, nothing stirred on the vacant parade ground.

Father. Dimly she remembered this afternoon's meeting. Yes, that must have been Father coming to meet her, although he looked a lot older and not at all handsome as she remembered him from her childhood.

He hadn't wanted her or her mother then as he didn't want Winnifred now. She had known that for certain this afternoon by the disapproving hardness in his bright blue eyes, the grim line of his mouth.

Everyone thought she didn't understand anything anymore — she could tell by the pitying glances, the way they talked in front of her as if she didn't speak English and wouldn't comprehend. If only she could get some peaceful sleep, perhaps she wouldn't be so confused.

Every time she closed her eyes, shrieking dark men came out of the recesses of her brain to hurt and humiliate her. They seemed always to be screaming in her ears although sometimes she reached up and found her own mouth open.

Maybe she was going crazy like Mama. Winnifred wrapped her arms around herself and stared out the window. More than anything, she was afraid of ending up in a madhouse, screaming her life away as Mama had done. All she really needed was some uninterrupted sleep and then she could straighten out her confused thoughts.

Why didn't you kill yourself as any respectable white woman would have done? She heard Father's accusing, angry voice, turned quickly, but there was no one there. He had been disappointed in her again. Always she was a disappointment to her parents. Once when she was little, Mama had snarled at her: *Why couldn't you have been a boy? If you had been a boy, I might have been able to hang on to him. He wanted a son and I didn't give him one.*

What was she going to do? Winnifred rocked back and forth on her heels, so very, very tired but terrified to close her eyes except with medication, and then it was a drugged, troubled sleep with shrieking savages chasing her through garishly colored nightmares. She had never dreamed in color before. Blood looked so bright in dreams. Somehow it was always her blood. The war paint and the dark skin seemed so terrifyingly real.

Strange how things worked out. Like her father, she had a fascination for dark skin. As an idyllic school girl, she had read *Uncle Tom's Cabin* and all those tales about the Noble Savage. She had lusted after the dark Pawnee scout. But why hadn't it occurred to her those warriors would smell of dirt and grease and gunpowder? There had been nothing noble about the way they had taken turns on her like dogs on a bitch in heat.

366

Very softly, she began to weep. She must get some sleep. Soon she would be going with Father to Denver and there would be parties in her honor and young men vying with each other to dance with her. She looked down at herself.

Silly, you can't go to a ball like that, you're in your nightdress. Don't you have a lovely dress?

Of course she did. She had a genuine Worth gown, imported from Paris, bought especially to be worn to parties in Denver. Father had sent the money to buy it.

Winnifred ran barefoot to the wardrobe. Yes, there it hung, ready to be packed for her trip to Denver. She smiled, stroking the pink fabric that complimented her eyes.

Had it really been only a couple of weeks ago that she had worn it to a party right here at the fort? She smiled at the memory. Ah, yes. She had been the belle of the ball. All the young officers had clustered around, begging for the next dance, even that young snob, Carter Osgoode, who had finally deserted. At least he was missing.

She put on the fine gown and carefully tied the wide sash. Voices from outside seemed to be calling to her. She couldn't find her shoes, but somehow, it didn't seem to matter.

Humming tunelessly to herself, she went outside. The officers' hall seemed to be dark. *How could that be when they were having a party in her honor?*

She stopped, the dirt coarse and gritty beneath her bare feet. It was all so very confusing. If the nightmares would stop, she might get some rest and then maybe she could straighten out her thoughts.

Winnifred leaned against the corner of the building and closed her eyes. Immediately, red-painted savages came at her from all directions, screaming in her ears. She stood trembling, hands clasped over her own mouth to hold back the sound. If she did that, people would come running, just as they used to when Mama screamed in the madhouse. All Winnifred wanted was blissful sleep, tranquil nights.

She thought she heard her mother calling her.

"Mama?" She began to walk toward the officers' mess hall. She was sure she had heard a whimper. *Or was it only the wind?*

A party. The officers of the post were having a party in her honor. She had been rescued off a train and carried by a tanned man to a horse. Noble Savage. Dark skin attracted her. She was her father's daughter after all.

If there was a party here tonight, why was the place so dark? Maybe it was a surprise party. She smiled to herself, clapped her hands in glee as she tried the unlocked door, and tiptoed into the deserted hall. *Yes, that was it! Any moment now, everyone would come out from the shadows and yell: Surprise! Surprise!*

She waited in the center of the deserted room for everyone to jump out, for the lights to come on. Dusty, faded decorations still hung from the crossbeams overhead.

Hadn't she been the belle of the ball that night with that pitiful Luci watching wistfully? Winnifred remembered that now with a smile. All Indian women were harlots, luring young officers away from their wives. Yes, that had been what her parents had been arguing about that night long before the war—the night Father went away forever.

"An unspeakable disease, Manning! That's what you've brought me home this time!"

And handsome, dashing Father in his captain's uniform, screaming back, "If you weren't such an ugly, cold bitch, I wouldn't keep leaving. I wouldn't need to find a real woman to share my bed!"

"Don't use that as an excuse! You were only after my money to begin with, and I was too stupid and smitten with you to realize it!"

"You haven't got much money left."

"Thanks to your wild ways and womanizing! Which one of your whores gave you this, Manning?"

And father shrugging. "How should I know? I've slept with dozens of black and Injun gals since I was home last. Only one it couldn't have been was that pretty little Cheyenne. She was a virgin."

And Mama in a storm of weeping. "I didn't ask for details that would break my heart."

"Oh, yes, you did, Clara! I'm sick of you, you hear? Sick of your whining and cold bed! I hear there's gold being found in Colorado, so I'm going there!"

"You?" Mama sneered. "You're too lazy to dig for gold."

He was reaching for his hat. "Dig? I didn't say 'dig.' It's easier to take the money away from them who've already dug it."

369

"What about your daughter? What about Winnifred?"

Father actually yawned. "What about her? A man wants sons, Clara. You couldn't even do that for me. Daughters are a dime a dozen. Why, even Sunrise gave me one."

"Get out! Get out!" Mama screamed.

He brushed past Winnifred, not even bothering to speak as he strode from the house, banging the door behind him.

Winnifred jumped at the slam of the door. *Where were Mama and Father?* A shutter banged again in the wind and she realized she stood barefoot in a deserted hall, all dressed up for a party.

What had happened to Mama? Oh, yes, Winnifred remembered. In the years that passed, her mother seemed to gradually lose her mind and had to be placed in the madhouse. Something horrible had happened there. Winnifred thought about it, but couldn't quite remember.

She smirked, thinking of Luci. She owed that half-breed the humiliation for all those squaws and Nigras who had slept with Father, who had stolen him away from her and Mama.

If Winnifred could just get some uninterrupted sleep, things would be better in the morning. But what about the ball? Where were the musicians, the laughing crowds? She realized suddenly that she stood all alone. But then, she had been all alone ever since Mama. . . .

Funny how things work out, she thought disinterestedly. Here she had planned the ultimate revenge—she had planned to put Father in a madhouse just as soon as possible, then possess all his power and money. From the look of his face, he was planning the same thing for Winnifred.

She shook her head violently. She did not want to end up like her mother. If she could just get some rest, she would be fine. All she wanted was quiet oblivion without nightmares.

She closed her eyes, remembering. Winnifred had been the one to find Mama at the madhouse. She had torn a bed sheet into strips.

She opened her eyes and looked up at the beams of the deserted hall. Mama had used the cross bars of the window of her little cell.

She saw Mama suddenly, beckoning to her. *I've waited for you a long time, daughter. Come with me to a place where there is no terror or pain or rejection.*

"Mama?"

The only answer was the sultry breeze blowing around the deserted building.

Come with me, Winnifred. I'm going now . . .

"No, Mama, don't go without me!" She tried to hold back her hysteria. "Mama? I'm coming!" Hurriedly, she dragged a chair over to one of the open beams. "I'm coming! Wait for me!"

She took off the wide silk sash, looped it up over the beam, then tied it around her neck.

Father, now you won't get the pleasure of putting me in a madhouse as you did Mama. I can keep you from doing it.

For a moment more, she stood on the chair. All she wanted was peace and tranquility. Ghostly music seemed to echo around her. Couples waltzed by, laughing and talking. Punch cups clinked.

But when she closed her eyes, from somewhere

in her tortured mind, savages came at her again. She had to escape from them before they caught her.

Winnifred stepped off the chair and kicked it out from under herself as she went. In that split second she regretted her action, reached frantically for the overturned chair with flaying feet, and grabbed vainly with frantic fingers at the sash around her neck. *I didn't mean it, I regret . . .*

She hit the end of the sash with her full weight and felt her neck snap. In that heartbeat of eternity, gigantic savages came screaming up out of the flames of hell and surrounded her. . . .

When they searched every building for the missing girl the next day, it was Johnny Ace who finally found her hanging stiffly from the ceiling beam.

"Oh, my God!" For a long moment, he could only stare at the hideous, discolored face, the expression of terror etched there. What had she seen in that very last second?

He wished suddenly that every silly girl who had ever pictured a romantic death by suicide could see Winnifred's distorted face, mouth hanging open in one last vain scream. In death, a body's muscles relax. Winnifred's fine dress was soaked with urine.

Johnny took a deep breath of the scent of her and staggered outside, gagging. He must not let the other women of the fort or her father see this. He went to find Major North. Together, they got the body down and covered it with a blanket before they sent word to the doctor and Manning Starrett that Winnifred had been found.

They buried her that afternoon in the little windswept cemetery outside the fort walls.

Frank North thought it was the saddest little procession he had ever participated in. Besides an honor guard, a chaplain, and a few curious people from the fort, there was only Johnny Ace, Manning Starrett, and himself walking along behind the horse-drawn wagon.

Starrett, hobbling with his cane, looked more annoyed than bereaved.

Only a plain, pine coffin, North noted to himself as the procession stopped and the soldiers lifted it off the wagon. Winnifred would be annoyed at such a crude box, such undistinguished company. He looked over at the grave next to it. Someone had carved out a wooden marker with a sun coming up over the prairie and the name.

The soldiers lowered the coffin into the grave that was waiting and the chaplain began his eulogy.

Frank North brushed away a fly that buzzed around his sweating face in the hot day. His body sweltered under the uniform. Would the minister never end? People were already shifting their feet restlessly, looking with longing eyes back toward the fort, sorry that they had let curiosity bring them out in the heat when there was beer and cold water from the well back up the path.

Finally the minister droned to a halt, shook hands with Manning Starrett, and mumbled his condolences. Then he and the curious began the walk back to the fort while the soldiers filled in the grave.

North watched Johnny Ace pick wild flowers along the neglected picket fence of the cemetery. The scout took a bunch over to place on Sunrise's grave, and then as the grave diggers finished, he put a small bouquet on the fresh mound.

Johnny Ace. Of course he had carved the headboard—or had it done. It might seem strange to anyone else, a Pawnee making a marker for a Cheyenne's grave, but then, Johnny was in love with Sunrise's daughter.

The soldiers climbed up on the wagon. The scout looked at him. "Major?"

North shook his head. "You men go on back. I'll stay here a few minutes with Mr. Starrett."

"But God damn it to hell, send a buggy back out here!" Starrett snapped. "I'm not in any shape to walk!"

"Do it." North nodded, and watched the wagon drive away. "I am sorry, Mr. Starrett, I never thought about your legs until too late. It's such an ingrained custom, walking behind the coffin—"

"Never mind! Just another example of bureaucratic bungling!"

North sighed and managed to control his temper. He must remember they were all very hot and tired and under stress;— particularly the father of the unfortunate girl. He said, "I'm so sorry about Winnifred. You have my deepest sympathy."

Manning Starrett only grunted and leaned on his cane, staring at the fresh grave with its pitiful little bouquet of wild flowers as if he did not quite

374

believe it.

North didn't know what else to say, so he stood there awkwardly, hoping the soldier hurried back with the buggy.

Somewhere in the silence, a quail called in the prairie grass: Bob white. Bob, bob white . . .

The breeze picked up a little. It felt good on his sweating face. On the flat Nebraska prairie, heat waves danced in the air when North looked out across the rippling waves of grass.

"Who's this?" Manning Starrett stared at the next grave and reached out with his cane to tap the carved marker.

"Sunrise Woman." North shrugged, wondering what difference it made. Was this bigot one of those who would insist on a segregated cemetery? Southerners had those, he remembered, "Mr. Starrett, I hope you aren't about to object to Winnifred being buried next to a Cheyenne woman. We're pretty democratic here at the fort—"

"Sunrise Woman?" Starrett leaned closer to stare at the marker. "Common enough name among Indians, I suppose."

Why in the goddamn hell would he care? *Watch it, Frank, you're beginning to think like that bastard.*

"She was just one of those Indian women who hang around Forts," North said by way of explanation. "She died a few weeks ago."

"Did she have a child?"

How did he know that? North nodded. "Yes, a very pretty girl named Luci. It means 'Morning Star.'"

Starrett didn't say anything for a long moment.

"She couldn't speak English well enough to say my name," he whispered almost regretfully. "That's what she called me."

"Who?"

"Is this daughter about seventeen or eighteen?" Starrett looked at him.

Morning Star. Manning Starrett. The major stared back into the bright blue eyes, and recognized suddenly why the man had looked so familiar to him. Had he been blind not to see the resemblance between Starrett, Winnifred — and Luci? "You lousy sonovabitch!" He said without thinking.

But Starrett only smiled. "Major, we've got a lot of talking to do. Sounds to me like I've got a relative after all to look after me as I get worse."

"And that's all she is to you — a free nurse."

"Don't make moral judgments, Major." He grinned, leaning on his cane. "I can offer her so much in exchange for looking after me."

Now it was Frank North's turn to grin. "Starrett, you're too late with your generosity. Your daughter isn't here. Luci's run away to her mother's people!"

But later, as they sat together in his office, North regretted his harshness toward Manning Starrett. Pouring his guest a drink, the major asked, "I suppose you'll be going back to Denver now?"

The man didn't even appear to have heard him. "Don't know what got into Winnifred," he said. "Crazy like her mother, I reckon."

376

What did it matter, North thought, but for a moment he said nothing, he only sipped his drink. And then he let his indignation voice itself. "All these years, you could have come for Sunrise and her child, and you didn't bother."

"I was a married man," Manning said, sipping his own drink. "What in the goddamn hell would you expect? Soldiers do it all the time and will always do it;—take up with any pretty girl until it's time to move on."

"Did you know there was a child?" He watched the other man's once handsome face for some sign of human kindness or caring.

Starrett shrugged. "I heard. But I had no need of her. After all, I already had a legitimate daughter. Of course, if she had been a boy, I might have been tempted."

"She's a beauty, and a feisty girl—the kind of daughter any man should be proud to claim."

Manning stared into his glass. "My only child," he muttered. "I wonder if I found her, gave her my name everything that goes with it—"

"You'd be better off to hire a nurse."

"Kin might not put me in a madhouse," Manning whispered. "I'm horrified of dying in a madhouse like my wife. A daughter might find it hard to put me there."

"You amaze me," North said, standing up. "You just buried one daughter with no more emotion than if you'd buried a dog, and now you talk about the other one as if she'd rush to claim you as her father—"

"Wouldn't she?" It was Starrett's turn to grin as he leaned on his cane. "If she knew her rich

377

father wanted to take her away to Denver to live like a princess, don't you think she'd say yes?"

There was no doubting human nature. He thought about Johnny Ace. "I'm sure she'd jump at the chance," he admitted.

"Well, then, Major." Starrett put his glass down, rubbing his hands together with satisfaction. "You're going out after Cheyenne. If you find her, tell her I'm here, and everything I've got to offer."

His smugness infuriated North. But before he could answer, there was a rap at the door. "Come in,"

Johnny Ace came halfway in the door. "Oh, excuse me, Major. I didn't know you had company." He looked at Starrett. "Sorry about your daughter."

Starrett made a gesture of sneering dismissal. "I don't need pity from an Injun."

Johnny's face turned a deep, angry color and North noticed his hands shook as he rolled a cigarette. "I felt sorry for her, not you."

North said, "Johnny, there's a new development about Luci."

Johnny paused with the cigarette halfway to his lips. He must not appear too interested. "What about her?"

The major had never felt as sorry for anyone as he did for Johnny Ace at that moment. His eyes strayed to his bookshelf. At least in this case, Romeo and Juliet wouldn't kill themselves. "Johnny," he said as gently as he could, "it appears that Mr. Starrett here may be her father."

"No!" Johnny lashed out, throwing the cigarette across the room. "Hell, no!"

378

Starrett looked from one to the other. "What's this all about?" And then a knowing look came into his eyes. "Oh, I begin to see—"

"No, you don't see, you selfish old bastard!" Johnny shouted but North caught his arm. "All these years, she and her mother waited and you never came for her, and now that I love her—"

"Love!" Starrett sneered. "Love is the most overrated thing in the world! You're Pawnee, aren't you? Even I know no miracle can work out between those two tribes!"

It was true, even Frank North knew it. God, he would give anything to change that!

Johnny stood feet wide apart, playing with the hilt of his knife, not looking either of them in the face. "What difference does it make?" he said. "Now that she's gone back to her people."

Starrett nodded. "I know that. But the Fifth Cavalry's going after the Cheyenne. There's a good chance you'll find her, and bring her back."

"What makes you think she'd come?" Johnny said.

Starrett grinned. "Human nature. I'd be willing to bet that the minute the major tells her I've come to take her to Denver and be my heir, she won't be able to get back here fast enough. Want to bet on it?"

Major North snapped, "Shut up, Starrett. Can't you see he's in love with her?"

"Wouldn't work," the older man grunted. "Too many things against it, him being Pawnee and all. Besides, boy, you think given a chance to choose, she'd take you over all my money?"

North looked at the sadness that came to Johnny's eyes, and at that moment, he hated Starrett as he had never hated a man. "Get out of my office before I throw you out!"

"You'd hit a sick man?" Starrett whined, getting to his feet. "I'm going to wire my associate in Denver, Major, and tell him I'm staying to see if you can bring her back."

"We'll probably be gone for weeks," North said to discourage him.

Starrett shrugged. "Doesn't matter. My partner can take care of business in Denver. I'll wire him I'm going to be delayed. He has the power of attorney to handle my business and I trust him."

Johnny said, "Why don't you go home and let us wire you if and when we find her?"

"You'd like that, wouldn't you, you savage, you! You'd never tell her I was looking for her, that's what. You'd try to carry her off and never let her know she had money and all waiting for her in Denver!"

"Don't tempt me," Johnny snapped.

"No, I'll just wait here for the Fifth's return." Starrett leaned on his cane. "Besides, it's a long, hard trip to Denver and I'm not up to making it too many times. Now you bring in my daughter, Major, you hear?"

Starrett turned and went out, limping down the path.

Johnny rolled another cigarette. His hands still shook a little as he lit it. "It isn't fair that he should turn up now just because he needs a daughter to look after him and give him some grandchildren."

It isn't fair when you love her so much, North

380

thought, but he didn't say anything for a long moment. Finally he said, "Orders came through. We're going out after the Dog Soldiers tomorrow, Johnny."

"It'll be a long, bad campaign," Johnny said as he smoked in silence, the smoke drifting between them. "We're outnumbered and they're better armed than we are."

North nodded. "But the Dog Soldiers are the key. If we can defeat them, the other hostiles will surrender and go back to the reservations."

Neither said anything for a long moment, but from Johnny's expression, North knew they were thinking the same. "Johnny, you think she's with the Dog Soldiers?"

"Probably. That means she might be in danger if we attack them."

"I don't know what I can do about that." North clasped his hands behind his back and paced up and down. "I can't keep from attacking if we run into them just because Luci may be with them."

"I know that, Major."

North had never seen such pain on a man's face and he had never felt as sorry for anyone as he felt now for this star-crossed pair of lovers. "Johnny, I tell you what I'll do. No one knows about this but the two of us. If we find her and rescue her, I'm not going to tell. Your enlistment's almost up. I'm going to let you make this decision."

"What?"

"I'm telling you that if you want to and if she's willing, you can take that girl and ride away with her. She need never know that she had a chance to become a rich princess with a castle in Denver and all that goes with it."

Johnny studied the glowing tip of his cigarette. "That wouldn't be fair to Luci, would it? Not give her a choice?"

North shrugged. "All's fair in love and war and I'm not sure anymore which is which. If you want her, take her away. I sure as hell won't tell her about Starrett."

"It's underhanded," Johnny said uncertainly.

"I don't give a damn about that and you shouldn't either if you want her, Johnny. Do you want to be ethical or do you want that girl?"

Johnny took a deep puff of smoke. "I want her, all right. I want her enough to do anything to get her!"

"Then that's your decision to make. I'll just tell the old bastard we didn't find her."

"Somebody in the troops might tell him different."

North laughed. "What could he do if the two of you disappeared without a trace?" North went over to his desk and looked at the map spread there. "Now get Cody and my brother in here. General Carr is waiting for a report. The whole Fifth Cavalry's going after the Dog Soldiers!"

Chapter Twenty-one

Friday, May 28. A day Luci would never forget. Snake's war party joined Tall Bull's south of the Saline River in Kansas. Whenever she looked back, the memory was as fresh and horrible as the day it happened.

The war party she rode with had finally linked up with her uncle's renegades coming up from the south. At first, Tall Bull hadn't been too friendly.

"You are a half-breed because my sister chose a white lover over a Cheyenne husband." He stood under a cottonwood tree, as the war party made plans. "Where is Sunrise Woman?"

Luci looked back at the gray-haired, war-painted brave, trying to decide how to tell him. She still couldn't think of Sunrise Woman without swallowing a lump in her throat. "My—my mother is dead this spring. She got out in the wet and cold too much, and caught the coughing and congestion in the chest."

"Dead?" He seemed almost to flinch at her words, then his painted face was stoic again, betraying nothing. "I warned Sunrise Woman that the whites, that the soldier, would bring her nothing but heartbreak, but she was stubborn and headstrong, probably like you are yourself."

She would not deny it. "But I think perhaps I am wiser than my mother was."

"Let us hope so." Tall Bull sighed. "My sister had a stupid idea that she could bridge the gap between two cultures when we all know it is hopeless."

Of course it was. And yet . . .

"Maybe in a few cases, if both people care enough, it could happen."

Tall Bull laughed without mirth, leaning on his lance. "You speak now with your heart, not your head. Have you a man?"

Her heart said yes, but she shook her head. Certainly if the leader of the Dog Soldiers had disapproved of a white lover, what would he think about an enemy Pawnee? "I want to wait a long time." She sneaked a glance at Snake's ugly face. He squatted over by the fire, cleaning and reloading a shiny Winchester. "But perhaps someday—"

" 'Someday' is not a good answer for a people who are running out of time to replenish their numbers," Tall Bull scoffed, looking at Snake.

"No, I—"

"I will choose a worthy Dog Soldier from among my warriors for you, since you have no father. The mistake my sad sister made will not be repeated," her uncle said with satisfaction, ignoring her interruption. "When we have gathered at the meeting place and have time to think of such things. But today, I have news. Not far from here, are some of the steel rails that carry the Iron Horse through our buffalo range. We attack it today!"

The Kansas Pacific, Luci thought, now laying track toward Denver. "Uncle, the whites will fight to protect their Iron Horse, and people will die—"

"We all die sooner or later," the warrior shouted at her, "but the warriors of our people, the Tsistsistas, will die with weapons in their hands, not on their knees, begging for white man's food!"

The listening warriors set up a chant of approval. "Yes! Yes! We will attack the whites who help bring the Iron Horse into our country to kill our game and steal our land!"

What to do? Whose side was she on? There was nothing Luci could do to stop them. All she could do was watch as they began the ceremony involved with taking the war trail.

A brave had managed to kill one lonely buffalo when, several years back, there might have been thousands. While the war party made medicine, Luci was ordered to cook the meat. She had to follow careful rituals. Dog Soldiers on a war party could not eat certain parts of the animal. The taboos and the rituals were many.

Tall Bull sent out scouts, called "wolves" even by the Cheyenne. They came back, rode in a ritual circle around the camp, then jumped from their already painted horses.

385

"We have seen white men working on the track not far from here."

"How many?" Snake leaned forward eagerly.

"Not more than six or seven."

"Are there soldiers to guard them? Are there Pawnee with them?" Tall Bull put his fingers up behind his head in the familiar sign that signified Pawnee.

"No, some of them do not even seem to have guns and those who do have left them carelessly on that small wheeled thing they ride down the rails."

Luci must try to stop this attack. "Do not fire on them," she said. "They will send a message over the wire and many soldiers will come."

The men glared at her in silent disapproval that she, a mere woman, had spoken at this war council.

Tall Bull scowled. "My niece has been too long among the whites. She forgets her place."

The scout said, "I saw no singing wires. I think they may not have gotten them yet."

"Good!" Tall Bull grunted. "We will butcher them and leave them lying in their own blood!"

Bear Cub had said nothing, sitting away from the circle, sketching on the white man's paper, but he gave Luci a sympathetic look.

She could stand it no longer. "No!" she began and then stopped when the braves glared at her.

Snake looked from Tall Bull to Luci and smiled. "All your niece needs is a proper husband to teach her what a Cheyenne girl is supposed to know."

Luci shuddered at the thought but Tall Bull stared into the fire and nodded. "That is true. We will discuss this more when we finally camp at that place whites call Summit Springs and we have time for other thoughts besides war."

After much ritual and pipe smoking, the warriors spread out on their buffalo robes and dropped off to sleep.

Luci waited until they were asleep, then sneaked to the horse herd. As usual, the crippled boy had been assigned sentry duty. He called out in a hoarse whisper, "Who is there?"

She gestured him to silence. "It's only me, Luci."

"What do you want?"

"I—I couldn't sleep." She hesitated. Bear Cub cared for her, she had seen it in his eyes. No doubt, she could convince him to give her a horse and help her escape. But what would happen to the crippled boy tomorrow for doing that? No doubt he would be whipped severely . . . or worse. She decided she couldn't be responsible for that.

Even in the moonlight, as he sat his horse, he sketched pictures.

"Bear Cub, about tomorrow—are you afraid?"

"Yes," he admitted, "but if I can prove that I am as good as any warrior, perhaps I, too, can become a Dog Soldier. Maybe many years from now when the Old Ones tell tales around the campfire, they will remember my bravery in their songs and stories."

"I'm sure they will," she said to comfort him. *What could a crippled half-grown boy do that might endure in Cheyenne legends?*

There was nothing to do but go back over the rise to the camp. She wanted very much to relieve herself and wash a little dust from her perspiring body. Now that the men were all asleep, she felt safe in doing that. Luci walked to the creek, wondering what she could do about tomorrow's attack. She could neither warn the railroaders nor escape without a horse. The prairie was too vast.

She pulled off her ragged dress and waded into the creek. The cool water felt good on her hot skin. Too bad she had no soap. She splashed awhile, washing herself, then came up out of the water, reaching for the dress she had left hanging over a sumac bush. A hand reached out of the darkness and handed her the dress.

With a gasp, she grabbed the cloth and held it in front of her as she stumbled backward.

Snake stepped out of the shadows, grinning at her. "Yes, now that I have seen you naked, I think I would like very much to have you for my third wife!"

"How dare you!" She wrapped the dress around herself, knowing she would have to show her nakedness if she attempted to slip it over her head. "I should scream for my uncle!"

But he reached out, grabbed her, and pulled her to him. "Don't do that! A Dog Soldier isn't supposed to touch a woman before he goes into battle, you know that? It takes his strength and medicine from him. But in this case, maybe it's worth the risk of bad luck!"

Before she could scream, he had his mouth on hers, hot and wet, his dirty hands on her naked body. His skin was slick with sweat in the heat of the night and he smelled of dirt, smoke, and blood.

She struggled and he clamped his hand over her mouth. "If you scream, your uncle will be angry with me, yes, but being a man, he will understand. Besides, to save the family honor, he would force you to marry me."

It was probably true. She managed to pull away from him, but she didn't scream for help. Snake had the dress in his hand and she could only try to cover herself with her own hands. "Stay away from me, Snake! I don't want to be your woman."

"I have many horses and am considered a rich man." He threw the dress to the ground, put his hand on her bare shoulder. "Because I already have two wives to do the work of curing hides and drying meat, you would not have to do much work. Mostly you would warm my blankets at night until I put a baby in your belly."

"That thought sickens me." She backed away from him. "Besides, this is not proper talk between a man and an unmarried maiden."

"So now you want to behave like a proper Cheyenne girl," he sneered. Before she could stop him, he grabbed her and ran his hands over her bare body while she struggled. "Probably some soldier has already taken your virginity."

"That's not true!" But she couldn't break away from him no matter how hard she struggled. To the Cheyenne, chastity was very important in a bride. Most of the Cheyenne girls wore a chastity belt to protect their virtue from overeager males until marriage. His hands were all over her, pawing at her, feeling her breasts. She struggled to get away, but she was small and he was a big man. He pulled her hard against him so that she could feel his hard maleness pulsating against her belly.

He forced his tongue between her lips, his hot, dirty hands stroking her wet body. She bit him and he struck her. But he didn't let go of her. "When you are my bride, I will teach you proper behavior," he snarled. "I will beat you until you will be glad to lie down on my buffalo robe and let me do anything I want to you! Anything!"

His tone scared her. There was probably no end to the sexual cruelties he could think of to inflict. Would he rape her tonight, even if it meant nullifying the magic powder, *sihyainoeisseeo,* that he had already sprinkled on himself for good medicine? The way he was looking at her, he evidently thought it worth the risk.

She'd have to trick him. She smiled invitingly at him. "Perhaps I have been too hasty. But then, what would you think of me if I didn't protest a little? Maybe I should consider you after all. Let us lie down together here in the shadow of these bushes."

Studying her in the moonlight, he looked suspicious at first, but as she sat down on the grass, he did, too. "Now, Snake, lie back and let me show you what the white whores do."

He grinned, nodded willingly, and lay down on the grass. Luci was waiting for her chance. Like a flash, she jumped up, grabbed her dress, and ran madly toward the campfire.

No one stirred. Quickly, she slipped on the dress and lay down on her blanket near her uncle. Snake strode back, glowered at her across the campfire, but even he wouldn't risk rape with her uncle so close. She heard him curse as he lay down on the other side of the circle.

Trembling, she lay sleepless, considering her future. What would she do after all the Cheyenne had gathered at Summit Springs? There when the renegades camped and rested, she would no doubt be forced into marriage with the ugly warrior. Besides being a friend of her uncle's, Snake was a rich man of many ponies. No doubt Tall Bull would look with favor on him when he came to ask for her as a bride.

Johnny Ace. Her mind went to his torrid, but gentle lovemaking. How she longed for the protection of his strong arms, the security of his embrace. If he had been here, he would have killed Snake for daring even to touch her. But he wasn't here. He was back at the fort, making plans to lead the soldiers against the Cheyenne.

There was nothing she could do tonight, but sometime in the next few days, maybe she could sneak away and escape.

And go where? she thought. There seemed to be no refuge for someone caught between two worlds, two civilizations.

Friday, May 28. The Dog Soldiers mounted up to ambush the men working on the track.

The war party, with Luci along, rode within a quarter mile of the crew, and saw them laughing and talking as they worked on the rails. Sure enough, they weren't all armed, and those who had guns appeared to have left them on the handcar a few hundred feet down the track.

Luci thought they probably hadn't dealt with any Indian attacks in a long time so they were getting careless; or maybe they hadn't heard the

Cheyenne had bolted the reservation and were raiding through Kansas.

Before they could be seen, Tall Bull motioned the war party down into a nearby gully. The work crew moved slowly closer to them. In the heat of the day, Luci felt the perspiration run down between her breasts. Her mouth tasted dry and salty, but she was hesitant to reach for the canteen of tepid water on her saddle. She needed both hands on her reins if, in the outbreak of gunfire, her roan horse should bolt.

There was little breeze in the gully. The horses stamped at flies and somewhere a cicada buzzed rhythmically in the heat. Faintly, she heard the workmen laughing and talking as they moved nearer. She took a deep breath, wondering what she could do to save them. She smelled the scent of sweating horses and men, the dry dust of the Kansas prairie.

The crew talked about what might be waiting for them for supper back at the station. *Fossil Creek Station. Some of them were not going to live to eat that supper,* she thought desperately, looking for help toward Bear Cub. He was armed, although she wondered how good a shot he was. At least he was brave enough to try. But his precious sketch book was tied up in the bundle behind his saddle.

She must do something, but what? If the workmen only had some idea the Indians were in the gully, they would run for the handcart, get on it, and try to get back to the station. If they ran away, she could save lives on both sides. An idea came to her. It was dangerous for herself, but she didn't care anymore if she could stop this massacre.

She dug her heels into her nervous pony's flanks. At once it began to buck and dance. "I—I can't stop it!" she screamed at the surprised Cheyenne. "It's running away with me!" And she gave the pony its head, letting it gallop up out of the gully, dancing and pitching across the prairie.

She heard the surprised exclamations of the rail workers, the shouts of dismay behind her that the advantage of surprise had been lost. Then all around her was noise and shots and confusion.

"Injuns! Run for it!"

"Aiee! Attack! Attack!" The Dog Soldiers galloped up out of the gully, trying to make up by speed for the edge that was gone.

Mostly she remembered the open-mouthed surprise of the white men as they stared for a heart-stopping moment. Then they scrambled toward the handcart parked up the track a few hundred feet away.

Shots rang out. The acrid scent of powder and smoke swirled around her as the Dog Soldiers returned fire with the new Winchesters.

All she could do was sit her nervous, dancing pony, watching the bright blur of colors as the action happened. The white men ran for the handcart; the Indians tried to stop them with a barrage of gunfire. A white man screamed out but managed to keep running as the others reached the cart and grabbed for their guns.

One young boy seemed no older than Bear Cub. He looked frightened and his hands shook. His rifle jammed as he tried to put too many cartridges in it. Only three others had rifles, she noted, but they were the repeating Spencers such as the ones she heard the men at Beecher's Island had carried. But one of the men didn't seem to have any ammunition for his. He kept looking around and begging the others, but they must not have any spare ammunition, she thought.

In the confusion, both sides fired back and forth at each other without much effect; the white men seemed too terrified to take proper aim, the braves too unaccustomed to the fine rifles to use them properly.

With all seven of the whites finally on the handcart, they tried to get under way, back toward the refuge of the station. The braves, seeing what they were attempting to do, rode in circles around the handcart to prevent that.

After a heart-stopping moment, the white men got the hand cart moving slowly, some working the handles, others firing at the Indians.

A brave cried out, grasped the spurting wound in his painted chest as if to hold his life inside. But it was already running out, hot and red between his fingers. He slid down the dun pony, leaving a scarlet smear as he fell.

Even as she watched, a white man shrieked, pitched forward, and fell from the cart. The others looked too busy to try to pull him back on as they got the handcart moving again.

There was nothing she could do but watch. Bear Cub raced about, firing, but she doubted that he knew enough about a rifle to hit anyone with it. A grin of pure delight lit Snake's ugly, painted features as he took careful aim at the creaking cart

394

inching its way along the track.

When he pulled the trigger, another white man screamed and tumbled from the cart to lie crumpled between the rails behind it. Immediately, the warriors dashed in to touch the body and count coup. She wasn't sure the men were even dead when Snake, ignoring the deadly rifle fire, rushed in, leaned over to count coup on the bodies, and began to scalp them.

She must be more white than Indian after all, Luci thought. At the sight and scent of blood, she rode off to one side, became very sick, and had to swallow hard to keep from vomiting.

Could she escape in all this confusion of battle? She looked around, but decided it was impossible. Her pony wasn't the best and the warriors would easily ride her down and recapture her.

The barrage of shots continued. Another brave yelled and fell from his horse. On the handcart, two of the white men dripped blood from wounds. They had the handcart going again with the Cheyenne keeping a more respectful distance from the deadly fire of the Spencers, but still attempting to stop them from reaching the station.

Fossil Station. A mere dugout a few hundred yards down the track. The despairing look on the white men's faces told her they didn't think they'd make it.

If only Snake would get hit or even her uncle, that might discourage the war party. They would take it as a sign of bad medicine and pull back. But the firing and shouting and screaming continued, with the crew working their way a few feet before they stopped and fired again, then labored yet closer to the dugout.

So near and yet so far. But about that time, a man ran out of the station and began firing. He was well armed and a good shot.

"Come on, boys!" he waved wildly. Encouraged, they got the cart moving again while he held the Indians off.

Luci began to urge them on, wanting them to make it. It was then she realized she wasn't Cheyenne deep in her heart where it counted most.

The white men struggled to get the handcart farther down the track while the man from the station laid a covering fire. Then they jumped and ran for it, half dragging, half carrying the wounded.

They were safe inside! Luci forgot herself and cried out in relief, but Snake cursed and shouted, shook his fist at the dugout, and was answered with a volley of rifle fire from inside.

The Cheyenne rode out of range and conferred. Snake said, "Let us keep attacking until we overrun them!"

But Tall Bull shook his head. "Would you kill all my men? No doubt the whites have plenty of ammunition and food inside. We could attack a long time before we killed them. It is not worth the cost in Cheyenne blood! There's easier prey along the river not far from here!"

Snake rode over to Luci. "Your bucking horse cost us the surprise and the win!"

She tried to look innocent. "I think maybe a bee stung him. I couldn't help it! Would you call Tall Bull's niece a liar?"

He seemed to consider. Even he was obviously

not that brave. "Your uncle is right. There are unsuspecting farmers all over this area. They have food, hidden gold, and soft women! We will attack them!"

But Tall Bull shook his head. "For a day or two, we must find a place to camp and rest. We have wounded to attend to. Then we will hit the farmers when it is so quiet, they think we have ridden out of the area and they are safe!"

They camped along a river that tasted a little salty, so Luci thought it must be the Saline. Mercy! She wrung her small, reddened hands. Was there any way to warn the innocent settlers? Luci knew she was watched too closely to sneak off and spread the alarm.

Sunday, May 30. Luci remembered the dates to keep herself occupied. When was it the Fifth Cavalry was riding out after the Dog Soldiers? The first or second week in June? Would they change their plans and move faster when reports of the new raids to the south began to filter in?

What a beautiful Sunday afternoon to die, she thought sadly as the Dog Soldiers made their plans, then split up near a farmhouse. Snake took his men to ambush the white people of that farm while she stayed with her uncle. There was nothing she could do to help those settlers or stop the attack, she knew that. Yet she tried desperately to think of some way, even as she heard the shots echoing and the screams.

Luci clasped her hands over her ears, not wanting to hear the shrieks, but was unable to keep them out. Her uncle looked at her and frowned. "I think my sister has given me a niece more white than red."

"I hate the killing," she wept. "I don't want to see anyone die!"

Bear Cub looked at her sympathetically and went on sketching a battle scene in the ledger book.

After a few minutes, there was only silence. Then Snake rode back in with his warriors, all shouting in triumphant. On an extra horse, he led a pregnant white girl who wept hysterically.

Seeing Luci, she cried out, "They've killed my children! Help me! Oh, please, for the love of God!"

Snake grinned. "She can't help you, white girl! You are a prize to be shared among the warriors!"

Luci threw all caution to the winds and galloped over to her uncle. "What cruelty is this? Do our warriors fight children? Let the woman go!"

"They have killed some of *our* children," Tall Bull reminded Luci grimly. "Remember Sand Creek? Our babies were massacred there and a dozen other places! Besides, we will be moving fast and can't be slowed down by children who might give away our position with their crying!"

There was nothing Luci could do as the whole group took off down the creek at a gallop, leading the white girl's horse. Luci managed to ride close to the sobbing, pretty, girl. "I'll try to help you," she whispered in English. "Who are you?"

The woman managed to pull herself together at the sound of the familiar tongue. "Susanna. Susanna Alderdice. My—my husband . . . gone for the day. . . . I—I walked over to visit the neighbors. . . ." She broke into sobs.

Now some of the warriors dismounted and were searching along the riverbanks. Luci was baffled. She turned to Susanna. "What do they search for?"

The girl shook with sobs. "Mrs. Kine and her baby managed to get away. . . . They're probably hiding. . . . Oh, dear God! I can't believe this has happened!" She covered her face with her hands and gave way to hysterics.

Luci wanted to reach out and comfort her, but there was no time for that now. Was there anything she could do to help the missing white woman? Sick at heart, she watched the Cheyenne braves checking along the muddy banks of the river, searching for a footprint or some other clue that the woman might have tried to cross there.

And then Luci saw her. Close to the bank where Luci sat her horse, there was a weedy, overgrown place. Luci saw the trembling white woman hiding in the muddy water up to her neck, her baby's face just barely out of the water. The woman had her hand clamped tightly over the baby's mouth to keep it from crying.

Luci's heart beat faster. Snake would kill that baby if he found it and take the woman captive as he had done poor Susanna. Luci must stop that from happening.

The woman realized that Luci had seen her. With her eyes, she begged for mercy. Luci couldn't do anything to help Susanna at this moment, but she might be able to save Mrs. Kine and her baby. She rode along the water, then shouted and pointed even farther up the river. "I saw a movement! I think I saw someone running into the brush from the water up ahead!"

Immediately the warriors took off at a gallop farther up the creek and fanned out, searching the brush and farther up along the river. They found nothing.

Snake scowled at Luci. "I thought you said you saw something move."

"I did! Can I help it if your warriors are so slow, they let her get away?" She defended herself gamely. If they realized what she had done, they might kill her, but it was worth it if she could save the woman and her child. "Why don't we ride farther up the river and look some more? Maybe she has gotten away. Or maybe the white woman fell in the creek and drowned. You know with all those long skirts they wear, that could happen easily."

Snake snorted disagreeably. "We've wasted too much time already! We can't spend the whole day looking for one woman when there are other farms to be raid!"

With a sigh of relief, Luci turned back. Now the war party took off across the country with Snake leading Susanna's horse. Luci tried to stay close and comfort her.

Bear Cub reined his horse alongside Luci. They rode along in silence. Then he said softly. "I know what you did. I, too, saw the woman hiding in the water."

Luci stiffened and looked at him. "Oh, Bear, don't tell!"

"I won't!" The boy shook his head. "I have no stomach for this. I would fight to defend my own people, but killing women and children is wrong, whatever race."

She gave him a warm smile. At least she had found a true friend, even though the way he looked at her said it was more to him than that. He gave her an encouraging nod and rode back to check on the straggling herd of horses that the Cheyenne had gathered up.

Susanna rode like a lifeless doll, no expression, no movement. The shock had put her almost into a trance, Luci thought sympathetically, wishing she could do something more for the poor woman. She didn't even want to think about the children.

But when they paused momentarily on the trail, Susanna managed to stir and leaned closer. "I—I saw what you did back there for Mrs. Kine. Who are you and why would you help us?"

"I'm Luci from Fort McPherson. I thought these were my people, but they are only savage strangers after all." It was true. Up ahead, the braves had paused. She saw a small house and plowed fields in the distance. The Indians were planning strategy and there was nothing she could do.

Susanna said, "What will happen to me?"

"I—I don't know," Luci lied, not looking the pitiful girl in the face. She knew full well that any soldier, white or brown, considered a captured woman a prize to be enjoyed.

The prairie would be soaked with blood before this outbreak ended and there was nothing she could do to stop it. The best she could hope for was that she might manage to free Susanna and help her escape later tonight.

Susanna retreated to her mental trance. "My husband was gone for the day. . . . My babies.

401

They killed my babies." She said it over and over again in a toneless voice as if she could not quite believe everything that had happened, and if she kept talking, sooner or later she would wake up and find it wasn't true.

The war party hit the farmhouse. The unsuspecting whites never had a chance. All Luci and Susanna could do was sit there under guard by a couple of Dog Soldiers while the rest attacked the farm.

Luci was almost in a daze herself. She sat her horse, hot, sweaty, and thirsty, closing her eyes so she couldn't see the attack. But she heard it, all the screams and shouts and shots. And finally, the triumphant yells of the warriors and a woman screaming.

They came riding back with a beautiful blond girl slung across a horse. Her clothes were ripped and she was wide-eyed in horror. When she saw the other two women, she wept and screamed at them in a language Luci didn't understand. Luci looked over at Susanna, who only blinked and shook her head. "German, maybe. There are a lot of immigrants among the farmers."

Immigrants who only wanted to make a small home for themselves on the plains, Luci thought in anguish. But at the expense of the Indians. *Who was right and who was wrong?*

Could she do anything to help these two unfortunate women? At least she had gotten herself into this mess, but these two white girls were innocent. She looked at the German girl, who was not much older than herself. This girl didn't look like an ordinary farmgirl. Her clothes were better than average and her hands were soft and fine as if she came from a better-educated class of people than the average immigrant.

But now there was no more time to think or talk. The Cheyenne war party took off at a gallop toward the north, yelling to each other that the whole area had probably been alerted by these raids and soldiers might be sent in soon. The Indians wanted to reach a safer place before they stopped to rest and count their loot. Luci heard Snake bragging about all the gold coins he had found on the last man's body.

Luci looked at the weeping blond girl, wondering if the body had been her husband's and if she had seen him die. No time to think about that now. If only Johnny Ace and the cavalry would show up. Then she almost laughed. Why had she thought of the enemy coming to rescue her? He was several hundred miles away, making plans to help lead the army to kill her people. Only she wasn't sure who her people were anymore.

The Cheyenne rode hard until after dark before they finally decided it might be safe enough to camp for the night, rest, and water the lathered horses.

While the braves built a fire, Luci helped the white girls from their horses. Both of them, but especially the pregnant one, were so sore and stiff, they fell when she helped them down and over to a willow tree.

Susanna grabbed her hand. "Can we escape?"

Luci looked around. A pair of Dog Soldiers leaned against a cottonwood in the shadows, watching the trio. "Not tonight, at least. Maybe

403

later when they let down their guard."

The foreign one jabbered at them in her native tongue and Luci shook her head to show neither of them understood her, but patted her own chest. "Luci," she said. She pointed at the pregnant girl. "Susanna. Susanna."

A flash of understanding lit the blond girl's pretty face. "Maria." She touched her own chest again. "Maria." Then she burst into tears.

Luci put her arms around her and hugged her.

Susanna said again without expression, "They killed my children. I saw them kill my children."

Luci wondered if the woman was going mad. To occupy herself, she patted the sobbing Maria's back and wondered if Mrs. Kine had made her way out of the creek and to safety.

Susanna said, "My husband . . . where is my husband?"

Luci patted her arm. "He's probably all right. Try not to think about it. Try to think about escaping and getting back to your husband."

At that, Susanna stared at her without blinking. "I don't know if he's even still alive. He and my younger brother had ridden off to look at land they were thinking about trying to buy if we could get the money." She studied her calloused, work-worn hands. "Farming is hard work," she said to no one. "It's all so ironic. My husband and my little brother were at Beecher's Island against the Cheyenne last September. Lots of men were killed, but they made it back. Now maybe the Indians have killed them when they least expected it."

"Maybe not," Luci said a little too brightly. "Maybe they are just fine and are searching everywhere for you."

"Do you think so?" Susanna grabbed Luci's arm like a drowning man grabbing a floating stick. "Do you think so?"

"Of course," Luci said. "Now let me see if I can get us something to eat." It took all her strength to pull away from the half-crazed woman and Maria, who clung to her skirt. She made eating motions to the German girl, pointing to the men gathered around the fire.

She passed Bear Cub sitting with his sketch book on a log. He looked up at her. "I hated what happened today."

"I know." She looked down at his drawings, wondering if David Van Schuyler would think the boy had talent, if there was anything he could do to help the crippled boy. Certainly there was no future for him here. There was no future for anyone among the Cheyenne, she thought suddenly, certainly not among the Dog Soldiers. Why hadn't she remembered this warrior society was the suicide group who expected to die in battle?

She went over, gathered up some dried beef and captured hardtack, and looked at her uncle and the others, who sat with bloodstained booty before them. "Is it all right if I feed the prisoners?"

Her uncle nodded, his face showing his good humor. "It was a successful raid, my niece. Perhaps you have brought us good luck."

The shaman frowned. "Let us hope so. I told you of my vision after Snake spilled blood at the place of the Balanced Rock."

Snake glared at him with contempt. "Superstition! You have misunderstood the omen, old man."

While they argued over what the vision meant, Luci slipped back to the two captives with the food. They ate ravenously although Luci herself was too worried to eat much. She had seen the way the men kept glancing at the captured women. Their bellies were full and they felt safe enough to camp here at least for the night.

Snake stood up, looking their way.

Susanna looked at him, then at Luci. "What will happen? What do you think he'll do now?"

Some of the other men stood up, too, looking toward the captives.

Was there anything she could do to protect these pitiful women? She'd have to try. Maybe if she pleaded with her uncle. . . .

"They're coming over here," Susanna said. "What do they want?"

Luci said it before she thought. "As pretty as you are, don't you know?"

Chapter Twenty-two

The following weeks were a blur of misery to Luci. All through the month of June, she and the two white women captives moved with the Dog Soldiers as the warriors raided across Nebraska, Kansas, and eastern Colorado Territory.

She hadn't realized she could be so unhappy, exhausted, and dirty, yet still manage to live without losing her mind.

The days were a blur of hard riding, hunger, and hot June weather, the sun beating down on the Cheyenne and their captives as they roamed the desolate and hostile prairie.

Susanna Alderdice and Maria Weichell were in bad condition and having a worse time than she was, Luci thought sympathetically as the group dismounted to camp for the night. She herself was bone tired from the killing pace the warriors had set all day but Maria and Susanna both collapsed in the shade of a tree and didn't move when they dismounted. She went over to see about them, taking them some water. The pregnant Susanna looked as if the mental strain was almost more than she could bear.

She had to cheer them up. "Sooner or later, the cavalry will find us," she whispered. "Think about home."

Immediately, she knew that was the wrong thing to say. It reminded Susanna of her murdered children and she began to weep.

Luci put her arm around her. "Remember what we discussed to keep our minds busy?"

Susanna nodded almost mechanically. Her eyes looked as if she were past thinking. "You said we must teach Maria English. Otherwise, she'll be helpless when she's finally rescued, with no one to understand her."

Maybe it was a ridiculous thing to be doing, Luci thought with a sigh, but it did pass the time and the German girl would need the language eventually—if they were ever rescued.

One of the Cheyenne women called to Luci to help with preparing food, and Luci went. If she didn't, they would punish her by not feeding the captives, which was more than Luci could bear. She was treated well, of course, since she was Tall Bull's niece. In reality, many times there wasn't enough food even for the Cheyenne themselves because of the vanishing buffalo herds and the white hunters.

The pace had been intense, attacking lonely ranches, outrunning cavalry patrols. All the United States army appeared to be combing the plains for the renegade Dog Soldiers and the net seemed to be closing around them.

Later, Luci tried to reason again with her uncle. "If you would surrender and free the captives, the women and children of this band would at least live. No doubt the government would let most of the warriors return to the reservation."

"Existing is not living." His calm logic was as tragic as his face. "The time for our people to roam wild and free as they have always done is drawing to a close. I see it, we all see it, none knows what to do, nor can we change."

"In that case, the army will hunt you down, a few at a time. Would you rather see the people die than return to the Indian Territory?"

He stared into the fire, a sad man who had outlived his time. "Each man must decide for his own family. As for mine, we will take our chances, and if cornered, we will fight. I will not be locked up in a barred cage, which is what they will do to the leaders this time."

Perhaps in his place, she would not do anything different, she thought, understanding him though she could not condone what he had done. She looked over at the exhausted captives. "If you freed the white women, the bluecoats and their Pawnee scouts might not hunt you so relentlessly."

Snake walked up just then. "I say *no!* The women have been providing amusement for some of our warriors."

Tall Bull shrugged. "What is more important than that is that we have them as hostages to barter if we should be cornered by the soldiers."

"And if we cannot exchange them," Snake said, squatting on his haunches by the fire, "we will kill them. Knowing that, the army will be cautious about attacking us!"

She tried to think of another way to reason with them. When she looked up, the ugly warrior stared at her with hunger in his eyes.

"Tall Bull," he said without taking his eyes off Luci, "when may I marry your niece? I want a son by her crying in a cradleboard next year."

Luci tried not to register disgust at the image that came to her mind of the big savage driving hard between her thighs. "I—I don't think I am ready to think of marriage."

Her uncle looked at her as if the opinion of a mere woman was less than important. "Snake is right. Time is what we are running out of. If our people are to survive at all against overpowering odds, we must breed big, strong sons to fight the bluecoats!"

She started to say that by the time that son would be old enough to fight, it would all be over, the West closed down, and the Indians on reservations. She saw the future clearly and it did not show free-roaming Indians riding at will, attacking each other and white ranchers.

Tall Bull stared into the fire. "We are headed up to Summit Springs to rest and let our ponies grow fat on the tall grass for a few weeks. I do not think the army knows this place. That would be a good place to celebrate a marriage."

She knew better than to argue. Somehow she would have to figure out a way to escape before that wedding took place. She had no idea how she would do it. The two white women were too sick and weak to escape and she wasn't sure that she was hard-hearted enough to leave them behind.

Snake stood up, scratching his privates. "I see some of my men looking over the captives. I have a hunger on me for a woman, too, until I can properly marry Morning Star."

"No," Luci protested, "the women have been raped almost every night by some of the warriors. Don't let them!"

But Tall Bull's mouth was a grim line. "Some of our women and children begged at Sand Creek and it did them no good." He looked over at the crippled Bear Cub, who sat his horse up on the ridge, guarding the pony herd. "Captive women are a spoil of war to be enjoyed by the victors. Do you expect my men to be any more noble than the soldiers?"

The white girls looked up, saw the warriors coming, and began to weep. There was nothing Luci could do to stop it.

Luci watched the cruel Snake take first one girl, then the other. When he stood up, another warrior waited to take his place between the captive's white thighs. The Indian women were disinterested as they went about their chores. Men had always behaved like that and captured women should be expected to serve a man's needs. Certainly some of them had at various times in the past been captured and raped.

There was nothing she could do to help the two; she couldn't even help herself. In a few days, probably during the hottest days of July, the Cheyenne would be at Summit Springs and Luci would be forced to wed Snake.

She watched the savagery, wept, and wondered if

411

the cavalry would ever find them. Surely they must be searching the plains. That meant sooner or later there would be a battle. The Cheyenne would die fighting rather than surrender. They were her people and she could understand their primitive way of life though she didn't condone it.

Luci had no hope of surviving such an attack. She only hoped she might get one last look at Johnny Ace before she died. That alone would have to be enough. Otherwise, she tried not to think of him. It made her too sad to keep going and she had to try to help Susanna and Maria. Johnny Ace. She thought of him every waking moment.

July. The sun beat down mercilessly on Johnny and Cody as they scouted ahead of the Fifth along a creek. They found the ashes of an old campfire and the tracks of many unshod ponies. Johnny felt his pulse quicken with hope.

Cody looked over at him. "Dog Soldier camp?"

Johnny nodded. "Yes," he said, and squatted to examine the print of a small shoe in the mud of the creek bank. "And they've got at least one white woman with them." He wondered if it might be Luci.

"There's at least two missing," Cody shook back his long locks. "Alderdice says his wife was taken and the neighbors who found Weichell's body say he had a pretty blond bride."

Johnny didn't even want to think about what would happen to the two women. At least if the Cheyenne had Luci, she wouldn't be harmed since

412

she was Tall Bull's niece. The other thought that haunted him night and day as he scouted ahead of the Fifth was whether she, too, was being held captive or did she ride with them willingly because of some handsome warrior whom she had fallen in love with? The thought of her in another man's arms drove him nearly crazy as they rode back to report to the major and General Carr.

The general wiped the sweat from his portly face and cursed. "We've been out on this wild-goose chase for almost a month now and we never seem to get any closer! Our food and oats for the horses are almost exhausted. Some of the men are worn to a nub or sick."

Johnny didn't answer—it wasn't his decision to make—but he didn't envy General Carr the choice. As he had said, many of the men and animals were no longer fit to travel and the Fifth was short on everything—except hostiles.

Pani Le-shar pulled at his mustache. "What do you think, sir?"

The general looked at Johnny. "You know Cheyenne as well as anyone, the major tells me. Where do *you* think the Dog Soldiers are headed?"

Johnny considered a long moment while slowly rolling a cigarette. Here in northeastern Colorado Territory, it was a long way between watering holes. There were only so many places the Cheyenne could camp.

Should he lead the Fifth on a wild-goose chase? At least Luci wouldn't be caught in the midst of a heated battle. But suppose she was being held against her will? And what of the other captives? He wanted Luci to live, but he had his duty.

413

"Summit Springs," he said thoughtfully. "If I were the Cheyenne, I'd be headed for Summit Springs to rest up. Not many whites know where it is."

Major North pushed his hat to the back of his head. "Then they won't be expecting us to find them there?"

Johnny nodded, lit the cigarette, and watched the smoke curl. "Of course, they'll have scouts out, too, and there's not much cover on that prairie. Unless we travel all night at a killing pace, they'll know we're coming before we get there."

Major North leaned on his saddle horn and looked over the exhausted troops behind him. "Not many of our men and horses are up to making a ride like that, General Carr."

The portly general looked from one to the other, then back to Johnny. "How far?"

"Too far," Johnny said, "in the shape we're in, but it can be done."

Cody forgot himself and groaned aloud, and even the two officers looked bleak.

General Carr looked at North. "This is your man and you swear by him, so I'll have to have that kind of faith in him, too. Major, order your officers to choose only the best of the horses and men. We're traveling light and we're traveling fast! We'll leave the majority of the Fifth behind."

Johnny studied the glowing tip of his cigarette. "We may come up against a superior force out there ahead since we don't know if other war parties might be joining up with them. I think you should realize that."

General Carr mopped his sweating brow again.

414

"If we don't hit them soon and hit them hard," he said, "we're going to have to give up on this campaign and return to the fort. The men and horses are worn out. Major, pass the word! Right now, all I can think about is cold water—lots and lots of cold water."

Luci splashed cold water from the spring on her face and then took a gourd full to the two exhausted white women who sprawled under a tree. With the killing pace the Dog Soldiers had set the last few days getting here, she hadn't been sure Susanna and Maria would make it through the heat without collapsing.

How long had she been with the Dog Soldiers? She shook her head, knowing she had lost all track of time. While it seemed an eternity, she thought it had only been five or six weeks.

"Where are we?" Susanna asked dully, sipping the water.

"Summit Springs," Luci said, pitying the girl. Her belly was big with child, but that didn't keep her from being raped. Luci looked at the pretty blond, Maria, wondering if she was pregnant by some Dog Soldier, but she kept silent. The girl had enough trouble without being reminded of that possibility.

Summit Springs. Her own time had run out. Probably in the next day or two, she would be forced to wed Snake and be at the mercy of his sexual appetites. She thought wistfully of Johnny. Did he know or care where she was? What a fool she had been!

To keep herself from thinking about Snake, she distracted the two women by teaching Maria English. "You'll need it when we're rescued."

"Rescued?" the pretty blond asked in her thick German accent, looking from one woman to the other.

Susanna seemed to forget her own problems then. "Yes, 'rescued,' Maria. We'll explain and see if we can teach you some more words."

Luci sighed and looked around. There was a small, treeless valley around the springs and a bunch of bluffs toward the back that made good places for sentries to watch off to the southeast. Surely if they were going to be attacked, the soldiers would come from the direction of Fort Sedgewick or Fort McPherson. The Indians must think that, too, since guards were always posted to watch the landscape to the southeast.

Tonight little Bear Cub sat up there on a rock, sketching in the lavender and pink twilight while keeping guard over the horses.

Luci managed to get enough smoked jerky to share with the white girls and took it to them. But when she went back to the big campfire and Snake looked her over, said to her uncle, "I weary of waiting for your niece to share my blankets."

Luci glared at him. "You have two wives already."

He grinned. "You know the taboos. When my son sucks at your breast, I will not touch you either until he's weaned."

Tall Bull sipped his strong, black coffee, munched dried jerky, and considered. "You are right, Snake. There is no reason to put it off now

416

that we will be here a few days. We will have the marriage tomorrow night."

Luci's heart sank and she didn't look at the ugly warrior. In her mind, she imagined him humping between her thighs, his wet mouth on her breast. Tomorrow night. That meant tonight would surely be her last chance to escape.

And go where? Her heart told her back to Johnny Ace, but her brain told her that was impossible. She'd figure out what to do once she got away.

Now that darkness had fallen, the old medicine tales could be told. It was taboo to tell the magic stories in the daylight; to do so would make one hump-backed. To the Cheyenne, a story was a possession like a blanket or a rifle. No man could tell another's story. The medicine tales were passed down from father to son, although sometimes a man might make a gift of a story to a special friend.

She sat near the fire and listened. An old one stood and told a tale of the long ago time when the Cheyenne, the Tsistsistas, first got the horse, which freed them to ride across the great prairies when they had had to walk before. Finally, he said, "That is my story. Can anyone tie another to it?"

Then a second warrior stood and began to tell a tale connected to the first, how the horse helped on the hunt with the buffalo so that the people were better fed. When he finished, he, too, offered to let someone tie a tale on to his. Sometimes the telling went on all night, Luci knew. But the sacred tales must end by dawn. It was forbidden to tell the magic stories in the daylight.

Tonight, however, Tall Bull cut the stories short. "We have to see if the shaman has had any new visions to guide us so that we will know what we are to do."

The gnarled and bent old man came from his lodge and settled himself before the crackling fire. He accepted a pipe from Tall Bull and smoked thoughtfully while he stared into the flames. On his chest were scars of the sun dance, denoting that a long time ago, he had been one of the bravest of the brave, who had survived that ritual torture.

She took a deep breath of the campfire smoke and the scent of the pungent mixture of tobacco and *kinnikinnik,* the red willow bark, which the old man smoked before he passed the pipe to the man on his right. It was so quiet as the people waited, that Luci could hear a cricket chirping over behind a far rock.

The old shaman cleared his throat and everyone leaned forward expectantly. "Yes, I have had a medicine vision; the same one I had before. I say, beware of the storm and the thunder from the north. I say, beware of the white horse."

Everyone waited expectantly as if for an explanation, but the old man only stared into the fire.

Tall Bull shrugged. "What nonsense is this? Can you not explain? We all know the storms blow out of the west from the shining mountains whites call the Rockies."

"I only tell you what the spirits whispered in my ear," the old man said.

"Beware of the storm and the thunder to the

north," Snake repeated thoughtfully. "Beware of the white horse. Perhaps when we think on it, we will understand its meaning."

Luci's mind went to a big, black horse. If the shaman was to be believed, obviously Katis and Johnny wouldn't be riding in to rescue her and the two captives.

The pipe continued to make its rounds. Tall Bull stared into the darkness. "We must all think on the shaman's words," he agreed. "Perhaps as Snake says, the message will be revealed to us."

At that, the council broke up and everyone bedded down for the night.

But Luci didn't go to sleep, though she wrapped herself in her blankets and pretended to. Tomorrow night, Tall Bull would force her to wed Snake. By this time a whole day from now, she would be spread-eagled in Snake's tipi while he put his mouth all over her, forced himself between her thighs, and sucked her breasts. She shuddered at the thought, knowing she had to escape tonight. Would Bear Cub help her? If he wouldn't, no one else would.

She waited until the camp slept, then sneaked up to where Bear Cub sat on a rock, keeping guard on the horses and watching the prairie to the southeast.

"Sooner or later," she said, "the Fifth Cavalry will send the troops and we will all die."

He nodded a little sadly. "I think we all know that, but we seem to have no choice. What I dream of is painting pictures of all my memories, the prairie when the sun is setting, new colts galloping with their mothers."

"There is a man among the soldiers," she said, "a gentle man who paints pictures, too. I think David would help you with your art."

For a moment, the boy's face lit up, then the hope faded and he shook his head. "It is too late for me, too late for the Cheyenne. We will be hunted down. My sketch book will be destroyed, I will be forgotten for all time."

Her heart went out to him. "Perhaps not."

He laughed without mirth. "The warriors will be remembered, but no one would remember a crippled herd boy who sketched pictures of his people's history." He hesitated a long moment as if building his nerve. "Do—do I hear right, that Tall Bull will give you to Snake tomorrow?" The hurt in his voice made her wince.

"That is what is planned."

"If I were a proper warrior, one with many ponies and war honors, I would ask for you myself." He hesitated as if expecting her to laugh.

She reached out and put her hand on his shoulder. "If I had my choice and if things were different, I would be honored. But I love a man who rides with the bluecoats."

He did not ask for any details, and tears came to Luci's eyes as she thought of Johnny. Yes, she loved him. No matter the chasm between them, no matter that it could never work out, she couldn't dictate to her heart.

Bear Cub looked at her soberly. "You have been so very kind to me. I—" He hesitated a long moment then blurted out, *Hahoo naa ne-mehotatse.*" Thank you and I love you.

He would aid her, no matter what kind of

420

punishment it brought down on him. "Bear Cub, will you help me escape from here?"

"You know how much I care for you, Morning Star," the boy said. "Whatever it is you want, I will help you."

She thought then of the white captives, turned, and looked back toward the camp. They were tied up in a tipi below. She might slip away from the camp, but not with two sick captives who needed rest and food to travel hard. There was no way she could take Susanna and Maria with her. "I'll have to leave them behind," she thought aloud.

Bear Cub said, "Then Snake will be so mad about your leaving, he may torture and kill them."

That was true. She had to admit that as she thought about it. Why should they be her responsibility? Each of them would have to look after herself. Didn't she have a right to think of herself first? And what of Bear Cub? There was no telling what Snake would do to him for helping Luci escape.

"Luci, decide quickly what you will do," the boy said urgently. "In a few minutes, a new guard comes to take my place and then your chance will be lost forever. I don't care what happens to me; I want to help you."

But she had already made her choice. She couldn't escape when it would cost the others such cruel punishment, maybe death. "I've changed my mind," she said reluctantly, standing up. But before she turned and ran down the path, she leaned over and kissed the surprised boy lightly on the cheek. *"Hahoo naa ne-mehotatse."*

She went back to her tipi and lay sleepless most

of the night, thinking of Johnny but knowing that this time tomorrow, she would be lying there weeping and smeared with Snake's seed. For the first time, she noticed a fresh tear in her faded dress. It didn't matter—tomorrow night she would be wearing fancy new buckskin.

Johnny squatted down to peer at a scrap of calico caught on a bush. Was that from Luci's dress? Hope beat harder in his heart. She was with them! He examined horse droppings and decided how long ago they had stopped at this site. Turning back to look up at Cody who leaned on his saddle horn, Johnny said, "This campsite is not more than a day or two old. We're gaining on them."

"That's what you've been saying for more'n a month now," Cody grumbled as Johnny swung up on Katis and they turned to ride back to report to General Carr and Major North. The troops waited in the scant shade of some straggly cottonwoods.

Johnny didn't answer. It was true that July now beat down on the luckless cavalry with all its heat while the so-called Republican River campaign chased the Dog Soldiers all over eastern Colorado Territory and western Nebraska. They were low on supplies, the men and horses tired and thin. If the Fifth didn't see action soon, they'd have to give up the chase and return to the fort.

He and Cody reported back. "Sir, I think they've split their forces to confuse us."

General Carr shifted his weight in the saddle. "Then all we can do is split our forces and follow both trails so we don't take a chance on losing them."

Major North pulled at his mustache thoughtfully. "Sir, with all due respect, the majority of my men are too ill and weary to go another step and our horses are down to half rations. We can't pick up the pace any in this heat."

"Then we'll take the men and horses who can keep up and leave the rest behind." The portly officer turned to Johnny and looked at him keenly. "What do you think, scout?"

"That's not my decision to make, sir. What you suggest could be dangerous if we run into a hornet's nest of Dog Soldiers."

"But that's what you'd do, isn't it?"

Johnny had to nod in agreement. "I suppose it's worth the risk." He thought of Luci, who might be riding with them. There was no help for that. "There's not much cover in the direction we seem to be heading and they'll have scouts out, too, just like us. There's not much chance of surprising them."

Major North reached for his canteen and took a drink. "Johnny, from your experience, do you still think you know where they're headed?"

"Could be several places." Johnny rolled a cigarette thoughtfully, and brushed a fly away. "One of those trails is bound to be a fake to lead us astray. They'll all meet up ahead someplace."

"You said before you thought that would be Summit Springs. Do you still think that?" General Carr wiped his sweating face again.

Johnny lit his smoke and shook out the match. The success of this campaign might depend on his judgment. Suppose he led them on a wild-goose chase and the Cheyenne weren't there?

"Well?" Major North prompted.

"I still feel it's Summit Springs," Johnny said. "I'd wager my life they're headed up to the northeastern part of the Colorado Territory. There's water and plenty of grass for the horses."

"Do we have a chance of surprising them?" North said.

Johnny shrugged, blowing smoke toward the sky. "The forts lie to the southeast, so that's where they'll be watching. We could make a wide circle, come around behind them, and maybe catch them by surprise."

"That's what we'll do then," the general said. "Major, you take some men and follow that one trail away from here; I'll follow the other. I hope your scout isn't wrong."

Major North grinned. "I doubt he'll be wrong. I have complete confidence in Johnny Ace."

"Johnny Ace? Funny name for an Indian."

"The soldiers can't remember my Pawnee name, Asataka, so they call me that."

"Asataka," the general mused. "What does it mean?"

"White Horse," Johnny said.

Chapter Twenty-three

Sunday, July 11, 1869. The cavalry had covered 150 miles in the past four days. It had been a long, hard ride in the heat. Now thunderheads built off to the west, angry, black clouds piling up behind the horizon. Thunder rumbled and echoed far away and a cool breeze blew against sweating faces. When they circled around behind the low-lying hills, they concealed themselves in a gully.

Johnny crept up the slope. On the hill between him and the camp, the Cheyenne horse herd grazed. There were nearly a hundred lodges, Johnny noted. It was a big camp, bigger than Johnny had expected.

General Carr sent a rider to find the other force and bring it posthaste. He had said he wanted to attack at dawn, but the sun moved relentlessly across the July sky and he grew more and more nervous, as did Johnny.

"General, the longer we hide here in this gully,

the better chance we have of being discovered and losing the element of surprise."

"You're right. What a helluva way to spend a Sunday afternoon! Take another look and report back. If the others don't get here soon, we'll attack without them!"

Johnny, like the other Pawnee, had stripped down to his breechcloth and moccasins. Because a bare-backed horse carried less weight and could run faster, the scouts all took their saddles off. It was revenge time for them against an old enemy. But he felt no thrill in it. Luci might be in that camp and he wasn't sure how to save her.

He crawled up the slope and looked around. The giant herd of horses grazed on the hill, watched over by a guard on horseback who seemed to be marking in a ledger book. He paused occasionally to gaze off toward the southeast, the direction from which an attack could surely be expected. If the camp was under attack, the guard would try to drive the herd into the camp so the warriors could get mounted. A brave on foot was not much threat. That sentry would have to be killed to keep him from giving early warning.

Johnny reached for his knife. With a good throw, he could hit the sentry in the back, straight through the heart. Forever silenced. But the guard turned and Johnny saw he was only a boy and a crippled one at that. Very slowly, he took his hand off his knife, cursing himself for his softness.

In the camp beyond, children laughed and ran about, women stood in groups to gossip, and warpainted warriors strolled or sat in groups, talking.

A dog barked somewhere and again the thunder rolled and echoed faintly to the west. The scent of campfires and cooking meat drifted to his nostrils.

Where was Luci? He pulled out the scrap of cloth. Was she in this camp? He strained to see the small figures in the distance. Johnny watched, torn between half hoping, half dreading he would see her. Then almost as if in answer to his thoughts, she came out of a tipi, walked over to a kettle hanging over a fire, and dished up some food.

He had to restrain himself from jumping up and shouting at her. Yes, it was her small, slight form all right. She took two bowls of food and disappeared into the tipi.

Where were the two white women captives who were supposed to be held prisoner by this band? He looked around, but saw no sign of them. Could they be the ones Luci carried food to? When the soldiers attacked the camp, he'd check that lodge first. His beloved was in danger. But what could be done about that? If the Fifth launched an attack, Luci and the women prisoners might be either executed by the vengeful Indians or caught in the deadly crossfire.

With a sigh of foreboding, Johnny returned to the officers and reported. General Carr shifted his big frame restlessly.

"We're going to have to go on with it! It's only a matter of luck we haven't been seen already. If we can hit that camp, catch those warriors by surprise, we've got a real advantage if they're afoot."

The decision made, orders passed softly through

the waiting cavalry. As always, the Pawnee scouts would lead the charge because they preferred to be the first to ride in, kill, and count coup on their old enemies.

How could he save Luci and the other captives? Johnny thought as he smeared war paint on his muscular, almost naked frame. He had the best horse in the bunch. If he rode out in front, ahead of even the Pawnee scouts, he stood a good chance of being killed, but he also had a better chance of arriving as the shooting started, saving his love.

Was it foolish to risk his life to save a girl who, given the choice, would surely go on to Denver with her rich father when she was rescued? More and more, he decided Pani Le-shar was right. His enlistment was up. The smart thing to do was take Luci away without ever giving her a chance to hear about Manning Starrett. He'd have to save her first.

Behind him, he heard the jingle of bridles as the Fifth readied itself for the charge. They'd come up out of the draw, cut off that pony herd from galloping into the village and then attack the camp itself. Without ponies, those Dog Soldiers were almost helpless.

He felt sweat run down his broad chest in the scorching July heat, smearing his scarlet and ochre war paint. Off to the west, the angry clouds piled layer on layer, the thunder rumbling ominously, echoing across the plains. The wind picked up suddenly ahead of the coming storm, blowing cool against his painted face.

Was that a raindrop on his cheek or a tear?

428

Warriors do not weep, he reminded himself sternly, but he didn't know if he was crying for himself, out of fear for Luci, or for the lives that were about to be lost. He was getting too soft to be a soldier.

The sky darkened now as the boiling lavender and gray clouds pushed his way, driven by the wind. Would the rain hit before the battle ended? He had never fought in a rainstorm before. It could only make it harder, galloping through mud, his vision blurred by driving rain. Lightning flashed in the west, making a jagged tear in the dark sky from ground to heaven.

His heart beat hard as he led the scouts up the slope. The crippled boy still sat his pony, marking in the book, looking occasionally off toward the southeast, oblivious to the threat coming up behind him from the north.

Now Major North's troops rejoined them. The bugle charge cut through the rumbling thunder. A cry went up from hundreds of throats as the Fifth Cavalry charged up the slope, determined to keep the pony herd from being driven into the camp.

The herdboy looked up suddenly as the scouts charged toward him. Always Johnny would remember the shock and disbelief in his eyes, the way his mouth opened in surprise. He turned and, still holding his ledger book, quirted his white pony, shouted at the grazing herd. He galloped through the milling horses, heading toward the village to warn his people.

He must not be allowed to reach the camp, Johnny thought, raising his pistol. The boy shouted a warning, but the thunder rolled again and drowned him out. *Or was it thunder?* Those in the camp below might think so, Johnny realized, but in reality, it was the drumming hooves of the hundreds of Fifth Cavalry horses making their charge.

Even as he aimed at the crippled youth, Johnny hesitated. He no longer saw him as a hated enemy, but as a young boy, a human being with a long life ahead of him. Their eyes met for a split second as the boy looked back over his shoulder. Johnny couldn't do it. He couldn't pull the trigger on a crippled boy. But in the moment that followed, someone else did.

A shot rang out, drowned by the rolling thunder of hooves to all but those riding in the forefront of the charge. A splotch of crimson soaked the back of the slight form. For only a heartbeat more, the boy clung to his horse, obviously determined to make it to the camp to warn his people. He cried out faintly, then fell from his running pony and was lost beneath the hooves of the running herd.

Johnny felt a sudden loss as if a little piece of himself had died with the enemy youth. Now his thoughts went to Luci, somewhere in that camp ahead. "Cut off that herd!" he shouted with a wave of his arm "Don't let it reach the camp!"

Charging riders raced to do his bidding and Johnny spurred his great horse, galloping into the edge of the camp in the front of the attack.

Behind him, the Pawnees raised a savage war cry, exulting in the coming fight. Once he, too, would have been eager to kill, ready to dip his lance in old enemies' blood, take their hair to

430

hang on his pony's bridle, and dance the scalp dances. But now as the first shots rang out, he thought of his enemies only as fellow human beings who, like himself, wanted more than anything to live. He cursed, thinking how a blue-eyed half-breed girl had ruined him as a warrior forever. *Beloved enemy.*

People ran out of their tipis as he galloped into the edge of the camp ahead of the cavalry charge. "Luci? Luci, where are you?"

His voice was drowned out by the roll of thunder, the echoing shots, shouts, and screams of confusion.

Luci sat in Tall Bull's tipi with the captives, listening to the growing thunder. If there were a terrible storm, would tonight's marriage to Snake be called off? Probably not. She should have escaped last night when she had that chance. Even as she thought that, she knew she could not have taken it, not when it would have brought punishment to Bear Cub, Susanna, and Maria.

The thunder boomed louder. "It must be a terrible storm," she shouted to the two women. *A storm.* She remembered the old Shaman's warning. *Beware of the storm and the thunder from the north. Beware of the white horse.* Such nonsense! And yet she shivered as the noise outside the tipi seemed to build to a roar. Now there were screams and shouts and loud noises, almost like shots echoing all around the camp.

Mercy! What on earth? Luci ran outside, followed by the two white girls. The camp was under

431

attack! She saw a blur of garishly painted brown bodies, then blue uniforms coming down the slope behind the braves. For a split second, she stood there, not quite sure what to do, or which way to run in the shooting and confusion. The cavalry, Luci realized suddenly. The camp was under attack by the cavalry! "We're saved!" She turned to yell at the captives, "The army has found us! We're—Tall Bull, no!"

Her uncle had run up behind the captives. Even as Luci screamed her protest and ran to stop him, it was already too late. The flashing lightning reflected off his tomahawk as he swung it. "Soldiers never get captives alive!"

Maria and Susanna turned and threw up their hands to ward off the blows even as Luci risked her own life, grabbing at his arm. He shoved her to one side and tomahawked Susanna as he shot Maria.

"No!" Luci screamed, kneeling beside the bloody bodies. "Oh, my God, not now! Not when rescue is so close!"

Tall Bull turned, grabbed up his Appaloosa's reins, and took off at a gallop.

She must get help! How? Where? All around her were noise and confusion as people ran and horses charged past. The acrid scent of gunpowder made her cough. Her ears rang with the shots. A very few of the pony herd made it into the camp, and Dog Soldiers grabbed the mounts as they ran past, then swung up on them using their long manes to guide them.

Was someone calling her name? Dimly, Luci heard a voice over the roar around her. *Luci,* it

432

seemed to call *Luci, where are you?*

"Johnny?" Through the swirling smoke, she saw a big brave on a giant black horse. "Oh, my God, Johnny! I thought you'd never come!"

But even as she ran toward him, a galloping horseman leaned over and lifted her before him on to a pinto pony. "Morning Star, I'll take you out of here!"

"Snake, let go of me! I don't want to go with you!" Luci struggled, but she was helpless in the ugly Dog Soldier's grasp. He spurred his horse around and took off at a gallop through the camp.

"We'll live to fight another day!" Snake shouted and hung on to her as his pony galloped toward the edge of the camp. If he could make it out of the camp, he might escape across the prairie.

"The captives are hurt!" she screamed, and fought him, but he held her easily. "Snake, don't you hear me? Our own people are hurt. They need help! You can't just run!"

But he didn't slow his pony. "I don't care about anyone but you! We can escape!"

In the swirling smoke Johnny saw first the bloody captives lying on the ground and then Luci being grabbed up by a galloping Dog Soldier. Frantically, he waved for a medic and watched a split second to see David Van Schuyler rushing to aid the women. Then Johnny took off at a gallop after the Dog Soldier.

The smoke from gunfire and flaming tipis burned his eyes and nostrils. His ears rang with screams and the neighs of dying horses. Half-naked children and old women ran before him. The storm to the west rumbled again, blowing a chill breeze across his sweating face and bringing a new scent across the camp—warm blood.

"Luci?" He heard her scream somewhere ahead of him, and spurred his horse forward. Some of the Dog Soldiers had grabbed weapons, caught horses, and were fighting back. Oblivious to his own safety, Johnny cared only about saving the beloved enemy girl.

He charged after the ugly Cheyenne, who galloped out of camp toward a draw. But Johnny's horse was fast. He was rapidly gaining on the other man, and the Dog Soldier seemed to know it, too. He glanced back over his shoulder, but he didn't relax his grip on the screaming, fighting girl. Then as he chased the Cheyenne into a blind canyon, the man seemed to realize he was trapped. For a heartbeat, he attempted to turn his horse, but the mount stumbled and threw them both in the dirt.

The Cheyenne had a rifle and Johnny had only his knife and a pistol. The other brave had the advantage of a longer range. And even as Johnny fired, the hammer clicked harmlessly; all six chambers were empty.

But the other had heard the sound, too. The Dog Soldier came up grinning. "So now you die, Pawnee coyote!"

Luci grabbed the man's arm, pleading with him. "Let him live, Snake! I'll go with you!"

The ugly Cheyenne laughed, shaking her hand away. "So you care that much for this wolf for the

434

bluecoats! I'll enjoy his death twice as much and you'll still go with me, Lucero. I intend to have you for my woman!"

Could he bargain with Snake to save Luci? Johnny dismounted slowly, tossing away the useless Colt. "Let her go. Kill me, take my horse, but let the girl go!"

Snake laughed, dragging Luci along by the arm as he advanced on Johnny, rifle ready. "You have nothing to bargain with, scout! I want your life, and your horse, and your woman! Tonight, while ants and vultures fight over your rotting carcass, I will lie between Lucero's thighs. Think about that now, scout. As you die, think about how I will enjoy her!"

That thought was more terrible to him even than his own death. As the ugly Cheyenne dragged the weeping girl forward, Johnny tried to decide what to do. All he had was his knife. To save his own life, he would not risk Luci's.

What could she do to save her love? Luci tried desperately to think of something as Snake dragged her toward the big stallion. All Johnny had was a knife, and that wasn't much good against a rifle. If she grabbed the barrel, and held it against her, the shot would kill her, but give Johnny time to make a move. *Beloved enemy.* Yes, it was worth the sacrifice to save the man she loved!

"Step away from that horse, Pawnee!"

Slowly, Johnny obeyed.

Snake paused only a few feet away. With a laugh, he brought the rifle up and aimed it at Johnny's chest. "And now you die, wolf!"

And in that moment, Luci grabbed the barrel and jerked with all her strength. "No!"

The rifle barrel was hot in her hands as she fought for it, determined to stop him. Snake swore and cursed as they fought over the gun, then he struck her.

She went down, her vision a blur of pain, saw his snarling expression and then a sudden warm gurgle of crimson as Johnny's big knife sang through the air and caught Snake in the throat.

The Cheyenne tried to cry out, tried to bring the rifle up to fire, but that moment she had delayed him had cost him the fight and his life. Even as he tried to pull the trigger, Johnny raced forward, struck him and jerked the rifle from his hands. Snake crashed to the dirt and lay there, his life pumping out into the canyon dust.

Then she was in Johnny's arms, weeping against his chest while he held her. "It's all right, Star Eyes! It's all right now!"

But she couldn't stop sobbing. "You would have let him kill you, you big, stupid Pawnee!"

"I suppose that's what I am," he said softly, rubbing his ear, "but what are you for risking your life to save mine?"

A fool in love with an enemy brave, she thought, burying her face against his chest. A fool because there was no future in it—had never been, and could never be. The chasm between them was still too deep and wide; nothing could bridge it.

The thunder rolled again and a cool drop of rain fell on her face. The noise from the camp had faded to a few shouts, a shot now and then.

Luci sat up suddenly. "Susanna and Maria! My

uncle killed them! And Bear Cub—I must see about him!"

He helped her to her feet. "David is looking after the women. I don't know who Bear Cub is."

"The crippled herd boy." She wiped her eyes as Johnny retrieved his weapons. "He's an artist. I hope David will help him—"

"I'm afraid he's beyond help, Luci." His voice was soft and gentle as he mounted, then reached down a hand to her.

A chill seemed to sweep over her as she realized his meaning. "Did you—?"

"I couldn't. I should have, but at the last minute, I saw his face. Even though he was an enemy who was trying to stop us, all I could think of was that he was a human being. You've ruined me as a killing machine, Star Eyes."

The tears blinded her again, but she said nothing as he lifted her up before him and they rode back to the camp.

The battle was all but over. Here and there tipis burned and a stray horse or two wandered about aimlessly. Many of the women and children had caught horses and escaped, but a few had been taken prisoner.

Dead Dog Soldiers lay everywhere, mute evidence that they had sought valiantly to defend the camp, fighting to the death rather than be captured and returned to the reservation. The group had been almost wiped out, Luci realized. Some would be hunted down and sent back to the Indian Territory. A few would escape to join up with other Cheyenne bands or their friends, the Sioux, and continue their hopeless fight against the white man's encroachment.

One thing was certain: there was no compromise with the fierce Cheyenne. They could never live peacefully on reservations, no matter how many treaties were signed.

General Carr sat his lathered horse in the center of the camp. "What happened to the chief?"

Almost in answer, Major North and Cody galloped back out of the canyon. "We had to kill him," Cody said as he reined in and dismounted. "He was determined not to be taken alive!"

"He swore he wouldn't return to the reservation." Luci felt only pity for her uncle, nothing else. He had lived and died the only way he knew.

Luci saw David bending over the two women along with Dr. Tesson. Johnny helped her dismount. "Are they all right? Is there anything I can do?"

The doctor looked up at her and she saw raindrops on his weathered face. *Or were those tears?*

"I just lost the pregnant one," he said. "I think the other one will live."

Luci fell to her knees next to Susanna. She looked at peace now, the tired lines gone from her face. "She grieved for her children. I think she wanted to join them."

Maria made a soft sound and her eyes flickered open. Luci took one of her hands, noting that David already held the other. "It's all right, Maria, you're safe now."

"Yes, safe," David whispered, and he leaned over and brushed the long blond hair from the girl's forehead. Her blue eyes sought his face. The strength and serenity she seemed to seek was in his

438

eyes, Luci thought.

David said, "Does she have anyone? Anyone at all?"

Luci shook her head. "She's an immigrant. She only speaks the little English I taught her. With her husband dead, she has no one."

"You're wrong," the medic said with conviction. "She's got me. I'll look after her." He reached over and took her other hand from Luci's so that he clasped them both.

Maria smiled at him and then dropped off into a peaceful sleep.

The doctor said, "We've got to get her under cover. I think the sky is finally going to break open and we'll get that storm."

A storm. Thunder from the north. There was only one thing missing. And somehow, suddenly she knew. She stood up and faced Johnny Ace. "Our shaman saw a vision. What does Asataka mean?"

His somber gaze swept her face. "Somehow, I think you know already."

"Come then, White Horse. I must find my little friend." The wind whipped strands of ebony hair about her face, the thunder rolled again, and the rain began in earnest. *Bear Cub. She must find Bear Cub.*

Behind her as she ran, she heard General Carr shouting orders, "Get everyone under cover! Looks like this will be a bad one! We'll camp here until morning!"

She ran up the slope toward the hilltop, the rain pelting her so hard, it stung her skin. She found the precious ledger book first, grabbed it up, and

439

protected it against her body. "Bear Cub?"

A crash of lightning drowned out her voice. But she thought she heard someone whisper her name. "Bear Cub?"

She saw him then, all crumpled and bloody, almost hidden by the wind-whipped grass. "Oh, Bear Cub!"

She knelt, weeping, as she gathered him into her arms. Blood ran out his mouth and he reached up one feeble hand to touch her face. "Don't cry, Morning Star . . . don't cry for me. I'm going up the Ekutsihimmiyo, the Hanging Road to the Sky, to Seyan, the Land of the Spirits."

"Oh, Bear Cub, I can't stand to lose you!" She held him close as if the warmth of her body could keep life in his, even though she could feel the flame of his life flickering in her grasp.

"I—I won't have to go back to the reservation now," he whispered "I'll be free . . . free . . . . Maybe in the Spirit Land, I'll have two good legs like the other warriors . . . my drawings . . ."

"I have them, Bear Cub." She held the ledger up before his failing sight. "I'll see that they're not lost, that others see them, and know our history. And you are braver than any warrior, giving your life to try to warn our people."

"Will I—will I be remembered?"

She wept openly now, hugging him to her. "Always!" she promised. "A hundred years from now, the Cheyenne will still tell medicine tales of the brave boy who gave his life to save his people!"

"No one can ask for more than that." He sighed and then he smiled and looked off in the distance as if those he had lost at Sand Creek were beckoning to him. "I — I'm coming!" he said, and then he was gone.

"Bear Cub! Don't go! Don't leave me!" She held on to him and the sketch book, rocking back and forth in an agony of grief as the rain pelted down and the lightning cracked.

"Luci?"

She looked up. Johnny Ace stood there. "You've got to get out of this storm."

"No, I can't leave him here!"

He dragged her to her feet and spread a poncho over the small body. "You're gonna get hit by lightning if you don't get under cover! Come on! I'll help you give him a proper warrior's burial in the morning."

Holding on to the sketch book, she felt too numb to do anything but let Johnny swing her up in his arms and carry her through the storm back to camp.

Everyone had taken shelter. Johnny dragged her into an army tent that had been set up. She stood there, wet and shivering, looking up at him as the rain poured down outside. "The victor always gets the loser's women," she said softly. "Where do you want me?"

For a moment, he glared at her and a nerve twitched in his jaw. In that instant, she saw a terrible fury in his face and thought he would strike her. Then very slowly, he opened his arms to her. "Here," he whispered, and she saw moisture in his dark eyes, "I want you right here."

She didn't think, she reacted. With a cry of grief and pain, she went into his arms and let him crush her against his massive chest. There was no

441

future for them, so tomorrow didn't matter. All they had was tonight in an army tent on a rain-soaked battleground. She wouldn't ask for more.

Her arms went up around his neck and she let him hold her wet, trembling body against his powerful, warm one. She turned her face up to his. "No"—he shook his head—"not that way, Luci. Not if you don't want me—"

And then her mouth cut off his words as she molded herself against him. "Tonight is all we've got," she said. "I don't even want to think about tomorrow."

His hands were hot as coals on her body through her wet clothes. "Take those things off. You'll catch pneumonia."

She stripped and turned back to him in the dim light, shivering slightly. "Warm me."

He seemed to need no urging. With a groan, he gathered her against him, his hands and mouth and body burning into hers. She lay down on a pile of captured buffalo robes, the fur silky against her bare skin. "Warm me," she said again.

He began taking off his clothes, but his gaze never left her face. "Nothing can come of this, because tomorrow . . . " He broke off, stood over her, trembling as if holding himself back.

Because why? He didn't love her? He had decided to go back to that Pawnee girl? Whatever the reason, at least he was being honest. "It—it doesn't matter." She held out her arms to him. "Can't we have tonight?"

With a moan, he fell to his knees and gathered her into his arms as if trying to pull her inside himself. She hadn't realized how cold she was until the hot iron bar of his maleness drove deep into her and his kisses covered her face. This was all the time they would ever have. But they had until dawn, she thought, returning his passion. Like it or not, that would have to be enough.

Chapter Twenty-four

The next morning, the cavalry surveyed the battle scene. Fifty-two Dog Soldiers lay dead; the rest were scattered to the four winds and would never again be an organized threat. Many of the women and children had fled; others would be gathered up and sent back to their reservation. Piles of supplies and confiscated weapons were heaped up and burned. Several hundred dollars taken in raids were found in tipis and General Carr instructed that this be given to Maria Weichell so she would have a little to live on until she decided what to do.

Johnny helped Luci give Bear Cub a warrior's funeral. They wrapped him in a fine buffalo robe and placed him on a burial platform high on a rolling hill. The cavalry buried Susanna Alderdice and made ready to ride out. Because Maria needed medical attention, General Carr gave orders that the Fifth would head for the nearest fort, Sedgewick.

Johnny had lain sleepless through most of the rainy night, holding Luci against his heart, wrestling with the decision that was his to make. But with the dawn, he knew what he must do. True, he might be able to take Luci away with him and maybe she would never discover that her rich father had wanted to claim her. But if he did that, Johnny would always live with the fear that someday she would find out and he would lose her anyway. Besides, it wasn't fair not to tell her when he knew how she had hungered to find her father.

"Luci," he said when they had a few minutes alone before the cavalry began their march back, "I—I've got something I need to tell you."

She looked up at him with those bright blue eyes and he weakened, almost changing his mind. He loved her so!

"Luci, if you could have any wish answered, what would it be?"

She hesitated a long moment, then looked away. "I suppose it would be to finally find my father."

Had he expected anything else?

"Sit down a minute." He sighed. "There's a lot to tell, but your wish has been granted!"

It was a dream come true, Luci thought, almost in a daze as she rode with the Fifth Cavalry to Fort Sedgewick. Just like in the fairy tales, her real father had finally appeared to take her away from her miserable existence. And yet . . .

Up ahead of her at the front of the column rode Johnny Ace with Will Cody. She couldn't stop herself from watching him, thinking about him, even though in a couple of days, she would be saying good-bye to this life forever. What if Manning Starrett had not turned up—what choices would she have made then?

What difference did that make now? She chided herself and shifted her weight in the creaking saddle. Even though the major and Johnny had both hinted that her father was a difficult person, she was determined to love him, to make him gradually love her. And now she would have a last name: Starrett. Luci Starrett. In Colorado Territory, the money and power that went with that name would change her life to one of luxury and privilege.

She tried to concentrate on her future, how happy she should be that things would change for her. But on the long ride back, she often grieved for Bear Cub, Susanna, and the few friends she had made among the Cheyenne. The Dog Soldiers had been almost completely destroyed in the attack on Summit Springs. Now the Cheyenne would have no choice but to return to the reservations. A few stubborn ones might join up with the Sioux and continue this hopeless fight.

Who were the victims and who the villains? She thought about it a lot on the long ride to the fort. Both sides had killed and taken losses. As in most wars, women and children took a big brunt of the suffering.

The Indians were caught in a vain attempt to turn back the clock to the way things had been long ago. They did not want to change their way of life. But could she fault starving immigrants and residents of crowded ghettos in Eastern cities who also wanted to live, to make a better life for their own children by farming land the Indians only roamed and ran buffalo on?

The two cultures could not live peacefully side by

side, no matter how good their intentions, no matter how many treaties were signed. Plains warriors were trained for war and hunting, and would not sit idly on reservations. But farmers could not grow crops with the braves stealing their livestock and attacking their settlements for the glory of war. When Luci tried to think about who was right and who was wrong, she realized there was no black and white to it, no easy answers.

On the last night on the trail before they would reach the fort, she approached the Pawnee at the picket line as he brushed his horse.

"Johnny, when I go to Denver, will you — will you ever come see me?"

He paused, brush in hand, his dark face impassive. "What is it you want from me, Luci? I doubt I'll have much reason to be in Denver and the society you'll be moving in wouldn't welcome an Indian scout."

She bit her lip, staring at him in the moonlight — big and wide-shouldered in his buckskin shirt, moccasins and cavalry pants. No, he wouldn't fit into Denver society. *Would she?*

A panic arose in her that must have shown in her face, because Johnny gave her a gentle, encouraging, smile. "Don't worry, Luci, you'll do fine. With your natural beauty, plus your father's money to dress you and hire a tutor to teach you which fork to use, and the latest dances, you'll take Denver by storm."

"And what are you going to do? Stay with the cavalry?"

He shook his head, patting Katis's neck. "I'm weary of killing. Maybe it's your Cheyenne influence. Even the enemy are beginning to look like human beings to me. I noticed at Summit Springs, I hesitated each time I pulled the trigger. That could get a man killed."

"You didn't hesitate when Snake —"

"Your life was in danger then, Star Eyes. I wouldn't hesitate where you were involved."

She felt her face burn, watching him curry his horse. "You were a big hero; everyone says so."

He shrugged. "Who needs it? Traveling Bear was a big hero. Major North will probably see he gets a Congressional Medal of Honor. I'm weary to the bone of all this."

She wanted to ask him a thousand things that they had never talked about; she wanted to know him deeply. But all she had ever done was argue with him. And make passionate love to him. "So what will you do now?"

"My enlistment is up. I have a little money saved. I had some loco idea about my own spread — I even had a brand designed — but I'll have to make some changes in it now."

"Can an Indian own land?"

He laughed. "I don't even know. Maybe if his wife was part white, he could. I may just become an illegal squatter. With millions of acres, how would the government know where I was? Cattlemen have done it for years."

The vision came again. It would be sundown. Johnny would ride Katis into the corral and she would be waiting on the porch of the ranch house. Behind her, there'd be a fire in the fireplace and . . .

"Have you had supper?" Johnny said.

Luci started, realizing he had stopped with brush in hand and stood looking at her as she stared vacantly into space. "No, I— I'll go get something."

She struggled against a terrible urge to reach out, put her hand on his arm, and ask if he had ever dreamed a dream like hers. Then she shrugged. What difference did it make? He had never asked for any kind of lasting commitment from her, even when he was making love to her. His idea of a little private Eden somewhere in the wilderness didn't seem to include her.

If you could have a wish granted, he had said, *what would it be?* She had almost said, "To be your wife." But of course the chasm between them was too deep, so she had answered, "To finally find my father."

Sadly, Luci turned away, trying to concentrate on all the eligible men who would be waiting to court her in Denver. Could she ever be thrilled by another man's kisses the way the big enemy scout had excited her to wild abandon? Even now, she hungered for him to take her in his embrace and press her hard against the shelter of his wide chest. For one crazed moment, she pictured him swinging her up in his arms, and carrying her off in the brush. She wanted to hold him prisoner between her slim thighs, lock him in her Cheyenne caress, and kiss him until they were both breathless.

The images her thoughts provoked made her tremble. Could any other man ever do that to her? She watched his hands handle the brush and remembered how they had felt on her own skin. *Beloved enemy.*

Without a word, she turned and headed back to camp. In the darkness outside the main camp, she saw a small campfire and paused to look. Maria

Weichell lay by that fire, gently protected by David Van Schuyler. Luci watched, touched by the scene.

The sensitive blond man sat holding Bear Cub's beloved sketch book. A knot grew in Luci's throat and threatened to choke her. The crippled Cheyenne boy had died trying to make it back to camp to save her—save the others. She was glad she had put his drawings into the hands of a fellow artist who could appreciate them.

David stared at the drawings. "These need to be in a museum of some kind, and saved for future generations to see," he said to Maria. "By looking at these, I can follow the history of the Dog Soldiers over the past several years."

"Oh?" Maria said softly, but her gaze was on David's face, not the drawings.

"Scenes of the Kidder Massacre, Beecher's Island, and some of the other big battles are drawn here."

"It's all so ironic—" Maria seemed to struggle with the English words. "Susanna told me her husband and her younger brother were both with Forsythe's Scouts at Beecher's Island last year in that fight. They killed Cheyenne and now the Cheyenne have killed her." She began to weep softly and David laid the sketch book down and took the girl's hand.

"Maria, what do you intend to do now?"

"I—I don't know. My husband is dead, and I know few people in this country. Maybe I should go back across the ocean where I have friends—"

"You have friends here." He brought her fingertips to his lips hesitantly. "This is the wrong time and the wrong place to discuss this, Maria, but in time, perhaps you could learn to care for me."

"You only feel pity for me." She turned her face away and tried to withdraw her hand, but David held on to it.

He reached down and turned her tear-stained face back to his. "No, I've grown to love you in just this short time, Maria. When this is all over, when you've recovered from your ordeal, I'd like to marry you."

"David, don't you understand?" Her voice trembled, "I—I've been raped by a dozen warriors! I'm expecting a half-Cheyenne child. God only know who fathered it—"

But he leaned over and kissed her gently, interrupting her words. "We can start fresh—somewhere where no one knows either one of us. I'll raise the child as my own, if you want to keep it."

She laughed sadly. "With your blond hair and blue eyes? The child will know; everyone will know. You know how white men feel about women who've been raped by Indians. They think we should kill ourselves rather than submit. You'll be ridiculed."

"I'm a secure person." He brushed her hair out of her eyes. "I can live with it if you can. What I haven't told you, Maria, is that my father is a rich man, and although he has disinherited me because I won't let him plan my life, I have a small income of my own from investments."

For the first time in the firelight, Luci saw hope in the girl's tragic face. "If I could only think we might make it, far from anyone who knew us!"

"We can. Trust me, we can." He looked down into her eyes. "I'm an artist at heart, Maria, and maybe a pretty good one. I never had much of a chance to find out. There's lots of beautiful country out there waiting for me to put it on canvas, and my enlistment will be up soon."

She put her small hand on his face. "They tell me I'll be in the hospital a couple of weeks. When you leave, David, if you still want me then, I'll go with you."

"I'll still want you." He leaned over and kissed her forehead.

Luci's vision blurred as she watched and she realized suddenly that she was crying. A happy ending—David and Maria were going to have a happy ending out of this tragedy. And wasn't she herself going to get a happy ending—a Cinderella finish with gold and a Colorado castle?

Then why was she crying? Because she was so weary and overcome by everything that had happened, she convinced herself as she tiptoed past the pair and on to the main campfire.

They arrived at Fort Sedgewick on a hot day in July.

As they rode in, Luci and Major North dismounted in front of the office where a once handsome older man leaned on a cane out front.

Luci's heart beat faster. No one had to tell her who he was. She saw her own features, Winnifred's features, in his face along with the bright blue eyes. "Father?"

But his attention turned to Major North. "Where in the goddamn hell have you been? When I said I'd wait at the fort, I didn't know you intended to be gone a month!"

"Sorry I can't arrange Indian wars to be convenient for you," North said dryly as he turned to

Luci. "Miss Starrett, this pleasant gentleman is your grief-stricken father, who's come to take you back to Denver."

She paused uncertainly, waiting for him to hold out his arms and embrace her. Instead, he leaned on his cane and looked her over. "You're mine, all right. If I had any doubts, I don't now. You look more like me than you do Sunrise."

Soldiers and settlers turned to look and listen.

Major North cleared his throat. "Out here in public is no place for this meeting. I think the officers of Fort Sedgewick wouldn't mind if we used their office." He turned and handed the reins of his and Luci's horses to Johnny Ace.

She looked back over her shoulder at the big Pawnee, but his dark, impassive face gave her no clue, no emotion, as he took the horses, hesitated, then turned and led them away.

All over the parade ground, weary, dusty troopers dismounted, and curious settlers and other soldiers crowded around to hear the battle details. Maria was carried past on a stretcher, headed for the infirmary. David Van Schuyler walked by her side, holding her hand.

For a moment, Luci envied the girl the devotion on the man's face and stared longingly after Johnny Ace's broad back as he strode away with the horses.

Then she realized her father was staring at her. She turned and went with them into the heat of the office.

I'm the luckiest girl alive, she thought as she accepted a chair. *Then why did she suddenly envy Maria?*

Major North helped Manning Starrett to a chair

and stood looking down at him. "I warned you I didn't know when the Fifth would return. It was your choice to wait."

"I almost went back to Denver," Starrett grumbled, "but I wasn't sure I felt like making the trip twice. At least you sent a message to McPherson so I could get here."

She smiled at him. "Father, I hope your business didn't suffer because of this." She yearned for him to reach out, pat her hand, and give some sign that he really was glad to claim her. Instead he only frowned.

"My associate, Billy Reno, is looking after things back in Denver. I trust him enough to give him my power of attorney so he can keep things running. He's as much like me as a son." He looked at her and she had a sudden feeling he was terribly disappointed that she and poor Winnifred had not been boys.

"In that case, I'll be looking forward to meeting Mister Reno," she said politely. She had been warned, but somehow, she hadn't been expecting such a disagreeable man.

"You'll meet him all right." Starrett laughed, leaning on his cane. "It's my fondest wish that you and Billy will marry so I'll have grandsons to inherit my empire."

She tried to look enthused although her mouth felt dry. It was all happening too quickly. "Well, maybe when I meet Billy, Father, if I like him, then maybe someday—"

"I haven't got a lot of time left!" Starrett snapped.

Major North pulled at his mustache. "Luci, I don't think your father was *asking*, I think he was issuing you *orders*. He's an important man, used to people doing what they're told."

"You got a goddamn helluva lot of nerve, Major!" The handsome face turned scarlet. "She'll like Billy! But first, I'll let all Denver society entertain her, give big balls and parties in her honor." He smiled at her. "You'd like that, wouldn't you—lots of pretty clothes and everything you ever dreamed of?"

She nodded at this prince of commerce who had, through some magic, turned out to be her father.

"Time I don't have, Luci." He glared at her. "I—I'm a sick man. I need someone to look after me—that'll be you and Billy right there in my mansion. We'll be one big, happy family."

He didn't care about her after all. Like Winnifred had said, he only wanted blood kin whom he perceived as doing a better job than hired nurses. And yet, with her kind heart, she pitied him. For only an instant, she wondered what he was dying of. What difference did it make? He was her father, and surely they would come to care about each other.

She reached out and patted his coat sleeve. "Maybe we can make up for the past, Father, and make a fresh start. And if it's your dearest wish that I marry Mr. Reno, maybe—"

"What about Johnny Ace?" the major blurted as he sat down behind the desk.

"What about him?" She kept her voice cold, her eyes averted. He had not made a commitment to her nor asked for one from her. "I'm going to Denver with my father and start life all over."

"That's a smart girl!" Manning Starrett smirked. "You won't regret it, Luci. Why, wait 'til you see

455

the trunk of clothes I brought from Denver for you and there's more back at the mansion."

She couldn't help clapping her hands in delight. "Dresses for me?"

"Anything you want, my dear. I can well afford it. By the way, the stage leaves at nine tomorrow morning for Denver. Let's not miss it."

An aide came in, saluted.

Major North sighed and gave him a halfhearted salute. "What is it?"

"The ladies of the fort sent me to extend an invitation to a grand party tonight in Miss Starrett's honor."

"I presume General Carr and the officers of this fort are aware of this?"

"Oh, yes, sir!" The handsome officer smiled at Luci and she felt herself blush.

Major North grinned in spite of himself. "We all need a little relaxation. I hope Miss Starrett and her father will join us." He looked at Luci.

She flinched, remembering the last time. "Father, is there a party gown in that trunk?"

"As a matter of fact, there's an original all the way from Paris, France," Starrett said with self-satisfaction. "It'll knock the ladies' eyes out. The goddamn thing cost enough to buy this place, lock, stock, and barrel!"

"Then of course, Major," she said, "we'd be delighted to let the ladies of the fort entertain us!"

The aide smiled at her again, saluted smartly, and left.

The major steepled his fingers, looking at her. "Well, Luci, you've done it. All the most important people in these parts will be here tonight, groveling at your feet because of you sudden power and

456

wealth. I hope what you've chosen is going to bring you happiness."

She nodded, although she didn't feel very happy. The Pawnee scout would be hanging around looking through the windows while officers fought to dance with her.

"You're goddamn right she's happy, Major." Starrett's eyes gleamed. "Maybe she's just like her old man after all. I can't blame you, gal. These people humiliated you? We'll make them crawl and fawn, just like they do me in Denver!"

She didn't want people fawning and bowing and scraping to her because of her father's money. She realized he must be one of the most hated and feared men in the Colorado Territory, and as his daughter, she would rule Denver society and be hated and feared, too.

Luci felt suddenly weary and depressed. She stood up and the men stood, too. "If you'll excuse me, I want to rest up and get ready for the party. Major, will you look after my father?"

"Of course. See you tonight." The slightly built officer bowed gallantly as Luci turned and went out.

It was more than a dream, Luci thought, as she opened up the big trunk her father had sent to her room. Like a treasure chest, it overflowed with elegant dresses, jewelry, shoes, and the finest of dainty lace undergarments.

She lay dress after dress across her bed, and knew immediately which one she would wear tonight. There was a full-skirted blue silk, just the color of her eyes, that matched priceless blue sapphire earrings and necklace. What a contrast tonight was going to be to that other party!

Luci took a bath in some of the imported soap she found in the trunk and did her ebony hair up in an elaborate cascade of curls on the back of her neck. There was even rich lotion for her work-worn hands. A few weeks away from the constant laundry tub and they would be pretty.

Her father had said he wasn't up to attending the party and stayed in his room. But that didn't deter Luci from going, and her heart beat fast with breathless anticipation as the buggy pulled up out front for her.

A dozen eager young officers waited out front of the hall and almost fought each other for the privilege of helping her from the buggy.

On the porch, Johnny Ace lounged against the wall, smoking a cigarette. He alone didn't rush to her side. His face was shadowed, so she couldn't see his expression, but the tip of the cigarette glowed in the darkness, and for a moment, she thought she saw his eyes, dark and moody.

She decided to ignore him. Laughing gaily with first one officer and another as they clustered around, she went inside to the dance. The crowd began to applaud as she came in and ladies came over, hinting that they might be in Denver sometime and would just love to be invited to the Starrett mansion for tea.

The young officers all begged to dance with her and more than one kissed her fingertips, swearing eternal devotion and asking permission to call on her when next they came to that city.

As one of the senior officers, Major North demanded the privilege of her first dance.

As he whirled her out onto the floor, he smiled. "My! Money does make a difference to the crowd hereabouts, doesn't it?" His voice was wry and slightly disapproving.

"Mercy! It certainly is different than last time," she admitted and was suddenly melancholic, remembering the one man to whom it hadn't made any difference.

"Of course I can't fault you for making this decision," North said, and he looked toward the windows.

She only mumbled something and twisted in his arms to see if there was a dark face looking in from outside. Once she thought she saw Johnny, but, she decided it was only a shadow. He must have left the porch.

She danced every dance, the belle of the ball, laughing and joking with each man who flirted with her. By the end of the evening, she had had half a dozen proposals of marriage from young men she remembered had sneered at her or treated her badly when she was only a poor half-breed girl named Lucero.

Johnny wasn't outside when she finally left the party in the wee hours of the morning, escorted by three young lieutenants who fought over who got to sit next to her in the buggy. She didn't know whether she was relieved or disappointed that he wasn't standing in the shadows. Probably she had seen him for the last time. With the Indians defeated, the stages could run again. She'd be leaving for Denver at nine o'clock in the morning.

She lay sleepless a long time, thinking. At long last, she was going to have the dream she and her mother had often dreamed together. The Pawnee scout had no place in that vision of wealth and privilege. Luci pushed him from her mind, thinking of fancy clothes and a mansion. She thought as she dropped off to sleep: *Denver, here I come!*

Chapter Twenty-five

Major North sat behind the borrowed desk, yawning as he sipped his first cup of coffee of the morning. Last night's party had kept everyone up a lot later than usual. Every unattached officer on the post had danced with Luci, and had begged permission to court her in Denver. But the major had noticed her glance strayed often to the window to see if the scout were there. He hadn't been. No doubt he couldn't bear to watch other men embrace her.

He pulled out his watch and looked at it. Eight twenty-five A.M. The stage to Denver would come through at nine o'clock and this whole drama would be ended.

He savored the strong brew and smiled. David Van Schuyler had just left the office. He was glad to hear of David and Maria's plans. Not that he hadn't expected it of course, since he was always a quiet observer of the scene around him. He hated to lose the sensitive, caring young officer, but he couldn't blame David. Maybe he and that tragic girl could lose themselves somewhere in the West and make a new start once Maria was able to travel.

He reached for a handkerchief and wiped his face. It was always hot on the plains in July, but it seemed unusually warm for early morning. "Frank, you're getting old," he said aloud, and then laughed because he was not yet thirty. This life had a way of aging a man, though. He ought to leave it. But he knew he wouldn't as long as there were hostiles to corral. Besides, who would protect his beloved Pawnee from those hordes if he weren't here?

He'd brought along his small volume of Shakespeare on this campaign. He got it out and began to read.

There was a rap at the door.

"Come in."

Johnny Ace came in hesitantly and stood with feet wide apart, his hand on the hilt of his knife. "I've come to say good-bye, Pani Le-shar."

"So you're really going to go?" He asked automatically although he and the scout had already talked. He had been unable to dissuade Johnny. "You're leaving before the stage comes through?"

Johnny stared at the floor. "You know why, don't you?"

"I can guess." He closed the book. "Did you ever even ask her, Johnny? Give her a chance to make a decision?"

"She's made her choice. You were there last night. Didn't she look like a princess in that dress surrounded by all those slobbering young officers?"

"I noticed that she kept looking out the window."

The big Pawnee shrugged. "Wishful thinking on your part, Major. You're trying to find a happy ending to that story." He nodded toward the book in North's hand.

North sighed. "I suppose you're right. Maybe I've seen as happy an ending as a Cheyenne and a Pawnee can handle. At least you're both alive, which is more than Romeo and Juliet got."

He laid the book aside, thinking he was a little bit disappointed in Luci. Maybe he had expected too much of the girl. It was absolutely insane to think she might throw all that money away to go into the arms of a penniless enemy.

"Good-bye, Johnny, keep in touch." He stood up and came around to shake hands.

"Sure." The hand that held North's trembled slightly. They both knew they might never meet again. "I'm sick of killing, Major. When I kill a Cheyenne now, I see her face and I hesitate. I think of them as people, not just enemies."

North turned away. "That haunts me, too, but I've got my orders. Maybe someday when peace finally comes to the plains . . ." He shrugged, pulling at his mustache. "I'm not sure what Luther and I will do; maybe go into business. Some fella who was in here early this morning wanted to write me into a book as the hero of Summit Springs."

"You're too modest for your own good, Pani Leshar." Johnny grinned. "That must be the same man who just found Cody asleep under a wagon out there, and says he can write books about him. Fella's name is Ned Buntline."

"Yeah, that's the one." North laughed, eager to avoid the tension of two comrades about to part forever. "That Cody! He'll probably end up the most famous of us all!"

"Knowing Cody, that's just what he'd like. Buffalo Bill Cody, Hero of the Old West." Johnny stood there and the silence felt heavy and awkward in the early heat.

"Well" — Johnny turned toward the door — "I've got to saddle Katis and leave. The stage will be here soon. I — I don't want to see her go."

Romeo and Juliet, Indian style, North thought, but he only extended his hand again. "Good luck to you, Johnny. I hope you find peace and happiness somewhere."

A sadness crossed the handsome, dark face as they shook hands. "My happiness is catching the nine o'clock stage. Good-bye, Pani Le-shar." He turned abruptly and walked out across the grass toward the stable.

North's heart ached for him as he watched the man disappear into the barn. He pulled out his watch. Given the choice, what would any ordinary girl take?

He went back to his desk and picked up the coffee. It tasted cold and bitter. He slammed the cup down.

Again, someone rapped on the door.

Damn it, where were all these people coming from so early this morning when he didn't feel much like carrying on business as usual? "Come in."

A sergeant entered and saluted. "This message came late last night for Mr. Starrett, but everyone was already asleep, so the operator hesitated to wake him." He held out the paper. "He thought you should give it to him. I hope that was the right thing to do, sir."

North grinned and accepted the crumpled paper. "Knowing Mr. Starrett's lovable disposition, I can see why the telegrapher hesitated. I'll see that Starrett gets it. He's due to catch the stage in a few minutes."

He glanced at the message and whistled low

464

under his breath. "Well, I'll be damned! You read this, Sergeant?"

The beefy man colored. "You know most of us can only read well enough to sign our names, sir."

"The telegrapher show this to anyone?"

"No sir. Like I said, everyone was asleep."

That meant North and the telegrapher were the only ones at the fort at this moment who knew this information.

"In that case, that'll be all, Sergeant. I'll give this message to Mr. Starrett myself in a few minutes when he comes out to catch the stage."

The sergeant saluted and left. North read the message again, smiling a little. Across from his office, he saw Manning Starrett and his daughter come out of the guest quarters, with soldiers carrying all her trunks and baggage.

North checked his watch again. It was almost time for the stage. He folded the message, put it in his pocket, and went out the door.

Out of the corner of his eye, he saw Johnny Ace riding from the barn. If the scout had hoped to leave the fort without running into Luci, he was in for a disappointment. *Or had Johnny been unable to resist one last look at her?*

North glanced from one to the other as he walked. This was going to be the final scene of this little drama and he wanted to be right there to witness it.

He patted the note in his pocket absently. This might affect her decision—if Johnny gave her a chance to make one—but North intended to hold on to the message until the very last minute. She'd have to make the choice from deep within her own heart.

North walked up on the steps of the sutler's store,

nodded to the pair, leaned against a post, and waited to see what would unfold before him.

Johnny acted almost as if he would ride by without speaking, but at the last moment, he reined in his horse and sat looking down at her. His face betrayed the fact that he was aware of nothing in this world but the slight girl in an expensive dress waiting for the stage.

Luci felt as if her heart would burst as she stood looking up at the big man on the black stallion. *What was it he wanted?*

"Good-bye, Johnny Ace. I—I want to thank you for everything you've done for me." She started to say something else in English, but was afraid she couldn't without weeping. *"Hahoo naa ne-meho-tatse,"* she whispered in Cheyenne, but she wasn't sure he heard her. *Thank you and I love you.*

He looked away. "Be happy, Star Eyes. I know how much being a rich, respectable white girl means to you. That's why I told you, and brought you back here. I hope life in the city is everything you ever dreamed of."

She looked at him and had to blink back tears. *Why was she crying? Wasn't she about to realize the one dream that had sustained her all these years?*

True, Manning Starrett was a cold, selfish man, but someday, she would be his heir. And there'd be young white men in Denver who would want to marry the wealthy heiress. She could have her choice of all the men in Colorado.

Starrett pulled out his watch and frowned, looking at the distant coach, visible with its cloud of dust, move through the fort gates. "Here comes the Denver stage. Let's not stand lollygagging here with

466

this Injun buck."

"I — I'm not sure . . ." In her mental agony, Luci didn't move. She had eyes only for Johnny's grim face.

"Star Eyes, he's right. Go on to Denver. You'll have clothes and money, things I could never hope to give you."

Luci swallowed hard. "I don't suppose we could have made a go of it. Maybe the gulf is too great, maybe our two tribes being bitter enemies was something that could never be overcome."

Johnny's dark face contorted and he seemed to be struggling for control. He only nodded, then turned his horse slowly around toward the fort gates.

Once upon a time . . . It seemed so long ago that she had dreamed of this. It was supposed to end: *and they lived happily ever after* . . . not with the girl going off to live in a fancy castle with her selfish and evil father,

She felt a terrible urge to delay Johnny. Luci ran and caught his stirrup, and looked up at him while the stage to Denver swung along the dusty road and stopped before the trading post. "I — you must come visit me some time."

He nodded, but she knew from his eyes that he wouldn't.

Behind her, her father yelled, "Girl, they're loading our luggage! Come on!"

Luci half turned, looking at the man who had deserted her mother, then back up at Johnny.

Behind her, Manning Starrett grumbled again and the stage horses jingled their harness, impatient to be off.

But she had eyes only for the face of the man in the saddle. "Johnny, do you . . . do you really think

467

that love can survive anything?"

He frowned. "What difference does it make what I think? Hurry! Denver and all it has to offer are waiting for you!"

"I believe in love, Johnny." The tears rolled unchecked down her face now. "I believe that real love can overcome any obstacle, no matter if it's background, tribe, or anything else. Nothing—nothing endures forever like true love! Take me with you, Johnny Ace! We'll turn our backs on it all—make our own little Eden—carve out a ranch someplace."

"No." He shook his head, trying to pull away from her hand holding on to his stirrup. "I'm afraid that sooner or later, you'd regret your choice and want to go back to everything your father has. It's hard enough now. I couldn't bear to worry that someday you might want to leave me and return to Denver."

Starrett leaned on his cane and cursed. "Well, you can stop worrying about that! I wouldn't give her a second chance!" Then to Luci, he said, "Girl, think hard before you make a loco decision you'll regret. Love!" he snorted in derision. "Gold, power, that's what counts, and that's what you'll have if you go with me! I'm warning you, you won't get another chance! If you don't go with me now, you can kiss my money good-bye!"

Johnny nodded. "He's right, Luci, you don't love me that much."

But she had made her choice. "Oh, but I do!" She looked up at him now, her heart beating hard. "Tell me you don't love me, Johnny Ace. Tell me I mean nothing to you and I'll turn and get on that stagecoach! I love you, I'll always love you! There's no obstacle too big for love to overcome! Now tell me you don't love me—you don't want me!"

His big hands clenched and unclenched on the reins. "It's—it's too big a sacrifice for you to make. I can't ask you to give everything you ever dreamed of for a big, stupid Pawnee scout!"

"Ask me! Oh God, ask me!" She wept openly now as she challenged him.

He was the bravest of the brave in battle, but now fear and uncertainty etched the lines of his rugged face. He was afraid to believe she might really love him; afraid even to hope. She saw him swallow hard, Then his voice came in a ragged whisper. "Star Eyes, would you . . . will you be my wife?"

"Beloved . . . enemy no more." She held up one small, trembling hand and he reached down, took it, and lifted her up before him on the saddle.

Starrett leaned on the head of his cane, glaring at them. "What the hell does this mean?"

Major North grinned as he lounged against the hitching post. "I think it means that it's come down between a choice of *your* money or *his* love. Looks like you lose, Starrett!" The delight in his voice was evident. He gave Johnny a casual salute. "Lots of luck to you both, scout. I hope you'll be very happy!"

But Starrett hobbled toward them, waving his cane. "Girl, have you gone mad? In a couple of years, I'll be gone and you'll have all my fortune and my fine house! You'll have any man you choose! Why trade all that for a penniless Injun buck?"

Because she loved him so. Luci buried her tear-streaked face against Johnny's wide chest. He held her against him tightly, and she heard his heart beat hard as he embraced her. Whatever lay ahead, they would have each other and their love. There was no obstacle too great, nothing they faced that love couldn't conquer.

"Let's go," she whispered. "I've made my decision," She had no pity for her father. Two women had loved him and he had broken both their hearts. To be alone now that he needed someone was all he deserved.

The Pawnee kissed her hair and she heard the tremor in his voice as if he still not believe she cared enough to go with him. "Forever, Star Eyes?"

"Yes, beloved, forever!" Luci didn't look back as Johnny held her close.

Then he urged the black into a walk toward the fort gates with Starrett yelling threats behind them.

Major North grinned with pleasure, watching the pair ride toward the gates. He liked happy endings. Maybe he'd go back in his office and tear out the last few pages of *Romeo and Juliet*.

Starrett cursed and waved his cane at him. "What the goddamned hell are you smiling about? That damned Injun savage is kidnapping my daughter and you aren't trying to stop him? I'll see that my friends in Washington hear about this!"

"It appears to me," North said, watching the figures grow smaller as they approached the gates, "it appears to me she's hanging on to him like she doesn't ever intend to let go. I don't think she's being kidnapped. Oh, by the way, this wire came for you." He held out the crumpled paper.

He watched the angry face turn pale with fury as Starrett read, but of course, North had the message almost memorized.

To Manning Starrett: Found the money hidden

470

*on stage like you said. Stop. Gave some to
your housekeeper and old Josh who both left
town. Stop. Kept the rest and used your power
of attorney to sell everything you own. Stop.
Lily and I are running away together with all
of it. Stop.*

   Billy

   *P.S. You're right, Manning, I'm just like
you. Stop. For that reason, you shouldn't have
trusted me. Stop.*

North had not known a sick man could curse and
scream so much, but the two lovers were already
too far away to hear what was going on behind
them.

Johnny could hardly believe he actually held her
in his arms. He pulled Luci against him and reined
in just outside the gate. "Where to, Star Eyes?"

She looked up at him, tears making crooked trails
down her cheeks. Luci reached to caress his face.
"Anywhere you are is home to me, my love! You
said something about a small ranch?"

"With an ace and a star for a brand," he whispered, and kissed her as if he would never let her
leave his arms for a moment.

Neither looked back as he nudged the big horse
into a lope and they rode away toward the untamed
frontier that waited for them.

To My Readers

The battle of Summit Springs happened much as I have described it. The battle is remembered not only because it was the last great Indian battle in the Colorado Territory, but because the circumstances were so unusual. The crack warriors of the Dog Soldiers were indeed taken by surprise and defeated in broad daylight when they should have seen the soldiers coming. The Cheyenne had fled from the southeast and expected the trailing cavalry to attack from that direction. Instead, the Fifth Cavalry circled around and came out of the north, taking the Cheyenne by surprise.

However, as far as I know, no whites were guilty of gun running on this particular occasion. I added that.

There was so much public interest in this battle, that Charles Schreyvogel painted the scene and called it "Rescue at Summit Springs." That painting hangs today at the Buffalo Bill Historical Center in Cody, Wyoming.

You have already met "Buffalo Bill" in my last

Zebra Hologram romance, *Nevada Nights,* #2701-X. That novel told of the Pony Express and the Paiute Indian war. Cody actually was a Pony Express rider in its short eighteen-month existence.

As legend has it, a writer named Ned Buntline did show up at Fort McPherson several days after the Summit Springs fight, met Cody, and decided to write dime novels about him. The young Chief of Scouts was on his way to fame and fortune both in books and with his Wild West Show. At one time, Frank North and his brother Luther, plus "Wild Bill" Hickok and Sitting Bull, would be part of that show, playing to European royalty. One of the other stars was a sharpshooter named Annie Oakley. But then you know all that if you've seen the musical or the movie *Annie Get Your Gun.*

Cody would make and lose a fortune in his lifetime. In 1914, he even tried his hand at silent movies, using General Miles as an actor. You'll remember General Miles as the rescuer of the little German girls during the Red River Uprising of 1874 led by Quanah Parker, which I told about in my third Zebra Hologram romance, *Comanche Cowboy,* #2449-5. This novel was chosen by *Affaire De Coeur* Magazine in their annual Readers' Poll as a winner in the list of Top Historical Romances of the year 1988.

The giant Castle Rock actually exists in the town by that name, approximately thirty miles south of Denver. According to the U.S. Weather Bureau, this area draws the second largest number of lightning strikes in the country. The storms blow in from the front range of the Rockies. The area of the country that draws the most lightning strikes is the Florida coast, if you're curious. In 1988, only 68 lightning deaths were reported in America, the lowest number in a decade. Nine of these were in Florida, six in Colorado.

As far as the Morning Star, it's not a star at all, but the planet, Venus. The Pawnees did have a star map painted on a buffalo robe, so accurate that present-day astronomers can tell by the positions of the major planets that it dates back to the time of Columbus. There is a photo of it in the July 1944 issue of *National Geographic* Magazine. That map is now in the Chicago Natural History Museum.

I have walked the rolling hills of the Summit Springs battleground on a hot summer afternoon while a storm built up on the horizon. With a chill of foreboding, I realized that the day was almost exactly as it had been that fateful time long ago when a summer storm blew in as the soldiers attacked, actually killing a cavalry horse that was struck by lightning.

There's not much to see but a few cows grazing in that lonely, isolated spot, a few miles from the little town of Sterling. Susanna Alderdice was indeed slain by the Dog Soldiers as the troops attacked, and is buried somewhere on the site. The marking of the grave has been lost. I am sorry to say the Indians did kill three of her small children. The fourth survived his wounds.

According to the legends, the other captive, Maria Weichell, married one of the army medics. When she left the Fort Sedgewick hospital with him on August 4, 1869, she disappeared into the pages of history forever.

The Kansas woman who hid in the water and thus escaped capture, Mrs. Kine, never quite recovered from her mental stress and ended up in an asylum for the insane at Leavenworth.

There are two marble monuments on the Summit Springs site, one telling the details of the battle, the other dedicated to the bravery of a Cheyenne boy about fifteen years old who was on guard at the horse herd when the soldiers approached. According to witnesses, the boy sacrificed his own life by galloping back to warn his people of the approaching danger.

The sketch book actually exists, although no one knows which Cheyenne drew the pictures. The ledger was picked up after the battle by a soldier as it lay abandoned in the rain. It was indeed a pictorial history of all the battles of the past several years. Today the book is on exhibit at the historical museum in downtown Denver, along with many other fascinating items of Western history.

No soldiers were killed at Summit Springs, but at least one Pawnee scout got a Congressional Medal of Honor, our country's highest award for bravery. The official records show the medal was awarded to Mad Bear, Co-rux-te-chod-ish. But Luther North, who should know, always said there was a mistake and that it was actually meant for and awarded to Traveling Bear, Co-rux-a-kah-wadde, for his bravery at Summit Springs.

Yes, there really was a white teacher named Elvira Platt who took a group of mostly orphaned Pawnee children and tried to turn them into little white children. In my intensive research, I found a rather sanctimonious article by her called "A Teacher Among the Pawnees," written in 1900, long after she had retired.

It may surprise some of my younger readers to know that the incidence of syphilis was once comparable to today's AIDS epidemic. Over the centuries, it killed or took the sanity of millions of people. There was no cure for it until the development of penicillin about the time of World War II. You'd think mankind would finally learn that irresponsible sex can be deadly, whatever the time period.

Frank North, the Pawnees' beloved Pani Le-shar, only lived to be forty-five, dying in 1885. He had never been in good health and was badly injured in 1884 in a freak accident while riding in Buffalo Bill's Wild West show.

Luther North would outlive Frank by fifty years and Buffalo Bill by seventeen. He managed to go see his old Pawnee scouts one last time just a few years before he died in 1935. Frank and Luther's father did freeze to death in a Nebraska blizzard, as I told you.

After the Indian trouble of 1869, the Pawnee scouts would be called into action only one more time, seven years later, to help track down the Cheyenne and Sioux who had just wiped out Custer and the Seventh Cavalry.

In the meantime, in 1873, their old enemies, the Sioux, caught the tribe out on a buffalo hunt and slaughtered hundreds of them. This massacre, plus pressure from greedy Nebraska farmers who wanted the land the Pawnees occupied, finally led to the tribe's accepting a reservation in northern Oklahoma in 1874.

Many of their descendants are still there, near the town of Pawnee, county seat of Pawnee County, about fifty miles northwest of Tulsa. One of the largest free powwows in the country takes place there every summer. Check with the Chamber of Commerce for exact dates if you decide to attend.

The Pawnee were traditional enemies of the Cheyenne and Sioux. I have already told you of the death of KiriKuks, Johnny's father, in my first Zebra Heartfire book, *Cheyenne Captive*. At the moment, that book has sold out its printing, but if the editor gets enough requests, I'm sure it will finally be reprinted. Some of you have written to ask if I have extra copies and I'm sorry to say I don't. Certainly if any of us had dreamed the book would be such a hit, Zebra would have printed more.

That bestseller also won awards from both *Romantic Times* Magazine and *Affaire De Coeur* Magazine. *Captive* was the first book of my Panorama of the Old West series, which may take dozens of books to complete as I attempt to tell much of the history of the Old West.

My second book, *Cheyenne Princess,* Heartfire #2176-3, was also a bestseller about the Great Plains' Indian Outbreak of 1864.

The rest of the series have all been Zebra Holograms. Book four concerned Colonel McKinzie's 1873 raid into Mexico against the warring Kickapoo, Mescalero, and Lipan Apache. That book was called *Bandit's Embrace*, #2596-3.

The book you hold in your hands is book six. You can order any of the above books from your bookstore or directly from Zebra. Follow the instructions in this book for ordering. Send the author's name, the title, the ISBN number, and a check or money order for cost plus 50¢ postage.

I'm getting a lot of mail wanting to know about Georgina Gentry. No, I'm not Indian but my husband is a mixed-blood Choctaw and my brother-in-law is a well-known Chickasaw. I'm a petite blonde with pale blue eyes, I'm left-handed, and my sign is Virgo.

My husband, "Murph," and I have three children, two girls and a boy. All have been active in 4H and Future Farmers of America. We live among the blackjack oak trees in the old Cross Timbers area of central Oklahoma.

I personally answer all mail and send bookmarks.

If you want to write me, send your letter in care of Zebra and my editor will forward it. Please include a long, stamped, self-addressed envelope and be patient. It may take several months, both to receive and to answer if I'm at work on a new book.

Some of you have asked about unfinished stories I left dangling in other books. Believe me, I haven't forgotten those characters. Everyone wants to know when Iron Knife and Summer Sky and their children will re-enter this saga. Depending on what my editor thinks, they may make a small appearance in the next book. In subsequent novels, Iron Knife will eventually find his missing sister, Cimarron, and we will also follow the lives of each of his children.

I will try to do two books a year, all with either an Indian or a Western title. The Panorama of the Old West is probably the longest series ever written by one author and will take many books to complete. Sooner or later, I will pick up all those unfinished story lines and weave them together like threads in a Indian blanket.

I am telling my stories the way the Cheyenne do when they gather around their campfires at night. An Ancient One will stand and tell a legend, and when he finishes, he will say, "That is my tale. Can anyone tie another to it?"

Then someone will tie a story to his and end by saying, "That, too, is my story, can someone tie another to it?"

Oh yes, Old One, this daughter of Oklahoma has heard your stories told by the flickering campfires. I can tell a tale and tie endless others to it, as long as there is an audience out there who listen with their hearts.

For my seventh tale, I'm going to tell Colorado's most beloved legend. The Coloradoans among you will know exactly what I mean. There are many variations of this old story that dates back to the Civil War; I'm going to tell you my version.

In that state, there is a magnificent mountain near the ghost towns of Alma and Buckskin Joe. This mountain has an unusual name and is surely the only one in the world named for a saloon girl. Ah, she was a great beauty, this laughing girl with silky hair and soft eyes! A shy, mixed-blood Cherokee miner loved this dancing girl from a distance. Afraid she might scorn him, he didn't voice his love. Instead he gave her a pair of shoes with real silver heels made from ore from his own mine. But then the Civil War started, and . . .

Well, I'd like to tell you what happened, but you'll have to wait for my next book, coming in a few months. Join me for a thrilling story of the Rocky Mountains, Indians, and action, but most of all, for a tale of eternal love and devotion. It's my version of the old Colorado legend of a saloon girl called Silver Heels!

And for those of you who read my novels and listen with your hearts, I say to you . . .

Hahoo naa ne-mehotatse,
Georgina Gentry

As always, I put an enormous amount of research into my books. Here are just a few of the many sources I used that you may find at your public library.

THE FIGHTING CHEYENNE
by George B. Grinnell, University of Oklahoma Press

MAN OF THE PLAINS, *The Recollections of Luther North*
Intro. by George B. Grinnell, University of Nebraska Press

PAWNEE, BLACKFOOT, AND CHEYENNE
by George B. Grinnell, Charles Scribner's Sons
THE PAWNEE INDIANS
by George E. Hyde, University of Oklahoma Press
WOLVES FOR THE BLUE SOLDIERS
by Thomas W. Dunlay, University of Nebraska Press